PENGUIN BOOKS

THE PENGUIN BOOK OF
CONTEMPORARY WOMEN'S SHORT STORIES

Susan Hill was born in Scarborough, Yorkshire, in 1942. She was educated at grammar schools there and in Coventry, and studied at King's College, London. Her works include *Gentleman and Ladies*, *A Change for the Better*, *I'm the King of the Castle* (Somerset Maugham Award), *The Albatross and Other Stories* (John Llewellyn Rhys Memorial Prize), *Strange Meeting*, *The Bird of Night* (Whitbread Award), *A Bit of Singing and Dancing*, *In the Springtime of the Year*, *The Woman in Black*, *Lanterns across the Snow*, *Air and Angels* and *Mrs de Winter*, a sequel to Daphne du Maurier's *Rebecca*. Her non-fiction books include the illustrated *Shakespeare Country*, *The Spirit of the Cotswolds*, *Through the Garden Gate* and *Through the Kitchen Window*. She has also written books for children, including *One Night at a Time*, *Mother's Magic*, *Can It Be True?* (Smarties Prize) and *Suzy's Shoes*, and two autobiographical books, *The Magic Apple Tree* and *Family*. In addition, she has edited Thomas Hardy's *The Distracted Preacher and Other Tales* for Penguin Classics and *The Penguin Book of Modern Women's Short Stories*. She is a regular broadcaster and book reviewer.

Susan Hill is married to the Shakespeare scholar Stanley Wells, and they have two daughters and live in Gloucestershire.

Contemporary
Women's Short Stories
AN ANTHOLOGY

SELECTED AND INTRODUCED BY
Susan Hill

PENGUIN BOOKS

PENGUIN BOOKS

Published by the Penguin Group
Penguin Books Ltd, 27 Wrights Lane, London W8 5TZ, England
Penguin Books USA Inc., 375 Hudson Street, New York, New York 10014, USA
Penguin Books Australia Ltd, Ringwood, Victoria, Australia
Penguin Books Canada Ltd, 10 Alcorn Avenue, Toronto, Ontario, Canada M4V 3B2
Penguin Books (NZ) Ltd, 182–190 Wairau Road, Auckland 10, New Zealand

Penguin Books Ltd, Registered Offices: Harmondsworth, Middlesex, England

First published as *Contemporary Women's Short Stories* by Michael Joseph 1995
Published under the present title in Penguin Books 1995
1 3 5 7 9 10 8 6 4 2

The acknowledgements on pp. vii–viii constitute an extension of this copyright page

The moral right of the editor has been asserted

Printed in England by Clays Ltd, St Ives plc

Contents

CONTENTS

Acknowledgements

The editor and publishers wish to thank the following for permission to use copyright material:

Bloomsbury Publishing Ltd for Candia McWilliam, 'Sweetie Rationing' from *Soho Square*; and with Penguin Canada Ltd for Nadine Gordimer, 'Some are Born to Sweet Delight' from *Jump and Other Stories*. Copyright © Felix Licensing BV 1991;

Leonora Brito for 'Body and Soul', *Stand Magazine*, Autumn 1993;

Curtis Brown Ltd, London, on behalf of The Chichester Partnership for Daphne Du Maurier, 'The Pool' from *The Breaking Point*. Copyright © Daphne Du Maurier 1959; and on behalf of the author for Janet Frame; 'Swans' from *The Lagoon*. Copyright © 1951, 1991 by Janet Frame;

Judith Condon for 'Scorched Earth' from *The Word Party*, Centre for Creative Performing Arts, University of East Anglia, 1990;

Constable Publishers for Mary Lavin, 'Lilacs' from *The Stories of Mary Lavin, Vol. III*, 1964;

Andre Deutsch Ltd for Grace Paley, 'The Immigrant Story' from *Enormous Changes at the Last Minute*, 1975;

Faber & Faber Ltd for Sylvia Plath, 'The Fifteen Dollar Eagle' from *Johnny Panic and the Bible of Dreams*, 1977; and with Sheil Land Associates on behalf of the author for Ellen Gilchrist, 'Revenge' from *The Blue-Eyed Buddhist and Other Stories*, 1981. Copyright Ellen Gilchrist;

The Jane Gregory Agency on behalf of the author for Judy Corbalis, 'The Bridesmaid' from *Exposure*, Centre for Performing Arts, University of East Anglia, 1991;

David Higham Associates on behalf of the authors, for Olivia

Manning, 'Innocent Pleasures' from *A Romantic Hero*, Heinemann, 1966; and Penelope Gilliatt, 'The Redhead' from *What's It Like Out*, Secker & Warburg, 1968;

John Johnson Ltd on behalf of the author's Estate for Frances Towers, 'Violets' from *Tea With Mr Rochester and Other Stories*, Virago;

Penguin Books Ltd for Alice Munro, 'The Peace of Utrecht' from *Dance of the Happy Shades* (Allen Lane, 1973). Copyright © Alice Munro, 1968.

Peters Fraser & Dunlop Group Ltd on behalf of the author for Mary Gordon, 'The Thorn';

Random House UK Ltd for Maeve Binchy, 'Shepherd's Bush' from *London Transport*, Century Hutchinson, 1978;

Reed Consumer Books Ltd for Helen Simpson, 'What Are Neighbours For' from *Four Bare Legs in a Bed*, Heinemann, 1990; and Janice Galloway, 'Frostbite' from *Blood*, Secker & Warburg, 1991;

Rogers, Coleridge & White Ltd on behalf of the author, for Angela Carter, 'Peter and the Wolf', Chatto and Windus, 1985;

Richard Scott Simon Ltd on behalf of the author, for Mavis Gallant, 'Up North' from *Home Truths*. Copyright © 1956, 1959, 1963, 1965, 1966, 1968, 1971, 1975, 1976, 1977, 1978, 1981 by Mavis Gallant;

Serpent's Tail for Mary Scott, 'Language' from *Nudists May Be Encountered*, 1991;

Sheil Land Associates Ltd on behalf of the author for Moy McCrory, 'The Wrong Vocation' from *Bleeding Summers*, Jonathan Cape, 1991;

Virago Press for Christa Wolf, 'June Afternoon' from *What Remains and Other Stories*, trans. Heike Schwarzbauer and Rick Takvorian, 1993. Translation copyright © 1993 by Farrar Straus & Giroux, Inc. Originally published in German under the title *Gesammelte Erzahlungen*. Copyright © 1974, 1980 by Aufbau-Verlag.

Introduction

Aspiring fiction writers often assume that simply because it *is* shorter, the short story is an easier form for a beginner than the novel; a trial run, a preparation for the longer work. Not so. A serious short story is an extremely difficult form in which to succeed, at every level. Form is all-important, but there must be content too, a point and a point of view. For it to be satisfying to read, a short story must have a shape – it needs to attract the attention, set a scene, convey character, attitude, emotion, subtlety and a denouement, all without the sense of greater space and more generous time scheme afforded by the novel. The story may be slight, its subject matter of no great moment, yet still every word must tell – there is no margin for error, no room for in-filling, no time in which to falter and dawdle, then to recover before the final sprint. It is, in short, an unforgiving form. Bad writing shows up. Clichés jar. Everything must be sharply in focus, unambiguous though never unsubtle, crystal clear. Small wonder that although entries are usually many for all the short story competitions which abound, a high percentage are dross: great wonder that there are always the few outstanding stories; brilliant, assured, electrifying, from confident new voices, always surprises, talent is everywhere evident.

There are relatively few outlets for short stories now – magazines publish few, small literary periodicals have dwindled in number. Yet publishers do from time to time show confidence by issuing collections of stories by unknown writers and sales are not always dismal. Of those women in the present selection, Janice Galloway, Helen Simpson and Mary Scott, for example, have had great critical success and very decent sales of their first volumes of short stories.

Very few short story writers do not also produce novels at some time – Katharine Mansfield, arguably the greatest practitioner of the form in the English language, was a rare exception. But the short stories of, say, Muriel Spark, Elizabeth Bowen or Edna O'Brien are not inferior to their novels, nor were they produced at the start of those writers' careers, before they graduated to higher things: they can be regarded as simply different, but equal, branches of the same corpus of work, which are mutually illuminating and complementary.

Young writers do not need to feel under an obligation to produce novels if they can say what they have to in the way that suits them most happily within the form of the short story. Those whose names appear here, next to those already established writers, have arrived; they are already accomplished. There is no competition within these pages and no order of merit, but, most of all, no allowances have had to be made. My brief was to follow the previous volume, *The Penguin Book of Modern Women's Short Stories*, by spreading my editorial net rather wider and catching in it both writers in English from countries other than Great Britain and those whose work had only recently begun to appear. They have in common only the fact that all are women and all have written a superb story, worthy of inclusion in a volume of some of the best contemporary writing.

Names such as Alice Munro, Mavis Gallant, or Maeve Binchy need no introduction and represent older generations of highly acclaimed and respected writers of the short story. All are alive and at the height of their powers. Others died recently and prematurely – Angela Carter, Penelope Gilliatt, but their names are still fresh, they are in every sense contemporary women's voices of our time, distinguished and utterly distinctive.

Some of the rising generation of young women writers

included here have published short story collections and also novels and become prominent over the past decade — Janice Galloway, Helen Simpson and Moy McCrory. Other names are quite new. Leonora Brito from England won a prize in a recent *Stand* short story competition and her work is most exciting, strong, memorably original but completely accessible. Others, too, are new and have so far written comparatively little — Judith Condon, Judy Corbalis, Mary Scott have outstanding stories here, written with confidence and assurance by authors sparkling with talent. Set beside them, again, are stories by two major twentieth-century women writers, Sylvia Plath's powerful and extraordinary 'The Fifteen Dollar Eagle' and, in a totally different style and mood, the New Zealand writer Janet Frame's classic 'Swans', a most tender, moving and perceptive account involving the minutiae of everyday provincial life, which are both ordinary and life changing.

The range of these women writers is astonishing; there are domestic stories, stories about love and accidentally momentous meetings, the tormented relationships between parents and children, stories about growing up and about memory, old age and slick city living. The peculiar and the bizarre are set beside the banal: settings range equally far and wide, from small town America, to London and Glasgow, an Italian village to wolf-haunted mountain country. Language is stretched, explored, manipulated and once or twice made almost the subject matter of the story itself. Emotions are explored — passion, fear, tenderness, jealousy, wonder, rage and there are marvellous evocations of the ennui and longueurs of adolescence, the trivialities and pettiness of claustrophobic family squabbles, the tiny frustrations, sadnesses and small, necessary activities that form the warp and woof of female lives.

But what marks the stories out as having been written by women is some indefinable, yet definite, sixth sense at work; probing, identifying, dissecting, sympathising, explaining, revealing, and finally understanding. The stories may be angry or tragic, but they are never cold; concerned with detail, yet never trivial. Each one earns its place for some individual quality, some flavour, some strength unique to itself as well as by virtue of sheer, interesting, exciting, good writing. Several have already stood the test of time, the rest will quite surely do so and be seen to have done so, many years from now.

Susan Hill
1995

MAEVE BINCHY

Shepherd's Bush

People looked very weary, May thought, and shabbier than she had remembered Londoners to be. They reminded her a little of those news-reel pictures of crowds during the war or just after it, old raincoats, brave smiles, endless patience. But then this wasn't Regent Street where she had wandered up and down looking at shops on other visits to London, it wasn't the West End with lights all glittering and people getting out of taxis full of excitement and wafts of perfume. This was Shepherd's Bush where people lived. They had probably set out from here early this morning and fought similar crowds on the way to work. The women must have done their shopping in their lunch-hour because most of them were carrying plastic bags of food. It was a London different to the one you see as a tourist.

And she was here for a different reason, although she had once read a cynical article in a magazine which said that girls coming to London for abortions provided a significant part of the city's tourist revenue. It wasn't something you could classify under any terms as a holiday. When she filled in the card at the airport she had written 'Business' in the section where it said 'Purpose of journey'.

The pub where she was to meet Celia was near the tube station. She found it easily and settled herself in. A lot of the accents were Irish, workmen having a pint before they went home to their English wives and their television programmes. Not drunk tonight, it was only Monday, but obviously regulars. Maybe not so welcome as regulars on Friday or

Saturday nights, when they would remember they were Irish and sing anti-British songs.

Celia wouldn't agree with her about that. Celia had rose-tinted views about the Irish in London, she thought they were all here from choice, not because there was no work for them at home. She hated stories about the restless Irish, or Irishmen on the lump in the building trade. She said people shouldn't make such a big thing about it all. People who came from much farther away settled in London, it was big enough to absorb everyone. Oh well, she wouldn't bring up the subject, there were enough things to disagree with Celia about . . . without searching for more.

Oh why of all people, of all the bloody people in the world, did she have to come to Celia? Why was there nobody else whom she could ask for advice? Celia would give it, she would give a lecture with every piece of information she imparted. She would deliver a speech with every cup of tea, she would be cool, practical and exactly the right person, if she weren't so much the wrong person. It was handing Celia a whole box of ammunition about Andy. From now on Celia could say that Andy was a rat, and May could no longer say she had no facts to go on.

Celia arrived. She was thinner, and looked a little tired. She smiled. Obviously the lectures weren't going to come in the pub. Celia always knew the right place for things. Pubs were for meaningless chats and bright, non-intense conversation. Home was for lectures.

'You're looking marvellous,' Celia said.

It couldn't be true. May looked at her reflection in a glass panel. You couldn't see the dark lines under her eyes there, but you could see the droop of her shoulders, she wasn't a person that could be described as looking marvellous. No, not even in a pub.

'I'm okay,' she said. 'But you've got very slim, how did you do it?'

'No bread, no cakes, no potatoes, no sweets,' said Celia in

a business-like way. 'It's the old rule but it's the only rule. You deny yourself everything you want and you lose weight.'

'I know,' said May, absently rubbing her waistline.

'Oh I didn't mean *that*,' cried Celia horrified. 'I didn't mean that at all.'

May felt weary, she hadn't meant that either, she was patting her stomach because she had been putting on weight. The child that she was going to get rid of was still only a speck, it would cause no bulge. She had put on weight because she cooked for Andy three or four times a week in his flat. He was long and lean. He could eat for ever and he wouldn't put on weight. He didn't like eating alone so she ate with him. She reassured Celia that there was no offence and when Celia had gone, twittering with rage at herself, to the counter, May wondered whether she had explored every avenue before coming to Celia and Shepherd's Bush for help.

She had. There were no legal abortions in Dublin, and she did not know of anyone who had ever had an illegal one there. England and the ease of the system were less than an hour away by plane. She didn't want to try and get it on the National Health, she had the money, all she wanted was someone who would introduce her to a doctor, so that she could get it all over with quickly. She needed somebody who knew her, somebody who wouldn't abandon her if things went wrong, somebody who would lie for her, because a few lies would have to be told. May didn't have any other friends in London. There was a girl she had once met on a skiing holiday, but you couldn't impose on a holiday friendship in that way. She knew a man, a very nice, kind man who had stayed in the hotel where she worked and had often begged her to come and stay with him and his wife. But she couldn't go to stay with them for the first time in this predicament, it would be ridiculous. It had to be Celia.

It might be easier if Celia had loved somebody so much that everything else was unimportant. But stop, that wasn't fair. Celia loved that dreary, boring, selfish Martin. She loved him so much that she believed one day he was going to get things organized and make a home for them. Everyone else knew that Martin was the worst possible bet for any punter, a Mammy's boy, who had everything he wanted now, including a visit every two months from Celia, home from London, smartly-dressed, undemanding, saving away for a day that would never come. So Celia did understand something about the nature of love. She never talked about it. People as brisk as Celia don't talk about things like unbrisk attitudes in men, or hurt feelings or broken hearts. Not when it refers to themselves, but they are very good at pointing out the foolish attitudes of others.

Celia was back with the drinks.

'We'll finish them up quickly,' she said.

Why could she never, never take her ease over anything? Things always had to be finished up quickly. It was warm and anonymous in the pub. They could go back to Celia's flat, which May felt sure wouldn't have even a comfortable chair in it, and talk in a business-like way about the rights and wrongs of abortion, the procedure, the money, and how it shouldn't be spent on something so hopeless and destructive. And about Andy. Why wouldn't May tell him? He had a right to know. The child was half his, and even if he didn't want it he should pay for the abortion. He had plenty of money, he was a hotel manager. May had hardly any, she was a hotel receptionist. May could see it all coming, she dreaded it. She wanted to stay in this warm place until closing-time, and to fall asleep, and wake up there two days later.

Celia made walking-along-the-road conversation on the way to her flat. This road used to be very quiet and full of retired people, now it was all flats and bed-sitters. That road was nice, but noisy, too much through-traffic. The houses in the road over there were going for thirty-five thousand, which was ridiculous, but then you had to remember it was fairly central and they did have little gardens. Finally they were there. A big Victorian house, a clean, polished hall, and three flights of stairs. The flat was much bigger than May expected, and it had a sort of divan on which she sat down immediately and put up her legs, while Celia fussed about a bit, opening a bottle of wine and putting a dish of four small lamb chops into the oven. May braced herself for the lecture.

It wasn't a lecture, it was an information-sheet. She was so relieved that she could feel herself relaxing, and filled up her wineglass again.

'I've arranged with Doctor Harris that you can call to see him tomorrow morning at 11. I told him no lies, just a little less than the truth. I said you were staying with me. If he thinks that means you are staying permanently, that's his mistake not mine. I mentioned that your problem was . . . what it is. I asked him when he thought it would be . . . em . . . done. He said Wednesday or Thursday, but it would all depend. He didn't seem shocked or anything; it's like tonsillitis to him, I suppose. Anyway he was very calm about it. I think you'll find he's a kind person and it won't be upsetting . . . that part of it.'

May was dumbfounded. Where were the accusations, the I-told-you-so sighs, the hope that now, finally, she would finish with Andy? Where was the slight moralistic bit, the heavy wondering whether or not it might be murder? For the first time in the eleven days since she had confirmed she was pregnant, May began to hope that there would be some normality in the world again.

'Will it embarrass you, all this?' she asked. 'I mean, do you feel it will change your relationship with him?'

'In London a doctor isn't an old family friend like at home, May. He's someone you go to, or I've gone to anyway, when I've had to have my ears syringed, needed antibiotics for flu last year, and a medical certificate for the time I sprained my ankle and couldn't go to work. He hardly knows me except as a name on his register. He's nice though, and he doesn't rush you in and out. He's Jewish and small and worried-looking.'

Celia moved around the flat, changing into comfortable

sitting-about clothes, looking up what was on television, explaining to May that she must sleep in her room and that she, Celia, would use the divan.

No, honestly, it would be easier that way, she wasn't being nice, it would be much easier. A girl friend rang and they arranged to play squash together at the weekend. A wrong number rang. A West Indian from the flat downstairs knocked on the door to say he would be having a party on Saturday night and to apologise in advance for any noise. If they liked to bring a bottle of something, they could call in themselves. Celia served dinner. They looked at television for an hour, then went to bed.

May thought what a strange empty life Celia led here far from home, miles from Martin, no real friends, no life at all. Then she thought that Celia might possibly regard her life too as sad, working in a second-rate hotel for five years, having an affair with its manager for three years. A hopeless affair because the manager's wife and four children were a bigger stumbling-block than Martin's mother could ever be. She felt tired and comfortable, and in Celia's funny, character-less bedroom she drifted off and dreamed that Andy had discovered where she was and what she was about to do, and had flown over during the night to tell her that they would get married next morning, and live in England and forget the hotel, the family and what anyone would say.

Tuesday morning. Celia was gone. Dr Harris's address was neatly written on the pad by the phone with instructions how to get there. Also Celia's phone number at work, and a message that May never believed she would hear from Celia. 'Good luck.'

He was small, and Jewish, and worried and kind. His examination was painless and unembarrassing. He confirmed what she knew already. He wrote down dates, and asked general questions about her health. May wondered whether he had a family, there were no pictures of wife or children in the surgery. But then there were none in Andy's office, either.

Perhaps his wife was called Rebecca and she too worried because her husband worked so hard, they might have two children, a boy who was a gifted musician, and a girl who wanted to get married to a Christian. Maybe they all walked along these leafy roads on Saturdays to synagogue and Rebecca cooked all those things like gefilte fish and bagels.

With a start, May told herself to stop dreaming about him. It was a habit she had got into recently, fancying lives for everyone she met, however briefly. She usually gave them happy lives with a bit of problem-to-be-solved thrown in. She wondered what a psychiatrist would make of that. As she was coming back to real life, Dr Harris was saying that if he was going to refer her for a termination he must know why she could not have the baby. He pointed out that she was healthy, and strong, and young. She should have no difficulty with pregnancy or birth. Were there emotional reasons? Yes, it would kill her parents, she wouldn't be able to look after the baby, she didn't want to look after one on her own either, it wouldn't be fair on her or the baby.

'And the father?' Dr Harris asked.

'Is my boss, is heavily married, already has four babies of his own. It would break up his marriage which he doesn't want to do . . . yet. No, the father wouldn't want me to have it either.'

'Has he said that?' asked Dr Harris as if he already knew the answer.

'I haven't told him, I can't tell him, I won't tell him,' said May.

Dr Harris sighed. He asked a few more questions; he made a telephone call; he wrote out an address. It was a posh address near Harley Street.

'This is Mr White. A well-known surgeon. These are his consulting-rooms, I have made an appointment for you at 2.30 this afternoon. I understand from your friend Miss . . .' He searched his mind and his desk for Celia's name and then gave up. 'I understand anyway that you are not living here, and don't want to try and pretend that you are, so that you want the termination done privately. That's just as well, because it would be difficult to get it done on the National Health. There are many cases that would have to come before you.'

'Oh I have the money,' said May, patting her handbag. She felt nervous but relieved at the same time. Almost exhilarated. It was working, the whole thing was actually moving. God bless Celia.

'It will be around £180 to £200, and in cash, you know that?'

'Yes, it's all here, but why should a well-known surgeon have to be paid in cash, Dr Harris? You know it makes it look a bit illegal and sort of underhand, doesn't it?'

Dr Harris smiled a tired smile. 'You asked me why he has to be paid in cash. Because he says so. Why he says so, I don't know. Maybe it's because some of his clients don't feel too like paying him after the event. It's not like plastic surgery or a broken leg, where they can see the results. In a termination you see no results. Maybe people don't pay so easily then. Maybe also Mr White doesn't have a warm relationship with his Income Tax people. I don't know.'

'Do I owe you anything?' May asked, putting on her coat.

'No, my dear, nothing.' He smiled and showed her to the door.

'It feels wrong. I'm used to paying a doctor at home or they send bills,' she said.

'Send me a picture postcard of your nice country sometime,' he said. 'When my wife was alive she and I spent several happy holidays there before all this business started.' He waved a hand to take in the course of Anglo-Irish politics and difficulties over the last ten years.

May blinked a bit hard and thanked him. She took a taxi which was passing his door and went to Oxford Street. She wanted to see what was in the shops because she was going to pretend that she had spent £200 on clothes and then they had all been lost or stolen. She hadn't yet worked out the details of this deception, which seemed unimportant compared to all the rest that had to be gone through. But she would need to know what was in the shops so that she could say what she was meant to have bought.

Imagining that she had this kind of money to spend, she examined jackets, skirts, sweaters, and the loveliest boots she had ever seen. If only she didn't have to throw this money away, she could have these things. It was her savings over ten months, she put by £30 a month with difficulty. Would Andy have liked her in the boots? She didn't know. He never said much about the way she looked. He saw her mostly in uniform when she could steal time to go to the flat he had for himself in the hotel. On the evenings when he was meant to be working late, and she was in fact cooking for him, she usually wore a dressing-gown, a long velvet one. Perhaps she might have bought a dressing-gown. She examined some, beautiful Indian silks, and a Japanese satin one in pink covered with little black butterflies. Yes, she would tell him she had bought that, he would like the sound of it, and be sorry it had been stolen.

She had a cup of coffee in one of the big shops and watched the other shoppers resting between bouts of buying. She wondered, did any of them look at her, and if so, would they know in a million years that her shopping money would remain in her purse until it was handed over to a Mr White so that he could abort Andy's baby? Why did she use words like that, why did she say things to hurt herself, she must have a very deep-seated sense of guilt. Perhaps, she thought to herself with a bit of humour, she should save another couple of hundred pounds and come over for a few sessions with a Harley Street shrink. That should set her right.

It wasn't a long walk to Mr White's rooms, it wasn't a pleasant welcome. A kind of girl that May had before only seen in the pages of fashion magazines, bored, disdainful, elegant, reluctantly admitted her.

'Oh yes, Dr Harris's patient,' she said, as if May should

have come in some tradesman's entrance. She felt furious, and inferior, and sat with her hands in small tight balls, and her eyes unseeing in the waiting-room.

Mr White looked like a caricature of a diplomat. He had elegant grey hair, elegant manicured hands. He moved very gracefully, he talked in practised, concerned clichés, he knew how to put people at their ease, and despite herself, and while still disliking him, May felt safe.

Another examination, another confirmation, more checking of dates. Good, good, she had come in plenty of time, sensible girl. No reasons she would like to discuss about whether this was the right course of action? No? Oh well, grown-up lady, must make up her own mind. Absolutely certain then? Fine, fine. A look at a big leather-bound book on his desk, a look at a small notebook. Leather-bound for the tax people, small notebook for himself, thought May viciously. Splendid, splendid. Tomorrow morning then, not a problem in the world, once she was sure, then he knew this was the best, and wisest thing. Very sad the people who dithered.

May could never imagine this man having dithered in his life. She was asked to see Vanessa on the way out. She knew that the girl would be called something like Vanessa.

Vanessa yawned and took £194 from her. She seemed to have difficulty in finding the six pounds in change. May wondered wildly whether this was meant to be a tip. If so, she would wait for a year until Vanessa found the change. With the notes came a discreet printed card advertising a nursing home on the other side of London.

'Before nine, fasting, just the usual overnight things,' said Vanessa helpfully.

'Tomorrow morning?' checked May.

'Well yes, naturally. You'll be out at eight the following morning. They'll arrange everything like taxis. They have super food,' she added as an afterthought.

'They'd need to have for this money,' said May spiritedly.

'You're not just paying for the food,' said Vanessa wisely.

It was still raining. She rang Celia from a public phonebox. Everything was organized, she told her. Would Celia like to come and have a meal somewhere, and maybe they could go on to a theatre?

Celia was sorry, she had to work late, and she had already bought liver and bacon for supper. Could she meet May at home around nine? There was a great quiz show on telly, it would be a shame to miss it.

May went to a hairdresser and spent four times what she would have spent at home on a hair-do.

She went to a cinema and saw a film which looked as if it were going to be about a lot of sophisticated witty French people on a yacht and turned out to be about a sophisticated witty French girl who fell in love with the deck-hand on the yacht and when she purposely got pregnant, in order that he would marry her, he laughed at her and the witty sophisticated girl threw herself overboard. Great choice that, May said glumly, as she dived into the underground to go back to the smell of liver frying.

Celia asked little about the arrangements for the morning, only practical things like the address so that she could work out how long it would take to get there.

'Would you like me to come and see you?' she asked. 'I expect when it's all over, all finished you know, they'd let you have visitors. I could come after work.'

She emphasized the word 'could' very slightly. May immediately felt mutinous. She would love Celia to come, but not if it was going to be a duty, something she felt she had to do, against her principles, her inclinations.

'No, don't do that,' she said in a falsely bright voice. 'They have telly in the rooms apparently, and anyway, it's not as if I were going to be there for more than twenty-four hours.'

Celia looked relieved. She worked out taxi times and locations and turned on the quiz show.

In the half light May looked at her. She was unbending, Celia was. She would survive everything, even the fact that

Martin would never marry her. Christ, the whole thing was a mess. Why did people start life with such hopes, and as early as their mid-twenties become beaten and accepting of things. Was the rest of life going to be like this?

She didn't sleep so well, and it was a relief when Celia shouted that it was seven o'clock.

Wednesday. An ordinary Wednesday for the taxi-driver, who shouted some kind of amiable conversation at her. She missed most of it, because of the noise of the engine, and didn't bother to answer him half the time except with a grunt.

The place had creeper on the walls. It was a big house, with a small garden, and an attractive brass handle on the door. The nurse who opened it was Irish. She checked May's name on a list. Thank God it was O'Connor, there were a million O'Connors. Suppose she had had an unusual name, she'd have been found out immediately.

The bedroom was big and bright. Two beds, flowery covers, nice furniture. A magazine rack, a bookshelf. A television, a bathroom.

The Irish nurse offered her a hanger from the wardrobe for her coat as if this was a pleasant family hotel or great class and comfort. May felt frightened for the first time. She longed to sit down on one of the beds and cry, and for the nurse to put her arm around her and give her a cigarette and say that it would be all right. She hated being so alone.

The nurse was distant.

'The other lady will be in shortly. Her name is Miss Adams. She just went downstairs to say goodbye to her friend. If there's anything you'd like, please ring.'

She was gone, and May paced the room like a captured animal. Was she to undress? It was ridiculous to go to bed. You only went to bed in the day-time if you were ill. She was well, perfectly well.

Miss Adams burst in the door. She was a chubby, pretty girl about twenty-three. She was Australian, and her name was Hell, short for Helen.

'Come on, bedtime,' she said, and they both put on their nightdresses and got into beds facing each other. May had never felt so silly in her whole life.

'Are you sure we're meant to do this?' she asked.

'Positive,' Helen announced. 'I was here last year. They'll be in with the screens for modesty, the examination, and the pre-med. They go mad if you're not in bed. Of course that stupid Paddy of a nurse didn't tell you, they expect you to be inspired.'

Hell was right. In five minutes, the nurse and Mr White came in. A younger nurse carried a screen. Hell was examined first, then May for blood pressure and temperature, and that kind of thing. Mr White was charming. He called her Miss O'Connor, as if he had known her all his life.

He patted her shoulder and told her she didn't have anything to worry about. The Irish nurse gave her an unsmiling injection which was going to make her drowsy. It didn't immediately.

Hell was doing her nails.

'You were really here last year?' asked May in disbelief.

'Yeah, there's nothing to it. I'll be back at work tomorrow.'

'Why didn't you take the Pill?' May asked.

'Why didn't you?' countered Hell.

'Well, I did for a bit, but I thought it was making me fat, and I then anyway, you know, I thought I'd escaped for so long before I started the Pill that it would be all right. I was wrong.'

'I know.' Hell was sympathetic. 'I can't take it. I've got varicose veins already and I don't really understand all those things they give you in the Family Planning clinics, jellies, and rubber things, and diaphragms. It's worse than working out income tax. Anyway, you never have time to set up a scene like that before going to bed with someone, do you? It's like preparing for a battle.'

May laughed.

'It's going to be fine, love,' said Hell. 'Look, I know, I've been here before. Some of my friends have had it done four or five times. I promise you, it's only the people who don't know who worry. This afternoon you'll wonder what you were thinking about to look so white. Now if it had been terrible, would I be here again?'

'But your varicose veins?' said May, feeling a little sleepy.

'Go to sleep, kid,' said Hell. 'We'll have a chat when it's all over.'

Then she was getting onto a trolley, half-asleep, and going down corridors with lovely prints on the walls to a room with a lot of light, and transferring onto another table. She felt as if she could sleep for ever and she hadn't even had the anaesthetic yet. Mr White stood there in a coat brighter than his name. Someone was dressing him up the way they do in films.

She thought about Andy. 'I love you,' she said suddenly.

'Of course you do,' said Mr White, coming over and patting her kindly without a trace of embarrassment.

Then she was being moved again, she thought they hadn't got her right on the operating table, but it wasn't that, it was back into her own bed and more sleep.

There was a tinkle of china. Hell called over from the window.

'Come on, they've brought us some nice soup. Broth they call it.'

May blinked.

'Come on, May. I was done after you and I'm wide awake. Now didn't I tell you there was nothing to it?'

May sat up. No pain, no tearing feeling in her insides. No sickness. 'Are you sure they did me?' she asked.

They both laughed.

They had what the nursing-home called a light lunch. Then they got a menu so that they could choose dinner.

'There are some things that England does really well, and this is one of them,' Hell said approvingly, trying to decide between the delights that were offered. 'They even give us a small carafe of wine. If you want more you have to pay for it. But they kind of disapprove of us getting pissed.'

Hell's friend Charlie was coming in at six when he finished work. Would May be having a friend too, she wondered? No. Celia wouldn't come.

'I don't mean Celia,' said Hell. 'I mean the bloke.'

'He doesn't know, he's in Dublin, and he's married,' said May.

'Well, Charlie's married, but he bloody knows, and he'd know if he were on the moon.'

'It's different.'

'No, it's not different. It's the same for everyone, there are rules, you're a fool to break them. Didn't he pay for it either, this guy?'

'No. I told you he doesn't know.'

'Aren't you noble,' said Hell scornfully. 'Aren't you a real Lady Galahad. Just visiting London for a day or two, darling, just going to see a few friends, see you soon. Love you darling. Is that it?'

'We don't go in for so many darlings as that in Dublin,' said May.

'You don't go in for much common sense either. What will you gain, what will he gain, what will anyone gain? You come home penniless, a bit lonely. He doesn't know what the hell you've been doing, he isn't extra-sensitive and loving and grateful because he doesn't have anything to be grateful about as far as he's concerned.'

'I couldn't tell him. I couldn't. I couldn't ask him for £200 and say what it was for. That wasn't in the bargain, that was never part of the deal.'

May was almost tearful, mainly from jealousy she thought. She couldn't bear Hell's Charlie to come in, while her Andy was going home to his wife because there would be nobody to cook him something exciting and go to bed with him in his little manager's flat.

'When you go back, tell him. That's my advice,' said Hell.

'Tell him you didn't want to worry him, you did it all on your own because the responsibility was yours since you didn't take the Pill. That's unless you think he'd have wanted it?'

'No, he wouldn't have wanted it.'

'Well then, that's what you do. Don't ask him for the money straight out, just let him know you're broke. He'll react some way then. It's silly not to tell them at all. My sister did that with her bloke back in Melbourne. She never told him at all, and she got upset because he didn't know the sacrifice she had made, and every time she bought a drink or paid for a cinema ticket she got resentful of him. All for no reason, because he didn't bloody know.'

'I might,' said May, but she knew she wouldn't.

Charlie came in. He was great fun, very fond of Hell, wanting to be sure she was okay, and no problems. He brought a bottle of wine which they shared, and he told them funny stories about what had happened at the office. He was in advertising. He arranged to meet Hell for lunch next day and joked his way out of the room.

'He's a lovely man,' said May.

'Old Charlie's smashing,' agreed Hell. He had gone back home to entertain his wife and six dinner guests. His wife was a marvellous hostess apparently. They were always having dinner parties.

'Do you think he'll ever leave her?' asked May.

'He'd be out of his brains if he did,' said Hell cheerfully.

May was thoughtful. Maybe everyone would be out of their brains if they left good, comfortable, happy home set-ups for whatever the other woman imagined she could offer. She wished she could be as happy as Hell.

'Tell me about your fellow,' Hell said kindly.

May did, the whole long tale. It was great to have somebody to listen, somebody who didn't say she was on a collision course, somebody who didn't purse up lips like Celia, someone who said, 'Go on, what did you do then?'

'He sounds like a great guy,' said Hell, and May smiled happily.

They exchanged addresses, and Hell promised that if ever she came to Ireland she wouldn't ring up the hotel and say, 'Can I talk to May, the girl I had the abortion with last winter?' and they finished Charlie's wine, and went to sleep.

The beds were stripped early next morning when the final examination had been done, and both were pronounced perfect and ready to leave. May wondered fancifully how many strange life stories the room must have seen.

'Do people come here for other reasons apart from . . . er, terminations?' she asked the disapproving Irish nurse.

'Oh certainly they do, you couldn't work here otherwise,' said the nurse. 'It would be like a death factory, wouldn't it?'

That puts me in my place, thought May, wondering why she hadn't the courage to say that she was only visiting the home, she didn't earn her living from it.

She let herself into Celia's gloomy flat. It had become gloomy again like the way she had imagined it before she saw it. The warmth of her first night there was gone. She looked around and wondered why Celia had no pictures, no books, no souvenirs.

There was a note on the telephone pad.

'I didn't ring or anything, because I forgot to ask if you had given your real name, and I wouldn't know who to ask for. Hope you feel well again. I'll be getting some chicken pieces so we can have supper together around 8. Ring me if you need me. C.'

May thought for a bit. She went out and bought Celia a casserole dish, a nice one made of cast-iron. It would be useful for all those little high-protein, low-calorie dinners Celia cooked. She also bought a bunch of flowers, but could find no vase when she came back and had to use a big glass instead. She left a note thanking her for the hospitality, warm enough to sound properly grateful, and a genuinely warm remark about how glad she was that she had been able to do it all through nice Dr Harris. She said nothing about the time in the nursing-home. Celia would prefer not to know. May just said that she was fine, and thought she would go back to Dublin tonight. She rang the airline and booked a plane.

Should she ring Celia and tell her to get only one chicken piece? No, damn Celia, she wasn't going to ring her. She had a fridge, hadn't she?

The plane didn't leave until the early afternoon. For a wild moment she thought of joining Hell and Charlie in the pub where they were meeting, but dismissed the idea. She must now make a list of what clothes she was meant to have bought and work out a story about how they had disappeared. Nothing that would make Andy get in touch with police or airlines to find them for her. It was going to be quite hard, but she'd have to give Andy some explanation of what she'd been doing, wouldn't she? And he would want to know why she had spent all that money. Or would he? Did he even know she had all that money? She couldn't remember telling him. He wasn't very interested in her little savings, they talked more about his investments. And she must remember that if he was busy or cross tonight or tomorrow she wasn't to take it out on him. Like Hell had said, there wasn't any point in her expecting a bit of cosseting when he didn't even know she needed it.

How sad and lonely it would be to live like Celia, to be so suspicious of men, to think so ill of Andy. Celia always said he was selfish and just took what he could get. That was typical of Celia, she understood nothing. Hell had understood more, in a couple of hours, than Celia had in three years. Hell knew what it was like to love someone.

But May didn't think Hell had got it right about telling Andy all about the abortion. Andy might be against that kind of thing. He was very moral in his own way, was Andy.

Body and Soul

'J'ai deux amours, I have two loves' – remember that song? But she won't be singing that at the funeral. In fact, although the crowds have gathered like moths around this candle-lit Church just to hear her sing, Sarah Vaughan won't be singing at Dooley Wilson's funeral at all.

I will, for I am what's known as a 'godly' singer. I sing at funerals. Chapel or Church, Pentacostal or Congregational – I go where I'm asked. Though the Church of the Blessed Mary remains my funeral singing home, so to speak. 'Mrs Silva has never put red to her lips, she does not smoke, or blaspheme, or take strong drink. And when she lifts up her voice, it is to sing God's praises in his house.'

Father Farrell is a nice enough man. His face is moist and white as an unbaked loaf, risen and unwrapped for the oven. His face has that unwrapped look, though his eyes are very dark and sincere. When he says his little piece I go along with it. Shake my head, pull down the corners of my mouth in a little smile. I worry about other things like are my new shoes too tight for my feet, and did I remember to take the price labels from the backs? Today, especially, I'm worried that the creases will start to show in my skirt, which is a size sixteen and on the small side for my ampleness. Vanity is mine.

I take my seat about half-way down. 'His Eye Is On The Sparrow', I am hymn number three on the hymn-board. A few rows in the front have been left empty for the family – what family there is. Most of the people have packed them-selves in at the back, with the crowds stretching out into the road. In the end, he was one of us; a local entertainer who paved the way for others – meaning Sarah Vaughan – to reach the heights.

I can feel the sway of bodies behind me, hear their breathing, sense the noisy hush of excitement. It's the one thing I don't like about funerals today; this excitement over death, the leaning in on grief; and they won't hold back.

I'm getting too emotional; but then I knew Dooley Wilson before he was Dooley Wilson. When he had a room in my father's boarding house just after the war. He was known as Archibald something or other then; and he played piano, wonderful piano: in between features at the Bug-House; or up at the young peoples' club – the Rainbow Club on the bridge. All the popular tunes of the day, whatever you cared to ask for he'd oblige. And he could imitate all the stars, with that wonderful singing voice of his. 'I'm the sheik, of Ar-ooby!' Wonderful voice, wonderful smile. We all admired him, especially us girls.

He was a smart-looking man. Big built, but smart-looking, with a beautiful razor moustache, and a fine, preacher-blue suit which he always wore on Sundays when he played the piano in our front parlour with the family gathered round. Old fashioned songs like 'No, John, No,' or quiet hymns and spirituals – 'Ezekiel Saw The Wheel'; 'There Is A Balm In Gilead' – songs which pleased my father and mother, especially.

I sang along with the others, but I liked to watch him play. His wide dark hands had pretty fingernails that shone like pearly shells as they struck the key-board. He used pomade on his hair, too, which he kept in a green jar by his bedside along with a flat-backed hairbrush and four or five lavender-coloured tablets of toilet soap. His room had its own specially-scented smell. We used to argue amongst ourselves, one girl and two boys, for the privilege of cleaning it out on a Saturday – as I've said, we all admired him but from a distance – I was only a young girl then and he was a grown man, almost a god in my young, fifteen-year-old eyes.

It was enough for me to lean my mop and bucket against the chest of drawers and run my fingers over the things that were left on top: the hairbrush, with its smooth wooden back; the green fluted jar, the leather manicure case that opened out to show all the silvery instruments he kept inside for keeping his nails nice; for keeping himself nice – trimming his moustache, for instance, or plucking away nose hairs. I'd never seen such shiny, beautiful things before, all inlaid with mother-of-pearl and strange, and beautiful to me, as I held them in my hands.

When he changed his name to 'Dooley Wilson' it was a shock. I remember he told us he was 'hitching his wagon to an unknown star'. We'd never heard of anyone changing their names before. Our silence around the supper table made him laugh. My father, who was a member of the Abyssinian Brethren, said something about the leopard not changing his spots, the Ethiopian his skin. But that just made him laugh all the more, but pleasantly, because he was a same island man, like my father. Still, he threw back his head and laughed, so that the shirt-button came undone at his throat, and I remember how his collar opened up around his wide dark neck, like the white wings of a bird.

After that he became Dooley Wilson. Dooley Wilson? You must remember him – the coloured fellow in the white suit. The one who rolls his eyes when he plays piano in that famous film and sings that famous song, so doleful! As if he already knew, even as he was singing it, poor dab, that he was destined to be forgotten.

Except in our dockland part of the city. You needed an American-sounding name in those days to help with the bookings. And I think it made him laugh, the man lying down there in the coffin; stepping into someone else's shoes and trying to make them fit. Especially as he was a different type of coloured man altogether, really – our Dooley was broader, taller, darker – much darker than the gold-skinned chap in the film; and with a much sweeter singing voice. Not that anyone seemed to notice; and after a while, I don't think he noticed himself. His act fell into more of a comic routine in the end and that kept him popular in all the local clubs long after the days with Sarah Vaughan.

Close my eyes and I can see him now. I saw him once, on my birthday, a couple of years ago. A big fleshy man, decked out in a white, satiny suit. A real professional, flashing his teeth in a smile while his fingers plinked out tunes on the piano: 'You must remember this'. And this, and this – then he'd go into his act, putting on all the voices, pulling faces:

> 'Dot boy over der, what's his name?
> That boy? Why that's Sam, Miss Ilsa. Sam.
> Dey sho is goan be trouble Mister Rick –
> Play it Sam! Sing it Sam!
> Please keep away from him Miss Ilsa; you bad
> luck to 'im!'

The voice was all honey and molasses as he rolled his eyes, and drooped his mouth to make us laugh. Under the amber-coloured spotlights his black skin had a silky-looking sheen to it, still. Like black taffeta, cool, under the spotlights. Of course, I stayed at the back with the girls from work; I didn't come forward at the end to introduce myself. From that distance his heavy-lidded eyes looked dull and small, like two black dots on a pair of ivory dice . . .

Though what I was remembering was the time when he stopped playing piano in our front parlour and told me I had a voice. 'Drink To Me Only With Thine Eyes' I sang, looking at the dried flowers inside the glass dome on the sideboard; then at the black iron archway of the fireplace, with the blue piece of sugar paper folded inside because it was Sunday. It was cold in the room, but the paper seemed to blaze blue when he said that: 'Gracie girl, you've gotta voice!'

He had tossed me that compliment like a flower, and I kept it for a long time, close to my heart.

Once I start remembering I can't control things. The

memories spin around in my head like a big roulette wheel.
Black and red, blue and gold, and I can't control them. I
never know when the wheel is going to stop – it drives my
old man Frank to distraction.

'Sweetness, don't you go sorrowing for that man. It will
only upset you, and for what?'

I was standing in front of the old-fashioned mirror that
hangs over our mantelpiece when Frank said that. I didn't say
anything; just moved my hand along the mantel searching for
the tortoise-shell combs to put in my hair, as if I'd forgotten
where I'd left them, or hadn't heard him right. But I could
see his eyes, looking at me through the mirror. They've got
the same sort of gleam as the television set he sits in front of,
my Frank's eyes. That greenish grey sort of gleam, when it
hasn't been switched on yet.

After a minute or two, when he saw there wasn't going to
be an argument, he picked up the newspaper on his lap and
turned to the horse-racing. Frank knows full well I cry at
funerals; I always cry a little bit, no matter who's it is. But
he's jealous, Frank. He's gotten jealous in his old age. I know
how it is with him, that's why I never bother saying much.
Except I remembered to ask him what he was having for his
tea, before I went through the door. He looked up and
yawned like a baby; both cheeks bellied out, bright as a brass
tea-pot. But inside I thought, corroded. Green. Because I
know, exactly.

'Oh don't you worry about me,' he said. 'I'll fry up the
fish.'

I had taken the fish out of the fridge earlier. Cleaned them
myself, because he says the market girls don't clean them
properly. I don't like cleaning them, but I did it. I took the
knife with the long shining blade, and slit open the soft,
silvery under-belly, scraping out the wraggle of guts. The
blood spilled dark red, like wine, and the fish felt like
something carved, under my hand. I cut the head off, slicing
behind the fins. I was concentrating on how pretty the fish

scales looked towards the tail end; they had a pearly sheen on them, where they caught the light. The fin opened out, shadowy like a bird-wing, when I picked it up between my fingers and threw the head to next-doors cats. I did that twice.

'Are you sure now?' I had to ask, about the tea.

'Sure I'm sure. You go on and bury the dead.'

He looked at me then and showed his teeth, brown between the ivory, in a smile. 'We've all got fish to fry, haven't we?'

'You come with me, then,' I said, as nicely as I could. 'Just to show your face. Frank?'

But he wouldn't budge. So I left him there, sat in front of the television set, waiting for the two o'clock at Sandown. Yet something touched my heart to see him sat, upright, with a hand on each knee of his dark pin-striped trousers. The trousers from what used to be his best suit thirty years ago. And I saw how the hair on his head had gone white and grey, and soft as cigarette ash to the touch. Because I had to rest my hand on his head for a moment before I went through the door.

My thoughts spin round. If the girls on my section could see my eyes fill up they wouldn't know me.

At work I keep my head down and just get on with it. I'm a roller in the cigar factory. I cut tobacco leaf on the machines. I'm a skilled machinist, cutting the leaf – soft brown, or gold, or tawny – on the metal die as the drum turns round. The drum is as big as a silver wheel with twenty-four dents in it. The drum turns round; each silver dent is filled with tobacco that has been wrapped once by the girl at the other end. My leaf is the second wrapping, the one that shows.

The wheel of the drum turns round and round. The clamp picks up the cigars; picks up the cigars, and places them in the dents; on and on. The cigars roll down the belt and I pick them up five at a time, scoop them up with my free hand. Bin the bad ones, and pack them, row upon row in the tins, without stopping. None of that stopping and starting. Not for me. It's very rare for me to have to take my foot off the pedal. Very rare. Five hundred cigars per tin, ten tins to reach my target: that's five thousand cigars minimum, and then move on to bonus. And always cutting my leaf to get my number out!

I've been rolling cigars for years. Though these days I'm on part-time. It's a well enough paid job, part-time. There's nothing romantic or exotic or steamy about it, except in other people's imaginations, other people's bad minds, as Frank would say. Sometimes, during the summer months, when it gets really hot – when the machines are roaring and the generator's going full blast, the girls will ask me to give them the lead in a song. 'Grace, give us a song,' they'll say. 'Please!' And I'll often come out with a Christmas Carol – 'In The Bleak Mid-Winter' perhaps, or 'See Amidst The Winter's Snow'. Christmas Carols have a cooling effect, when you're singing them in August and you're stuck there, in a forest of palm-green overalls, trying to cut your leaf to get your number out.

When I was a young girl I sang different songs – 'I Don't Want To Set The World On Fire!' That was one of our favourites – I laugh when I think of it now. We formed a group, me and Baby Cleo and Sarah Vaughan. And practised singing in work time. Our first and last performance was at the Rainbow Club, one Bonfire Night. Those two hoofing across the stage, doing the high stepping and the 'Whoo-ooh-whoo-oohs' behind me, while I stood still and sang, happy not to have to shake too much because of my bulk. The three of us wore wrap-over pinnies, yellowy white, and brown berets. We called ourselves, 'The Safety Matches'.

Dooley Wilson played piano for everyone who was performing. 'Bye-bye Black Bird', that was our encore! It was me and Baby who had the idea for it; then we had to have Sarah to make the number up.

Hark at me, sat inside this darkened Church with my mind wandering. But that's always the way with funerals, isn't it? The emotion comes and goes, like God's grace, or the light falling in on us now from the high windows. It comes and goes. Walking down the road towards the Church the sun was shining, where a minute before it had been raining. Warm spring rain. Standing by the kerb, waiting to cross, I saw white cloud and blue sky mirrored in the black water as it ran into the gutter. So clear, it make me think; to see the sky beneath my feet as if the earth had gone.

There were quite a few mourners waiting outside the Church. I counted more women than men, standing under the trees in silent clumps of black. The wreaths had been propped against the funeral car windows. I saw two red hearts and a cross made up of curling, wax-white petals and I wondered who had sent them; these tokens of love and tribulation, love and trouble? He had no wife to speak of.

Baby Cleo came over to talk to me. Old friends. We stood by the black speared railings and talked a little bit. She said she'd heard a rumour that Sarah Vaughan had managed to telephone Dooley Wilson long distance, just the night before he died. Baby couldn't get over it. 'Imagine,' she kept saying as we walked through the gate and into the Church yard. 'After all them years, oh God love 'em.' She dabbed her eyes with a hanky.

It's like a film, I thought. But I didn't say anything. People see life down here like a film.

But it's different for Baby. She was one of the girls who joined the dance-troupe. The one Dooley Wilson got together and toured the Valleys with in the early fifties. 'Jolson's Jelly Jelly Babes' they were called, or some such; and Sarah Vaughan made her name in it. Blacking her face up and acting comic at the end of the line. If Al Jolson'd had an illegitimate daughter, the papers said, she'd have been it. Baby was one of the girls who came back on the charabanc, while Miss Sassy Vaughan ended up in a London show: swaying in front of a

coconut tree, under a pale yellow moon. Sarah Vaughan, the
coloured young lady with the Welsh name. The sepia celtic
siren they billed her as. That was her gimmick. Batting her
eye-lashes and telling reporters she was a native, of Cardiff.
Some of them thought she was American, but she didn't have
that good a voice.

I was glad not to have been part of the Valleys tour; the
other girls were all a bit downcast when they got off the bus.
Proud, but downcast.

Baby Cleo's put on a lot of weight since her time as a
dancer. It used to be just me who was the hefty one. Her face
is like a round beige moon, and she moves heavily. My face is
like a round dark moon and I stump along. Her face-powder
blows into the air as she walks. To my mind, the soft grains
seemed to cling to the decaying flowers in the grass, the
shrivelled clumps of daffodils and narcissi, the clusters of
moth-brown petals on the hydrangea bushes, and give them
scent and life. The Church garden is neglected, though if you
were to mention it to Father Farrell he would tell you that
he's here to tend his flock, not his pasture. A wreath of
poppies placed at the stony foot of the cross in late November
are the only spots of colour, like the last drops of blood
drained from the body of Christ that hangs above them.

I was surprised to see more people crowded around the side
entrance as we approached. But Baby said they were waiting
there just in case Sarah Vaughan were to turn up. It had said
over the local radio that she wouldn't, couldn't; but people
still hoped she might appear, unannounced, the way stars do.

He will always be remembered as the man who discovered
Sarah Vaughan, I think. That will be Dooley Wilson's epitaph,
discovering her. Like finding something valuable and precious
that no one else had even realized was there before. Mr
Columbus.

There's only a month between our birth signs, mine and
Sarah Vaughan's. Not that I believe in that sort of thing, but
it makes you wonder. We both started out over the cigar

factory on the same day, bunching and rolling tobacco leaf on the same machine, getting our numbers out – and singing together, high over the noise of the machinery . . . all those years ago. We were friends, I suppose. But it wasn't all cosy and sentimental. Oh no, because I was the roller and she was only the buncher. And she didn't like that, because I got paid more, I did more too, but you could never reason with her.

> 'Stuff it, I wanna go home!
> Stuff it, I wanna go,
> But they woan let me go,
> Stuff it, I wanna go home!'

Except that she used to sing other words, staring down the length of our machine Number 28, with cheek and daring in her eyes I used to think, as I scooped up the cigars and stacked them neatly. Always the calm and steady one; steady and responsible, that was me. And I think it used to provoke her, Sarah, into behaving worse. She was a wild one, one of those girls who wouldn't take a telling, not from the foreman, the supervisor or anyone.

'Keep your eyes off Norman, he's mine!' She was always threatening people. Or, 'Think I'm gonna spend the rest of my life in this place? Uh. Uh. Not me! So what if they pays better than the brush factory, or the box factory, so what!' And that was to the foreman. She didn't care, Sarah. Most of the other girls admired her for the way she acted. But I could see it for the put-on it was. She hadn't been brought up properly. Her father had left her mother to bring up three small kids; and they were dragged up, not brought up, like the rest of us. She wasn't sure about a lot of things; behind the loudness I could see. It was easy to get to her if you put your mind to it.

Some things she had going for her – she had a good figure. And she was tall for her age, with a jutting bosom and a narrow waist. But she wore her wiry hair swept over to one side, in imitation of some Hollywood film star or other – it used to curtain half her face, like the brown-gold webbing on the mouth of a wireless, unravelled. Sometimes she tied it back, and I thought that looked much nicer, neater. Not that you could tell her anything, though. Sarah Vaughan. She took that name Vaughan from the man her mother was living with at the time. Her real name was more common: Jones, everybody knew that. But — her eyes were brown like toffee, and her skin was bright like tin; and if she wanted to call herself after her mother's fancy man then she would.

The name-change came after the performance at the Rainbow Club. At first she hadn't wanted to waste a Saturday night at home in the dockland. 'The Rainbow Club!' she said when I asked her to make up our number. She curled her lip. 'Run Off Young Girls, Boys In View — it's run by the friggin' missionaries, ain it?' She came with us. She wanted to go to the American base in Brize Norton where the soldiers were. But her mother said no, for a wonder. So she ended up with us, performing with me and Baby down the club, because it was some kind of 'do' and she knew the song; we'd sung it in work often enough and the steps were easy.

It was raining that Bonfire Night. Everything was gleaming black with rain. And I can remember Sarah, standing at the end of the arched bridge, just in front of the club, frightened to go inside on her own. The tweed coat she had on was water-logged and rucked up at the back, and she'd straightened her hair too much at the front, greased it so that the drops of water stayed in her hair and glittered like small glass beads. A fringe of glittering cheap glass beads. Only it wasn't. But that's what I remember: the rain, and the sound of it running into the gutters and flowing under the bridge as we stood there. And the child's voice, reciting through the club's open door, '"Tiger, tiger, burnin bright, inna forest of the night . . ."'

On the Monday morning she was late for work.

'A grown-man, right? Wants to go out with me.'

All five of us sitting around the canteen table looked at her.

'What would he want with someone like you then, Sair, a grown man?'

But the women on the table were nudging one another and laughing. Sarah laughed along with them, then she pushed a scribble of brassy hair away from her face and took a swig from a bottle of Tizer. 'She knows him.' She nodded in my direction, smiling. 'He's a big feller, ain he?' She took another swig from the bottle and burped. 'An' he wears an awful blue suit I'd like to set alight to, with a match . . .'

The women around the table laughed and someone said, 'Well, madam, are you going to meet up with this one or not?' Sarah placed her elbows on the table and leaned forward, her eyes danced. 'Oh I'm definitely going! He wants to give me breathing lessons, doan he? Says it'll improve my singing voice.' She coughed.

They all thought that was funny, and they roared. Even Baby, though she had left the club with me and must have been as surprised as I was. We did our encore, 'Bye-bye Blackbird', and we left. People were clapping us out, because we'd been a hit. Funny. We were supposed to be funny, but it was Sarah who had been the funny one. Going cross-eyed in the background as I sang. She made them laugh as I was singing. I had to turn round, to see what they were laughing at. The piano was slow and lilting. It wasn't him; he played it right. But she made it funny, whipping another beret out of her pocket near the end and flinging it on top of the piano, to land as I came out with the last line: about wanting to start a flame in your heart. The beret wasn't brown but yellow, like sulphur, this time. I suppose that was the joke.

I watched her wipe her mouth with the back of her hand. She hadn't said anything nice about him, only nasty. She hadn't even mentioned his piano playing, or his smile, or his beautiful razor moustache. Nothing, only smut.

'An who'd you think you're looking at? she asked, still smiling. 'I'm looking at you,' I said in a steady voice. 'You've got no manners, have you? Sitting there with your elbows on the table, drinking out of a bottle!'

The others were embarrassed. To hear me coming out with something like that, out of the blue. Everyone stared at the Tizer bottle, mesmerized by the sudden shame of it. And Sarah's mouth opened and closed a few times before she leaned across the table with a little screech and dragged her fingernails down the side of my face, once.

Then she clip-clopped through the canteen doors and was gone before I'd even got to my feet. But I remember holding my hands to my breast and screaming after her: 'You tart! You tart, you!' I must have looked a pretty sight, standing there, screaming my head off with my cheek puffed up like pastry and the blood seeping through red, like jam.

A storm in a tea-cup. No one had any idea what it was all about, least of all Sarah Vaughan, who got the sack for it. One misdemeanour too many, or so they said. I was given a warning because I'd acted out of character, they said. I saw her later that afternoon at four o'clock. She was standing by the fire-bucket outside the foreman's office, waiting for her wages to be made up. I had to walk past her. She was wearing her old tweed coat with the rucked-up hem. She muttered something as I went past. When I got to the end of the corridor I looked round; she had taken her compact out of her bag and was busy putting lipstick on. Pulling her mouth over her teeth and making her lips into dark red wings.

If I felt guilty about her getting the sack the feeling didn't last long, because only a couple of months later she was off with him, touring the Valleys as a Jelly Babe. And the rest, as they say, is history. But not for me, my mind keeps going back to it.

I remember having to go up to his room on an errand, after the fight with Sarah. I knocked at the door, my face still smarting. I was holding the blue suit over my arm. My mother had had it cleaned and ironed for him. I was hoping he'd be out. But he was only getting ready to go out. He couldn't take the suit from me at the door; his hands were slick with pomade.

He left the door ajar and I walked in and draped the suit carefully over the chair. He had turned back to the mirror. The contents of the manicure case were spread out on top of the chest of drawers. All silvery and pretty, with the mother-of-pearl inlay along each handle. He'd been trimming his moustache, I could see that; prettifying himself.

He said something about starting up a dance-troupe. 'I want you to come with us,' he said, taking more pomade from the jar and smoothing it onto his head like green ice. 'A Jolson Jelly Babe!' He was laughing in front of the mirror. There was a white shirt on the bed, whiter than the one he had on. A tie had been placed alongside the shirt, ready for going out I supposed. The tie had a pattern of small red diamonds on it. Flashy, like a playing card, I saw.

'I'm Alabamy bound!' He waved his hands like a minstrel in front of the glass, laughing at his own reflection.

'Ok. Grace.' He could see that I wasn't smiling back. He took his own smile from the glass and turned to face me with it.

I remember him putting his hand to my cheek and stroking it in surprise, when he saw the marks. 'You're a nice girl,' he said, over and over again. 'A nice girl. Grace. Did you know that?' He stopped stroking my face and glanced towards the open door. Then he put his arms around my body and drew me close to him.

I felt his head against my neck.

'Ma-mmy . . .' he was crooning softly, singing against my neck.

'. . . Ma-mmy.' Leaning into my breasts, and singing, like Al Jolson '. . . mm mm.' I could see us in the mirror. His arms around the dark width of me, his face heavy against my neck.

And I held him to me, young as I was. I put my hands against his white-shirted back and held him, firmly. His shoulder blades parted under the pressure of my hands. I felt them opening out and spreading, under my hands, like the white wings of a bird. I heard him sigh. Then, still holding him with one hand, I put the other on top of the chest of drawers and picked up one of the silvery instruments. It was the one he used for trimming his moustache. I picked it up by the handle, the mother-of-pearl handle, and stabbed the shiny point into his back. Just once.

I let myself into his room after he'd left us. The blue suit was hanging up behind the door on a wire coat-hanger. I put my hand inside the pockets and drew out two lavender-coloured bus tickets and a card of matches. The pink had bled on the matches so I threw them into the empty fire-grate. Looking down, I saw his passport photo wedged between a crack in the oil-cloth and the clawed foot of the chest of drawers.

I eased it out with my thumb and looked at his face for a long time, but I didn't see it. The wound was only a flesh wound, like a small red diamond on his shirt, before it blossomed into a flower shape and had to be bandaged up. He had packed his bags himself, moving in with Sarah Vaughan that same night. But nothing came of it. Their love affair, so called. Which didn't survive her fame, how could it?

And now he was dead.

Love is a bird that flies where it will, that's what it says in the song. But I think we travel in flocks; different flocks, cut into by our shadows, our opposites flying the other way. And not just for love, but for life.

I tucked the tiny photograph inside the wooden frame of the mirror. I remember doing that and stepping back further and further into the darkness of the room until it looked as though a face had been imprinted on my forehead. His face. His eyes were just gashes of black – black with pin-points of light at the centres, like domino pieces. Then the photograph came unstuck, and dropped to the floor.

The Lord is my shepherd I shall not want.

Father Farrell bares his teeth in pearly-gated smile. A signal, but when I get up to sing I find that my heart isn't in it. My face is as dry as tobacco leaf. And my lungs feel heavy and empty at the same time, like the blackened boughs of a tree in winter. I picture my lungs like that. And yet. And yet . . . as soon as the organ music starts up those opening chords . . . I move my bulk and sing. The fat lady is singing.

'And I sing because I'm happy; and I sing because I'm free!' Vanity I think, as I sense the congregation perk up behind me. All is vanity. But Baby Cleo is smiling; smiling and crying at the same time. And myself?

I have hoarded my tears like a jewel thief, but one or two steal down my face now as I look towards the coffin for the first time. Sing! I think, even as my voice veers out of control, high as a bird's, a small falsetto; then deeper than the deepest tolling of the bell. A ruined voice; a factory girl's voice; cracked, but sincere.

ANGELA CARTER

Peter and the Wolf

At length the grandeur of the mountains becomes monotonous; with familiarity, the landscape ceases to provoke awe and wonder and the traveller sees the alps with the indifferent eye of those who always live there. Above a certain line, no trees grow. Shadows of clouds move across the bare alps as freely as the clouds themselves move across the sky.

A girl from a village on the lower slopes left her widowed mother to marry a man who lived up in the empty places. Soon she was pregnant. In October, there was a severe storm. The old woman knew her daughter was near her time and waited for a message but none arrived. After the storm passed, the old woman went up to see for herself, taking her grown son with her because she was afraid.

From a long way off they saw no smoke rising from the chimney. Solitude yawned round them. The open door banged backwards and forwards on its hinges. Solitude engulfed them. There were traces of wolf-dung on the floor so they knew wolves had been in the house but left the corpse of the young mother alone although of her baby nothing was left except some mess that showed it had been born. Nor was there a trace of the son-in-law but a gnawed foot in a boot.

They wrapped the dead in a quilt and took it home with them. Now it was late. The howling of the wolves mutilated the approaching silence of the night.

Winter came with icy blasts, when everyone stays indoors and stokes the fire. The old woman's son married the blacksmith's daughter and she moved in with them. The snow melted and it was spring. By the next Christmas, there was a bouncing grandson. Time passed. More children came.

When the eldest grandson, Peter, reached his seventh summer, he was old enough to go up the mountain with his father, as the men did every year, to let the goats feed on the young grass. There Peter sat in the new sunlight, plaiting the straw for baskets, until he saw the thing he had been taught most to fear advancing silently along the lea of an outcrop of rock. Then another wolf, following the first one.

If they had not been the first wolves he had ever seen, the boy would not have inspected them so closely, their plush, grey pelts, of which the hairs are tipped with white, giving them a ghostly look, as if they were on the point of dissolving at the edges; their sprightly, plumey tails; their acute, inquisitive masks.

Then Peter saw that the third wolf was a prodigy, a marvel, a naked one, going on all fours, as they did, but hairless as regards the body although hair grew around its head.

The sight of this bald wolf so fascinated him that he would have lost his flock, perhaps himself been eaten and certainly been beaten to the bone for negligence had not the goats themselves raised their heads, snuffed danger and run off, bleating and whinnying, so that the men came, firing guns, making hullabaloo, scaring the wolves away.

His father was too angry to listen to what Peter said. He cuffed Peter round the head and sent him home. His mother was feeding this year's baby. His grandmother sat at the table, shelling peas into a pot.

'There was a little girl with the wolves, granny,' said Peter. Why was he so sure it had been a little girl? Perhaps because her hair was so long, so long and lively. 'A little girl about my age, from her size,' he said.

His grandmother threw a flat pod out of the door so the chickens could peck it up.

'I saw a little girl with the wolves,' he said.

His grandmother tipped water into the pot, got up from the table and hung the pot of peas on the hook over the fire. There wasn't time, that night, but, next morning, very early, she herself took the boy back up the mountain.

'Tell your father what you told me.'

They went to look at the wolves' tracks. On a bit of dampish ground they found a print, not like that of a dog's pad, much less like that of a child's footprint, yet Peter worried and puzzled over it until he made sense of it.

'She was running on all fours with her arse stuck up in the air . . . therefore . . . she'd put all her weight on the ball of her foot, wouldn't she? And splay out her toes, see . . . like that.'

He went barefoot in summer, like all the village children; he inserted the ball of his own foot in the print, to show his father what kind of mark he would have made if he, too, always ran on all fours.

'No use for a heel, if you run that way. So she doesn't have a heel-print. Stands to reason.'

At last his father made a slow acknowledgement of Peter's powers of deduction, giving the child a veiled glance of disquiet. It was a clever child.

They soon found her. She was asleep. Her spine had grown so supple she could curl into a perfect C. She woke up when she heard them and ran, but somebody caught her with a sliding noose at the end of a rope; the noose over her head jerked tight and she fell to the ground with her eyes popping and rolling. A big, grey, angry bitch appeared out of nowhere but Peter's father blasted it to bits with his shotgun. The girl would have choked if the old woman hadn't taken her head on her lap and pulled the knot loose. The girl bit the grandmother's hand.

The girl scratched and fought until the men tied her wrists and ankles together with twine and slung her from a pole to carry her back to the village. Then she went limp. She didn't scream or shout, she didn't seem to be able to, she made only a few dull, guttural sounds in the back of her throat, and, though she did not seem to know how to cry, water trickled out of the corners of her eyes.

How burned she was by the weather! Bright brown all over; and how filthy she was! Caked with mud and dirt. And every inch of her chestnut hide was scored and scabbed with dozens of scars of sharp abrasions of rock and thorn. Her hair dragged on the ground as they carried her along; it was stuck with burrs and it was so dirty you could not see what colour it might be. She was dreadfully verminous. She stank. She was so thin that all her ribs stuck out. The fine, plump, potato-fed boy was far bigger than she, although she was a year or so older.

Solemn with curiosity, he trotted behind her. Granny stumped alongside with her bitten hand wrapped up in her apron. Once the girl was dumped on the earth floor of her grandmother's house, the boy secretly poked at her left buttock with his forefinger, out of curiosity, to see what she felt like. She felt warm but hard. She did not so much as twitch when he touched her. She had given up the struggle; she lay trussed on the floor and pretended to be dead.

Granny's house had the one large room which, in winter, they shared with the goats. As soon as it caught a whiff of her, the big tabby mouser hissed like a pricked balloon and bounded up the ladder that went to the hayloft above. Soup smoked on the fire and the table was laid. It was now about supper-time but still quite light; night comes late on the summer mountain.

'Untie her,' said the grandmother.

Her son wasn't willing at first but the old woman would not be denied, so he got the breadknife and cut the rope round the girl's ankles. All she did was kick, but when he cut the rope round her wrists, it was as if he had let a fiend loose. The onlookers ran out of the door, the rest of the family ran for the ladder to the hayloft but Granny and Peter both ran to the door, to shoot the bolt, so she could not get out.

The trapped one knocked round the room. Bang – over went the table. Crash, tinkle – the supper dishes smashed. Bang, crash, tinkle – the dresser fell forward upon the hard white shale of crockery it shed in falling. Over went the meal barrel and she coughed, she sneezed like a child sneezes, no different, and then she bounced around on fear-stiffened legs in a white cloud until the flour settled on everything like a magic powder that made everything strange. Her first frenzy over, she squatted a moment, questing with her long nose and then began to make little rushing sorties, now here, now there, snapping and yelping and tossing her bewildered head.

She never rose up on two legs; she crouched, all the time, on her hands and tiptoes; yet it was not quite like crouching, for you could see how all fours came naturally to her as though she had made a different pact with gravity than we have, and you could see, too, how strong the muscles in her thighs had grown on the mountain, how taut the twanging arches of her feet, and that indeed, she only used her heels when she sat back on her haunches. She growled; now and then she coughed out those intolerable, thick grunts of distress. All you could see of her rolling eyes were the whites, which were the bluish, glaring white of snow.

Several times, her bowels opened, apparently involuntarily. The kitchen smelled like a privy yet even her excrement was different to ours, the refuse of raw, strange, unguessable, wicked feeding, shit of a wolf.

Oh, horror!

She bumped into the hearth, knocked over the pan hanging from the hook and the spilled contents put out the fire. Hot soup scalded her forelegs. Shock of pain. Squatting on her hindquarters, holding the hurt paw dangling piteously from its wrist before her, she howled, in high, sobbing arcs.

Even the old woman, who had contracted with herself to love the child of her dead daughter, was frightened when she heard the girl howl.

Peter's heart gave a hop, a skip, so that he had a sensation of falling; he was not conscious of his own fear because he could not take his eyes off the sight of the crevice of her girl-child's sex, that was perfectly visible to him as she sat there square on the base of her spine. The night was now as dark as, at this season, it would go – which is to say, not very dark; a white thread of moon hung in the blond sky at the top of the chimney so that it was neither dark nor light indoors yet the boy could see her intimacy clearly, as if by its own phosphorescence. It exercised an absolute fascination upon him.

Her lips opened up as she howled so that she offered him, without her own intention or volition, a view of a set of Chinese boxes of whorled flesh that seemed to open one upon another into herself, drawing him into an inner, secret place in which destination perpetually receded before him, his first, devastating, vertiginous intimation of infinity.

She howled.

And went on howling until, from the mountain, first singly, then in a complex polyphony, answered at last voices in the same language.

She continued to howl, though now with a less tragic resonance.

Soon it was impossible for the occupants of the house to deny to themselves that the wolves were descending on the village in a pack.

Then she was consoled, sank down, laid her head on her forepaws so that her hair trailed in the cooling soup and so closed up her forbidden book without the least notion she had ever opened it or that it was banned. Her heavy eyelids closed on her brown, bloodshot eyes. The household gun hung on a nail over the fireplace where Peter's father had put it when he came in but when the man set his foot on the top rung of the ladder in order to come down for his weapon, the girl jumped up, snarling and showing her long yellow canines.

The howling outside was now mixed with the agitated dismay of the domestic beasts. All the other villagers were well locked up at home.

The wolves were at the door.

The boy took hold of his grandmother's uninjured hand. First the old woman would not budge but he gave her a good tug and she came to herself. The girl raised her head suspiciously but let them by. The boy pushed his grandmother up the ladder in front of him and drew it up behind them. He was full of nervous dread. He would have given anything to turn time back, so that he might have run, shouting a warning, when he first caught sight of the wolves, and never seen her.

The door shook as the wolves outside jumped up at it and the screws that held the socket of the bolt to the frame cracked, squeaked and started to give. The girl jumped up, at that, and began to make excited little sallies back and forth in front of the door. The screws tore out of the frame quite soon. The pack tumbled over one another to get inside.

Dissonance. Terror. The clamour within the house was that of all the winds of winter trapped in a box. That which they feared most, outside, was now indoors with them. The baby in the hayloft whimpered and its mother crushed it to her breast as if the wolves might snatch this one away, too; but the rescue party had arrived only in order to collect their fosterling.

They left behind a riotous stench in the house, and white tracks of flour everywhere. The broken door creaked backwards and forwards on its hinges. Black sticks of dead wood from the extinguished fire were scattered on the floor.

Peter thought the old woman would cry, now, but she seemed unmoved. When all was safe, they came down the ladder one by one and, as if released from a spell of silence, burst into excited speech except for the mute old woman and the distraught boy. Although it was well past midnight, the daughter-in-law went to the well for water to scrub the wild smell out of the house. The broken things were cleared up and thrown away. Peter's father nailed the table and the dresser back together. The neighbours came out of their houses, full of amazement; the wolves had not taken so much as a chicken from the hen-coops, not snatched even a single egg.

People brought beer into the starlight, and schnapps made from potatoes, and snacks, because the excitement had made them hungry. That terrible night ended up in one big party but the grandmother would eat or drink nothing and went to bed as soon as her house was clean.

Next day, she went to the graveyard and sat for a while beside her daughter's grave but she did not pray. Then she came home and started chopping cabbage for the evening meal but had to leave off because her bitten hand was festering.

That winter, during the leisure imposed by the snow, after his grandmother's death, Peter asked the village priest to teach him to read the Bible. The priest gladly complied; Peter was the first of his flock who had ever expressed any interest in learning to read.

The boy became very pious, so much so that his family were startled and impressed. The younger children teased him and called him 'Saint Peter' but that did not stop him sneaking off to church to pray whenever he had a spare moment. In Lent, he fasted to the bone. On Good Friday, he lashed himself. It was as if he blamed himself for the death of the old lady, as if he believed he had brought into the house the fatal infection that had taken her out of it. He was consumed by an imperious passion for atonement. Each night, he pored over his book by the flimsy candlelight, looking for a clue to grace, until his mother shooed him off to sleep.

But, as if to spite the four evangelists he nightly invoked to protect his bed, the nightmare regularly disordered his sleeps. He tossed and turned on the rustling straw pallet he shared with two little ones.

Delighted with Peter's precocious intelligence, the priest started to teach him Latin. Peter visited the priest as his duties with the herd permitted. When he was fourteen, the priest told his parents that Peter should now go to the seminary in the town in the valley where the boy would learn to become a priest himself. Rich in sons, they spared one to God, since his books and his praying made him a stranger to them. After the goats came down from the high pasture for the winter, Peter set off. It was October.

At the end of his first day's travel, he reached a river that ran from the mountain into the valley. The nights were already chilly; he lit himself a fire, prayed, ate bread and cheese his mother had packed for him and slept as well as he could. In spite of his eagerness to plunge into the white world of penance and devotion that awaited him, he was anxious and troubled for reasons he could not explain to himself.

In the first light, the light that no more than clarifies darkness like egg shells dropped in cloudy liquid, he went down to the river to drink and to wash his face. It was so still he could have been the one thing living.

Her forearms, her loins and her legs were thick with hair and the hair on her head hung round her face in such a way that you could hardly make out her features. She crouched on the other side of the river. She was lapping up water so full of mauve light that it looked as if she were drinking up the dawn as fast as it appeared yet all the same the air grew pale while he was looking at her.

Solitude and silence; all still.

She could never have acknowledged that the reflection beneath her in the river was that of herself. She did not know she had a face; she had never known she had a face and so her face itself was the mirror of a different kind of consciousness than ours is, just as her nakedness, without innocence or display, was that of our first parents, before the Fall. She was hairy as Magdalen in the wilderness and yet repentance was not within her comprehension.

Language crumbled into dust under the weight of her speechlessness.

A pair of cubs rolled out of the bushes, cuffing one another. She did not pay them any heed.

The boy began to tremble and shake. His skin prickled. He felt he had been made of snow and now might melt. He mumbled something, or sobbed.

She cocked her head at the vague, river-washed sound and the cubs heard it, too, left off tumbling and ran to burrow their scared heads in her side. But she decided, after a moment, there was no danger and lowered her muzzle, again, to the surface of the water that took hold of her hair and spread it out around her head.

When she finished her drink, she backed a few paces, shaking her wet pelt. The little cubs fastened their mouths on her dangling breasts.

Peter could not help it, he burst out crying. He had not cried since his grandmother's funeral. Tears rolled down his face and splashed on the grass. He blundered forward a few steps into the river with his arms held open, intending to cross over to the other side to join her in her marvellous and private grace, impelled by the access of an almost visionary ecstasy. But his cousin took fright at the sudden movement, wrenched her teats away from the cubs and ran off. The squeaking cubs scampered behind. She ran on hands and feet as if that were the only way to run towards the high ground, into the bright maze of the uncompleted dawn.

When the boy recovered himself, he dried his tears on his sleeve, took off his soaked boots and dried his feet and legs on the tail of his shirt. Then he ate something from his pack, he scarcely knew what, and continued on the way to the town; but what would he do at the seminary, now? For now he knew there was nothing to be afraid of.

He experienced the vertigo of freedom.

He carried his boots slung over his shoulder by the laces. They were a great burden. He debated with himself whether or not to throw them away but, when he came to a paved road, he had to put them on, although they were still damp.

The birds woke up and sang. The cool, rational sun surprised him; morning had broken on his exhilaration and the mountain now lay behind him. He looked over his shoulder and saw, how, with distance, the mountain began to acquire a flat, two-dimensional look. It was already turning into a picture of itself, into the postcard hastily bought as a souvenir of childhood at a railway station or a border post, the newspaper cutting, the snapshot he would show in strange towns, strange cities, other countries he could not, at this moment, imagine, whose names he did not yet know, places where he would say, in strange languages, 'That was where I spent my childhood. Imagine!'

He turned and stared at the mountain for a long time. He had lived in it for fourteen years but he had never seen it before as it might look to someone who had not known it as almost a part of the self, so, for the first time, he saw the primitive, vast, magnificent, barren, unkind, simplicity of the mountain. As he said goodbye to it, he saw it turn into so much scenery, into the wonderful backcloth for an old country tale, tale of a child suckled by wolves, perhaps, or of wolves nursed by a woman.

Then he determinedly set his face towards the town and tramped onwards, into a different story.

'If I look back again,' he thought with a last gasp of superstitious terror, 'I shall turn into a pillar of salt.'

JUDITH CONDON

Scorched Earth

At ten o'clock, feeling uneasy, I put aside my book and rake what's left of the coal to the front of the grate. Ash falls down and glows between the bars. I lift and lower the door-latch quietly, though there is no one to hear it but me. Out in the hall the cold is waiting. I feel it on my face and neck. I feel it rising through my slippers from the flagstones as I lift my coat from its peg. The sheepskin chills my shoulders at first, and my hands are already losing their warmth as I slip the buttons through the button holes. But I do it easily because the holes have stretched wide with the years.

The kitchen is warm enough. I stand for a moment at the window, looking out through the darkness. The farm cats are fighting again. Cold moonlight picks them out on the dry stone wall – the lean, buff-coloured tom and his young white rival. The white cat squeals, then drops into Hindley's field and out of sight.

I open the door of the Rayburn and shoot in some coal. It is foolish, perhaps, this keeping two fires alight. But I've no wish to huddle day and night in the kitchen. And the warmth will not be wasted. It will rise up the chimney breast and keep the night frost from my bedroom; it will warm the little pan of oatmeal I've already put to soak for my breakfast; and the coal laid on top of this coal tomorrow will in turn cook my dinner. Coal. What it meant to us once. So much it meant!

I push off my slippers, the right then the left, and slip my feet into my boots. The fur inside is warm from the stove.

Perhaps tomorrow I will leave my coat in here too. I can surely find an old hook somewhere, to screw into the cupboard door. Just while this cold spell lasts. I open the back door and step down into the garage. I squeeze past the old Mini, pull my gloves from my pockets, and go out through the open doorway.

Outside the air is sharp and still. Its coldness scours the inside of my nose. I've been indoors all day — it's only now I feel fully awake. The moonlight shows me where to place my feet. Where there was soft mud a week ago, there is now frozen earth, moulded in peaks and ruts that send fear through my ankles. I make my way up to the gate, where frost is forming on the top-most bar. I lift and pull it open just enough to slip through, and hear the metal clang as it falls back into place. Out on the stony track I turn left and head up towards the edge of the moor. I am anxious not to fall. But my eyes are good. I depend on my eyes.

Only at the top, at the last gate, do I turn. Up here in the quiet I am rarely afraid.

A crescent moon, huge and tipped back like a rocking chair, is lighting the hillside. It catches the telegraph poles, the wires, and the roof of my house below. Hindley's farm, on the lower road, is hidden by the curve of the hill. Miles across the valley, beyond the wood, two or three clusters of light mark where other people are — the villages, the town. They seem as remote as the stars. And such stars! The sky as clear and dark as I've ever known it — but brimful of them. Does the sky look this way when night settles on the desert? I catch myself shivering. And suddenly — a classroom — a row of faces. And at the very front an under-sized brown-haired child struggling to recite from memory. I know her anxiety, my heart goes out to her.

> 'On Wenlock's Edge the wood's in trouble;
>   His forest fleece the Wrekin heaves;'

A ragged chorus of voices takes over:

'The gale, it plies the saplings double,
And thick on Severn snow the leaves.'

My lips are moving, but no sound is coming from them. I
am not alone, then, after all.

I can't get into the old chest of drawers. I've been out in the
garage in search of a hook, but I can't open the drawers where
the tools and nails are because the Mini is parked up tight
against them on the far side. How long has it been like this? I
simply don't remember when that car was last out. Back in
the kitchen I've taken the odds-and-ends box from the dresser,
and emptied it onto a newspaper on the table. There's the
usual mess of items. I might even find a hook among them.
But no. Here are the keys, at least, their worn leather tag. I
step outside again. The driver's door is stiff and the seat
seems lower down than ever. Sure enough, as I turn the key, I
am reproached by a deathly rattle. I pull the choke out as far
as it will go, and try again. Again that awful sound, and
several times more. I think to release the hand brake and let
the car roll back a few inches. I'm not even certain what's
behind it. A miracle! Now that I try again, the engine groans
into life.

And with the engine, Jim. No miracle, I hear him say.
Good basic engineering. Always the same. Even propped on
hospital pillows, when we knew he'd never drive again – still
wanting to know how the old car was running. I could have
replaced it, it wasn't the cost. Mad to have moved up here
any way – didn't they all tell me so! – but an antique Mini?
On these ruts and stones? Hasn't it always been my way to
hold on to things too long?

It wouldn't have been my choice, this car. My right hand's
not so stiff this morning and I spread my fingers against the
glass of the sliding window. You always had to do that to
stop it falling out when you shut the door. The glass is dirty.
And now I can see him, leaning his hand on the bonnet.

'Move with the times, that's the thing!' It was a Saturday morning he went to collect it . . . drove off in the old Ford Prefect, and just before dinner time we heard him calling, 'Come and see!' There he is, leaning on the bonnet, shouting, never mind who hears him.

'Come out – come and see!'

'Look out the window, quick!' the boys are yelling. It might be a mirage and fade away. And we all have to get in, no arguments allowed. It's the big windows they like, the sense of space inside.

Cautiously I am pressing down the clutch and moving the gear lever forward. Like a learner driver, I am balancing my feet, listening for the right sound. Now it comes, a change of key. Unconsciously I lift the clutch and the car jumps up the slope. It shoots out through the doorway into bright sunlight – and stalls to a halt on the grass. Now I see just how filthy the windows are. I wipe the glass of the instrument panel with my handkerchief, and shade the dials with my hand. Seventy-four thousand miles. Seventy-four thousand miles up and down the county for the union and the party, for the good of the cause. And what do they all add up to, Jim?

The hook is a great success. I have awarded myself a gold star for putting it up so well. I cleaned it with Brasso and I turned it with pliers till it was tight. Now I am sitting by the stove with a cup of coffee, reading from *The Oxford Book of Nineteenth Century Verse*. I am very pleased with myself. My coat is hanging on the cupboard door. Every day, whenever I want, I can put on my warm coat and my warm boots and walk up the lane. I am breaking the habits of a lifetime. I will not watch the news any more.

I am reading up on Alfred Edward Housman, 'classical scholar and poet'. I've split an enormous piece of coal with the poker, and heat is blazing out of the fireplace. The curtains are drawn against the dark outside. When I look up I see red firelight flickering through the soft yellow glow of my solitary lamp and the colours consorting along the bevelled glass doors of the book-case, one of which – the one with the key – stands a little open.

Housman, I read, was a repressed and controversial man, emotionally scarred by a failed homosexual love affair in his youth. He was clearly painfully shy. And fascinated by soldiers. I turn the pages steadily. Always the same pleasure in learning new things. I scan his savage prefaces to Juvenal and Manilius, and make a start on the Shropshire poems. I read of young men being hanged, or dying in battle. His style is meticulous. The mood is brooding and ferocious.

It seems that I.A. Richards, coming out of Housman's lecture 'The Name and Nature of Poetry' in 1933, is reputed to have said: 'Housman has put the clock back thirty years!'

I dreamt in the night about Yuri Gagarin. Of all the things! Once round the world two hundred miles up in an hour and a half. I was there when he landed. It was so clear. He was stepping down from Vostok I – twenty-seven years old, so handsome, so proud. Why do I remember all this? His warm bright eyes, that gleaming row of fine white teeth? At my age too!

And here is his picture. Curiosity led me to take a stack of papers from the bottom of the old chest in the garage, and I have them spread on the kitchen table. There are all kinds of things, party publications, things we kept, well preserved in cardboard files. It's not the *Daily Worker* I'm looking at, but the *Daily Mirror*. The front page, April 13th, 1961. He has on a flying suit with a zip up the front – like those marvellous outfits little children wear nowadays. It fits snugly round his ears. 'Today the *Mirror* celebrates the greatest story of OUR lifetime . . . the greatest story of OUR century . . . MAN IN SPACE.' I am looking at a sweet smile, bowed lips with little curves at the ends. Boy in space, I am thinking. Babe in space.

What else is in here? Something I'd forgotten. July 13th,

the same year. We were there, in London, visiting. Now those eyes under a wide-peaked military hat. Major Gagarin on his world tour lays a wreath at the Cenotaph. Underneath the caption, a brief report. We were allies against the Nazis, he said. The USSR paid with twenty million dead. The world would never forget.

We were believers then, in peace and progress.

I am turning the cuttings one by one. August. A high wall is built through the middle of Berlin.

All day I've been grappling with history. Who would believe so much of life is wrapped up in the printed word! Having emptied the bottom drawer of the chest in the garage I simply couldn't stop. Mid-day came and went and I didn't feel hungry until now. I see we have been amateur archivists, believing we could learn from the past. Fabian pamphlets, _Tribune_, _The Daily Worker_, _The Daily Herald_ – these by the score. Critiques of Korea, Cyprus, Suez, Aden. Proceedings of the Labour Women's League, minutes from the NUT. Mementos of delegations. Papers of the Anglo-Soviet Friendship Society. Articles by Orwell, Doris Lessing, Tony Crosland. Nye Bevan's 'In Place Of Fear', Strachey's 'Why You Should Be A Socialist'. I have stuffed pile upon pile into cardboard boxes and carrier bags and these are now stacked at the garage doorway. They put me in mind of an eviction, but without bailiffs, without spectators. The only other creature with any interest in the proceedings has been Hindley's white cat. He stood for a short while, not venturing in, but sniffing the air. I think he was hoping I might disturb a mouse.

I am tired and cold from my outdoor exertions. Some lentil soup, some cheese on toast will do me well. They are quick to prepare, comforting, and the kitchen smells good.

The fire is ablaze and I have some red wine warming on the hearth. I am waiting for a concert on the radio. My dear friend Leni looks out at me from within a small wooden frame propped under the lamp. Sipping my wine, I take it in my hand and turn it to the light. She is walking down Kingsway and I am beside her – both of us in summer dresses with padded shoulders and half-length sleeves. We smile at having our photograph taken. Leni, it's plain to see, is full of confidence. Her people are intellectuals. They are among the lucky ones, the ones who got out. Talking loudly, we turn into the coffee shop at the corner of Aldwych. Our companion, who is walking ahead, holds open the door. There is a table free by the window. He lays his camera on it, and we squeeze into the space. By the time our coffee arrives, Leni dominates the conversation.

'Opening this second front is Hitler's biggest mistake,' she declares. 'It will be hard. It will be very hard. But the Russian people, the Russian winter will defeat him. First his soldiers will be cold. Then they will be hungry. Like Napoleon. Think of Tchaikovsky's overture, the first slow movement. If they advance further, the Russians will retreat. This they know how to do well. They will dismantle their factories. They will burn their food crops. They will leave nothing for the invading army. Then the Nazi soldiers will start dreaming of home. Then they will know they are beaten.'

The young man looks at her wistfully.

'And where will you go, Leni? When Hitler is finished, what will you do?'

'We will go back to Berlin. We will, how do you say it, spit on his grave.'

Her face is animated. Her hands are talking too. We do not ask who she means by 'we'. We are happy to drink our coffee and listen.

'What a mess there will be. We shall need to rebuild a whole society.'

'And what about you? Will you feel safe there?' the young man asks.

Leni answers without hesitating. 'Who is ever safe? But Germany must never be a land without Jews. Our presence will be their reminder.'

'Drink your coffee,' I say to her, touching her arm. 'Don't let it go cold.'

I look into her face, her twenty-year-old eyes already dark with experience, and remember how much I loved her. Beautiful Leni, who believed in believing, who had the courage to go back.

I shut my eyes as the music takes hold – I have never heard Prokofiev played better. Now the cellos summon Nureyev to my mind. He is displaying, advancing into the ball. Eyes meet through masks, promises are made. Now it is Fonteyn alone, raising one arm against the moon. She moves before and through and after the notes – was ever a dancer so fluent? Now Mercutio is dead and Lady Montague cries revenge. This story is an old one. Ten o'clock approaches. I rake the ashes in the grate.

Sometimes, lying in bed, I do not know whether I am awake or dreaming. The room is dark, I hear the clock ticking, and my thoughts go round and round. I am with Leni, in a restaurant. Something has prevented her from ever coming here before. The people opposite have paid their bill with a plastic card and I am trying to explain to Leni what it is. She has never used a cheque book, and my explanation is having to stretch to other matters. As I speak the table too appears slowly to be stretching between us, until Leni is so far away she can no longer hear me. Later I notice a square-faced man addressing a group of reporters. We are witnessing, he says, a new imperialism. Something is wrong. He is speaking the wrong language. I seem to remember him once before, his terrible school-boy French. But I am overcome with a sense of admiration for his courage . . . for his independence of mind. I try to say something but my own words seem obscure. I am offering a kind of toast. I freely ignore that winter when all the lights went out, I am saying. I forgive you the police horse that crushed me against a wall. But as I raise my glass I see that it is misted over with my own breath; then the mist begins to break up, and a pattern slowly forms. I realize the pattern is made of men's faces. I look behind me and find ranks of men in helmets, standing in a field. Drawing near, I ask one of them to explain to me what is happening. We are miners, he says. We are Ukrainians. As he speaks he turns, taking off his helmet. I see that his face bears blue scars, made by the coal. Perhaps you gathered here to receive medals, I say. Are you not the flower of the working class? Do you not produce a third of all the coal in the USSR? We are on strike, he says, turning back and pointing at his companions. All of us. He puts on his helmet and is beginning to walk away. We have no soap. I cannot be sure that I have heard him correctly. Later I turn over. Now I hear an American voice. I see a figure striding down the hillside. I recognize him at once. You are Noam Chomsky, I say, walking towards him. I heard you speak long ago in the time of the war in Vietnam. It was not so long ago, he says. Have you forgotten? I have not forgotten, I reply. But there are so many things I find confusing now. Perhaps you can help me? Look over there, he says, pointing to the hilltop. There is a new millennium not far away. America is staking its claim. Have you not noticed how strong Germany and Japan are growing? All at once his face dissolves and he is someone different. He is speaking in Latin yet I recognize the words. *'Tis the old wind in the old anger* he begins to chant.

There is a thin white layer over the garden and field. The snow began early, but it has stopped now, and the afternoon is raw. It is important to keep moving. I put on my warm boots and my warm coat and walk out to where the Mini still stands at the edge of the field. There is a spare can of petrol in the boot, kept for emergencies. I take it out, leaving the boot open. One by one I carry the boxes piled inside the garage doorway, and stow them into the car. When the boot is full, I open the door on the passenger side and stack them on the back seat. History, scrawling lines across the map, chaining the future to the mistakes of the past. Fossilised time, spilling into the sea and burning beneath the earth's crust. You smoulder in nationalism, fester in religion. You infect the young and mock the old. What would my sons do with all this except sigh, and exchange embarrassed glances? I am piling my thoughts with the boxes and bags into the car.

Once again I walk to the gate. And again it clangs as it falls into place. In the white of the lane the only marks are the ones I have made trailing behind me as I climb. My steps fall into a rhythm:

> 'The gale it plies the saplings double,
> It blows so hard, 'twill soon be gone.'

I reach the top gate and turn:

> 'Today the Roman and his trouble
> Are ashes under Uricon.'

I am thinking of petrol, soaking into paper, and of a match carefully posted through a sliding window. Perhaps the white cat will stand and watch with me. He will be barely visible against the snow.

JUDY CORBALIS

The Bridesmaid

When I was ten and she was fourteen Jennifer Hartley-Burns was my idol and mentor. Everything she said and did was bathed in divine light. I admired the way she walked, hung on her every word and cherished as icons the postcards and letters she had sent me in the holidays and the programme from the school concert with her name next to mine.

When she grew up Jennifer was going to either get married and have five children, three boys and twin girls, or be a nun. I was planning to get-married-and-live-happily-ever-after, having seen no other options bar the teachers at our school or the bag-lady who lived under Whetton Bridge in summer and in the doorway of Casey's Bottles o' Booze in winter.

'She turned down the prospect of a good sound man when she had one,' said Mumma, gleaming with self-righteousness. 'And look at her now!'

My brother Joseph and I were rather taken by the bag-lady's itinerant lifestyle but we had to agree that having no hot meals every night and no dear little children of your own seemed an unfortunate prospect. Neither of us thought to question who would be looking after the dear little children, or indeed, what constituted dear little children, which certainly couldn't have been us or anyone we knew. Nor whether the fact that the bag-lady would have been the one preparing, not receiving, the delicious hot meals, was what had driven her to baggery in the first place.

'A Tragic Waste,' said my mother, handing me a homemade

Cornish pasty as I went off to meet Jennifer. 'Here, give her this on your way.'

I hung from the top rail of the bridge. 'MILL-IE!' I called, leaning right over to see if I could spot her. I couldn't. I jumped up and down on the wooden slats. 'MI-LL-IE! I've brought you a homemade pasty.'

Millie appeared like a tortoise from under the shell of the bridge. She smiled at me, and showed her worrying missing teeth. There was a rumour in my school that Millie was a witch and so cunning that she didn't switch personalities till dusk, the better to snare her victims. It was all rubbish, I knew, but I gazed anxiously at the sun to reassure myself that it really was only four o'clock.

Millie took the pasty, smiling at me all the while. She poked the long end into her mouth, slobbered on it for a minute or two, then mashed it with her gums. She chewed with her whole cheeks and even her forehead working. I was compelled by revulsion to watch her eat the lot.

'She's disgusting!' I said excitedly, recounting it to Jennifer later.

'Poor thing,' said pious Jennifer. 'She doesn't know any better. You ought to be sorry for her, Mary.' Her halo grew before my worshipping gaze.

I was twelve before Jennifer decided to tell me about 'doing it'. She made me swear on the Bible not to pass the information on to a living soul, especially not to Joseph. This made sense. Joseph was only seven and a noted goody-goody who could not be trusted even with a bribe of threepence. I swore. 'You promise?' asked Jennifer solemnly. I nodded.

We were crouched under Whetton Bridge watching the turbulent muddy water bouncing over the rocks. It was spring, too early for Millie, and the thaw in the mountains twelve miles away had swollen the creek to three times its usual seasonal depth. This was causing me a lot of worry. The previous autumn my mother had knitted me a truly terrible cardigan in a colour she called oatmeal-flecked but which everyone in school knew as vomit-coloured. I'd put it on with a doomed heart and it had looked just as frightful as I had known it would.

'It's lovely,' I had lied politely, then, assuming a Jennifer expression, 'but it's much too nice for me. I'd like to be kind and give it to the Lepers.'

The Lepers were my mother's chosen charity. She had had a brief spell as a concerned community member driving the Handicapped School's bus but had been forced to retire ('I'm too sensitive. All those poor little mongols distress me so much!') and had taken up Mr Tombley's Mission to Lepers instead.

So far, the Lepers had had my best woolly monkey, my Rupert Rabbit with the bent wire in his ear, two of my dolls, some special books and my brother's plush tiger and his kookabura mascot.

Joseph and I hated the Lepers. It served them right losing all their fingers and toes when they stole other people's things like that. We pored over the Leper Man's frequent brochures, torn between the secret thrill of the whole-bodied at the sight of the amputee and the outside hope that we might catch a glimpse of Rupert or Tiger in the background, peeping from a hut window or relaxing under a palm. Joseph, being younger, had spent several tearful nights distraught about Tiger's reaction to life in the leper colony.

'It's too hot for him,' he explained between sobs.

'He's used to the heat,' I said. 'Tigers come from hot countries.'

'He's missing me,' wept Joseph. 'He's never been away without me before.'

'Let's look again,' I said, pulling open another concertinaed brochure. We scanned the pages.

HAPPY IN THE LOVE OF JESUS, MANUNU STILL CHEER-FULLY GATHERS COCONUTS USING HIS ELBOWS AND FEET, read the central page. No Tiger. We pored over the backdrops behind the earless leper playing the nose-flute and his friends washing the Mission laundry with their stumps. There were a lot of coconuts but definitely no Tiger.

I had asked Jennifer what I could do. 'Tell him his tiger ran away,' she had said. 'It's very happy, living in a cave.'

'He'll ask me how I know.'

'Tell him you had a letter.'

'Yes, but he'll ask to see it.'

'Tell him Marilyn ate it before you could stop her.'

It had worked, too. Everyone knew Marilyn, our nanny goat, would eat anything she could reach. Joseph had believed me completely.

My regard for Jennifer had risen but my conscience was troubled. 'That was a lie. What I told Joseph.'

'It was a good lie,' said Jennifer. 'Some lies are all right sometimes.'

'When?'

'When they make people feel better,' said Jennifer.

It seemed to me that all lies were told to make somebody feel better but I didn't want to challenge Jennifer's authority, so I didn't say so.

'Does God mind the good lies?'

'No,' said His spokeswoman unctuously. 'God understands.'

I began to wonder if God would consider the cardigan lie a kind and helpful one. Possibly. On the other hand, possibly not. Could I ask Jennifer? What if I did and she made me tell? She had done it before, the time David and I threw the mud balls at Mrs Benson's washing and the time I stole the chocolate fish from the sweet shop. Both times I had been smacked very hard but Jennifer had said at least my soul was clean and if I'd died in the night I'd have thanked her for being the one who'd made it possible for me to come face to face with Jesus without sin or stain. I wasn't very sure about coming face to face with Jesus. His hair looked a bit like Millie's. Loose and wild. But that was something else it might not be a good idea to say to Jennifer. If I told her about the cardigan and she refused to be my friend till I owned up, I'd have to tell, but if I didn't tell her . . .

'You're not listening,' said Jennifer irritably. I jerked to attention. The tumbling water scoured the banks, and the stones and soil where we crouched were damp and uncomfortable.

'I'm cold,' I complained.

'I think you're still too young to know about "doing it",' said Jennifer. 'Maybe I shouldn't tell you.'

'Yes. No, I'm not,' I said. 'I do want to hear. Really.' I searched for a proper explanation for my inattention. 'I was just thinking about Jesus actually.'

Jennifer began to giggle. 'You're *awful*, Mary,' she said. 'Fancy thinking about Jesus doing that! No one would believe you're only twelve.'

On the whole that seemed to be a compliment. 'I'm quite an advanced reader for my age,' I said.

I scanned the far bank as it crumbled into the swirling water. My mother had been deeply scathing that autumn about my offer to the Lepers. Not only did we not waste new things on lepers who, being natives, did not understand the difference between new and second-hand but what would someone in the tropics do with a heavy woollen garment? I had not thought of that. Defeated, I had slunk into my strait-jacket and set off for school.

And as I had been crossing the bridge, cursed and heavy-laden, salvation had descended on me. Unlike Saul, I had not gone blind, indeed my vision had seemed to clear to such an extent that the whole of the soft muddy autumn riverbank had refocused into a shimmering, beckoning vision. Twice before I had had these infant peak experiences when shining doorways had opened before me and showed me the true way forward. The first had been the time I had cut off beautiful baby Joseph's eyelashes with the bacon scissors, then jealously disposed of his shoulder-length ringlets. And the second had culminated when I bit right through Dr Weisenblum's hand as he approached to give me an injection. Whenever I thought about it, I could still taste the mixture of blood and satisfaction.

Since both these transcendental moments had been followed by retribution from either my mother or Dr Weisenblum, I had known what my ultimate fate would be. I had stood on the bridge wrestling. Long-term public humiliation or short-term private pain? The fools' gold in the rocks in the water winked at me: the mud had had a faint golden glow. Did I want to be an Occidental leper, mocked in the playground all winter? I had hesitated a moment, then clambered over the end of the bridge and dropped onto the calling bank. Screened by the bridge from prying eyes, I had slipped off the vomit-bag, compressed it into a bundle and buried it deep in the clay.

But had I buried it deep enough? It had seemed like a huge hole in autumn but I had forgotten the vicious revealing waters of spring. Would I now be exposed for the liar and cheat I was? If my mother crossed Whetton Bridge might she look down and see below her, oozing from its grave, an arm of the beautiful oatmeal-flecked cardigan she had so lovingly knitted for me? What would it look like now? What happened to wool when you buried it?

For iniquity had paid off. I had told my mother someone at school must have stolen the hideous thing and in a trembling voice had even suggested it might be some poor child who had no other warm winter garment. And she had believed me. Her belief was even more terrible to me than my own lie. To deceive your mother and *succeed*? What kind of wicked child was I? Worse, if I could lie to her so successfully, how could I believe in her ever again? If I could lie to her so easily how could I have any faith in her at all? All winter, to test her, I had stolen from her purse. She had not noticed once and consequently, she had shrunk before my eyes and I hated her for not finding me out. But if she found out now it would be a disaster. Whatever God might think about necessary lies, Mumma certainly didn't approve of them.

Jennifer flung a stone at the other bank. 'You're too young,' she said again.

'You just said I was old for twelve,' I said indignantly.

'Yes, but not old like that,' she said.

I could see she was losing interest in being with me. 'All right,' I said. 'Don't tell me then. Just don't expect me to be your bridesmaid, that's all.'

The bridesmaid fantasy was an old one and very well-known in my family. The first time Jennifer had mentioned it I was only nine, had thought she'd meant she was marrying right away and had gone home demanding an instant outfit. It had taken several phone calls to Jennifer's family to convince me I was wrong. In the ensuing three years, while Jennifer and I made wedding plans, I had been clothed variously in pale blue satin, an English Liberty flowered smock, an apple-green silk dress with a pink sash ('apple tree and apple blossom,' Jennifer had explained) and in pure white, like the bride, but with a Hartley-Burns tartan sash. 'A strangely little-known clan, the Hartley-Burns,' remarked my father. 'I expect old Cedric's the *Burn* of MacBurns if only we knew.'

My grandmother, who was staying with us again, told him to stop being unkind. 'Not unkind,' said my father. 'Realistic.'

'What's realism got to do with it?' said my grandmother. 'It's hardly Cedric's fault, after all.'

I knew Cedric was Jennifer's father. 'What's not Cedric's fault?' I asked.

My grandmother looked at my father. 'Pas devant,' she said. 'I told you.'

'Not before what?' I said.

'Christ,' said my father. 'They teach her French at that school? I thought it was all fashion and weddings.'

My grandmother turned on him sharply. 'I wish you'd stop

it,' she said. 'We all know what's the matter with you. And if you go on seeing her, you know just what the outcome will be. Really, a married man your age ought to have more sense.'

She looked at me. 'Go and do your homework, Mary.'

'I've done it already,' I said.

'As a matter of interest,' said my father, 'who's the bridegroom?'

'What bridegroom, Dada?'

'Jennifer's. I assume if she's getting married there is a husband. Or is she having a solo wedding?'

'I don't know,' I said. The idea of the bridegroom didn't really interest me. After all, he wouldn't be wearing a proper bridal outfit like me and Jennifer.

'Leave her alone,' said my grandmother. 'Go and find something to do, Mary.'

'What?' I said.

My father raised his eyes. 'Skipping?'

'It's raining, Dada.'

'Don't you start,' warned my grandmother, and to me she said, 'What would you like to do?'

I seized my chance. 'Please may I look at the Journal?'

It was the 'may' that did it. Even my father was impressed.

'Well, all right,' she said. 'But be very, very careful.'

'Promise, Ga,' I said, and I slipped off to get it before she could change her mind.

The Journal belonged to Ga because it had been her father's. He'd been away a lot when Ga was growing up so she hadn't known him very well but he'd left her the Journal when he died. It was a diary of his life when he was a war correspondent with the army fighting in the desert, Ga said. As well as what he'd written, there were a lot of photographs of Ga and Uncle Charles and Uncle Edward and Uncle Cecil and Poor Mama who died when Ga was thirteen. But best of all were the drawings. Palm trees, crocodiles, mud houses, camels, two men in a boat on a river, some pyramids, pots and vases, a man in a dress, men going into a cave – the Journal had dozens of tiny pictures drawn all the way through. I particularly liked the one of the crocodile eating the little boy.

I had a special system for looking at the Journal. I took it out of its silk cloth, laid it down carefully, then, closing my eyes, let it fall open at random. If it opened at the crocodile, it was a very good omen. That day, however, its stiff dust-smelling pages split apart at a whole page of writing and a photograph. The writing was in copper-plate and I could read it without too much difficulty but I was disappointed at the lack of a drawing. I thought about turning over but it would have been cheating. I looked at the photograph.

Nearly a century away, my great-grandfather sat with his elbow on his desk, his face shaded from the Empire sun by a solar topee. He contemplated his latest dispatches untroubled by the waterfall pouring from the left corner of the photograph to form a river in front of his desk. I knew this was how it must have been all along the Nile. Little desks set up by natives in the mud beside the cooling water. The gun propped by his chair would be for protection from the crocodiles. I had frequently heard the story of the Brave Little Egyptian Girl whom my great-grandfather had seen save her baby brother from a crocodile's jaws by pushing her thumbs into the wicked beast's eyes and blinding it: I understood the dangers of the riverbank. I had always had a secret worry that I should be unable to perform such a noble act if called upon to rescue Joseph and whenever we went on family picnics, I checked the banks for long stretches on either side of our site. My family had little sympathy with these precautions and my father constantly directed me back to the passage in the encyclopaedia which said that crocodiles did not live in temperate countries.

But I had secret knowledge of my own. What was a taniwha but a crocodile in disguise?

'There aren't any taniwhas,' said my father wearily.

'There could be. There might be one left over.'

'Not in this river.'

'But, Dada, what if there is?'

We repeated this at every picnic and at that point he would sigh or curse and leave me to get on with Crocodile Patrol.

I finished examining the photograph and began poring over the writing. Dada and Ga were arguing quite loudly. I could hear them even from that distance. 'She won't be back till you make a decision and stick by it,' said Ga.

'It's none of your business,' said Dada. I could tell he was starting to lose his temper. 'Stop interfering.'

'Interfering!' said Ga. 'I see. I should just let you get on with wrecking four people's lives and stay at home and say nothing.'

'If you didn't come rushing down as soon as she asked you, I might have been able to talk her round.'

'That's exactly why she asked me, I expect,' said Ga in a steely tone. 'Perhaps you'd better go away and think about it. I'm certainly not looking after your washing or cooking. I'm disgusted by the way you're going on. Like a boy of fourteen.'

I heard a door slam, then silence. I went back to the copperplate, half-listening to Ga taking bowls out of cupboards, flour out of drawers, thumping spoons, clacking the sifter. I went on reading till the air felt a bit quieter, then I went back into the kitchen.

Ga was rolling out scone dough. Cheese, not raisin. I could see the yellow worms in it.

'What's pro-cliv-eyety?' I asked.

'Proclivity. Whose?'

'Lord Kitchener's unfortunate.'

She took the kitchen knife and slashed the dough into nine large squares. 'A bad habit Lord Kitchener had.'

'Why was it unfortunate?'

'He probably wasted too much time on it. Like you with your questions.'

'Yes, but what was it?'

'I told you. A bad habit. He was rude to the natives sometimes.'

'The Maoris?'

'No. The Sudanese. In Africa. Just below the pyramids.'

'Were they cross about it?'

'Who?'

'The Sudanese.'

'More uncomfortable, I should think.' She pulled out the oven tray and lifted the scones onto it in one whole block. 'Did you put the Journal away properly?'

'Yes.'

'Good girl. Now go out to the greenhouse and look at the guava tree. There's one on it nearly ripe. If it smells ready, you can have it. Only if it's ready, mind.'

This was a great honour. Joseph would be really jealous. I raced outside and sniffed at the pale pink fruit, hoping to catch the lemony pear-tomato smell that showed it was ripe. It wasn't. I trailed back inside.

'It's not.'

My grandmother was lying upside-down on the ironing board which she'd wedged in a diagonal between the sink and the Kelvinator. She was in her Gayelord Hauser phase right then which meant she ate a lot of yoghurt and spinach and lay upside down on the ironing board at intervals every day chanting things like, *Every day in every way, I grow stronger and stronger*. Or, *Whatever happens is for the best in the best of all possible worlds*. It drove Dada crazy.

'Better than the Theosophists,' said Mumma.

'Christ,' said Dada, 'why can't I have normal relations like everybody else?'

Ga's eyes were shut. '*Beauty is Truth, Truth Beauty*,' she intoned. '*That is all ye know on Earth and all ye need to know*. I'm sorry, Mary. It looked as if it would be ready by today.'

'And I'm all wet,' I said accusingly.

Ga sat up on the ironing board and slung her legs onto the floor.

'I'll make a cup of tea,' she said. 'Just for you and me. And we'll have the best scones.'

'Can I have the guava tomorrow?'

'It's yours,' said Ga. She edged round the board to fill the kettle. I watched her. I loved Mumma, of course, but Ga was special. She wasn't like other people's grandmothers. Jennifer didn't even have any grandparents because her mother and father were old but Ga was so young that everyone thought she was our mother, not Mumma's. She smoked and wore slacks in the winter and a green bikini in summer. Not one single other person on the whole beach had a bikini. Sometimes, she and I took baths together. Ga's bosoms were little and crumpled up. 'Very fashionable,' said Ga. 'And very twenties. Not like those ugly great melons some women have. I was a beauty in the twenties, you know.' Ga had two boyfriends, Lance, an American who gave me chewing-gum, and Douglas who took us out in his boat. Joseph and I had automatically assumed that anyone who came courting Ga was obliged to make good with us. Lance had given Ga a black satin nightie. After our joint bath I was usually allowed to rub Ga's Elizabeth Arden Orange Skin Food into my face and neck, dab myself with her Arpège perfume (Douglas), climb into the satin nightie and spend the night in the spare double bed with her.

I watched her fondly as she buttered our scones. 'Can I sleep in your bed tonight?'

'I suppose so,' said Ga. 'But you'll have to try not to kick.' She passed me my tea and sat down with hers.

'How's Jennifer?' she said.

'All right. It's her birthday next week. I'm going to buy her a present in Woolworths.'

'That's nice,' said Ga. 'How old will she be this time?'

'Sixteen.'

'Mmmn,' said Ga. 'Are you missing Mumma?'

'No,' I said. 'It's better with you. But Joseph is.'

'Joseph's younger. Why is it better with me?'

I considered. 'Well, there's the nightie. And sleeping in your bed. And you don't make us be generous to the Lepers.'

My grandmother sighed. 'Watch out for the good people in this world,' she said. 'They're the ones who create all the problems for the rest of us.'

'I thought it was the poor,' I said. 'That's what they say at Sunday School. And the evil.'

'Oh, the evil,' said Ga. 'Well, at least they're enjoying themselves. It's the improvers that cause all the trouble. Don't turn into an improver, whatever you do.'

'Will I?'

'I doubt it,' said Ga. 'It usually skips a generation. Is Jennifer having a party?'

'No.'

'Just some friends around?'

'No, only me,' I said proudly. 'I'm her best friend. We're going to the Singing Kettle for tea.'

Ga revolved her cup. 'Doesn't she have any friends her own age?'

'No,' I said. 'She likes me best. And I'm old for nearly twelve. Everyone says so.'

'I know,' said Ga. 'But that's not the point. She ought to have some friends nearer her age. An eleven-year-old's too young for a sixteen-year-old.'

'Nearly twelve,' I repeated, hurt. 'And we've been best friends for ages.'

'Have you ever been to her house?'

'No, but she's come here lots of times. And I'm going to be her bridesmaid when she gets married.'

'I know,' said Ga, 'I know all about that. Here, take this scone to Joseph. He's in the shed.'

'Can I take one for Marilyn?'

'Marilyn doesn't know the difference between a scone and a tin can,' said Ga. 'If you want to feed Marilyn, take the scraps bucket with you out of the washhouse on your way. And mind she doesn't eat your raincoat.'

★

I bought Jennifer a china donkey pulling a china cart full of china flowers, and a box of Winning Post chocolates. It took all my pocket-money but she was so pleased, especially with the chocolates, it was worth it. 'I've never had a whole box all to myself before,' she said. We were having tea and fairy cakes in the Singing Kettle.

'Joseph and I always get one each at Christmas. From Ga. But they're all mint ones.'

'A box each?'

'Yes.'

She was impressed. 'I like your grandmother,' she said. 'But my mother thinks she shouldn't have boyfriends like that.'

I was torn between embarrassment that Ga should have offended Jennifer's mother and an urge to defend her. 'They're not really boyfriends,' I explained. 'They're just her unfortunate proclivity.'

Jennifer seemed satisfied by this. 'Well, that's different,' she said. She smiled at me. 'I've got a surprise.'

'For your birthday?'

'No. Not till next weekend. Because you're my best friend, Mother says I can ask you to stay.'

'At your house?'

'Yes. She'll pick you up on Friday and we can go to school on Monday together.'

I was ecstatic. A weekend at the house of my best friend!

'Will your mother let you come?'

'I'm always allowed to stay with people,' I said. 'That's wonderful!'

I had never been inside Jennifer's house. The Hartley-Burns lived a long way from us on the outskirts of town in one of the few two-storey houses I had ever seen. They had a tennis court at the front and a glasshouse at the side of the garden.

'Will we sleep upstairs?'

'Yes,' said Jennifer. 'In my room. Beatrix says she doesn't mind moving out.' Beatrix was her elder sister whom I'd met once or twice when the Hartley-Burns had come to collect or deposit Jennifer at our house. 'Bring your racquet,' she said. 'It's a bit late but we can still play if it doesn't rain.' I winged my way home to break the news. 'Guess what? I'm going to stay a whole weekend with Jennifer! Her mother said.'

Ga was still staying with us but Mumma was back home. 'I don't know about that, Mary,' she said.

I was taken aback. 'Mumma! Why not?'

'It's too much work for Jennifer's mother,' she said.

'But she asked me!'

'I don't think it's a good idea,' she said.

I was furious. 'She's my best friend! Why can't I go? You just want to spoil it for me. You're mean and nasty.'

'Mary!' said my mother warningly.

'Well, it's true. You are. You don't want me to have a good time. You're jealous just because she's my best friend.' My cheeks were hot with rage and frustration. 'You can't stop me. I'll pack my bags and go even if you don't let me. And if you don't watch out, I might stay there for good.'

'Then I'll be an only child,' said Joseph who'd been watching the scene with enjoyment.

'Goody goody,' I sneered.

He let out a wail. 'Mary's being mean.'

Ga's voice came booming out of the carpet. 'For Heaven's sake, be quiet both of you!' She was doing yoga and had to stand on her head or shoulders four times a day for her blood. She had her legs propped against the wall by the tea towel from bonnie Scotland and her slacks were all rucked up round her calves. Her voice sounded deeper upside-down.

'Why can't she go, Eleanor?'

'You know perfectly well why not.'

'I don't see that she'll come to any harm.'

'Jennifer's my friend,' I squawked. 'She likes me.'

'Be quiet, Mary!' snapped Ga. I shut up. 'She's got to find out sooner or later.'

'She's only eleven, Mother. Don't be ridiculous.'

'She's almost twelve, actually, and at twelve I delivered poor Mama's last baby when the doctor's trap overturned and he couldn't get there in time.'

'That was over forty years ago, Mother. Things are different now.'

'Not so different,' said Ga. 'I should let her go, Eleanor. She's a sensible child. She can cope.'

'I am sensible,' I broke in, 'Miss Carter said so today in class. And anyway, I don't know why you're all going on as if there's something wrong with going to Jennifer's. I thought you'd be pleased.' And I burst into tears.

'We are pleased,' said Ga. 'Aren't we, Eleanor? You go and have a good time. Your mother's got one or two things on her mind right now.'

I sniffed loudly. 'Can I use your Orange Skin Food?'

'Only a dab,' said Ga. 'I'm nearly out of it.'

The weekend after that I went to stay with Jennifer. I took my racquet and overnight case to school and Mrs Hartley-Burns picked us up in the Morris Minor. 'Jump in, girls,' she cried brightly. 'Super to see you, Mary.' We clambered in and squashed together in the back seat. As we swung in at their front gate, my blur of excitement was tinged with awe. A two-storey house. With stairs. An upstairs bedroom.

I had only ever lived in a single-storey house and the idea of a second floor above my head seemed romantic beyond dreams. I stood in the hall clutching my case and staring. A wooden staircase curved elegantly up and round to a landing above me. 'Show Mary up, Jen,' said her mother. We took my case and racquet and started the magic climb.

Jennifer's bedroom was the third room along. From behind the second door, which was closed, came loud snores. 'Daddy,' explained Jennifer. 'He gets tired easily.' She pushed her own door wide open. 'There,' she said expansively. I don't remember what I was expecting but I can still recall my acute disappointment at the sight of the two iron bedsteads covered with white candlewick bedcovers, the white chest of drawers and the ugly big wooden wardrobe. The curtains were striped and skimpy, there was a small rag rug on the floor. 'It's lovely,' I said, wanting to cry.

'I knew you'd like it,' said Jennifer. The snoring was coming through the wall. Jennifer rapped sharply on the plaster. 'Stop it, Daddy!' The snoring diminished. 'I'll show you the bathroom,' she said. 'Then we'll have supper.'

I can't remember much about the supper either but I had trouble swallowing owing to the lump in my throat. Somehow I had envisaged Jennifer in a completely different environment. I thought of Ga and a warm bath and the Orange Skin Food.

'Do you use Orange Skin Food?' I asked Mrs Hartley-Burns to be polite.

'Cosmetics are an unnatural affront to the Lord, Mary,' said Mrs Hartley-Burns. 'If God had meant us to have red lips, we'd have been born with them.'

Derek, Jennifer's brother, who came between her and Beatrix in age, looked at me. 'D'you play tennis?' he asked.

'I brought my racquet,' I said miserably.

'Good,' he said. 'It's going to be fine tomorrow. We can make up a four.'

Daddy was not at supper. 'Too tired, I'm afraid,' said Jennifer's mother. 'He'll catch up with you in the morning.' We played dominoes and consequences and Pelmanism round the kitchen table until it was time for bed.

The kitchen had seemed rather cold to me but the hall was icy. As we went upstairs, I leaned over the banisters and looked down at the chequer-board pattern of the hall floor. After all, I was going to be sleeping upstairs. That was something to have over Joseph. I began to cheer up and by the time Jennifer and I had changed and climbed between our frozen white sheets, I was feeling much better. We spent a long time giggling and talking in the dark. We completely altered my bridesmaid's outfit to peach satin with ecru crochet trim and dyed matching satin shoes.

'My grandmother's got a satin nightie,' I offered.

'Really?'

'Yes.'

'What colour?'

'Black. And I wear it sometimes.' Jennifer gave a sigh. Envy of luxury was inherent in it. 'You can try it on one day if you like.'

'Oh yes,' she said. 'Please. You are lucky, Mary.'

Jennifer's own pyjamas were thick men's ones. Her mother had been worried that my winceyette nightdress with pink floral rosebuds would not be warm enough but I'd reassured her. If I was cold in bed I would get out and put my jersey on. We talked and giggled and made plans as the beds slowly warmed up a few degrees, then finally we fell asleep.

I woke up to the disorientation of a strange bedroom. Jennifer was awake already and as I climbed out into the sharp-edged early autumn cold, she said, 'Make sure you put your jersey on. It's cold in the drawing-room.' The drawing-room! I was again transported to another world. Did the Hartley-Burns have breakfast in a drawing-room? The grandeur of it was overwhelming. My clothes felt damp and clammy and I had goosebumps on my arms. We went off and cleaned our teeth and washed our faces, then I followed Jennifer down the staircase and up to the double doors I'd noticed on the way in last night.

She pushed them apart. A freezing wave of air came swelling out and I shivered. There was no heating at all in the drawing-room. The fireplace was ghostly empty, its grate bars forlornly waiting to be stacked and heaped. On the slate hearth, to the left of its fireless yawn, was an enamel jug full of rosehips swaying dismally in the chimney's cold breath. At the side of the fireplace stood an old leather chair with buttons on its back and opposite was a large battered floral sofa. In the bay window was a pretty desk I knew Mumma would like and there was a half-circle table against the far wall.

Jennifer knelt down on the rug in front of the fireplace, her back to the grate. 'Just kneel by me,' she whispered. I moved to the side where the draught felt less cold and sank down next to her. I then realized that Beatrix was already kneeling in the bay window by the desk where a few beams of early April sun were filtering in. What was I supposed to do now?

Derek came sullenly in, his mother behind him, bright and eager.

'Good morning, girls,' she said. 'I hope you slept well, Mary.'

'Yes, thank you,' I replied, still baffled by the breakfast arrangements. At my house we had it at an ordinary kitchen table. 'Just waiting for Daddy,' said Mrs Hartley-Burns. She put her head round the door. 'Daddy!' There was a noise I couldn't identify, Mrs Hartley-Burns sank to her knees, the door opened again and Daddy came in.

I had never met Jennifer's father. It was always her mother who dropped her and collected her but that was normal enough. Most of the mothers did that. I had never even thought very much about the fact that she had a father. I assumed all fathers were much like my own. So I was not prepared for Daddy. He was very, very old with a blank baby's face and wispy grey hair at the sides of his head. He rocked as he walked and his head kept slipping sideways. There was drool bubbling at the side of his mouth. I thought of Millie and the pasty.

'This is Mary, Daddy,' said Mrs Hartley-Burns. 'Jennifer's friend.' Daddy looked at me with benign vacuity. 'He's absolutely thrilled to meet you at last,' said Mrs Hartley-Burns. 'Aren't you, Daddy? He's heard so much about you.'

'How do you do?' I said. 'I'm going to be Jennifer's bridesmaid.'

'Isn't that super?' said his wife.

Daddy looked at me from large empty dilated pupils. He was smiling into the far distance. 'Come over here, Daddy,' said Mrs Hartley-Burns. 'By me.'

Daddy moved towards her. As he walked he drifted from foot to foot and glided and swayed like a man underwater, aimlessly heading for an unknown goal. His wife caught him by the wrist and swung him towards her. He knelt down. 'Very good, Daddy,' said Beatrix and Jennifer encouragingly. I stole a look at everybody. Jennifer didn't seem to see anything odd about Daddy's behaviour and nor did Beatrix. Derek, however, looked awkward and embarrassed. Their mother was clearly preparing for something: she had a blue book open in front of her and an enthusiastic look on her face.

'Close your eyes!' she said in a singing voice. 'And let us pray! Oh, Jesus, who sees our every sin and every blemish, open our eyes to Thine ever-loving kindness. Make clean our hearts within us and mercifully hear us when we call upon Thee.'

'Amen,' said Derek, Beatrix and Jennifer. Jennifer nudged me. I opened my eyes. Mrs Hartley-Burns was looking at me with her eyebrow raised. 'Amen,' I croaked. She smiled. 'Oh, Jesus, Light of the World and Salvation of the Life to come, hear these Thy servants, Albinia, Cedric, Beatrix, Derek and Jennifer and our guest, Mary Fredrickson, as they call upon Thee to cleanse them from all sin and stain.'

My stomach rumbled loudly. Derek grinned at me. 'Imbue Thy servants with righteousness,' implored Mrs Hartley-Burns. 'And make Thy chosen people joyful.'

'Amen,' cried everyone, me included.

Mrs Hartley-Burns continued with a request for peace in the world, a lot of promises to Jesus to behave well and a wish for eternal life. She concluded that we all wanted to be made better people through Jesus and to become servants and missionaries of God. Mr Tombley was a missionary of God, I knew. I prayed silently and explained to God that it was all a mistake and that I did not ever want to be a missionary.

'We will now have an inward prayer,' said Mrs Hartley-Burns. 'Just ask God to grant you any little thing in your heart. But don't be greedy, please. God loveth not the greedy man.' I asked God for a new jar of Orange Skin Food for Ga. If it came soon, Ga would give me the old jar with the remains of the cream. 'And now for the hymn,' she said. *All Things Bright and Beautiful.'*

I knew it without the book but I felt really stupid singing it with just the six of us. Daddy didn't sing but made low crooning noises and smiled a lot.

Following their mother's lead, Beatrix, Derek and Jennifer got to their feet, Daddy and I close behind, and filed into the kitchen for breakfast. Daddy sat at the head of the table as Mrs Hartley-Burns took the bacon and eggs out of the Aga and set them down in front of us. 'Daddy's had his already,' she said. He sat smiling and drooling, watching us all eating. I chewed on my bacon and egg and tried not to stare at him. If I thought too much about the drooling, my stomach would start lurching and my throat would gag. I concentrated hard on the weather. The kitchen was wonderfully warm after the drawing-room. Derek and Beatrix were arguing about whether it would be too cold for tennis.

'It's a hard court,' said Derek. 'And the sun's out now.'

After we'd done the washing-up I went upstairs, got my racquet and went out to the court. Derek had said a foursome, so I was surprised to see his parents by the court with their racquets too. 'We'll all play,' said Beatrix. 'Mother and Daddy and I'll be at this end and Derek and Jennifer and Mary at the other.'

I'd never played in a sixsome before though I was good at tennis and went to a Saturday club in the season. 'You stand forward, Derek,' said Jennifer, 'and we'll go by the line.' We tossed a coin for service and Beatrix's end won. She served to me and I returned it. The ball fell gently next to Daddy's racquet.

'Come on, Daddy,' roared the Hartley-Burnses encouragingly. Daddy looked dazed, raised his racquet, batted it feebly at the air and smiled at us.

'Jolly good, Daddy!' called Mrs Hartley-Burns, swooping

in behind him and returning the ball which had bounced twice. 'Nearly got it that time.'

Even Joseph would have seen that was a lie. I was so engrossed in watching Daddy, I missed my own return shot.

'Hard luck, Mary!' cried Mrs Hartley-Burns.

It suddenly dawned on me that I was participating in a real-life school story. The people were not quite right but the language was clearly recognizable to anyone who had swallowed my diet of Brazil and Blyton. All my life I had longed to have a midnight feast in the dorm, to play lacrosse and eat tuck, and, unexpectedly, my wish had been granted. I had been precipitated into the school holiday version of my dream. Over the course of the game, I became so carried away by this idea that I found myself quite naturally shouting 'Tophole!' when Derek hit a decisive ace.

'Game!' said Beatrix.

'Don't forget a little rally for Daddy,' said Mrs Hartley-Burns starting to go inside. Was he her Daddy? I didn't like to be rude and ask.

'My father used to be a provincial tennis champion,' I told her as she went by. 'That's why I get coaching.'

'Terrific,' she said. 'Super. So just have a little to-and-fro with Daddy before I come and take him in.'

Daddy began to giggle. He put down his racquet and clapped his hands. Beatrix threw the ball to him and he shambled after it and clumsily picked it up. 'Come on,' said Jennifer. 'Let's go in and see what there is for lunch.'

Now I understood the nature of where I was, things slotted happily into place. Not even morning prayers seemed bizarre in that context. Even Daddy appeared somehow correct. I floated happily through the rest of the visit, murmuring appropriate responses from time to time and returned ecstatic to my family after school on Monday.

'Did you enjoy it?' asked my father.

'Super,' I said. 'Tophole, actually.' He groaned. 'Daddy's funny, though. But he likes me. Everybody noticed.'

'You see,' said Ga to Mumma. 'I told you.'

'Ga,' I said. 'Whose father is he?'

'Jennifer's, of course,' said Mumma.

'Why's he like that?'

'He was mustard-gassed in the First World War,' said Ga. 'He used to be quite normal before.'

'Heaven knows why Albinia married him,' said my mother.

'Some people,' said Dada, 'think he got the raw end of the deal. Did you have morning prayers, Mary?'

'Oh yes,' I said, 'and evening, too, on Sunday. And we changed my bridesmaid's dress. It's going to be pale peach satin with . . .'

'Somebody stop her,' said Dada. 'I can't stand it.'

'There's a boy in my school,' said Joseph, competing, 'who can whistle through his tummy button.'

'Navel,' said Ga who liked us to give things anatomical their proper names.

'Navel, then. He can whistle, *Oh I Do Like to be Beside the Seaside*. He's going to teach me.'

Our father got up from the table. 'Excuse me from the pudding,' he said. 'It's excitement. A professional bridesmaid and a navel virtuoso in the same family. It's too much glory for one householder to contain.' He went out.

Ga looked at Mumma. 'I know where he's going,' said Mumma miserably, 'but what can I do about it?'

'Away, you two,' said Ga. 'Right now. Off and play and don't come back till I call you.' We went.

Joseph was seven. He still believed in ghosts and the tooth fairy. 'Let's feed Marilyn,' he said, picking up some windfalls from under the apple tree.

'I'll tell you about Jennifer's house,' I said.

'I don't want to hear about her house,' said Joseph. 'Why was Mumma crying?'

'She wasn't, you big baby,' I said, even though I knew she had been.

★

As I sat under the bridge with Jennifer, I couldn't stop thinking about Mumma's crying and about how she didn't notice when I stole from her purse and how Lance had brought Joseph a wind-up car and only a silly baby doll for me and how often Dada wasn't at home and how I'd had to stop having baths with Ga because I didn't want her to see I'd started growing big ugly melon breasts. I felt overwhelmed with misery.

'Just don't expect me to be your bridesmaid, that's all,' I said nastily.

'Of course you will,' said Jennifer. 'You can be chief bridesmaid if you want.' She lowered her voice. 'When you're married you'll have to "do it", you know,' she whispered.

'I will not,' I said.

'You know what happens?' she asked.

'Ga told me,' I said.

'Have you seen Joseph's thing?'

'Of course I have.'

'When?'

'In the bath,' I said. 'Only I have baths by myself now.'

'Beatrix and I never have baths with Derek,' Jennifer said. 'But I saw his thing once when he was getting changed after tennis.' She snickered. 'That's what they use,' she said. 'That's how you get a baby.' Her face looked greedy and secret.

'I know that,' I said. 'Ga told me. And it isn't a thing. It's a penis.'

'*Mary*!' Jennifer was shocked. 'That's filthy! Fancy saying it out loud.'

'It is called that,' I said irritably. 'I saw it in *The Book of the Human Body*. Ga showed me.'

'Your grandmother must be disgusting, showing you that.'

'I thought you were going to tell me about "doing it",' I said. 'I know all that already.'

'Yes, but do you know what they actually do?'

I thought back to what Ga had said. 'The man's got a

penis and the woman's got a space,' I said. I couldn't remember the name of the space. 'And he puts his penis against her space and drops a seed in and then she gets a baby.'

I had a mental picture of a man in his suit, gabardine raincoat and hat, politely raising the hat as he pressed himself against the woman. She was wearing a print floral dress which she'd kindly lifted up to allow him to perform the clinical, perfunctory action which would yield them the baby they wanted now they were married. Jennifer looked at me triumphantly. 'I knew you didn't know! He doesn't just put it against her, stupid, he pokes it right inside her.'

It was the first time she had ever called me stupid. I looked at her, dazed and hurt. 'He does not!'

'Yes, he does,' she said, exultant. 'And what's more *your own mother and father* have done it. Twice, at least. They must have. They've got you and Joseph.'

I was absolutely disgusted. 'You're wrong,' I said loudly. 'It's not true.'

'Right inside her,' said Jennifer. 'And it is true. And you'll have to do it one day too.'

Somewhere deep down in myself I knew she was right. There had always been a secret that I hadn't known about, that Joseph didn't know about, that everyone in my class at school didn't know about, even though we all knew vaguely and namelessly that it existed.

'You're a filthy, wicked liar, Jennifer Hartley-Burns!' I shouted. 'And I'm going to tell on you.' I knew I sounded like Joseph but I couldn't help it. 'I hate you! And I'm never going to be your bridesmaid, ever!'

I cast about for some way to hurt her back. A movement at the top of the bank caught my eye. A shambling wild-haired figure laden with bags was picking her way down the bank to her spring and summer home under the bridge. She drooled and smiled to herself as she concentrated all her attention on keeping her bags clear of the damp soil.

'Well, your parents didn't do it,' I said spitefully. 'They couldn't have, could they? Not with your father like that.' I saw by her face that I had hit my target. 'He can't even pick up a tennis ball properly. He probably hasn't even got a penis.'

Her face crumpled. 'Millie ought to be your mother,' I said. 'She'd be exactly right for your father. Two mental people doing it. You ought to bring him to live under Whetton Bridge with her. They could slobber away together.'

I couldn't believe I was really saying it. I felt shocked and excited and cruel. Jennifer burst into tears. Power scoured the banks of my remaining decency and they crumbled. 'You'd better never have any children,' I said. 'They'll probably turn out like your father.' I tapped the side of my forehead with my forefinger.

Jennifer just sat there with tears running down her face. She looked awful. I couldn't see why I'd ever liked her. I got up and clambered up the bank, sticking out my tongue at Millie as I passed her.

I went straight home, my chest gripped with power and hate and grief. Joseph was playing in the yard. He had scraped out roads in the soil for his matchbox cars and was contentedly driving them round and round. I scuffed out some of the roads with my foot. 'Don't, Mary,' he said, re-making them.

'You listen to me, Joseph Frederickson,' I said. 'There's no tooth fairy and no Father Christmas, either.' Joseph looked at me, startled. 'There is so a tooth fairy,' he said. 'She gave me sixpence for my double tooth.'

'You're just dumb,' I said. 'Fancy believing that. It's not the tooth fairy, it's Mumma and Dada. And at Christmas, too. Father Christmas is for babies, Stupid.' He gave me a stricken look.

'And another thing,' I said. 'About Tiger. He's dead. He caught leper's disease and his legs and tail fell off and he starved to death. And that's the truth.' Joseph opened his mouth and began to scream. Ga would be out any moment now to see what the matter was. 'And I'll tell you what else,' I said. 'You're adopted. You don't really belong to us. Nobody round here wants you. They're sending you back to your real parents soon. Mumma told me.' The awful sobs and screams followed me as I stalked off inside to my bedroom.

I took my Chinese box off my dressing-table. It was red with a gold dragon on it. Jennifer had given it to me: it was my most treasured possession. Inside it were all her letters and postcards and a real gold locket with a picture of Ga as a baby. I opened the box, took out the locket, then shut the box again and went back outside with it. I could hear Joseph sobbing in the kitchen. The sound followed me all the way down the garden, right to the back.

Marilyn looked up as I approached. Her eyes were like the devil's and she had bad breath. She waggled her beard and bleated. I held out the box to her. 'Here you are, Marilyn,' I said. She seized the red lacquered end and began to crunch on it. For a split second I tried to pull it away but Marilyn jerked her head sideways wrenching it out of my fingers. I watched dry-eyed as she chewed up my box, my letters and my postcards, then I went back up to the house.

I felt so old I could hardly bear it. I veered away at the back door: I couldn't face what was going to happen inside. Instead, I went back to Whetton Bridge. And underneath it, with Millie incuriously laying out her belongings and setting up her spring and summer house opposite me, I sat and wept and wept for my red Chinese box and the buried cardigan and Tiger and the tooth fairy and Joseph and Jennifer and my big new melon breasts and because I could tell lies to Mumma and not be found out. But most of all, I wept for Crocodile Patrol which I knew I would never need to do again since I finally understood that crocodiles don't ever live in temperate countries.

DAPHNE DU MAURIER

The Pool

The children ran out on to the lawn. There was space all around them, and light, and air, with the trees indeterminate beyond. The gardener had cut the grass. The lawn was crisp and firm now, because of the hot sun through the day; but near the summer-house where the tall grass stood there were dew-drops like frost clinging to the narrow stems.

The children said nothing. The first moment always took them by surprise. The fact that it waited, thought Deborah, all the time they were away; that day after day while they were at school, or in the Easter holidays with the aunts at Hunstanton being blown to bits, or in the Christmas holidays with their father in London riding on buses and going to theatres – the fact that the garden waited for them was a miracle known only to herself. A year was so long. How did the garden endure the snows clamping down upon it, or the chilly rain that fell in November? Surely sometimes it must mock the slow steps of Grandpapa pacing up and down the terrace in front of the windows, or Grandmama calling to Patch? The garden had to endure month after month of silence, while the children were gone. Even the spring and the days of May and June were wasted, all those mornings of butterflies and darting birds, with no one to watch but Patch gasping for breath on a cool stone slab. So wasted was the garden, so lost.

'You must never think we forget,' said Deborah in the silent voice she used to her own possessions. 'I remember, even at school, in the middle of French' – but the ache then was unbearable, that it should be the hard grain of a desk under her hands, and not the grass she bent to touch now. The children had had an argument once about whether there was more grass in the world or more sand, and Roger said that of course there must be more sand, because of under the sea; in every ocean all over the world there would be sand, if you looked deep down. But there could be grass too, argued Deborah, a waving grass, a grass that nobody had ever seen, and the colour of that ocean grass would be darker than any grass on the surface of the world, in fields or prairies or people's gardens in America. It would be taller than trees and it would move like corn in a wind.

They had run in to ask somebody adult, 'What is there most of in the world, grass or sand?', both children hot and passionate from the argument. But Grandpapa stood there in his old panama hat looking for clippers to trim the hedge – he was rummaging in the drawer full of screws – and he said, 'What? What?' impatiently.

The boy turned red – perhaps it was a stupid question – but the girl thought, he doesn't know, they never know, and she made a face at her brother to show that she was on his side. Later they asked their grandmother, and she, being practical said briskly, 'I should think sand. Think of all the grains,' and Roger turned in triumph. 'I told you so!' The grains. Deborah had not considered the grains. The magic of millions and millions of grains clinging together in the world and under the oceans made her sick. Let Roger win, it did not matter. It was better to be in the minority of the waving grass.

Now, on this first evening of summer holiday, she knelt and then lay full-length on the lawn, and stretched her hands out on either side like Jesus on the Cross, only face downwards, and murmured over and over again the words she had memorized from Confirmation preparation. 'A full, perfect and sufficient sacrifice . . . a full, perfect and sufficient sacrifice . . . satisfaction, and oblation, for the sins of the whole world.'

To offer herself to the earth, to the garden, the garden that had waited patiently all these months since last summer, surely this must be her first gesture.

'Come on,' said Roger, rousing himself from his appreciation of how Willis the gardener had mown the lawn to just the right closeness for cricket, and without waiting for his sister's answer he ran to the summer-house and made a dive at the long box in the corner where the stumps were kept. He smiled as he lifted the lid. The familiarity of the smell was satisfying. Old varnish and chipped paint, and surely that must be the same spider and the same cobweb? He drew out the stumps one by one, and the bails, and there was the ball – it had not been lost after all, as he had feared. It was worn, though, a greyish red – he smelt it and bit it, to taste the shabby leather. Then he gathered the things in his arms and went out to set up the stumps.

'Come and help me measure the pitch,' he called to his sister, and looking at her, squatting in the grass with her face hidden, his heart sank, because it meant that she was in one of her absent moods and would not concentrate on the cricket.

'Deb?' he called anxiously. 'You are going to play?'

Deborah heard his voice through the multitude of earth sounds, the heartbeat and the pulse. If she listened with her ear to the ground there was a humming much deeper than anything that bees did, or the sea at Hunstanton. The nearest to it was the wind, but the wind was reckless. The humming of the earth was patient. Deborah sat up, and her heart sank just as her brother's had done, for the same reason in reverse. The monotony of the game ahead would be like a great chunk torn out of privacy.

'How long shall we have to be?' she called.

The lack of enthusiasm damped the boy. It was not going to be any fun at all if she made a favour of it. He must be firm, though. Any concession on his part she snatched and turned to her advantage.

'Half-an-hour,' he said, and then, for encouragement's sake, 'You can bat first.'

Deborah smelt her knees. They had not yet got the country smell, but if she rubbed them in the grass, and in the earth too, the white London look would go.

'All right,' she said, 'but no longer than half-an-hour.'

He nodded quickly, and so as not to lose time measured out the pitch and then began ramming the stumps in the ground. Deborah went into the summer-house to get the bats. The familiarity of the little wooden hut pleased her as it had her brother. It was a long time now, many years, since they had played in the summer-house, making yet another house inside this one with the help of broken deckchairs; but, just as the garden waited for them a whole year, so did the summer-house, the windows on either side, cobweb-wrapped and stained, gazing out like eyes. Deborah did her ritual of bowing twice. If she should forget this, on her first entrance, it spelt ill-luck.

She picked out the two bats from the corner, where they were stacked with old croquet-hoops, and she knew at once that Roger would choose the one with the rubber handle, even though they could not bat at the same time, and for the whole of the holidays she must make do with the smaller one, that had half the whipping off. There was a croquet clip lying on the floor. She picked it up and put it on her nose and stood a moment, wondering how it would be if for evermore she had to live thus, nostrils pinched, making her voice like Punch. Would people pity her?

'Hurry,' shouted Roger, and she threw the clip into the corner, then quickly returned when she was halfway to the pitch, because she knew the clip was lying apart from its fellows, and she might wake in the night and remember it. The clip would turn malevolent, and haunt her. She replaced him on the floor with two others, and now she was absolved and the summer-house at peace.

'Don't get out too soon,' warned Roger as she stood in the

crease he had marked for her, and with a tremendous effort of concentration Deborah forced her eyes to his retreating figure and watched him roll up his sleeves and pace the required length for his run-up. Down came the ball and she lunged out, smacking it in the air in an easy catch. The impact of ball on bat stung her hands. Roger missed the catch on purpose. Neither of them said anything.

'Who shall I be?' called Deborah.

The game could only be endured, and concentration kept, if Roger gave her a part to play. Not an individual, but a country.

'You're India,' he said, and Deborah felt herself grow dark and lean. Part of her was tiger, part of her was sacred cow, the long grass fringing the lawn was jungle, the roof of the summer-house a minaret.

Even so, the half-hour dragged, and, when her turn came to bowl, the ball she threw fell wider every time, so that Roger, flushed and self-conscious because their grandfather had come out on to the terrace and was watching them, called angrily, 'Do try.'

Once again the effort at concentration, the figure of their grandfather – a source of apprehension to the boy, for he might criticize them – acting as a spur to his sister. Grandpapa was an Indian god, and tribute must be paid to him, a golden apple. The apple must be flung to slay his enemies. Deborah muttered a prayer, and the ball she bowled came fast and true and hit Roger's off-stump. In the moment of delivery their grandfather had turned away and pottered back again through the French windows of the drawing-room.

Roger looked round swiftly. His disgrace had not been seen. 'Jolly good ball,' he said. 'It's your turn to bat again.'

But his time was up. The stable clock chimed six. Solemnly Roger drew stumps.

'What shall we do now?' he asked.

Deborah wanted to be alone, but if she said so, on this first evening of the holiday, he would be offended.

'Go to the orchard and see how the apples are coming on,' she suggested, 'and then round by the kitchen garden in case the raspberries haven't all been picked. But you have to do it all without meeting anyone. If you see Willis or anyone, even the cat, you lose a mark.'

It was these sudden inventions that saved her. She knew her brother would be stimulated at the thought of outwitting the gardener. The aimless wander round the orchard would turn into a stalking exercise.

'Will you come too?' he asked.

'No,' she said, 'you have to test your skill.'

He seemed satisfied with this and ran off towards the orchard, stopping on the way to cut himself a switch from the bamboo.

As soon as he had disappeared Deborah made for the trees fringing the lawn, and once in the shrouded wood felt herself safe. She walked softly along the alley-way to the pool. The late sun sent shafts of light between the trees and on to the alley-way, and a myriad insects webbed their way in the beams, ascending and descending like angels on Jacob's ladder. But were they insects, wondered Deborah, or particles of dust, or even split fragments of light itself, beaten out and scattered by the sun?

It was very quiet. The woods were made for secrecy. They did not recognize her as the garden did. They did not care that for a whole year she could be at school, or at Hunstanton, or in London. The woods would never miss her: they had their own dark, passionate life.

Deborah came to the opening where the pool lay, with the five alley-ways branching from it, and she stood a moment before advancing to the brink, because this was holy ground and required atonement. She crossed her hands on her breast and shut her eyes. Then she kicked off her shoes. 'Mother of all things wild, do with me what you will,' she said aloud. The sound of her own voice gave her a slight shock. Then she went down on her knees and touched the ground three times with her forehead.

The first part of her atonement was accomplished, but the pool demanded sacrifice, and Deborah had come prepared. There was a stub of pencil she had carried in her pocket throughout the school term which she called her luck. It had teeth marks on it, and a chewed piece of rubber at one end. This treasure must be given to the pool just as other treasures had been given in the past, a miniature jug, a crested button, a china pig. Deborah felt for the stub of pencil and kissed it. She had carried and caressed it for so many lonely months, and now the moment of parting had come. The pool must not be denied. She flung out her right hand, her eyes still shut, and heard the faint plop as the stub of pencil struck the water. Then she opened her eyes, and saw in mid-pool a ripple. The pencil had gone, but the ripple moved, gently shaking the water-lilies. The movement symbolized acceptance.

Deborah, still on her knees and crossing her hands once more, edged her way to the brink of the pool and then, crouching there beside it, looked down into the water. Her reflection wavered up at her, and it was not the face she knew, not even the looking-glass face which anyway was false, but a disturbed image, dark-skinned and ghostly. The crossed hands were like the petals of the water-lilies themselves, and the colour was not waxen white but phantom green. The hair too was not the live clump she brushed every day and tied back with ribbon, but a canopy, a shroud. When the image smiled it became more distorted still. Uncrossing her hands, Deborah leant forward, took a twig, and drew a circle three times on the smooth surface. The water shook in ever-widening ripples, and her reflection, broken into fragments, heaved and danced, a sort of monster, and the eyes were there no longer, nor the mouth.

Presently the water became still. Insects, long-legged flies and beetles with spread wings hummed upon it. A dragon-fly had all the magnificence of a lily leaf to himself. He hovered there, rejoicing. But when Deborah took her eyes off him for a moment he was gone. At the far end of the pool, beyond the clustering lilies, green scum had formed, and beneath the scum were rooted, tangled weeds. They were so thick, and had lain in the pool so long, that if a man walked into them from the bank he would be held and choked. A fly, though, or a beetle, could sit upon the surface, and to him the pale green scum would not be treacherous at all, but a resting-place, a haven. And if someone threw a stone, so that the ripples formed, eventually they came to the scum, and rocked it, and the whole of the mossy surface moved in rhythm, a dancing-floor for those who played upon it.

There was a dead tree standing by the far end of the pool. He could have been fir or pine, or even larch, for time had stripped him of identity. He had no distinguishing mark upon his person, but with grotesque limbs straddled the sky. A cap of ivy crowned his naked head. Last winter a dangling branch had broken loose, and this now lay in the pool half-submerged, the green scum dripping from the withered twigs. The soggy branch made a vantagepoint for birds, and as Deborah watched a nestling suddenly flew from the undergrowth enveloping the dead tree, and perched for an instant on the mossy filigree. He was lost in terror. The parent bird cried warningly from some dark safety, and the nestling, pricking to the cry, took off from the branch that had offered him temporary salvation. He swerved across the pool, his flight mistimed, yet reached security. The chitter from the undergrowth told of his scolding. When he had gone silence returned to the pool.

It was, so Deborah thought, the time for prayer. The water-lilies were folding upon themselves. The ripples ceased. And that dark hollow in the centre of the pool, that black stillness where the water was deepest, was surely a funnel to the kingdom that lay below. Down that funnel had travelled the discarded treasures. The stub of pencil had lately plunged the depths. He had now been received as an equal among his fellows. This was the single law of the pool, for there were no other commandments. Once it was over, that first cold headlong flight, Deborah knew that the softness of the welcoming water took away all fear. It lapped the face and cleansed the eyes, and the plunge was not into darkness at all but into light. It did not become blacker as the pool was penetrated, but paler, more golden-green, and the mud that people told themselves was there was only a defence against strangers. Those who belonged, who knew, went to the source at once, and there were caverns and fountains and rainbow-coloured seas. There were shores of the whitest sand. There was soundless music.

Once again Deborah closed her eyes and bent lower to the pool. Her lips nearly touched the water. This was the great silence, when she had no thoughts, and was accepted by the pool. Waves of quiet ringed themselves about her, and slowly she lost all feeling, and had no knowledge of her legs, or of her kneeling body, or of her cold, clasped hands. There was nothing but the intensity of peace. It was a deeper acceptance than listening to the earth, because the earth was of the world, the earth was a throbbing pulse, but the acceptance of the pool meant another kind of hearing, a closing in of the waters, and just as the lilies folded so did the soul submerge.

'Deborah . . .? Deborah . . .?' Oh, no! Not now, don't let them call me back now! It was as though someone had hit her on the back, or jumped out at her from behind a corner, the sharp and sudden clamour of another life destroying the silence, the secrecy. And then came the tinkle of the cowbells. It was the signal from their grandmother that the time had come to go in. Not imperious and ugly with authority, like the clanging bell at school summoning those at play to lessons or chapel, but a reminder, nevertheless, that Time was all-important, that life was ruled to order, that even here, in the holiday home the children loved, the adult reigned supreme.

'All right, all right,' muttered Deborah, standing up and thrusting her numbed feet into her shoes. This time the rather raised tone of 'Deborah?', and the more hurried clanging of the cowbells, brought long ago from Switzerland, suggested a more imperious Grandmama than the tolerant one who seldom questioned. It must mean their supper was already laid, soup perhaps getting cold, and the farce of washing hands, of tidying, of combing hair, must first be gone through.

'Come on, Deb,' and now the shout was close, was right at hand, privacy lost for ever, for her brother came running down the alley-way swishing his bamboo stick in the air.

'What *have* you been doing?' The question was an intrusion and a threat. She would never have asked him what he had been doing, had he wandered away wanting to be alone, but Roger, alas, did not claim privacy. He liked companionship, and his question now, asked half in irritation, half in resentment, came really from the fear that he might lose her.

'Nothing,' said Deborah.

Roger eyed her suspiciously. She was in that mooning mood. And it meant, when they went to bed, that she would not talk. One of the best things, in the holidays, was having the two adjoining rooms and calling through to Deb, making her talk.

'Come on,' he said, 'they've rung,' and the making of their grandmother into 'they', turned a loved individual into something impersonal, showed Deborah that even if he did not understand he was on her side. He had been called from play, just as she had.

They ran from the woods to the lawn, and on to the terrace. Their grandmother had gone inside, but the cowbells hanging by the French window were still jangling.

The custom was for the children to have their supper first, at seven, and it was laid for them in the dining-room on a hot-plate. They served themselves. At a quarter-to-eight their grandparents had dinner. It was called dinner, but this was a concession to their status. They ate the same as the children, though Grandpapa had a savoury which was not served to the children. If the children were late for supper then it put out Time, as well as Agnes, who cooked for both generations, and it might mean five minutes' delay before Grandpapa had his soup. This shook routine.

The children ran up to the bathroom to wash, then downstairs to the dining-room. Their grandfather was standing in the hall. Deborah sometimes thought that he would have enjoyed sitting with them while they ate their supper, but he never suggested it. Grandmama had warned them, too, never to be a nuisance, or indeed to shout, if Grandpapa was near. This was not because he was nervous, but because he liked to shout himself.

'There's going to be a heat-wave,' he said. He had been listening to the news.

'That will mean lunch outside tomorrow,' said Roger swiftly. Lunch was the meal they took in common with the grandparents, and it was the moment of the day he disliked. He was nervous that his grandfather would ask him how he was getting on at school.

'Not for me, thank you,' said Grandpapa. 'Too many wasps.'

Roger was at once relieved. This meant that he and Deborah would have the little round garden-table to themselves. But Deborah felt sorry for her grandfather as he went back into the drawing-room. Lunch on the terrace could be gay, and would liven him up. When people grew old they had so few treats.

'What do you look forward to most in the day?' she once asked her grandmother.

'Going to bed,' was the reply, 'and filling my two hot-water bottles.' Why work through being young, thought Deborah, to this?

Back in the dining-room the children discussed what they should do during the heat-wave. It would be too hot, Deborah said, for cricket. But they might make a house, suggested Roger, in the trees by the paddock. If he got a few old boards from Willis, and nailed them together like a platform, and borrowed the orchard ladder, then they could take fruit and bottles of orange squash and keep them up there, and it would be a camp from which they could spy on Willis afterwards.

Deborah's first instinct was to say she did not want to play, but she checked herself in time. Finding the boards and fixing them would take Roger a whole morning. It would keep him employed. 'Yes, it's a good idea,' she said, and to foster his spirit of adventure she looked at his notebook, as they were drinking their soup, and approved of items necessary for the camp while he jotted them down. It was all part of the day-long deceit she practised to express understanding of his way of life.

When they had finished supper they took their trays to the kitchen and watched Agnes, for a moment, as she prepared the second meal for the grandparents. The soup was the same, but garnished. Little croûtons of toasted bread were added to it. And the butter was made into pats, not cut in a slab. The savoury tonight was to be cheese straws. The children finished the ones that Agnes had burnt. Then they went through to the drawing-room to say good night. The older people had both changed. Grandmama had a dress that she had worn several years ago in London. She had a cardigan round her shoulders like a cape.

'Go carefully with the bathwater,' she said. 'We'll be short if there's no rain.'

They kissed her smooth, soft skin. It smelt of rose leaves. Grandpapa's chin was sharp and bony. He did not kiss Roger.

'Be quiet overhead,' whispered their grandmother. The children nodded. The dining-room was underneath their rooms, and any jumping about or laughter would make a disturbance.

Deborah felt a wave of affection for the two old people. Their lives must be empty and sad. 'We *are* glad to be here,' she said. Grandmama smiled. This was how she lived, thought Deborah, on little crumbs of comfort.

Once out of the room their spirits soared, and to show

relief Roger chased Deborah upstairs, both laughing for no reason. Undressing they forgot the instructions about the bath, and when they went into the bathroom – Deborah was to have first go – the water was gurgling into the overflow. They tore out the plug in a panic, and listened to the waste roaring down the pipe to the drain below. If Agnes did not have the wireless on she would hear it.

The children were too old now for boats or play, but the bathroom was a place for confidences, for a sharing of those few tastes they agreed upon, or, after quarrelling, for moody silence. The one who broke silence first would then lose face.

'Willis has a new bicycle,' said Roger. 'I saw it propped against the shed. I couldn't try it because he was there. But I shall tomorrow. It's a Raleigh.'

He liked all practical things, and the trying of the gardener's bicycle would give an added interest to the morning of next day. Willis had a bag of tools in a leather pouch behind the saddle. These could all be felt and the spanners, smelling of oil, tested for shape and usefulness.

'If Willis died,' said Deborah, 'I wonder what age he would be.'

It was the kind of remark that Roger resented always. What had death to do with bicycles? 'He's sixty-five,' he said, 'so he'd be sixty-five.'

'No,' said Deborah, 'what age when he got *there*.'

Roger did not want to discuss it. 'I bet I can ride it round the stables if I lower the seat,' he said. 'I bet I don't fall off.'

But if Roger would not rise to death, Deborah would not rise to the wager. 'Who cares?' she said.

The sudden streak of cruelty stung the brother. Who cared indeed ... The horror of an empty world encompassed him, and to give himself confidence he seized the wet sponge and flung it out of the window. They heard it splosh on the terrace below.

'Grandpapa will step on it, and slip,' said Deborah, aghast.

The image seized them, and choking back laughter they

covered their faces. Hysteria doubled them up. Roger rolled over and over on the bathroom floor. Deborah, the first to recover, wondered why laughter was so near to pain, why Roger's face, twisted now in merriment, was yet the same crumpled thing when his heart was breaking.

'Hurry up,' she said briefly, 'let's dry the floor,' and as they wiped the linoleum with their towels the action sobered them both.

Back in their bedrooms, the door open between them, they watched the light slowly fading. But the air was warm like day. Their grandfather and the people who said what the weather was going to be were right. The heat-wave was on its way. Deborah, leaning out of the open window, fancied she could see it in the sky, a dull haze where the sun had been before; and the trees beyond the lawn, day-coloured when they were having their supper in the dining-room, had turned into night-birds with outstretched wings. The garden knew about the promised heat-wave, and rejoiced: the lack of rain was of no consequence yet, for the warm air was a trap, lulling it into a drowsy contentment.

The dull murmur of their grandparents' voices came from the dining-room below. What did they discuss, wondered Deborah. Did they make those sounds to reassure the children, or were their voices part of their unreal world? Presently the voices ceased, and then there was a scraping of chairs, and voices from a different quarter, the drawing-room now, and a faint smell of their grandfather's cigarette.

Deborah called softly to her brother but he did not answer. She went through to his room, and he was asleep. He must have fallen asleep suddenly, in the midst of talking. She was relieved. Now she could be alone again, and not have to keep up the pretence of sharing conversation. Dusk was everywhere, the sky a deepening black. 'When they've gone up to bed,' thought Deborah, 'then I'll be truly alone.' She knew what she was going to do. She waited there, by the open window, and the deepening sky lost the veil that covered it, the haze disintegrated, and the stars broke through. Where there had been nothing was life, dusty and bright, and the waiting earth gave off a scent of knowledge. Dew rose from the pores. The lawn was white.

Patch, the old dog, who slept at the end of Grandpapa's bed on a plaid rug, came out on to the terrace and barked hoarsely. Deborah leant out and threw a piece of creeper on to him. He shook his back. Then he waddled slowly to the flower-tub above the steps and cocked his leg. It was his nightly routine. He barked once more, staring blindly at the hostile trees, and went back into the drawing-room. Soon afterwards, someone came to close the windows – Grandmama, thought Deborah, for the touch was light. 'They are shutting out the best,' said the child to herself, 'all the meaning, and all the point.' Patch, being an animal, should know better. He ought to be in a kennel where he could watch, but instead, grown fat and soft, he preferred the bumpiness of her grandfather's bed. He had forgotten the secrets. So had they, the old people.

Deborah heard her grandparents come upstairs. First her grandmother, the quicker of the two, and then her grandfather, more laboured, saying a word or two to Patch as the little dog wheezed his way up. There was a general clicking of lights and shutting of doors. Then silence. How remote, the world of the grandparents, undressing with curtains closed. A pattern of life unchanged for so many years. What went on without would never be known. 'He that has ears to hear, let him hear,' said Deborah, and she thought of the callousness of Jesus which no priest could explain. Let the dead bury their dead. All the people in the world, undressing now, or sleeping, not just in the village but in cities and capitals, they were shutting out the truth, they were burying their dead. They wasted silence.

The stable clock struck eleven. Deborah pulled on her clothes. Not the cotton frock of the day, but her old jeans that Grandmama disliked, rolled up above her knees. And a jersey. Sandshoes with a hole that did not matter. She was cunning enough to go down by the back stairs. Patch would bark if she tried the front stairs, close to the grandparents' rooms. The back stairs led past Agnes's room, which smelt of apples though she never ate fruit. Deborah could hear her snoring. She would not even wake on Judgement Day. And this led her to wonder on the truth of that fable too, for there might be so many millions by then who liked their graves – Grandpapa, for instance, fond of his routine, and irritated at the sudden riot of trumpets.

Deborah crept past the pantry and the servants' hall – it was only a tiny sitting-room for Agnes, but long usage had given it the dignity of the name – and unlatched and unbolted the heavy back door. Then she stepped outside, on to the gravel, and took the long way round by the front of the house so as not to tread on the terrace, fronting the lawns and the garden.

The warm night claimed her. In a moment it was part of her. She walked on the grass, and her shoes were instantly soaked. She flung up her arms to the sky. Power ran to her fingertips. Excitement was communicated from the waiting tree, and the orchard, and the paddock; the intensity of their secret life caught at her and made her run. It was nothing like the excitement of ordinary looking forward, of birthday presents, of Christmas stockings, but the pull of a magnet – her grandfather had shown her once how it worked, little needles springing to the jaws – and now night and the sky above were a vast magnet, and the things that waited below were needles, caught up in the great demand.

Deborah went to the summer-house, and it was not sleeping like the house fronting the terrace but open to understanding, sharing complicity. Even the dusty windows caught the light, and the cobwebs shone. She rummaged for the old lilo and the motheaten car rug that Grandmama had thrown out two summers ago, and bearing them over her shoulder she made her way to the pool. The alley-way was ghostly, and Deborah knew, for all her mounting tension, that the test was hard. Part of her was still body-bound, and afraid of shadows. If anything stirred she would jump and know true terror. She must show defiance, though. The woods expected it. Like old wise lamas they expected courage.

She sensed approval as she ran the gauntlet, the tall trees watching. Any sign of turning back, of panic, and they would crowd upon her in a choking mass, smothering protest. Branches would become arms, gnarled and knotty, ready to strangle, and the leaves of the higher trees fold in and close like the sudden furling of giant umbrellas. The smaller under-growth, obedient to the will, would become a briary of a million thorns where animals of no known world crouched snarling, their eyes on fire. To show fear was to show misunderstanding. The woods were merciless.

Deborah walked the alley-way to the pool, her left hand holding the lilo and the rug on her shoulder, her right hand raised in salutation. This was a gesture of respect. Then she paused before the pool and laid down her burden beside it. The lilo was to be her bed, the rug her cover. She took off her shoes, also in respect, and lay down upon the lilo. Then, drawing the rug to her chin, she lay flat, her eyes upon the sky. The gauntlet of the alley-way over, she had no more fear. The woods had accepted her, and the pool was the final resting-place, the doorway, the key.

'I shan't sleep,' thought Deborah. 'I shall just lie awake here all the night and wait for morning, but it will be a kind of introduction to life, like being confirmed.'

The stars were thicker now than they had been before. No space in the sky without a prick of light, each star a sun. Some, she thought, were newly born, white-hot, and others wise and colder, nearing completion. The law encompassed them, fixing the riotous path, but how they fell and tumbled depended upon themselves. Such peace, such stillness, such sudden quietude, excitement gone. The trees were no longer menacing but guardians, and the pool was primeval water, the first, the last.

Then Deborah stood at the wicket-gate, the boundary, and there was a woman with outstretched hand, demanding tickets. 'Pass through,' she said when Deborah reached her. 'We saw you coming.' The wicket-gate became a turnstile. Deborah pushed against it and there was no resistance, she was through.

'What is it?' she asked. 'Am I really here at last? Is this the bottom of the pool?'

'It could be,' smiled the woman. 'There are so many ways. You just happened to choose this one.'

Other people were pressing to come through. They had no faces, they were only shadows. Deborah stood aside to let them by, and in a moment they had all gone, all phantoms.

'Why only now, tonight?' asked Deborah. 'Why not in the afternoon, when I came to the pool?'

'It's a trick,' said the woman. 'You seize on the moment in time. We were here this afternoon. We're always here. Our life goes on around you, but nobody knows it. The trick's easier by night, that's all.'

'Am I dreaming, then?' asked Deborah.

'No,' said the woman, 'this isn't a dream. And it isn't death, either. It's the secret world.'

The secret world ... It was something Deborah had always known, and now the pattern was complete. The memory of it, and the relief, were so tremendous that something seemed to burst inside her heart.

'Of course . . .' she said, 'of course . . .' and everything that had ever been fell into place. There was no disharmony. The joy was indescribable, and the surge of feeling, like wings about her in the air, lifted her away from the turnstile and the woman, and she had all knowledge. That was it – the invasion of knowledge.

'I'm not myself, then, after all,' she thought. 'I knew I wasn't. It was only the task given,' and, looking down, she saw a little child who was blind trying to find her way. Pity seized her. She bent down and put her hands on the child's eyes, and they opened, and the child was herself at two years old. The incident came back. It was when her mother died and Roger was born.

'It doesn't matter after all,' she told the child. 'You are not lost. You don't have to go on crying.' Then the child that had been herself melted, and became absorbed in the water and the sky, and the joy of the invading flood intensified so that there was no body at all but only being. No words, only movements. And the beating of wings. This above all, the beating of wings.

'Don't let me go!' It was a pulse in her ear, and a cry, and she saw the woman at the turnstile put up her hands to hold her. Then there was such darkness, such dragging, terrible darkness, and the beginning of pain all over again, the leaden heart, the tears, the misunderstanding. The voice saying 'No!' was her own harsh, worldly voice, and she was staring at the restless trees, black and ominous against the sky. One hand trailed in the water of the pool.

Deborah sat up, sobbing. The hand that had been in the pool was wet and cold. She dried it on the rug. And suddenly she was seized with such fear that her body took possession, and throwing aside the rug she began to run along the alley-way, the dark trees mocking and the welcome of the woman at the turnstile turned to treachery. Safety lay in the house behind the closed curtains, security was with the grandparents sleeping in their beds, and like a leaf driven before a whirlwind Deborah was out of the woods and across the silver soaking lawn, up the steps beyond the terrace and through the garden-gate to the back door.

The slumbering solid house received her. It was like an old staid person who, surviving many trials, had learnt experience. 'Don't take any notice of them,' it seemed to say, jerking its head – did a house have a head? – towards the woods beyond. 'They've made no contribution to civilization. I'm man-made, and different. This is where you belong, dear child. Now settle down.'

Deborah went back again upstairs and into her bedroom. Nothing had changed. It was still the same. Going to the open window she saw that the woods and the lawn seemed unaltered from the moment, how long back she did not know, when she had stood there, deciding upon the visit to the pool. The only difference now was in herself. The excitement had gone, the tension too. Even the terror of those last moments, when her flying feet had brought her to the house, seemed unreal.

She drew the curtains, just as her grandmother might have done, and climbed into bed. Her mind was now preoccupied with practical difficulties, like explaining the presence of the lilo and the rug beside the pool. Willis might find them, and tell her grandfather. The feel of her own pillow, and of her own blankets, reassured her. Both were familiar. And being tired was familiar too, it was a solid bodily ache, like the tiredness after too much jumping or cricket. The thing was, though – and the last remaining conscious thread of thought decided to postpone conclusion until the morning – which was real? This safety of the house, or the secret world?

When Deborah woke next morning she knew at once that her mood was bad. It would last her for the day. Her eyes ached, and her neck was stiff, and there was a taste in her mouth like magnesia. Immediately Roger came running into her room, his face refreshed and smiling from some dreamless sleep, and jumped on her bed.

'It's come,' he said, 'the heat-wave's come. It's going to be ninety in the shade.'

Deborah considered how best she could damp his day. 'It can go to a hundred for all I care,' she said. 'I'm going to read all morning.'

His face fell. A look of bewilderment came into his eyes. 'But the house?' he said. 'We'd decided to have a house in the trees, don't you remember? I was going to get some planks from Willis.'

Deborah turned over in bed and humped her knees. 'You can, if you like,' she said. 'I think it's a silly game.'

She shut her eyes, feigning sleep, and presently she heard his feet patter slowly back to his own room, and then the thud of a ball against the wall. If he goes on doing that, she thought maliciously, Grandpapa will ring his bell, and Agnes will come panting up the stairs. She hoped for destruction, for grumbling and snapping, and everyone falling out, not speaking. That was the way of the world.

The kitchen, where the children breakfasted, faced west, so it did not get the morning sun. Agnes had hung up fly-papers to catch wasps. The cereal, puffed wheat, was soggy. Deborah complained, mashing the mess with her spoon.

'It's a new packet,' said Agnes. 'You're mighty particular all of a sudden.'

'Deb's got out of bed the wrong side,' said Roger.

The two remarks fused to make a challenge. Deborah seized the nearest weapon, a knife, and threw it at her brother. It narrowly missed his eye, but cut his cheek. Surprised, he put his hand to his face and felt the blood. Hurt, not by the knife but by his sister's action, his face turned red and his lower lip quivered. Deborah ran out of the kitchen and slammed the door. Her own violence distressed her, but the power of the mood was too strong. Going on to the terrace, she saw that the worst had happened. Willis had found the lilo and the rug, and had put them to dry in the sun. He was talking to her grandmother. Deborah tried to slip back into the house, but it was too late.

'Deborah, how very thoughtless of you,' said Grandmama. 'I tell you children every summer that I don't mind your taking the things from the hut into the garden if only you'll put them back.'

Deborah knew she should apologize, but the mood forbade it. 'That old rug is full of moth,' she said contemptuously, 'and the lilo has a rainproof back. It doesn't hurt them.'

They both stared at her, and her grandmother flushed, just as Roger had done when she had thrown the knife at him. Then her grandmother turned her back and continued giving some instructions to the gardener.

Deborah stalked along the terrace, pretending that nothing had happened, and skirting the lawn she made her way towards the orchard and so to the fields beyond. She picked up a windfall, but as soon as her teeth bit into it the taste was green. She threw it away. She went and sat on a gate and stared in front of her, looking at nothing. Such deception everywhere. Such sour sadness. It was like Adam and Eve being locked out of paradise. The Garden of Eden was no more. Somewhere, very close, the woman at the turnstile waited to let her in, the secret world was all about her, but the key was gone. Why had she ever come back? What had brought her?

People were going about their business. The old man who came three days a week to help Willis was sharpening his scythe behind the toolshed. Beyond the field where the lane ran towards the main road she could see the top of the postman's head. He was pedalling his bicycle towards the village. She heard Roger calling, 'Deb? Deb . . .?' which meant that he had forgiven her, but still the mood held sway and she did not answer. Her own dullness made her own punishment. Presently a knocking sound told her that he had got the planks from Willis and had embarked on the building of his house. He was like his grandfather; he kept to the routine set for himself.

Deborah was consumed with pity. Not for the sullen self humped upon the gate, but for all of them going about their business in the world who did not hold the key. The key was hers, and she had lost it. Perhaps if she worked her way through the long day the magic would return with evening and she would find it once again. Or even now. Even now, by the pool, there might be a clue, a vision.

Deborah slid off the gate and went the long way round. By skirting the fields, parched under the sun, she could reach the other side of the wood and meet no one. The husky wheat was stiff. She had to keep close to the hedge to avoid brushing it, and the hedge was tangled. Foxgloves had grown too tall and were bending with empty sockets, their flowers gone. There were nettles everywhere. There was no gate into the wood, and she had to climb the pricking hedge with the barbed wire tearing her knickers. Once in the wood some measure of peace returned, but the alley-ways this side had not been scythed, and the grass was long. She had to wade through it like a sea, brushing it aside with her hands.

She came upon the pool from behind the monster tree, the hybrid whose naked arms were like a dead man's stumps, projecting at all angles. This side, on the lip of the pool, the scum was carpet-thick, and all the lilies, coaxed by the risen sun, had opened wide. They basked as lizards bask on hot stone walls. But here, with stems in water, they swung in grace, cluster upon cluster, pink and waxen white. 'They're asleep,' thought Deborah. 'So is the wood. The morning is not their time,' and it seemed to her beyond possibility that the turnstile was at hand and the woman waiting, smiling. 'She said they were always there, even in the day, but the truth is that being a child I'm blinded in the day. I don't know how to see.'

She dipped her hands in the pool, and the water was tepid brown. She tasted her fingers, and the taste was rank. Brackish water, stagnant from long stillness. Yet beneath . . . beneath, she knew, by night the woman waited, and not only the woman but the whole secret world. Deborah began to pray. 'Let it happen again,' she whispered. 'Let it happen again. Tonight. I won't be afraid.'

The sluggish pool made no acknowledgement, but the very silence seemed a testimony of faith, of acceptance. Beside the pool, where the imprint of the lilo had marked the moss, Deborah found a kirby-grip, fallen from her hair during the night. It was proof of visitation. She threw it into the pool as part of the treasury. Then she walked back into the ordinary day and the heat-wave, and her black mood was softened. She went to find Roger in the orchard. He was busy with the platform. Three of the boards were fixed, and the noisy hammering was something that had to be borne. He saw her coming, and as always, after trouble, sensed that her mood had changed and mention must never be made of it. Had he called, 'Feeling better?', it would have revived the antagonism, and she might not play with him all the day. Instead, he took no notice. She must be the first to speak.

Deborah waited at the foot of the tree, then bent, and handed him up an apple. It was green, but the offering meant peace. He ate it manfully. 'Thanks,' he said. She climbed into the tree beside him and reached for the box of nails. Contact had been renewed. All was well between them.

The hot day spun itself out like a web. The heat haze stretched across the sky, dun-coloured and opaque. Crouching on the burning boards of the apple-tree, the children drank ginger beer and fanned themselves with dock-leaves. They grew hotter still. When the cowbells summoned them for lunch they found that their grandmother had drawn the curtains of all the rooms downstairs, and the drawing-room was a vault and strangely cool. They flung themselves into chairs. No one was hungry. Patch lay under the piano, his soft mouth dripping saliva. Grandmama had changed into a sleeveless linen dress never before seen, and Grandpapa, in a dented panama, carried a fly-whisk used years ago in Egypt.

'Ninety-one,' he said grimly, 'on the Air Ministry roof. It was on the one o'clock news.'

Deborah thought of the men who must measure heat, toiling up and down on this Ministry roof with rods and tapes and odd-shaped instruments. Did anyone care but Grandpapa?

'Can we take our lunch outside?' asked Roger.

His grandmother nodded. Speech was too much effort, and she sank languidly into her chair at the foot of the dining-room table. The roses she had picked last night had wilted.

The children carried chicken drumsticks to the summer-house. It was too hot to sit inside, but they sprawled in the shadow it cast, their heads on faded cushions shedding kapok.

Somewhere, far above their heads, an aeroplane climbed like a small silver fish, and was lost in space.

'A Meteor,' said Roger. 'Grandpapa says they're obsolete.'

Deborah thought of Icarus, soaring towards the sun. Did he know when his wings began to melt? How did he feel? She stretched out her arms and thought of them as wings. The fingertips would be the first to curl, and then turn cloggy soft, and useless. What terror in the sudden loss of height, the drooping power . . .

Roger, watching her, hoped it was some game. He threw his picked drumstick into a flowerbed and jumped to his feet.

'Look,' he said, 'I'm a Javelin,' and he too stretched his arms and ran in circles, banking. Jet noises came from his clenched teeth. Deborah dropped her arms and looked at the drumstick. What had been clean and white from Roger's teeth was now earth-brown. Was it offended to be chucked away? Years later, when everyone was dead, it would be found, moulded like a fossil. Nobody would care.

'Come on,' said Roger.

'Where to?' she asked.

'To fetch the raspberries,' he said.

'You go,' she told him.

Roger did not like going into the dining-room alone. He was self-conscious. Deborah made a shield from the adult eyes. In the end he consented to fetch the raspberries without her on condition that she played cricket after tea. After tea was a long way off.

She watched him return, walking very slowly, bearing the plates of raspberries and clotted cream. She was seized with sudden pity, that same pity which, earlier she had felt for all people other than herself. How absorbed he was, how intent on the moment that held him. But tomorrow he would be some old man far away, the garden forgotten, and this day long past.

'Grandmama says it can't go on,' he announced. 'There'll have to be a storm.'

But why? Why not for ever? Why not breathe a spell so that all of them could stay locked and dreaming like the courtiers in the *Sleeping Beauty*, never knowing, never waking, cobwebs in their hair and on their hands, tendrils imprisoning the house itself?

'Race me,' said Roger, and to please him she plunged her spoon into the mush of raspberries but finished last, to his delight.

No one moved during the long afternoon. Grandmama went upstairs to her room. The children saw her at her window in her petticoat drawing the curtains closed. Grandpapa put his feet up in the drawing-room, a handkerchief over his face. Patch did not stir from his place under the piano. Roger, undefeated, found employment still. He first helped Agnes to shell peas for supper, squatting on the back-door step while she relaxed on a lopsided basket chair dragged from the servants' hall. This task finished, he discovered a tin bath, put away in the cellar, in which Patch had been washed in younger days. He carried it to the lawn and filled it with water. Then he stripped to bathing-trunks and sat in it solemnly, an umbrella over his head to keep off the sun.

Deborah lay on her back behind the summer-house, wondering what would happen if Jesus and Buddha met. Would there be discussion, courtesy, an exchange of views like politicians at summit talks? Or were they after all the same person, born at separate times? The queer thing was that this topic, interesting now, meant nothing in the secret world. Last night, through the turnstile, all problems disappeared. They were non-existent. There was only the knowledge and the joy.

She must have slept, because when she opened her eyes she saw to her dismay that Roger was no longer in the bath but was hammering the cricket-stumps into the lawn. It was a quarter-to-five.

'Hurry up,' he called, when he saw her move. 'I've had tea.'

She got up and dragged herself into the house, sleepy still, and giddy. The grandparents were in the drawing-room, refreshed from the long repose of the afternoon. Grandpapa smelt of eau-de-Cologne. Even Patch had come to and was lapping his saucer of cold tea.

'You look tired,' said Grandmama critically. 'Are you feeling all right?'

Deborah was not sure. Her head was heavy. It must have been sleeping in the afternoon, a thing she never did.

'I think so,' she answered, 'but if anyone gave me roast pork I know I'd be sick.'

'No one suggested you should eat roast pork,' said her grandmother, surprised. 'Have a cucumber sandwich, they're cool enough.'

Grandpapa was lying in wait for a wasp. He watched it hover over his tea, grim, expectant. Suddenly he slammed at the air with his whisk. 'Got the brute,' he said in triumph. He ground it into the carpet with his heel. It made Deborah think of Jehovah.

'Don't rush around in the heat,' said Grandmama. 'It isn't wise. Can't you and Roger play some nice, quiet game?'

'What sort of game?' asked Deborah.

But her grandmother was without invention. The croquet mallets were all broken. 'We might pretend to be dwarfs and use the heads,' said Deborah, and she toyed for a moment with the idea of squatting to croquet. Their knees would stiffen, though, it would be too difficult.

'I'll read aloud to you, if you like,' said Grandmama.

Deborah seized upon the suggestion. It delayed cricket. She ran out on to the lawn and padded the idea to make it acceptable to Roger.

'I'll play afterwards,' she said, 'and that ice-cream that Agnes has in the fridge, you can eat all of it. I'll talk tonight in bed.'

Roger hesitated. Everything must be weighed. Three goods to balance evil.

'You know that stick of sealing-wax Daddy gave you?' he said.

'Yes.'

'Can I have it?'

The balance for Deborah too. The quiet of the moment in opposition to the loss of the long thick stick so brightly red.

'All right,' she grudged.

Roger left the cricket stumps and they went into the drawing-room. Grandpapa, at the first suggestion of reading aloud, had disappeared, taking Patch with him. Grandmama had cleared away the tea. She found her spectacles and the book. It was *Black Beauty*. Grandmama kept no modern children's books, and this made common ground for the three of them. She read the terrible chapter where the stable-lad lets Beauty get overheated and gives him a cold drink and does not put on his blanket. The story was suited to the day. Even Roger listened entranced. And Deborah, watching her grandmother's calm face and hearing her careful voice reading the sentences, thought how strange it was that Grandmama could turn herself into Beauty with such ease. She *was* a horse, suffering there with pneumonia in the stable, being saved by the wise coachman.

After the reading, cricket was an anticlimax, but Deborah must keep her bargain. She kept thinking of Black Beauty writing the book. It showed how good the story was, Grandmama said, because no child had ever yet questioned the practical side of it, or posed the picture of a horse with a pen in its hoof.

'A modern horse would have a typewriter,' thought Deborah, and she began to bowl to Roger, smiling to herself as she did so because of the twentieth-century Beauty clacking with both hoofs at a machine.

This evening, because of the heat-wave, the routine was changed. They had their baths first, before their supper, for they were hot and exhausted from the cricket. Then, putting on pyjamas and cardigans, they ate their supper on the terrace. For once Grandmama was indulgent. It was still so hot that they could not take chill, and the dew had not yet risen. It made a small excitement, being in pyjamas on the terrace. Like people abroad, said Roger. Or natives in the South Seas, said Deborah. Or beachcombers who had lost caste. Grandpapa, changed into a white tropical jacket, had not lost caste.

'He's a white trader,' whispered Deborah. 'He's made a fortune out of pearls.'

Roger choked. Any joke about his grandfather, whom he feared, had all the sweet agony of danger.

'What's the thermometer say?' asked Deborah.

Her grandfather, pleased at her interest, went to inspect it.

'Still above eighty,' he said with relish.

Deborah, when she cleaned her teeth later, thought how pale her face looked in the mirror above the wash-basin. It was not brown, like Roger's, from the day in the sun, but wan and yellow. She tied back her hair with a ribbon, and the nose and chin were peaky sharp. She yawned largely, as Agnes did in the kitchen on Sunday afternoons.

'Don't forget you promised to talk,' said Roger quickly.

Talk . . . That was the burden. She was so tired she longed for the white smoothness of her pillow, all blankets thrown aside, bearing only a single sheet. But Roger, wakeful on his bed, the door between them wide, would not relent. Laughter was the one solution, and to make him hysterical, and so exhaust him sooner, she fabricated a day in the life of Willis, from his first morning kipper to his final glass of beer at the village inn. The adventures in between would have tried Gulliver. Roger's delight drew protests from the adult world below. There was the sound of a bell, and then Agnes came up the stairs and put her head round the corner of Deborah's door.

'Your Granny says you're not to make so much noise,' she said.

Deborah, spent with invention, lay back and closed her

eyes. She could go no further. The children called good night to each other, both speaking at the same time, from age-long custom, beginning with their names and addresses and ending with the world, the universe, and space. Then the final main 'Good night', after which neither must ever speak, on pain of unknown calamity.

'I must try and keep awake,' thought Deborah, but the power was not in her. Sleep was too compelling, and it was hours later that she opened her eyes and saw her curtains blowing and the forked flash light the ceiling, and heard the trees tossing and sobbing against the sky. She was out of bed in an instant. Chaos had come. There were no stars, and the night was sulphurous. A great crack split the heavens and tore them in two. The garden groaned. If the rain would only fall there might be mercy, and the trees, imploring, bowed themselves this way and that, while the vivid lawn, bright in expectation, lay like a sheet of metal exposed to flame. Let the waters break. Bring down the rain.

Suddenly the lightning forked again, and standing there, alive yet immobile, was the woman by the turnstile. She stared up at the windows of the house, and Deborah recognized her. The turnstile was there, inviting entry, and already the phantom figures, passing through it, crowded towards the trees beyond the lawn. The secret world was waiting. Through the long day, while the storm was brewing, it had hovered there unseen beyond her reach, but now that night had come, and the thunder with it, the barriers were down. Another crack, mighty in its summons, the turnstile yawned, and the woman with her hand upon it smiled and beckoned.

Deborah ran out of the room and down the stairs. Somewhere somebody called – Roger, perhaps, it did not matter – and Patch was barking; but caring nothing for concealment she went through the dark drawing-room and opened the French window on to the terrace. The lightning searched the terrace and lit the paving, and Deborah ran down the steps on to the lawn where the turnstile gleamed.

Haste was imperative. If she did not run the turnstile might be closed, the woman vanish, and all the wonder of the sacred world be taken from her. She was in time. The woman was still waiting. She held out her hand for tickets, but Deborah shook her head. 'I have none.' The woman, laughing, brushed her through into the secret world where there were no laws, no rules, and all the faceless phantoms ran before her to the woods, blown by the rising wind. Then the rain came. The sky, deep brown as the lightning pierced it, opened, and the water hissed to the ground, rebounding from the earth in bubbles. There was no order now in the alley-way. The ferns had turned to trees, the trees to Titans. All moved in ecstasy, with sweeping limbs, but the rhythm was broken up, tumultuous, so that some of them were bent backwards, torn by the sky, and others dashed their heads to the undergrowth where they were caught and beaten.

In the world behind, laughed Deborah as she ran, this would be punishment, but here in the secret world it was a tribute. The phantoms who ran beside her were like waves. They were linked one with another, and they were, each one of them, and Deborah too, part of the night force that made the sobbing and the laughter. The lightning forked where they willed it, and the thunder cracked as they looked upwards to the sky.

The pool had come alive. The water-lilies had turned to hands, with palms upraised, and in the far corner, usually so still under the green scum, bubbles sucked at the surface, steaming and multiplying as the torrents fell. Everyone crowded to the pool. The phantoms bowed and crouched by the water's edge, and now the woman had set up her turnstile in the middle of the pool, beckoning them once more. Some remnant of a sense of social order rose in Deborah and protested.

'But we've already paid,' she shouted, and remembered a second later that she had passed through free. Must there be duplication? Was the secret world a rainbow, always repeating itself, alighting on another hill when you believed yourself beneath it? No time to think. The phantoms had gone through. The lightning, streaky white, lit the old dead monster tree with his crown of ivy, and because he had no spring now in his joints he could not sway in tribute with the trees and ferns, but had to remain there, rigid, like a crucifix.

'And now . . . and now . . . and now . . .' called Deborah.

The triumph was that she was not afraid, was filled with such wild acceptance . . . She ran into the pool. Her living feet felt the mud and the broken sticks and all the tangle of old weeds, and the water was up to her armpits and her chin. The lilies held her. The rain blinded her. The woman and the turnstile were no more.

'Take me too,' cried the child. 'Don't leave me behind!' In her heart was a savage disenchantment. They had broken their promise, they had left her in the world. The pool that claimed her now was not the pool of secrecy, but dank, dark brackish water choked with scum.

'Grandpapa says he's going to have it fenced round,' said Roger. 'It should have been done years ago. A proper fence, then nothing can ever happen. But barrow-loads of shingle tipped in it first. Then it won't be a pool, but just a dewpond. Dewponds aren't dangerous.'

He was looking at her over the edge of her bed. He had risen in status, being the only one of them downstairs, the bearer of tidings good or ill, the go-between. Deborah had been ordered two days in bed.

'I should think by Wednesday,' he went on, 'you'd be able to play cricket. It's not as if you're hurt. People who walk in their sleep are just a bit potty.'

'I did not walk in my sleep,' said Deborah.

'Grandpapa said you must have done,' said Roger. 'It was a good thing that Patch woke him up and he saw you going across the lawn . . .' Then, to show his release from tension, he stood on his hands.

Deborah could see the sky from her bed. It was flat and dull. The day was a summer day that had worked through storm. Agnes came into the room with junket on a tray. She looked important.

'Now run off,' she said to Roger. 'Deborah doesn't want to talk to you. She's supposed to rest.'

Surprisingly, Roger obeyed, and Agnes placed the junket on the table beside the bed. 'You don't feel hungry, I expect,' she said. 'Never mind, you can eat this later, when you fancy it. Have you got a pain? It's usual, the first time.'

'No,' said Deborah.

What had happened to her was personal. They had prepared her for it at school, but nevertheless it was a shock, not to be discussed with Agnes. The woman hovered a moment, in case the child asked questions; but, seeing that none came, she turned and left the room.

Deborah, her cheek on her hand, stared at the empty sky. The heaviness of knowledge lay upon her, a strange, deep sorrow.

'It won't come back,' she thought. 'I've lost the key.'

The hidden world, like ripples on the pool so soon to be filled in and fenced, was out of her reach for ever.

Swans

They were ready to go. Mother and Fay and Totty, standing by the gate in their next best to Sunday best, Mother with her straw hat on with shells on it and Fay with her check dress that Mother had made and Totty, well where was Totty a moment ago she was here?

'Totty,' Mother called. 'If you don't hurry we'll miss the train, it leaves in ten minutes. And we're not to forget to get off at Beach Street. At least I think Dad said Beach Street. But hurry Totty.'

Totty came running from the wash-house round the back.

'Mum quick I've found Gypsy and her head's down like all the other cats and she's dying I think. She's in the wash-house. Mum quick,' she cried urgently.

Mother looked flurried. 'Hurry up, Totty and come back Fay, pussy will be all right. We'll give her some milk now there's some in the pot and we'll wrap her in a piece of blanket and she'll be all right till we get home.'

The three of them hurried back to the wash-house. It was dark with no light except what came through the small square window which had been cracked and pasted over with brown paper. The cat lay on a pile of sacks in a corner near the copper. Her head was down and her eyes were bright with a fever or poison or something but she was alive. They found an old clean tin lid and poured warm milk in it and from one of the shelves they pulled a dusty piece of blanket. The folds stuck to one another all green and hairy and a slater with hills and valleys on his back fell to the floor and moved slowly along the cracked concrete floor to a little secret place by the wall. Totty even forgot to collect him. She collected things, slaters and earwigs and spiders though you had to be careful with earwigs for when you were lying in the grass asleep they crept into your ear and built their nest there and you had to go to the doctor and have your ear lanced.

They covered Gypsy and each one patted her. Don't worry Gypsy they said. We'll be back to look after you tonight. We're going to the Beach now. Goodbye Gypsy.

And there was Mother waiting impatiently again at the gate.

'Do hurry. Pussy'll be all right now.'

Mother always said things would be all right, cats and birds and people even as if she knew and she did know too, Mother knew always.

But Fay crept back once more to look inside the washhouse.

'I promise,' she called to the cat. 'We'll be back, just you see.'

And the next moment the three Mother and Fay and Totty were outside the gate and Mother with a broom-like motion of her arms was sweeping the two little girls before her.

O the train and the coloured pictures on the station, South America and Australia, and the bottle of fizzy drink that you could only half finish because you were too full, and the ham sandwiches that curled up at the edges, because they were stale, Dad said, and he *knew*, and the rabbits and cows and bulls outside in the paddocks, and the sheep running away from the noise and the houses that came and went like a dream, clackety-clack, Kaitangata, Kaitangata, and the train stopping and panting and the man with the stick tapping the wheels and the huge rubber hose to give the engine a drink, and the voices of the people in the carriage on and on and waiting.

'Don't forget Beach Street, Mum,' Dad had said. Dad was

away at work up at six o'clock early and couldn't come. It was strange without him for he always managed. He got the tea and the fizzy drinks and the sandwiches and he knew which station was which and where and why and how, but Mother didn't. Mother was often too late for the fizzy drinks and she coughed before she spoke to the children and then in a whisper in case the people in the carriage should hear and think things, and she said I'm sure I don't know kiddies when they asked about the station, but she was big and warm and knew about cats and the little ring-eyes, and Father was hard and bony and his face prickled when he kissed you.

O look the beach coming it must be coming.

The train stopped with a jerk and a cloud of smoke as if it had died and finished and would never go anywhere else just stay by the sea though you couldn't see the water from here, and the carriages would be empty and slowly rusting as if the people in them had come to an end and could never go back as if they had found what they were looking for after years and years of travelling on and on. But they were disturbed and peeved at being forced to move. The taste of smoke lingered in their mouths, they had to reach up for hat and coat and case, and comb their hair and make up their face again, certainly they had arrived but you have to be neat arriving with your shoes brushed and your hair in place and the shine off your nose. Fay and Totty watched the little cases being snipped open and shut and the two little girls knew for sure that never would they grow up and be people in bulgy dresses, people knitting purl and plain with the ball of wool hanging safe and clean from a neat brown bag with hollyhocks and poppies on it. Hollyhocks and poppies and a big red initial, to show that you were you and not the somebody else you feared you might be, but Fay and Totty didn't worry they were going to the Beach.

The Beach. Why wasn't everyone going to the Beach? It seemed they were the only ones for when they set off down the fir-bordered road that led to the sound the sea kept making forever now in their ears, there was no one else going. Where had the others gone? Why weren't there other people?

'Why Mum?'

'It's a week-day chicken,' said Mum smiling and fat now the rushing was over. 'The others have gone to work I suppose. I don't know. But here we are. Tired?' She looked at them both in the way they loved, the way she looked at them at night at other people's places when they were weary of cousins and hide the thimble and wanted to go home to bed. Tired? she would say. And Fay and Totty would yawn as if nothing in the world would keep them awake and Mother would say knowingly and fondly: The dustman's coming to someone. But no they weren't tired now for it was day and the sun though a watery sad sun was up and the birds, the day was for waking in and the night was for sleeping in.

They raced on ahead of Mother eager to turn the desolate crying sound of sea to the more comforting and near sight of long green and white waves coming and going forever on the sand. They had never been here before, not to this sea. They had been to other seas, near merry-go-rounds and swings and slides, among people, other girls and boys and mothers, mine are so fond of the water the mothers would say, talking about mine and yours and he, that meant father, or the old man if they did not much care but Mother cared always.

The road was stony and the little girls carrying the basket had skiffed toes by the time they came to the end, but it was all fun and yet strange for they were by themselves no other families and Fay thought for a moment what if there is no sea either and no nothing?

But the sea roared in their ears it was true sea, look it was breaking white on the sand and the seagulls crying and skimming and the bits of white flying and look at all of the coloured shells, look a little pink one like a fan, and a cat's eye. Gypsy. And look at the seaweed look I've found a round piece that plops, you tread on it and it plops, you plop this one, see it plops, and the little girls running up and down

plopping and plopping and picking and prying and touching
and listening, and Mother plopping the seaweed too, look
Mum's doing it and Mum's got a crab.

But it cannot go on for ever.

'Where is the place to put our things and the merry-go-
rounds and the place to undress and that, and the place to get
ice-creams?'

There's no place, only a little shed with forms that have
bird-dirt on them and old pieces of newspapers stuffed in the
corner and writing on the walls, rude writing.

'Mum, have we come to the wrong sea?'

Mother looked bewildered. 'I don't know kiddies, I'm
sure.'

'Is it the wrong sea?' Totty took up the cry.

It was the wrong sea. 'Yes kiddies,' Mother said, 'now
that's strange I'm sure I remembered what your Father told
me but I couldn't have but I'm sure I remembered. Isn't it
funny. I didn't know it would be like this. Oh things are
never like you think they're different and sad. I don't know.'

'Look, I've found the biggest plop of all,' cried Fay who
had wandered away intent on plopping. 'The biggest plop of
all,' she repeated, justifying things. 'Come on.'

So it was all right really it was a good sea, you could pick
up the foam before it turned yellow and take off your shoes
and sink your feet down in the wet sand almost until you
might disappear and come up in Spain, that was where you
came up if you sank. And there was the little shed to eat in
and behind the rushes to undress but you couldn't go in
swimming.

'Not in this sea,' Mother said firmly.

They felt proud. It was a distinguished sea oh and a lovely
one noisy in your ears and green and blue and brown where
the seaweed floated. Whales? Sharks? Seals? It was the right
kind of sea.

All day on the sand, racing and jumping and turning head
over heels and finding shells galore and making castles and

getting buried and unburied, going dead and coming alive like
the people in the Bible. And eating in the little shed for the
sky had clouded over and a cold wind had come shaking the
heads of the fir-trees as if to say I'll teach you, springing them
backwards and forwards in a devilish exercise.

Tomatoes, and a fire blowing in your face. The smoke
burst out and you wished. Aladdin and the genie. What did
you wish?

I wish today is always but Father too jumping us up and
down on his knee. This is the maiden all forlorn that milked
the cow.

'Totty, it's my turn, isn't it Dad?'

'It's both of your turns. Come on, sacks on the mill and
more on still.' Not Father away at work but Father here
making the fire and breaking sticks, quickly and surely, and
Father showing this and that and telling why. Why? Did
anyone in the world ever know why? Or did they just
pretend to know because they didn't like anyone else to know
that they didn't know? Why?

They were going home when they saw the swans. 'We'll go
this quicker way,' said Mother, who had been exploring.
'We'll walk across the lagoon over this strip of land and soon
we'll be at the station and then home to bed.' She smiled and
put her arms round them both. Everything was warm and
secure and near, and the darker the world outside got the
safer you felt for there were Mother and Father always, for
ever.

They began to walk across the lagoon. It was growing dark
now quickly and dark sneaks in. Oh home in the train with
the guard lighting the lamps and the shiny slippery seat
growing hard and your eyes scarcely able to keep open, the
sea in your ears, and your little bagful of shells dropped
somewhere down the back of the seat, crushed and sandy and
wet, and your baby crab dead and salty and stiff fallen on the
floor.

'We'll soon be home,' Mother said, and was silent.

It was dark black water, secret, and the air was filled with murmurings and rustlings, it was as if they were walking into another world that had been kept secret from everyone and now they had found it. The darkness lay massed across the water and over to the east, thick as if you could touch it, soon it would swell and fill the earth.

The children didn't speak now, they were tired with the dustman really coming, and Mother was sad and quiet, the wrong sea troubled her, what had she done, she had been sure she would find things different, as she had said they would be, merry-go-rounds and swings and slides for the kiddies, and other mothers to show the kiddies off too, they were quite bright for their age, what had she done?

They looked across the lagoon then and saw the swans, black and shining, as if the visiting dark tiring of its form, had changed to birds, hundreds of them resting and moving softly about on the water. Why, the lagoon was filled with swans, like secret sad ships, secret and quiet. Hush-sh the water said; rush-hush, the wind passed over the top of the water; no other sound but the shaking of rushes and far away now it seemed the roar of the sea like a secret sea that had crept inside your head for ever. And the swans, they were there too, inside you, peaceful and quiet watching and sleeping and watching, there was nothing but peace and warmth and calm, everything found, train and sea and Mother and Father and earwig and slater and spider.

And Gypsy?

But when they got home Gypsy was dead.

Up North

When they woke up in the train, their bed was black with soot and there was soot in his Mum's blondie hair. They were miles north of Montreal, which had, already, sunk beneath his remembrance. 'Do'you know what I sor in the night?' said Dennis. He had to keep his back turned while she dressed. They were both in the same berth, to save money. He was small, and didn't take up much room, but when he woke up in that sooty autumn dawn, he found he was squashed flat against the side of the train. His Mum was afraid of falling out and into the aisle; they had a lower berth, but she didn't trust the strength of the curtain. Now she was dressing, and sobbing; really sobbing. For this was worse than anything she had ever been through, she told him. She had been right through the worst of the air raids, yet this was the worst, this waking in the cold, this dark, dirty dawn, everything dirty she touched, her clothes – oh, her clothes! – and now having to dress as she lay flat on her back. She daren't sit up. She might knock her head.

'You know what I sor?' said the child patiently. 'Well, the train must of stopped, see, and some little men with bundles on their backs got on. Other men was holding lanterns. They were all little. They were all talking French.'

'Shut up,' said Mum. 'Do you hear me?'

'Sor them,' said the boy.

'You and your bloody elves.'

'They was people.'

'Little men with bundles,' said Mum, trying to dress again.

'You start your fairy tales with your Dad and I don't know what *he'll* give you.'

It was this mythical, towering, half-remembered figure they were now travelling to join up north.

Roy McLaughlin, travelling on the same train, saw the pair, presently, out of his small red-lidded eyes. Den and his Mum were dressed and as clean as they could make themselves, and sitting at the end of the car. McLaughlin was the last person to get up, and he climbed down from his solitary green-curtained cubicle conspicuous and alone. He had to pad the length of the car in a trench coat and city shoes – he had never owned slippers, bathrobe, or pajamas – past the passengers, who were drawn with fatigue, pale under the lights. They were men, mostly; some soldiers. The Second World War had been finished, in Europe, a year and five months. It was a dirty, rickety train going up to Abitibi. McLaughlin was returning to a construction camp after three weeks in Montreal. He saw the girl, riding with her back to the engine, doing her nails, and his faculties absently registered 'Limey bride' as he went by. The kid, looking out the window, turned and stared. McLaughlin thought 'Pest', but only because children and other men's wives made him nervous and sour when they were brought around camp on a job.

After McLaughlin had dressed and had swallowed a drink in the washroom – for he was sick and trembling after his holiday – he came and sat down opposite the blond girl. He did not bother to explain that he had to sit somewhere while his berth was being dismantled. His arms were covered with coarse red hair; he had rolled up the sleeves of his khaki shirt. He spread his pale, heavy hands on his knees. The child stood between them, fingertips on the sooty window sill, looking out at the breaking day. Once, the train stopped for a long time; the engine was being changed, McLaughlin said. They had been rolling north but were now turning west. At six o'clock, in about an hour, Dennis and his mother would have to get down, and onto another train, and go north once more.

Dennis could not see any station where they were now. There was a swamp with bristling black rushes, red as ink. It was the autumn sunrise; cold, red. It was so strange to him, so singular, that he could not have said an hour later which feature of the scene was in the foreground or to the left or right. Two women wearing army battle jackets over their dresses, with their hair piled up in front, like his mother's, called and giggled to someone they had put on the train. They were fat and dark – grinny. His mother looked at them with detestation, recognizing what they were; for she hated whores. She had always acted on the desire of the moment, without thought of gain, and she had taken the consequences (Dennis) without complaint. Dennis saw that she was hating the women, and so he looked elsewhere. On a wooden fence sat four or five men in open shirts and patched trousers. They had dull, dark hair, and let their mouths sag as though they were too tired or too sleepy to keep them closed. Something about them was displeasing to the child, and he thought that this was an ugly place with ugly people. It was also a dirty place; every time Dennis put his hands on the window sill they came off black.

'Come down any time to see a train go by,' said McLaughlin, meaning those men. 'Get up in the *night* to see a train.'

The train moved. It was still dark enough outside for Dennis to see his face in the window and for the light from the windows to fall in pale squares on the upturned vanishing faces and on the little trees. Dennis heard his mother's new friend say, 'Well, there's different possibilities.' They passed into an unchanging landscape of swamp and bracken and stunted trees. Then the lights inside the train were put out and he saw that the sky was blue and bright. His mother and McLaughlin, seen in the window, had been remote and bodiless; through their transparent profiles he had seen the yellowed trees going by. Now he could not see their faces at all.

'He's been back in Canada since the end of the war. He was wounded. Den hardly knows him,' he heard his mother say. 'I couldn't come. I had to wait my turn. We were over a thousand war brides on that ship. He was with Aluminium when he first came back.' She pronounced the five vowels in the word.

'You'll be all right there,' said McLaughlin. 'It's a big place. Schools. All company.'

'Pardon me?'

'I mean it all belongs to Aluminum. Only if that's where you're going you happen to be on the wrong train.'

'He isn't there now. He hates towns. He seems to move about a great deal. He drives a bulldozer, you see.'

'Owns it?' said McLaughlin.

'Why, I shouldn't *think* so. Drives for another man, I think he said.'

The boy's father fell into the vast pool of casual labour, drifters; there was a social hierarchy in the north, just as in Heaven. McLaughlin was an engineer. He took another look at the boy: black hair, blue eyes. The hair was coarse, straight, rather dull; Indian hair. The mother was a blonde; touched up a bit, but still blonde.

'What name?' said McLaughlin on the upward note of someone who has asked the same question twice.

'Cameron. Donald Cameron.'

That meant nothing, still; McLaughlin had worked in a place on James Bay where the Indians were named MacDonald and Ogilvie and had an unconquered genetic strain of blue eyes.

'D'you know about any ghosts?' said the boy, turning to McLaughlin. McLaughlin's eyes were paler than his own, which were a deep slate blue, like the eyes of a newly born child. McLaughlin saw the way he held his footing on the rocking train, putting out a few fingers to the window sill only for the form of the thing. He looked all at once ridiculous and dishonoured in his cheap English clothes – the little jacket, the Tweedledum cap on his head. He outdistanced his clothes; he was better than they were. But he was rushing on this train into an existence where his clothes would be too good for him.

'D'you know about any ghosts?' said the boy again.

'Oh, sure,' said McLaughlin, and shivered, for he still felt sick, even though he was sharing a bottle with the Limey bride. He said, 'Indians see them,' which was as close as he could come to being crafty. But there was no reaction out of the mother; she was not English for nothing.

'You seen any?'

'*I'm* not an Indian,' McLaughlin started to say; instead he said, 'Well, yes, I saw the ghost, or something like the ghost, of a dog I had.'

They looked at each other, and the boy's mother said, 'Stop that, you two. Stop that this minute.'

'I'll tell you a strange thing about Dennis,' said his mother. 'It's this. There's times he gives me the creeps.'

Dennis was lying on the seat beside her with his head on her lap.

She said, 'If I don't like it I can clear out. I was a waitress. There's always work.'

'Or find another man,' McLaughlin said. 'Only it won't be me, girlie. I'll be far away.'

'Den says that when the train stopped he saw a lot of elves,' she said, complaining.

'Not elves – men,' said Dennis. 'Some of them had mattresses rolled up on their backs. They were little and bent over. They were talking French. They were going up north.'

McLaughlin coughed and said, 'He means settlers. They were sent up on this same train during the depression. But that's nine, ten years ago. It was supposed to clear the unemployed out of the towns, get them off relief. But there wasn't anything up here then. The winters were terrible. A lot of them died.'

'He couldn't know that,' said Mum edgily. 'For that matter, how can he tell what is French? He's never heard any.'

'No, he couldn't know. It was around ten years ago, when times were bad.'

'Are they good now?'

'Jeez, after a *war*?' He shoved his hand in the pocket of his shirt, where he kept a roll, and he let her see the edge of it.

She made no comment, but put her hand on Den's head and said to him, 'You didn't see anyone. Now shut up.'

'Sor 'em,' the boy said in a voice as low as he could descend without falling into a whisper.

'You'll see what your Dad'll give you when you tell lies.' But she was halfhearted about the threat and did not quite believe in it. She had been attracted to the scenery, whose persistent sameness she could no longer ignore. 'It's not proper country,' she said. 'It's bare.'

'Not enough for me,' said McLaughlin. 'Too many people. I keep on moving north.'

'I want to see some Indians,' said Dennis, sitting up.

'There aren't any,' his mother said. 'Only in films.'

'I don't like Canada.' He held her arm. 'Let's go home now.'

'It's the train whistle. It's so sad. It gets him down.'

The train slowed, jerked, flung them against each other, and came to a stop. It was quite day now; their faces were plain and clear, as if drawn without shading on white paper. McLaughlin felt responsible for them, even compassionate; the change in him made the boy afraid.

'We're getting down, Den,' said his Mum, with great, wide eyes. 'We take another train. See? It'll be grand. Do you hear what Mum's telling you?'

He was determined not to leave the train, and clung to the window sill, which was too smooth and narrow to provide a grip; McLaughlin had no difficulty getting him away. 'I'll give you a present,' he said hurriedly. But he slapped all his pockets and found nothing to give. He did not think of the money, and his watch had been stolen in Montreal. The woman and the boy struggled out with their baggage, and

McLaughlin, who had descended first so as to help them down, reached up and swung the boy in his arms.

'The Indians!' the boy cried, clinging to the train, to air; to anything. His face was momentarily muffled by McLaughlin's shirt. His cap fell to the ground. He screamed. 'Where's Mum? I never saw *any*thing!'

'You saw Indians,' said McLaughlin. 'On the rail fence, at that long stop. Look, don't worry your mother. Don't keep telling her what you haven't seen. You'll be seeing plenty of everything now.'

Frostbite

Christ it was cold.

And only one glove as usual. The bare hand in the pocket, sweaty against the change counted out for the fare; the other inside the remaining glove, cramped stiff round the handle of the fiddle case. Freezing. Her feet were solid too; just a oneness of dead cold inside her boots in place of anything five-toed or familiar. She stamped them hard for spite, waiting and watching for the fingers of light smudging through the dark, the bus feeling its way up the other side of the hill. The last two had been full and driven straight on. No point getting angry. That was just the way of it.

Nothing yet.

Cloud came out of her mouth and she looked up. There on the other side of the road was the spire. Frame of royal blue, frazzled through with sodium orange, and the spire in the middle, lit from beneath by a dozen calendar windows: people working late. There was a hollow triangle of light above the tip; a clear opening in the sky where she could see the snow flurry and settle on the stone like white ivy. The University.

This was the best of the place now – the look of it. Still able to catch her out. As for the rest, it had not been what she had hoped. Her own fault, of course, expecting too much as usual. They said as much beforehand, over and over: it's no a job though, music willny keep you, it's no for the likes of you – cursing the teacher who had put the daft idea into her head in the first place. Still, she went, and she found they were right and they were not right. It wasn't her *likes* that bothered them, not that at all. Something much simpler. It was her excitement; all that gauche intensity about the thing. Total strangers wondered loudly who she was trying to impress. There was more than the music to learn: a whole series of bitter little lessons she never expected. It was hard. She learned to keep her ideas in check and her mouth shut, to carry her stifled love without whining much. But on nights like this, after compulsory practice that was all promise and no joy, cold and tired and waiting for a hypothetical bus, it was heavy and hard to bear. Even with her face to the sentimental spire, she wondered who it was she was trying to fool.

Low-geared growling turned her to the hill again. This time the effort paid off. Not one but two — jesus wasn't it always the way — sets of headlamps were dipping over the brow, coming on through the fuzzy evening smirr. She bounced the coins in her ungloved hand and watched as they nosed cautiously down through the slush. Then there was something else. A shape. A man lumping up and over the top of the hill, flapping after the buses. One was away already, had overtaken and gone ahead to let the other make the pick-up. She stood while it braked and sat shivering at the stop, one foot on the platform to keep the driver and let the wee man catch up. The windows were yellow behind the steam. She looked to see if he was nearer and he stumbled, slittered to the gutter, fell. The driver revved the engine. The man lay on, not moving in the gutter like an old newspaper. The driver drew her a look. She shrugged, embarrassed. The bus began sliding out from under her foot. Too late already. There was nothing else for it. She settled the case in a drift at the side of the pole and turned and made a start, picking carefully up the hill towards the ragged shape still lying near the gutter. An arm flicked out. She came nearer as he struggled onto his hands and knees, trying to stand. Then he crashed down again on the thin projections of his backside and groaned, knees angled up, fingers clutching at his brow in a pantomime of despair. By the time she reached him he was bawling like a wean. She could see blood congealed, red jam squeezing between the fingers. The line of his jaw was grey.

OK?

The man said nothing. Just kept sobbing away. He was a fair age too.

OK eh? What happened to you grandad?

She had never called anybody grandad in her life. And that voice. Like a primary teacher or something. She started to blush. Maybe she should get him onto his feet instead. Touch would calm him down and he might stop greeting to concentrate. She looked about first to check if there was another witness, hoping for a man. A man who would be shamed by her struggling on her own and come and do the thing for her, leave her clucking on the sidelines while he took over. But there was no one and she knew she had called the thing upon herself anyway. Fools rushed in right enough.

An acrid smell of drink, wool and clogged skin rose as she bent towards him, and she saw the knuckles scraped raw, the silted nails. Closing her eyes, she linked his arm and started pulling, hoping for the best. They must look ridiculous.

C'mon then, lets get you up. Need to get up. Catch your death sitting in the wet like this. Come on, up.

He acquiesced, child-like, letting himself be hauled inelegantly straight before he finished the rest for himself. He backed onto a low wall and waited while he caught his breath. O thanks hen, between wheezes, words vapourising in the cold. Am that ashamed, all no be a minute but am that ashamed. All be fine in a minute. Am OK hen.

★

He didn't look OK. He looked lilac and the sodium glare didn't do him any favours. He puffed on about being fine and ashamed while she foraged in her pocket for a paper hanky to pat at the bloody jelly on his temple, the sticky threads stringing across to his nose. She thought better of it and gave it to him instead – something to do, shut him up for a minute, maybe. But neither the idea nor the mopping up worked too well. His hand stopped at his brow only as long as she held it there. When he saw what it produced the whine started again. O my god hen, o hen see o look at that, as he dabbed and looked, dabbed and looked.

You're fine, fine. Just a wee bit surprised, thats all. Take your time and just relax OK? Relax. Where is it you're going anyway?

He kept patting and looked at her. Very pale eyes, coated like a crocodiles, the sockets over-big.

O he'll be that angry hen. He will and am that ashamed. Am a stupit old fool a am. Nothing but a stupit old man. The pale eyes threatened to leak. Who? Who'll be angry? The trick was to keep him talking and standing up. Every time he stumbled, he repeated what he'd just said. Between repetitions, she found he had been due at his son's house, due at a particular time and he was late. They were supposed to be going somewhere. It sounded like a pub. They were to set off from the son's house and he was chasing the bus because he was already late did she see? She tried to.

Och he'll not be mad. Just tell him you were running for the bus and you fell. How will that get him angry? You'll be fine.

He wasn't content yet. The specs but. A broke the specs hen. ∙

There was a lull. She looked about the tarmac and the pavement. There weren't any specs. Then his hand was into his pocket, fumbling out three pieces of plastic and glass: See? She broke ma specs.

She. He said *she*; *she* broke the specs. Right enough, that couldn't have happened just now. There had to be more to it, and she knew already she didn't want to hear it. All she had wanted was to make sure he was all right, get him on his feet and back on his way. But this was what she was getting and it was difficult to get out of now. It was her that had started it, her choice to come up that hill. This was part of it now.

Who broke your specs?

She knew it had to happen and it did. He started to cry. He howled for a good minute or so while she cursed silently and patted clumsily at his sleeve, shooshing. He caught enough breath to hiccup out some more: It's ma own fault hen. It was a bad woman, a bad woman. She hit me hen, o she killed me. She had to smile. The exaggeration wasn't just daft, it was reassuring too. He couldn't see her anyway.

Still, even as she told him he was fine, fine, she knew there was more coming she wasn't going to like. The story. A man's story about what he would call a *bad woman*, and he would tell it as though she wasn't a woman herself, as if she shared his terms. As though his were the only terms. And she wouldn't be expected to argue – just stand and listen. The smiling didn't last long. He told her about a pub, having a drink, then a bad woman, something about a bad woman but he hadn't known it at the time, and as they were leaving the pub together, going out the door, she hit him. Knocked him down in the street, hard, so it broke his specs. When he reached that part he gazed down at the bits he held in his hand, taking in the fact with a deep sigh that exhaled as cursing and swearing. He whooered and bitched till he was unsteady on his legs again then started whining. He was a stupit old fool and a silly old man, should never have had

anything to do with the bad woman. Bad bad bitchahell.
Then there were more tears.

She hadn't reacted once. And maybe it was worth it. He
seemed steadier ready to make off again for the stop. She let
him walk, moving slowly alongside to keep him straight while
he muttered and sobbed about himself. She knew better than
to ask but she wondered, step by step, steering him downhill.
She wanted to know about the woman. What had he said to
make her do that? Was that when he had been cut – where
the blood had come from? It must have happened right
enough: he would hardly make a thing like that up. But it
was hard to imagine this sorry, snivelling wee man provoking
it, being pushy or lewd-mouthed. It was in another place
though, with another woman altogether. He could have been
different. And he must have done something. Unless of course
there really were such bad women that went about hitting
old men for nothing. What the hell was a *bad woman* anyhow –
was it a prostitute he meant? The corner of her eye caught his
face, the mottled purple skin under grey veins and a big dreep
at the end of his nose. The very idea turned her stomach. Yet
she couldn't stop her chest being sore for the stranger: he
seemed so beaten, so genuinely surprised by what had hit him
not just once but twice that day. He was still muttering
when they reached the stop: broke ma specs, cow. She felt her
jaw sore with remembering to be quiet. Shhh.

Shh, forget about her eh? She's away now, forget about it.
Let's just get you to your boy's place. Get you on the bus.
    What else could she do?
    Canny be up to them hen. She realized this was a confi-
dence. Advice. Canny be up to them. A bad lot.
    Aye, a lot of it about. What bus is it you get?
    Aye, don't you worry. Get the bus. All be fine in a minute,
get the bus.

There was no point in keeping asking, best just to wait with him. The right bus would come and he would recognize it instinctively. Fair enough. Holding some of the weight, she kept her arm under his: the wet frosting on his sleeve burned the fingers of her gloveless hand. He was looking down at something, staring as though to work out what it was.

Violin hen. Eh — Violin? Nice, a violin. A like that stuff, classical music and that.

She shook her head thinking about it. Victorian melodrama as they chittered in the twilight under the university spire — Hearts and Flowers. But she said nothing. Knew enough by this time not to respond to remarks, even harmless ones, about being *on the fiddle* or *doing requests*, or any of the other fatuous to obscene things some men assumed a lassie carrying a violin case was asking for. Anyway, the bus was coming now: she could hear it. Good timing. She turned for the pleasure of watching it approach: twin haloes of deliverance.

This one do you? A 59?

She couldn't hear his answer for the searing of brakes. He seemed ready enough to get on, though; his hands stretching out full, paddling towards the pole to prepare for the assault on the platform. She shunted the case to one side with her foot and moved with him. The conductress hauled while she pushed till he was inside, clutching the pole. Then he swivelled suddenly to face her.

Cheerio hen and A have ti thank you very much, very much indeed. Yiv been kind ti me yi have that. He was leaning out dangerously and shaking her hand uncomfortably tightly in both of his, the pole propping his chest. She nodded in what she hoped was a reassuring way, weary. She hadn't the heart left to explain she had meant to get on too, this was her bus as well. She just kept patting and shaking at his hand; giving up to it. He felt daft enough already and it would take forever to pantomine through. She wasn't in any hurry, could easily wait for the next one.

Parting shot then. What's the name? What do they call you eh?

The conductress and driver looked but the engine continued to purr neutrally. Her smile was as much for them: indulge it a wee bit longer?

Me? He was pleased. Pat, am Pat Gallagher hen. Pat.

Cheerio then Pat. See and look after yourself a wee bit better in future eh?

His face changed then, remembering. He hesitated for a second, baring his teeth, then he spat, suddenly vicious.

Aye. Keep away from bastart women, thats what yi do. Filth. Dirty whooers and filth the lot a them, the whole bloody lot. Get away fi me bitchahell – and he lunged a fist. It wasn't well-aimed and she had enough of a glimpse to see it come. It didn't connect: just made her totter back a few steps; enough for the driver to seize this as his moment and drive off, chasing an already sliding schedule.

She stood on the pavement and watched till it went round the corner, then stood on watching the space where it had been. After a moment, she shut her mouth again and pulled up her coat collar. Warm enough now: just as well there was no one about, though she looked round to check and shrugged to be casual just in case. The spire was still there across the road; still beautiful, still peaceful. Snow feathered about and nothing moved behind the gates. No difference. Thankful, she leaned back against the stop: it would be a while yet. Then she remembered the case and stooped to lift it out of the snow, leaving a free-standing drift where it had been. Didn't want it to get too cold, go out of tune. Not as though it was her own. Then, unexpectedly, she felt angry; violently, bitterly angry. The money in her pocket cut into her hand. Who did he think he was, lashing out at people like that? And what sort of bloody fool was she, letting him? What right had he? What right had any of them? She'd show him. She'd show the whole bloody lot of them. Shaking, she snatched up the fiddle case and glared at the hill. To hell with this waiting. There were other ways, other things to do. Take the underground; walk, dammit. Walk.

She crossed the road, defying the slush underfoot, making a start up the other side of the hill.

ELLEN GILCHRIST

Revenge

It was the summer of the Broad Jump Pit.

The Broad Jump Pit, how shall I describe it! It was a bright orange rectangle in the middle of a green pasture. It was three feet deep, filled with river sand and sawdust. A real cinder track led up to it, ending where tall poles for pole-vaulting rose forever in the still Delta air.

I am looking through the old binoculars. I am watching Bunky coming at a run down the cinder path, pausing expertly at the jump-off line, then rising into the air, heels stretched far out in front of him, landing in the sawdust. Before the dust has settled Saint John comes running with the tape, calling out measurements in his high, excitable voice.

Next comes my thirteen-year-old brother, Dudley, coming at a brisk jog down the track, the pole-vaulting pole held lightly in his delicate hands, then vaulting, high into the sky. His skinny tanned legs make a last, desperate surge, and he is clear and over.

Think how it looked from my lonely exile atop the chicken house. I was ten years old, the only girl in a house full of cousins. There were six of us, shipped to the Delta for the summer, dumped on my grandmother right in the middle of a world war.

They built this wonder in answer to a V-Mail letter from my father in Europe. The war was going well, my father wrote, within a year the Allies would triumph over the forces of evil, the world would be at peace, and the Olympic torch would again be brought down from its mountain and carried to Zurich or Amsterdam or London or Mexico City, wherever free men lived and worshipped sports. My father had been a participant in an Olympic event when he was young.

Therefore, the letter continued, Dudley and Bunky and Philip and Saint John and Oliver were to begin training. The United States would need athletes now, not soldiers.

They were to train for broad jumping and pole-vaulting and discus throwing, for fifty-, one-hundred-, and four-hundred-yard dashes, for high and low hurdles. The letter included instructions for building the pit, for making pole vaulting poles out of cane, and for converting ordinary saw-horses into hurdles. It ended with a page of tips for proper eating and admonished Dudley to take good care of me as I was my father's own dear sweet little girl.

The letter came one afternoon. Early the next morning they began construction. Around noon I wandered out to the pasture to see how they were coming along. I picked up a shovel.

'Put that down, Rhoda,' Dudley said. 'Don't bother us now. We're working.'

'I know it,' I said. 'I'm going to help.'

'No, you're not,' Bunky said. 'This is the Broad Jump Pit. We're starting our training.'

'I'm going to do it too,' I said. 'I'm going to be in training.'

'Get out of here now,' Dudley said. 'This is only for boys, Rhoda. This isn't a game.'

'I'm going to dig it if I want to,' I said, picking up a shovelful of dirt and throwing it on Philip. On second thought I picked up another shovelful and threw it on Bunky.

'Get out of here, Ratface,' Philip yelled at me. 'You German spy.' He was referring to the initials on my Girl Scout uniform.

'You goddamn niggers,' I yelled. 'You niggers. I'm digging this if I want to and you can't stop me, you nasty niggers, you Japs, you Jews.' I was throwing dirt on everyone now.

Dudley grabbed the shovel and wrestled me to the ground. He held my arms down in the coarse grass and peered into my face.

'Rhoda, you're not having anything to do with this Broad Jump Pit. And if you set foot inside this pasture or come around here and touch anything we will break your legs and drown you in the bayou with a crowbar around your neck.' He was twisting my leg until it creaked at the joints. 'Do you get it, Rhoda? Do you understand me?'

'Let me up, ' I was screaming, my rage threatening to split open my skull. 'Let me up, you goddamn nigger, you Jap, you spy. I'm telling Grannie and you're going to get the worst whipping of your life. And you better quit digging this hole for the horses to fall in. Let me up, let me up. Let me go.'

'You've been ruining everything we've thought up all summer,' Dudley said, 'and you're not setting foot inside this pasture.'

In the end they dragged me back to the house, and I ran screaming into the kitchen where Grannie and Calvin, the black man who did the cooking, tried to comfort me, feeding me pound cake and offering to let me help with the mayonnaise.

'You be a sweet girl, Rhoda,' my grandmother said, 'and this afternoon we'll go over to Eisenglas Plantation to play with Miss Ann Wentzel.'

'I don't want to play with Miss Ann Wentzel,' I screamed. 'I hate Miss Ann Wentzel. She's fat and she calls me a Yankee. She said my socks were ugly.'

'Why, Rhoda,' my grandmother said. 'I'm surprised at you. Miss Ann Wentzel is your own sweet friend. Her momma was your momma's roommate at All Saint's. How can you talk like that?'

'She's a nigger,' I screamed. 'She's a goddamned nigger German spy.'

'Now it's coming. Here comes the temper,' Calvin said, rolling his eyes back in their sockets to make me madder. I threw my second fit of the morning, beating my fists into a door frame. My grandmother seized me in soft arms. She led me to a bedroom where I sobbed myself to sleep in a sea of down pillows.

The construction went on for several weeks. As soon as they finished breakfast every morning they started out for the pasture. Wood had to be burned to make cinders, sawdust brought from the sawmill, sand hauled up from the riverbank by wheelbarrow.

When the pit was finished the savage training began. From my several vantage points I watched them. Up and down, up and down they ran, dove, flew, sprinted. Drenched with sweat they wrestled each other to the ground in bitter feuds over distances and times and fractions of inches.

Dudley was their self-appointed leader. He drove them like a demon. They began each morning by running around the edge of the pasture several times, then practising their hurdles and dashes, then on to discus throwing and calisthenics. Then on to the Broad Jump Pit with its endless challenges.

They even pressed the old mare into service. Saint John was from New Orleans and knew the British ambassador and was thinking of being a polo player. Up and down the pasture he drove the poor old creature, leaning far out of the saddle, swatting a basketball with my grandaddy's cane.

I spied on them from the swing that went out over the bayou, and from the roof of the chicken house, and sometimes from the pasture fence itself, calling out insults or attempts to make them jealous.

'Guess what,' I would yell, 'I'm going to town to the Chinaman's store.' 'Guess what, I'm getting to go to the beauty parlour.' 'Doctor Biggs says you're adopted.'

They ignored me. At meals they sat together at one end of the table, making jokes about my temper and my red hair, opening their mouths so I could see their half-chewed food, burping loudly in my direction.

At night they pulled their cots together on the sleeping porch, plotting against me while I slept beneath my grandmother's window, listening to the soft assurance of her snoring.

I began to pray the Japs would win the war, would come marching into Issaquena County and take them prisoners, starving and torturing them, sticking bamboo splinters under their fingernails. I saw myself in the Japanese colonel's office, turning them in, writing their names down, myself being treated like an honoured guest, drinking tea from tiny blue cups like the ones the Chinaman had in his store.

They would be outside, tied up with wire. There would be Dudley, begging for mercy. What good to him now his loyal gang, his photographic memory, his trick magnet dogs, his perfect pitch, his camp shorts, his Baby Brownie camera.

I prayed they would get polio, would be consigned forever to iron lungs. I put myself to sleep at night imagining their laboured breathing, their five little wheelchairs lined up by the stores as I drove by in my father's Packard, my arm around the jacket of his blue uniform, on my way to Hollywood for my screen test.

Meanwhile, I practised dancing. My grandmother had a black housekeeper named Baby Doll who was a wonderful dancer. In the mornings I followed her around while she dusted, begging for dancing lessons. She was a big woman, as tall as a man, and gave off a dark rich smell, an unforgettable incense, a combination of Evening in Paris and the sweet perfume of the cabins.

Baby Doll wore bright skirts and on her blouses a pin that said REMEMBER, then a real pearl, then HARBOR. She was engaged to a sailor and was going to California to be rich as soon as the war was over.

I would put a stack of heavy, scratched records on the record player, and Baby Doll and I would dance through the parlours to the music of Glenn Miller or Guy Lombardo or Tommy Dorsey.

Sometimes I stood on a stool in front of the fireplace and made up lyrics while Baby Doll acted them out, moving lightly across the old dark rugs, turning and swooping and shaking and gliding.

Outside the summer sun beat down on the Delta, beating down a million volts a minute, feeding the soybeans and cotton and clover, sucking Steele's Bayou up into the clouds, beating down on the road and the store, on the pecans and elms and magnolias, on the men at work in the fields, on the athletes at work in the pasture.

Inside Baby Doll and I would be dancing. Or Guy Lombardo would be playing 'Begin the Beguine' and I would be belting out lyrics.

> 'Oh, let them begin . . . we don't care,
> America all . . . ways does its share,
> We'll be there with plenty of ammo,
> Allies . . . don't ever despair . . .'

Baby Doll thought I was a genius. If I was having an especially creative morning she would go running out to the kitchen and bring anyone she could find to hear me.

'Oh, let them begin any warrr . . .' I would be singing, tapping one foot against the fireplace tiles, waving my arms around like a conductor.

> 'Uncle Sam will fight
> for the underrr . . . doggg.
> Never fear, Allies, never fear.'

A new record would drop. Baby Doll would swoop me into her fragrant arms, and we would break into an improvisation on Tommy Dorsey's 'Boogie-Woogie.'

But the Broad Jump Pit would not go away. It loomed in my dreams. If I walked to the store I had to pass the pasture. If I stood on the porch or looked out my grandmother's window, there it was, shimmering in the sunlight, constantly guarded by one of the Olympians.

Things went from bad to worse between me and Dudley. If we so much as passed each other in the hall a fight began. He would hold up his fists and dance around, trying to look like a fighter. When I came flailing at him he would reach underneath my arms and punch me in the stomach.

I considered poisoning him. There was a box of white powder in the toolshed with a skull and crossbones above the label. Several times I took it down and held it in my hands, shuddering at the power it gave me. Only the thought of the electric chair kept me from using it.

Every day Dudley gathered his troops and headed out for the pasture. Every day my hatred grew and festered. Then, just about the time I could stand it no longer, a diversion occurred.

One afternoon about four o'clock an official-looking sedan clattered across the bridge and came roaring down the road to the house.

It was my cousin, Lauralee Manning, wearing her WAVE uniform and smoking Camels in an ivory holder. Lauralee had been widowed at the beginning of the war when her young husband crashed his Navy training plane into the Pacific.

Lauralee dried her tears, joined the WAVES, and went off to avenge his death. I had not seen this paragon since I was a small child, but I had memorized the photograph Miss Onnie Maud, who was Lauralee's mother, kept on her dresser. It was a photograph of Lauralee leaning against the rail of a destroyer.

Not that Lauralee ever went to sea on a destroyer. She was spending the war in Pensacola, Florida, being secretary to an admiral.

Now, out of a clear blue sky, here was Lauralee, home on leave with a two-carat diamond ring and the news that she was getting married.

'You might have called and given some warning,' Miss Onnie Maud said, turning Lauralee into a mass of wrinkles with her embraces. 'You could have softened the blow with a letter.'

'Who's the groom,' my grandmother said. 'I only hope he's not a pilot.'

'Is he an admiral?' I said, 'or a colonel or a major or a commander?'

'My fiancé's not in uniform, Honey,' Lauralee said. 'He's in real estate. He runs the war-bond effort for the whole state of Florida. Last year he collected half a million dollars.'

'In real estate!' Miss Onnie Maud said, gasping. 'What religion is he?'

'He's Unitarian,' she said. 'His name is Donald Marcus. He's best friends with Admiral Semmes, that's how I met him. And he's coming a week from Saturday, and that's all the time we have to get ready for the wedding.'

'Unitarian!' Miss Onnie Maud said. 'I don't think I've ever met a Unitarian.'

'Why isn't he in uniform?' I insisted.

'He has flat feet,' Lauralee said gaily. 'But you'll love him when you see him.'

Later that afternoon Lauralee took me off by myself for a ride in the sedan.

'Your mother is my favourite cousin,' she said, touching my face with gentle fingers. 'You'll look just like her when you grow up and get your figure.'

I moved closer, admiring the brass buttons on her starched uniform and the brisk way she shifted and braked and put in the clutch and accelerated.

We drove down the river road and out to the bootlegger's shack where Lauralee bought a pint of Jack Daniel's and two Cokes. She poured out half of her Coke, filled it with whiskey, and we roared off down the road with the radio playing.

We drove along in the lengthening day. Lauralee was chain-smoking, lighting one Camel after another, tossing the butts out the window, taking sips from her bourbon and Coke. I sat beside her, pretending to smoke a piece of rolled-up paper, making little noises into the mouth of my Coke bottle.

We drove up to a picnic spot on the levee and sat under a tree to look out at the river.

'I miss this old river,' she said. 'When I'm sad I dream about it licking the tops of the levees.'

I didn't know what to say to that. To tell the truth I was afraid to say much of anything to Lauralee. She seemed so splendid. It was enough to be allowed to sit by her on the levee.

'Now, Rhoda,' she said, 'your mother was matron of honour in my wedding to Buddy, and I want you, her own little daughter, to be maid of honour in my second wedding.'

I could hardly believe my ears! While I was trying to think of something to say to this wonderful news I saw that Lauralee was crying, great tears were forming in her blue eyes.

'Under this very tree is where Buddy and I got engaged,' she said. Now the tears were really starting to roll, falling all over the front of her uniform. 'He gave me my ring right where we're sitting.'

'The maid of honour?' I said, patting her on the shoulder, trying to be of some comfort. 'You really mean the maid of honour?'

'Now he's gone from the world,' she continued, 'and I'm marrying a wonderful man, but that doesn't make it any easier. Oh, Rhoda, they never even found his body, never even found his body.'

I was patting her on the head now, afraid she would forget her offer in the midst of her sorrow.

'You mean I get to be the real maid of honour?'

'Oh, yes, Rhoda, Honey,' she said. 'The maid of honour, my only attendant.' She blew her nose on a lace-trimmed handkerchief and sat up straighter, taking a drink from the Coke bottle.

'Not only that, but I have decided to let you pick out your own dress. We'll go to Greenville and you can try on every dress at Nell's and Blum's and you can have the one you like the most.'

I threw my arms around her, burning with happiness, smelling her whiskey and Camels and the dark Tabu perfume that was her signature. Over her shoulder and through the low branches of the trees the afternoon sun was going down in an orgy of reds and blues and purples and violets, falling from sight, going all the way to China.

Let them keep their nasty Broad Jump Pit I thought. Wait till they hear about this. Wait till they find out I'm maid of honour in a military wedding.

Finding the dress was another matter. Early the next morning Miss Onnie Maud and my grandmother and Lauralee and I set out for Greenville.

As we passed the pasture I hung out the back window making faces at the athletes. This time they only pretended to ignore me. They couldn't ignore this wedding. It was going to be in the parlour instead of the church so they wouldn't even get to be altar boys. They wouldn't get to light a candle.

'I don't know why you care what's going on in that pasture,' my grandmother said. 'Even if they let you play with them all it would do is make you a lot of ugly muscles.'

'Then you'd have big old ugly arms like Weegie Toler,' Miss Onnie Maud said. 'Lauralee, you remember Weegie Toler, that was a swimmer. Her arms got so big no one would take her to a dance, much less marry her.'

'Well, I don't want to get married anyway,' I said. 'I'm never getting married. I'm going to New York City and be a lawyer.'

'Where does she get those ideas?' Miss Onnie Maud said.

'When you get older you'll want to get married,' Lauralee said. 'Look at how much fun you're having being in my wedding.'

'Well, I'm never getting married,' I said. 'And I'm never having any children. I'm going to New York and be a lawyer and save people from the electric chair.'

'It's the movies,' Miss Onnie Maud said. 'They let her watch anything she likes in Indiana.'

We walked into Nell's and Blum's Department Store and took up the largest dressing room. My grandmother and Miss Onnie Maud were seated on brocade chairs and every saleslady in the store came crowding around trying to get in on the wedding.

I refused to even consider the dresses they brought from the 'girls' department.

'I told her she could wear whatever she wanted,' Lauralee said, 'and I'm keeping my promise.'

'Well, she's not wearing green satin or I'm not coming,' my grandmother said, indicating the dress I had found on a rack and was clutching against me.

'At least let her try it on,' Lauralee said. 'Let her see for herself.' She zipped me into the green satin. It came down to my ankles and fit around my midsection like a girdle, making my waist seem smaller than my stomach. I admired myself in the mirror. It was almost perfect. I looked exactly like a nightclub singer.

'This one's fine,' I said. 'This is the one I want.'

'It looks marvellous, Rhoda,' Lauralee said, 'but it's the wrong colour for the wedding. Remember I'm wearing blue.'

'I believe the child's colour-blind,' Miss Onnie Maud said. 'It runs in her father's family.'

'I am not colour-blind,' I said, reaching behind me and unzipping the dress. 'I have twenty-twenty vision.'

'Let her try on some more,' Lauralee said. 'Let her try on everything in the store.'

I proceeded to do just that, with the salesladies getting grumpier and grumpier. I tried on a gold gabardine dress with a rhinestone-studded cumberbund. I tried on a pink ballerina-length formal and a lavender voile tea dress and several silk suits. Somehow nothing looked right.

'Maybe we'll have to make her something,' my grandmother said.

'But there's no time,' Miss Onnie Maud said. 'Besides first we'd have to find out what she wants. Rhoda, please tell us what you're looking for.'

Their faces all turned to mine, waiting for an answer. But I didn't know the answer.

The dress I wanted was a secret. The dress I wanted was dark and tall and thin as a reed. There was a word for what I wanted, a word I had seen in magazines. But what was that word? I could not remember.

'I want something dark,' I said at last. 'Something dark and silky.'

'Wait right there,' the saleslady said. 'Wait just a minute.' Then, from out of a prewar storage closet she brought a black-watch plaid recital dress with spaghetti straps and a white piqué jacket. It was made of taffeta and rustled when I touched it. There was a label sewn into the collar of the jacket. *Little Miss Sophisticate*, it said. *Sophisticate*, that was the word I was seeking.

I put on the dress and stood triumphant in a sea of ladies and dresses and hangers.

'This is the dress,' I said. 'This is the dress I'm wearing.'

'It's perfect,' Lauralee said. 'Start hemming it up. She'll be the prettiest maid of honour in the whole world.'

All the way home I held the box on my lap thinking about how I would look in the dress. Wait till they see me like this, I was thinking. Wait till they see what I really look like.

I fell in love with the groom. The moment I laid eyes on him I forgot he was flat-footed. He arrived bearing gifts of music and perfume and candy, a warm dark-skinned man with eyes the colour of walnuts.

He laughed out loud when he saw me, standing on the porch with my hands on my hips.

'This must be Rhoda,' he exclaimed, 'the famous red-haired maid of honour.' He came running up the steps, gave me a slow, exciting hug, and presented me with a whole album of

Xavier Cugat records. I had never owned a record of my own, much less an album.

Before the evening was over I put on a red formal I found in a trunk and did a South American dance for him to Xavier Cugat's 'Poinciana'. He said he had never seen anything like it in his whole life.

The wedding itself was a disappointment. No one came but the immediate family and there was no aisle to march down and the only music was Onnie Maud playing 'Liebestraum'.

Dudley and Philip and Saint John and Oliver and Bunky were dressed in long pants and white shirts and ties. They had fresh military crew cuts and looked like a nest of new birds, huddled together on the blue velvet sofa, trying to keep their hands to themselves, trying to figure out how to act at a wedding.

The elderly Episcopal priest read out the ceremony in a gravelly smoker's voice, ruining all the good parts by coughing. He was in a bad mood because Lauralee and Mr Marcus hadn't found time to come to him for marriage instruction.

Still, I got to hold the bride's flowers while he gave her the ring and stood so close to her during the ceremony I could hear her breathing.

The reception was better. People came from all over the Delta. There were tables with candles set up around the porches and sprays of greenery in every corner. There were gentlemen sweating in linen suits and the record player playing every minute. In the back hall Calvin had set up a real professional bar with tall, permanently frosted glasses and ice and mint and lemons and every kind of whiskey and liqueur in the world.

I stood in the receiving line getting compliments on my dress, then wandered around the rooms eating cake and letting people hug me. After a while I got bored with that and went out to the back hall and began to fix myself a drink at the bar.

I took one of the frosted glasses and began filling it from
different bottles, tasting as I went along. I used plenty of
crème de menthe and soon had something that tasted heav-
enly. I filled the glass with crushed ice, added three straws,
and went out to sit on the back steps and cool off.

I was feeling wonderful. A full moon was caught like a kite
in the pecan trees across the river. I sipped along on my
drink. Then, without planning it, I did something I had never
dreamed of doing. I left the porch alone at night. Usually I
was in terror of the dark. My grandmother had told me that
alligators come out of the bayou to eat children who wander
alone at night.

I walked out across the yard, the huge moon giving so
much light I almost cast a shadow. When I was nearly to the
water's edge I turned and looked back toward the house. It
shimmered in the moonlight like a jukebox alive in a meadow,
seemed to pulsate with music and laughter and people,
beautiful and foreign, not a part of me.

I looked out at the water, then down the road to the
pasture. The Broad Jump Pit! There it was, perfect and
unguarded. Why had I never thought of doing this before?

I began to run toward the road. I ran as fast as my Mary
Jane pumps would allow me. I pulled my dress up around my
waist and climbed the fence in one motion, dropping lightly
down on the other side. I was sweating heavily, alone with
the moon and my wonderful courage.

I knew exactly what to do first. I picked up the pole and
hoisted it over my head. It felt solid and balanced and alive. I
hoisted it up and down a few times as I had seen Dudley do,
getting the feel of it.

Then I laid it ceremoniously down on the ground, reached
behind me, and unhooked the plaid formal. I left it lying in a
heap on the ground. There I stood, in my cotton underpants,
ready to take up pole-vaulting.

I lifted the pole and carried it back to the end of the cinder
path. I ran slowly down the path, stuck the pole in the

wooden cup, and attempted throwing my body into the air, using it as a lever.

Something was wrong. It was more difficult than it appeared from a distance. I tried again. Nothing happened. I sat down with the pole across my legs to think things over.

Then I remembered something I had watched Dudley doing through the binoculars. He measured down from the end of the pole with his fingers spread wide. That was it, I had to hold it closer to the end.

I tried it again. This time the pole lifted me several feet off the ground. My body sailed across the grass in a neat arc and I landed on my toes. I was a natural!

I do not know how long I was out there, running up and down the cinder path, thrusting my body further and further through space, tossing myself into the pit like a mussel shell thrown across the bayou.

At last I decided I was ready for the real test. I had to vault over a cane barrier. I examined the pegs on the wooden poles and chose one that came up to my shoulder.

I put the barrier pole in place, spit over my left shoulder, and marched back to the end of the path. Suck up your guts, I told myself. It's only a pole. It won't get stuck in your stomach and tear out your insides. It won't kill you.

I stood at the end of the path eyeballing the barrier. Then, above the incessant racket of the crickets, I heard my name being called. Rhoda . . . the voices were calling. Rhoda . . . Rhoda . . . Rhoda . . . Rhoda.

I turned toward the house and saw them coming. Mr Marcus and Dudley and Bunky and Calvin and Lauralee and what looked like half the wedding. They were climbing the fence, calling my name, and coming to get me. Rhoda . . . they called out. Where on earth have you been? What on earth are you doing?

I hoisted the pole up to my shoulders and began to run down the path, running into the light from the moon. I picked up speed, thrust the pole into the cup, and threw myself into the sky, into the still Delta night. I sailed up and was clear and over the barrier.

I let go of the pole and began my fall, which seemed to last a long, long time. It was like falling through clear water. I dropped into the sawdust and lay very still, waiting for them to reach me.

Sometimes I think whatever has happened since has been of no real interest to me.

PENELOPE GILLIATT

The Redhead

When the skulls in the crypt of St Bride's Church were disinterred the wisps of hair remaining on them were found to have turned bright orange. The earth lying under the paving stones of Fleet Street had apparently had some extravagant chemical effect. This was what Harriet's hair looked like. When she was born she had two sprouts of what seemed to be orange hay on her head. It was shocking in its coarseness and to her gentle Victorian mother alarmingly primitive, nearly pre-moral. It gave the infant's presence the power of some furious Ancient Briton lying in the crib.

Neither the colour nor the texture ever changed. The hair stayed orange, and to the end of her life it was as tough as a rocking horse's. When she was a child it was left uncut and grew down well below her waist. The tangles were tugged out three times a day by a Norland nurse who attacked the mane in a moral spirit as though it were some disagreeable piece of showing-off. By the time she was thirteen the routine of agony and rebellion on one side and vengeful discipline on the other had worn everyone out and she was taken to a barber. The barber took a knife to the thicket, weighed it when it was off, and gave her $2\frac{1}{2}$ lb of hair wrapped up in tissue paper which the nurse briskly took from her as soon as they were outside because she didn't believe in being morbid.

The operation had several effects. One of them was that the nurse, robbed of her pleasure in subduing the hair, turned her savagery more directly on to Harriet and once in a temper broke both of her charge's thumbs when she was forcing her into a new pair of white kid gloves for Sunday School. Another was that the child, who had always been sickly and scared, as though all her fortitude were going into the stiff orange fence hanging down her back, seemed to begin another kind of life as soon as it was cut off. She grew four inches in a year. Her father, a dark, sarcastic, pharisaically proud man whom she worshipped, started to introduce her to people as 'My fat daughter'.

She wasn't really fat at all. With her hair cut off she didn't even look like any normal Victorian parent's idea of a daughter. She looked more like Swinburne steaming up Putney Hill. Her lavender-scented mother began to watch her distastefully, as though she were a cigar being smoked in the presence of a lady without permission. Mrs Buckingham's dislike gave Harriet a sort of bristling resilience. She had from the beginning an immunity to other people's opinion of her, which isn't a characteristic that is much liked in women. Later in her life it made her impossible. Her critics thought it crude of her not to care what they thought of her. It meant that she started off at an advantage, for as soon as they imagined they had caused her misery they found that they were only confirming her grim and ribald idea of the way things would always be. She lay in wait for pain, expecting no rewards from people, and this made her a hopelessly disconcerting friend. Her peculiar mixture of vehemence and quietism caused people discomfort. If she had had any talent, if she had been born in another period and perhaps if her spirit had been lodged in the body of a man, she might just have been heroic. As it was, her flamboyance struck people as unbecoming and her apparent phlegm as not very lovable. The only person who might have respected her independence was her father, and he was the one being in whose presence she lost it. His mockery, which he meant as love, frightened and cut her to the bone. At thirteen she felt trapped by the system of growing into a woman, which seemed to be separating them, and longed more than ever to be his son.

A year later her back began to hurt. At the girls' establishment where she had been sent at huge expense to learn music and French and to carry out the ornate disciplines conceived by the headmistress – including communal teethwashing in the gardens, winter and summer, and then communal gargling into the rosebeds, which the headmistress regarded as a form of manure-spreading – the pain was put down to growing too fast. It was only after she had fainted at tennis that her father took her to a specialist who found that she had an extra vertebra. For the next two years she was supposed to spend five hours a day lying flat on her back on an old Flemish seat in the hall of her parents' London house. Formal education was shelved, which was a relief, because the unctuous kind of diligence expected of her at school had convinced her that she was both stupid and sinful. The physical privation of lying for hours on cold wood suited her mood. She began to feel that she would like to become a Roman Catholic, partly to frighten her mother, who was one of the pioneer Christian Scientists in England, and partly because the rigorousness of the experience attracted her. Her father was a Presbyterian and when she confronted him with her decision, doing it as pugnaciously as usual in spite of her nerves, they had a furious and ridiculous quarrel: a man of fifty for some reason threatened by the vast religious longings of a fifteen-year-old. She found herself capable of a courage that startled her. Maybe it was temper. She went upstairs, emptied her jewelbox into her pockets and left the house.

In 1912 this was an extraordinary thing to do. For two nights she slept on the Thames Embankment. It was really the misleading start to her whole punishingly misled life, because it gave her an idea of herself that she was absolutely unequipped to realize. She started to think that she had a vocation for taking heroic decisions, but it was really nothing more sustaining than a rabid kind of recklessness that erupted suddenly and then left her feeling bleak and inept. As a small child, sick with temper when she was forced to do something against her will or even when she was strapped too tightly into a bed, she had risen to heights of defiance that genuinely alarmed her family. She had a ferocious and alienating attachment to independence, but very little idea of what to do with it. The row about Catholicism got her out of the house and carried her through two euphoric days, during which she thought about the Trinity, existed on lollipops and stared at the Celebration of the Mass from the back of Westminster Cathedral. After that, the fuel was spent.

The priest whom she eventually accosted took one look at her, an ill-proportioned, arrogant child with cheap clips in her gaudy hair, and started grilling her for an address. She was furious that he refused to talk about religion except in terms of duty to her parents; what she wanted was a discussion of Peter Abelard and an immediate place in a convent. She had an exhaustive knowledge of Sunday Schools and it was depressing to find him full of the same bogus affability that she detected on every Sabbath of the year. She wanted harshness, remote ritual, a difficult kind of virtue; what she got was an upholstered smile and an approach like a cosy London policeman's to a well-bred drunk on Boat Race night.

Declining to lie, she let the priest take her home, planning to swear the maid to secrecy and slip out of the back door again as soon as he had gone. When she got there she found that her father was dying. The truancy was forgotten. Her mother, supported by two Christian Science practitioners, was in another room 'knowing the truth' and trying to reconcile her hysteria with Mary Baker Eddy's teaching that passing on is a belief of moral mind. The child was allowed into the bedroom and for two hours she watched her father die. He was in coma, and as he breathed he made a terrible bubbling sound. The nurse and the doctor left the room together for a moment and she grabbed him by the shoulders and shook him desperately, with an air-lock in her throat as though she were in a temper. When his bubbling stopped and he was dead, it seemed to her that he suddenly grew larger. He looked enormous, like a shark on the sand.

After that no one in the family really bothered about her. Though it was Edwardian England and though Harriet was the sort of upper-class child who would normally have been corseted with convention, Mrs Buckingham's resolve collapsed after her husband's death. Her natural passivity, encouraged by her religion and perhaps by the fact that she was pregnant, committed her to a mood of acceptance that was sweetly and hermetically selfish. The nurse was sacked to keep down the bills and the incoming maternity nurse was not interested in an unattractive fifteen-year-old. It was agreed by Mrs Buckingham, who had always resisted the false belief about the pain in her daughter's back, that Harriet should stop lying around on the hall seat and go to a school founded in the 1840s for the further education of gentlewomen. Having lost some of the true Christian Scientist's sanguinity about money and the faith that good Scientists should be able to demonstrate prosperity, she suggested faintly that Harriet had better take a secretarial course and equip herself to earn what she called a hat allowance, by which she meant a living.

The classes that Harriet in fact chose to go to were logic, history, English literature and Greek. Logic, when she came to it, seemed to her as near to Hell as she had ever been. She felt as though her brain were clambering around her skull like a wasp trying to get out of a jam jar. History was taught by a whiskery professor who thundered about the Origin and Destiny of Imperial Britain. His ferocious idealism made her think over and over again in terror of what her father would have said to her, and what she would have replied, if he had woken up when she shook him.

The English master baffled her. She hated Lamb, who was his favourite writer, and once terrified the class by saying so by mistake. Her own tastes were all wrong for the times; she liked the flaying moral tracts of the Christian Socialists and a kind of violent wit that had hardly existed since Pope. She felt a thousand miles away from the gentle professor, who used to cross out the expletives in Sheridan and even bowdlerized *Macbeth*. 'Ladies,' he said sweetly to the class one day, 'before proceeding further we will turn to the next page. We will count one, two, three lines from the top. We will erase or cross out the second word and substitute the word "thou". The line will then read: "Out, out thou spot. Out I say!"'

To begin with she made friends. There was one girl called Clara whom she used to meet in the lower corridor an hour before classes began: they had long discussions about Tolstoy, Maeterlinck and Ibsen, and were suspected of immorality. But soon she began to detach herself from the girls sitting hand in hand in the Bun Shop and from their faintly rebuking way of going at their books. Life, she felt vaguely but powerfully, was more than fervent chats about great literature. Life as she wanted it to be was momentarily embodied by the don who taught her Greek, a brave and learned man who fought the Turks in Modern Greece. As usual her excitement burnt out fast, like her courage. She had no gift for academic work; she simply longed to be able to dedicate her life to it.

Six months later she went to prison as a suffragette, having lied about her age and enrolled as a militant. It was the only time in her life when she was free of Doubts. She had found a cause, and the cause wasn't yet debased by her own incapacity to believe. She was thrilled with the suffragettes' tenacity and the expression it gave to her feelings about being in some kind of sexual trap.

But feminism, far from letting her out of the trap, turned out to be a hoax. She suddenly saw herself and her comrades not as prophets but as a howling and marauding mob. She prayed for faith, addressing a God whom she had never altogether managed to believe in, but clinging to the structure of the Roman Catholic Church as though it might do instead. During a hunger strike she asked to go to Confession. The prison doctor refused unless she agreed to drink a cup of tea and eat a piece of bread and butter. Confused, she agreed, and wrote a letter confessing the weakness to a friend outside, asking her not to tell the stonyhearts at Suffragette Headquarters. When she came back from Confession, uncomforted, she found her cell mate kicking the doctor who was trying to feed her, and at the same time yelling that he should take his hat off in the presence of a lady.

For Harriet this was the end of Votes for Women. She had no idea what she wanted, but it wasn't a licence to have it both ways. She left cold and fraudulent. After making several trips to Headquarters in Lincoln's Inn and each time letting the bus take her on to Aldgate East, she managed to resign from the movement. Characteristically, she did it in the most abrasive and insulting way possible. Everyone was disagreeable.

Six months later the Great War had broken out and she had found a new cause. She became a ward maid in a hospital. For a girl brought up in a Christian Science home there was a certain frightening kind of excitement about medicine, like drink for a teetotaller; but otherwise she found the work harrowing and repellent. Everyone else seemed to be roused by the War, but she saw it as a giant emotional hoax. The romanticism of the period upset her more than the blood. All the house surgeons started to avoid her, preferring the pretty VADs. Her unnecessary decision to do the dirtiest work in the place struck them as alarming. By now she was six feet tall and to the patients she looked like Boadicea with a bedpan; none of them found her calming, and the sisters regarded her hair with secret fear. The people she liked best were the consultants. Longing as usual with her spirit to enact the role that her flesh shrank from, she pined to be a doctor. She knew that the one thing that her mother would never provide money for was a training in medicine, so she wrote eventually to the *Boys' Own Paper* to ask them how to go about it, inventing a letter that was supposed to come from a badly-off boy whom she thought would enlist their sympathy. The bullying answer appeared in the correspondence columns: 'Medical training is long and arduous. It is unsuitable for the working boy. Our advice is that you learn a trade.'

So the huge, blundering, privileged girl, now seventeen, went back to her mother's comfortable house. She prayed, and took up vegetarianism, more as an extra religion than as part of the war effort; after a while she made herself go back to the hospital, and eventually she found Higher Mathematics. She bought textbooks, studied in bed at dawn, and went every night to evening classes given by a frockcoated seer who spoke about calculus as though it were a way of life. 'The language of Newton!' he cried, scribbling figures on the blackboard and immediately wiping them off with a damp rag as though he were doing vanishing tricks. 'O Newton!' He was the only living person whom she had ever heard using the vocative case. He talked as though he had learnt Latin constructions before English. 'To read the language by which Galileo explored the harmony of the celestial system! To look backward to the time when first the morning stars sang together!' He treated the mad redhead as though she were a fellow-spirit, and she responded, until the moment when she finally admitted she was incapable of understanding a word he was saying. After two months she loosened her grasp on the subject like a drowning man giving himself up to the sea.

Slogging away at the military hospital, sickened by the pain she saw and more muddled than ever, she decided that when the war was over she would become a tramp. She thought of it first when she spent her two nights on the Embankment, which was littered as soon as dark fell with sad, wild men and women stuffing bread into their mouths out of brown paper bags or staring at the barges on the river. She was attracted by the privation of the life, which she always linked with virtue, and she liked its sexual freedom. One woman derelict told her that after living with three husbands for twenty-five years she had decided to give them up and devote herself to the task of viewing the Cathedrals and Abbeys of the British Isles. This woman also had a passion to visit Russia, and she seemed to look on herself as a sort of tramp reformer. Besides being keen on Bolshevism she was deeply religious, and a great admirer of the Court of St James. She told Harriet that she often met King Edward VII in her dreams and thought of him as a kind of uncle.

At the end of the war the Buckinghams decided that something had to be done; not Mrs Buckingham, who was still repining, but Harriet's vast web of paternal relations. At Christmas her Uncle Bertie assembled the clan at his manor house in Wiltshire and announced that as a start she had better be presented at Court.

'But I don't want to be,' she said.

Girls didn't speak like that then.

'Nonsense,' he said breezily. 'Fun for you. Get you out of yourself for a bit. Put some roses in your cheeks.' And he bore down on her and pinched them, smelling of horse-sweat and sherry. 'Agnes will see to it, won't you?'

His wife stopped eating marrons glacés and nodded grimly.

'It's a waste of money,' said Harriet, looking out of the window at the parkland, which seemed lush enough to feed the whole of the East End of London until the next war. She remembered going to harangue working women in the East End when she was in the Suffragettes: their pale, pinched faces, dulled with years of lost endeavour. She had told them that once women got the vote everything would be all right: 'Poverty will be swept away! Washing will be done by municipal machinery!' Not that she knew anything about washing. At home she had never been aware of it. But it seemed to her that the women in the East End never got away from it: everlasting wet linen in the kitchen, smells of flat-irons and scorching, burns on their knuckles and puffy skin up to their elbows.

Bertie was furious. His performance of the lecherous uncle collapsed. His glass eye – he had lost the original when he was cleaning a gun – seemed to swivel further out of true than usual and stared pleasantly at the fire; the real one looked like a razor.

'Waste of money! Question of yield, my girl. £1,000 for a season and we might get you married off. No £1,000 and your mother might find herself supporting you all her life. How much do you think you cost in a year? Eh? Add it up. Add it up.' The married women in the room looked righteous as though they had made the unselfish decision. Harriet's Aunt Gertrude, a nervy spinster who lived with Uncle Bertie's household, sat as still as possible.

When they got back to London Harriet packed and left forever. The fact that she had no money of her own didn't strike her as an obstacle; the Suffragettes had reinforced her natural contempt for people who worried about money. One of her few friends in the movement, whom she used to meet at Lockharts in the Strand for a poached egg once a week, had come down from a mill town in Lancashire in 1916 with nothing but two brown paper parcels. (The smaller was her private luggage; the larger, which she called her public luggage, was full of pamphlets.) Harriet got a job as a dentist's receptionist and lived on lentils and poached eggs in a hostel until the dentist asked her to marry him. To her surprise, she said yes.

She was surprised, because she had thought that she had a vocation not to marry. Her heroines were Queen Elizabeth and Mary Wollstonecraft and Edith Cavell and, when she was miserable, Mary and Martha, the maiden ladies of Bethany. Queen Victoria, whom she made perpetual coarse jokes about in a way that struck people as uncalled for, had put her off marriage in the same way that she had put her off Scotland. But the dentist supplied her with a religion for a while: the religion of giving up everything for someone else. As she saw it, this meant becoming as drab and acquiescent as possible, and until her temper and gaiety erupted again it worked.

They lived in a depressing house in Finchley. She cooked abominably: boiled meat and blancmanges. After the birth of her second child, during the Depression, she began to dream violently of Hell and her father and the Book of Revelation.

The Queen Victoria jokes got more ferocious and they upset the dentist a great deal. There was one terrible day when she came into his surgery and found him sitting beside the gramophone playing *Soldiers of the Queen* with tears pouring down his face. She launched into a long mocking invention about patriotism and monarchists and the Army, inspiring herself with hatred and feeling pleasurably like a pianist going into a cadenza. Afterwards she repented it bitterly, but she was hopeless at apologizing: instead of retracting her feelings, what she always did was to say that she was sorry for expressing them, a kind of amends that costs nothing and carries the built-in rebuke that the other person is unable to bear the truth.

The fanatic voice of Revelation built up in her head like the air in a pressure chamber. 'Nevertheless I have somewhat against thee, *because thou hast left thy first love.*' She went over the final quarrel with her father again and again, and left her present loves to fend for themselves. She brought up her children in her sleep; her husband, who was a silent, kindly man, did a lot of the work. In the front room she started to hold prayer meetings that were almost like séances. Presently she found that she had the gift of tongues: notions of sacrifice and immolation and of a saviour with hair of sackcloth poured out of her mouth like a river of lava.

When the war began her husband was too old to be called up. He became an Air Raid Warden and they kept allotments. She made touching things for the children called mock devil's-food-cakes, concocted out of cocoa, golden syrup, carrots and soya flour. Her back by now was giving her constant pain. She looked more odd than ever and her movements were beginning to stiffen. She smoked cheap cigars, and the ash lay on her cardigans like catkins. On her fortieth birthday, in 1943, she was taken to hospital for a cancer operation and no one expected her to live. When she found she had survived she felt like Lazarus. She noticed that everyone was slightly embarrassed by her; she reminded them too much of the death around them, and they put on brutish cheerful voices with her. She felt, as so often, fraudulent, a corpse stuck together with glue.

In 1944, when she was out shopping, a flying bomb killed her elder child. It fell on a crowded school, and when she ran to the site from the High Street she could see some bodies still moving. The youngest children had been out in the playground; some of them survived. She found one little girl of about four under a pile of masonry. The child was on her back, unconscious. Just before she died she began to bicycle furiously with her legs, like a bee not quite crushed under a knife. Harriet carried the memory around with her as an image of horror, like the sickness in her own body.

After the war it became clear to her that the one heroic thing she was even faintly equipped to do with her life was to teach herself to die honourably, by which she meant without fear. This meant grappling with a panic that was like an asphyxiation. Her wisps of belief in an after-life had deserted her irrevocably with the flying bomb. 'It is not death that is frightening, but the knowledge of death': she started from this. After cooking her watery stew one night and seeing her younger daughter into bed she went to the public library and looked up 'Death' in a concordance. She brought home piles of books every week: Seneca and the Stoics and 'Measure for Measure' and the Jacobeans. Her husband watched her reading and finally lost touch with her. The daughter fidgeted through her long wild monologues and wished she wore prettier clothes. People said that she had become nicer, quieter, but harder to get at than ever, if you knew what they meant.

'I really must go up to Harriet's tonight.'

'Oh God, she's so unrewarding.'

'You feel you have to. She might be gone next week.'

'I thought they got it out when they operated.'

'You never know, do you.'

'But she's as tough as old boots.'

'I can't bear her really, but I feel sorry for her husband.'

'How can people make such a *mess* of themselves?'

She is still alive. When she dies I think she is going to be more frightened than she expects. It is an absurd ideal, really: a huge carcass inhabited by a blundering speck of dust and hoping to die as well as Nelson.

I put this down only because I have heard her daughter's friends call her 'mannish', and her own generation 'monstrous'. This is true, perhaps, but not quite the point.

NADINE GORDIMER

Some Are Born to Sweet Delight

Some are Born to sweet delight,
Some are Born to Endless Night.

WILLIAM BLAKE, *Auguries of Innocence*

They took him in. Since their son had got himself signed up
at sea for eighteen months on an oil rig, the boy's cubbyhole
of a room was vacant; and the rent money was a help. There
had rubbed off on the braid of the commissionaire father's
uniform, through the contact of club members' coats and
briefcases he relieved them of, loyal consciousness of the
danger of bombs affixed under the cars of members of parlia-
ment and financiers. The father said 'I've no quarrel with
that' when the owners of the house whose basement flat the
family occupied stipulated 'No Irish'. But to discriminate
against any other foreigners from the old Empire was against
the principles of the house owners, who were also the mother's
employers — cleaning three times a week and baby-sitting
through the childhood of three boys she thought of as her
own. So it was a way of pleasing Upstairs to let the room to
this young man, a foreigner who likely had been turned away
from other vacancies posted on a board at the supermarket.
He was clean and tidy enough; and he didn't hang around the
kitchen, hoping to be asked to eat with the family, the way
one of their own kind would. He didn't eye Vera.

Vera was seventeen, and a filing clerk with prospects of

advancement; her father had got her started in an important firm through the kindness of one of his gentlemen at the club. A word in the right place; and now it was up to her to become a secretary, maybe one day even a private secretary to someone like the members of the club, and travel to the Continent, America – anywhere.

– You have to dress decently for a firm like that. Let others show their backsides. –

– Dad! – The flat was small, the walls thin – suppose the lodger heard him. Her pupils dilated with a blush, half shyness, half annoyance. On Friday and Saturday nights she wore T-shirts with spangled graffiti across her breasts and went with girl-friends to the discothèque, although she'd had to let the pink side of her hair grow out. On Sundays they sat on wooden benches outside the pub with teasing local boys, drinking beer shandies. Once it was straight beer laced with something and they made her drunk, but her father had been engaged as doorman for a private party and her mother had taken the Upstairs children to the zoo, so nobody heard her vomiting in the bathroom.

So she thought.

He was in the kitchen when she went, wiping the slime from her panting mouth, to drink water. He always addressed her as 'miss' – Good afternoon, miss – He was himself filling a glass.

She stopped where she was; sourness was in her mouth and nose, oozing towards the foreign stranger, she mustn't go a step nearer. Shame tingled over nausea and tears. Shame heaved in her stomach, her throat opened, and she just reached the sink in time to disgorge the final remains of a pizza minced by her teeth and digestive juices, floating in beer. – Go away. Go away! – her hand flung in rejection behind her. She opened both taps to blast her shame down the drain. – Get out! –

He was there beside her, in the disgusting stink of her, and he had wetted a dish-towel and was wiping her face, her dirty mouth, her tears. He was steadying her by the arm and sitting her down at the kitchen table. And she knew that his kind didn't even drink, he probably never had smelled alcohol before. If it had been one of her own crowd it would have been different.

She began to cry again. Very quietly, slowly, he put his hand on hers, taking charge of the wrist like a doctor preparing to follow the measure of a heart in a pulse-beat. Slowly – the pace was his – she quietened; she looked down, without moving her head, at the hand. Slowly, she drew her own hand from underneath, in parting.

As she left the kitchen a few meaningless echoes of what had happened to her went back and forth – are you all right yes I'm all right are you sure yes I'm all right.

She slept through her parents' return and next morning said she'd had flu.

He could no longer be an unnoticed presence in the house, outside her occupation with her work and the friends she made among the other junior employees, and her preoccupation, in her leisure, with the discothèque and cinema where the hand-holding and sex-tussles with local boys took place. He said, Good afternoon, as they saw each other approaching in the passage between the family's quarters and his room, or couldn't avoid coinciding at the gate of the tiny area garden where her mother's geraniums bloomed and the empty milk bottles were set out. He didn't say 'miss'; it was as if the omission were assuring, Don't worry, I won't tell anyone, *although I know all about what you do*, everything, I won't talk about you among my friends – did he even have any friends? Her mother told her he worked in the kitchens of a smart restaurant – her mother had to be sure a lodger had steady pay before he could be let into the house. Vera saw other foreigners like him about, gathered loosely as if they didn't know where to go; of course, they didn't come to the disco and they were not part of the crowd of familiars at the cinema. They were together but looked alone. It was some-

thing noticed the way she might notice, without expecting to
fathom, the strange expression of a caged animal, far from
wherever it belonged.

She owed him a signal in return for his trustworthiness.
Next time they happened to meet in the house she said – I'm
Vera. –

As if he didn't know, hadn't heard her mother and father
call her. Again he did the right thing, merely nodded politely.

– I've never really caught your name. –

– Our names are hard for you here. Just call me Rad. – His
English was stiff, pronounced syllable by syllable in a soft
voice.

– So it's short for something? –

– What is that? –

– A nickname. Bob for Robert. –

– Something like that. –

She ended this first meeting on a new footing the only way
she knew how: – Well, see you later, then – the vague
dismissal used casually among her friends when no such
commitment existed. But on a Sunday when she was leaving
the house to wander down to see who was gathered at the
pub she went up the basement steps and saw that he was in
the area garden. He was reading newspapers – three or four of
them stacked on the mud-plastered grass at his side. She
picked up his name and used it for the first time, easily as a
key turning in a greased lock. – Hullo, Rad. –

He rose from the chair he had brought out from his room.
– I hope your mother won't mind? I wanted to ask, but she's
not at home. –

– Oh no, not Ma, we've had that old chair for ages, a bit of
fresh air won't crack it up more than it is already. –

She stood on the short path, he stood beside the old rattan
chair; then sat down again so that she could walk off without
giving offence – she left to her friends, he left to his reading.

She said – I won't tell. –

And so it was out, what was between them alone, in the

family house. And they laughed, smiled, both of them. She walked over to where he sat. – Got the day off? You work in some restaurant, don't you, what's it like? –

– I'm on the evening shift today. – He stayed himself a moment, head on one side, with aloof boredom. – It's something. Just a job. What you can get. –

– I know. But I suppose working in a restaurant at least the food's thrown in, as well. –

He looked out over the railings a moment, away from her. – I don't eat that food. –

She began to be overcome by a strong reluctance to go through the gate, round the corner, down the road to The Mitre and the whistles and appreciative pinches which would greet her in her new flowered Bermudas, his black eyes following her all the way, although he'd be reading his papers with her forgotten. To gain time she looked at the papers. The one in his hand was English. On the others, lying there, she was confronted with a flowing script of tails and gliding flourishes, the secret of somebody else's language. She could not go to the pub; she could not let him know that was where she was going. The deceptions that did for parents were not for him. But the fact was there was no deception: she *wasn't* going to the pub, she suddenly wasn't going.

She sat down on the motoring section of the English newspaper he'd discarded and crossed her legs in an X from the bare round knees. – Good news from home? –

He gestured with his foot towards the papers in his secret language; his naked foot was an intimate object, another secret.

– From my home, no good news. –

She understood this must be some business about politics, over there – she was in awe and ignorance of politics, nothing to do with her. – So that's why you went away. –

He didn't need to answer.

– You know, I can't imagine going away. –

– You don't want to leave your friends. –

She caught the allusion, pulled a childish face, dismissing them. – Mum and Dad . . . everything. –

He nodded, as if in sympathy for her imagined loss, but made no admission of what must be his own.

– Though I'm mad keen to travel. I mean, that's my idea, taking this job. Seeing other places – just visiting, you know. If I make myself capable and that, I might get the chance. There's one secretary in our offices who goes everywhere with her boss, she brings us all back souvenirs, she's very generous. –

– You want to see the world. But now your friends are waiting for you –

She shook off the insistence with a laugh. – And you want to go home! –

– No. – He looked at her with the distant expression of an adult before the innocence of a child. – Not yet. –

The authority of his mood over hers, that had been established in the kitchen that time, was there. She was hesitant and humble rather than flirtatious when she changed the subject. – Shall we have – will you have some tea if I make it? Is it all right? – He'd never eaten in the house; perhaps the family's food and drink were taboo for him in his religion, like the stuff he could have eaten free in the restaurant.

He smiled. – Yes it's all right. – And he got up and padded along behind her on his slim feet to the kitchen. As with a wipe over the clean surfaces of her mother's sink and table, the other time in the kitchen was cleared by ordinary business about brewing tea, putting out cups. She set him to cut the gingerbread: – Go on, try it, it's my mother's homemade. – She watched with an anxious smile, curiosity, while his beautiful teeth broke into its crumbling softness. He nodded, granting grave approval with a full mouth. She mimicked him, nodding and smiling; and, like a doe approaching a leaf, she took from his hand the fragrant slice with the semicircle marked by his teeth, and took a bite out of it.

★

Vera didn't go to the pub any more. At first they came to look for her – her chums, her mates – and nobody believed her excuses when she wouldn't come along with them. She hung about the house on Sundays, helping her mother. – Have you had a tiff or something? –

As she always told her bosom friends, she was lucky with her kind of mother, not strict and suspicious like some. – No, Ma. They're okay, but it's always the same thing, same things to say, every weekend. –

– Well . . . shows you're growing up, moving on – it's natural. You'll find new friends, more interesting, more your type. –

Vera listened to hear if he was in his room or had had to go to work – his shifts at the restaurant, she had learnt from timing his presence and absences, were irregular. He was very quiet, didn't play a radio or cassettes but she always could feel if he was there, in his room. That summer was a real summer for once; if he was off shift he would bring the old rattan chair into the garden and read, or stretch out his legs and lie back with his face lifted to the humid sun. He must be thinking of where he came from; very hot, she imagined it, desert and thickly-white cubes of houses with palm trees. She went out with a rug – nothing unusual about wanting to sunbathe in your own area garden – and chatted to him as if just because he happened to be there. She watched his eyes travelling from right to left along the scrolling print of his newspapers, and when he paused, yawned, rested his head and closed his lids against the light, could ask him about home – his home. He described streets and cities and cafés and bazaars – it wasn't at all like her idea of desert and oases. – But there are palm trees? –

– Yes, nightclubs, rich people's palaces to show tourists, but there are also factories and prison camps and poor people living on a handful of beans a day. –

She picked at the grass: I see. – Were you – were your family – do you like beans? –

He was not to be drawn; he was never to be drawn.

– If you know how to make them, they are good. –

– If we get some, will you tell us how they're cooked? –

– I'll make them for you. –

So one Sunday Vera told her mother Rad, the lodger, wanted to prepare a meal for the family. Her parents were rather touched; nice, here was a delicate mark of gratitude, such a glum character, he'd never shown any sign before. Her father was prepared to put up with something that probably wouldn't agree with him. – Different people, different ways. Maybe it's a custom with them, when they're taken in, like bringing a bunch of flowers. – The meal went off well. The dish was delicious and not too spicy; after all, gingerbread was spiced, too. When her father opened a bottle of beer and put it down at Rad's place, Vera quickly lifted it away. – He doesn't drink, Dad. –

Graciousness called forth graciousness; Vera's mother issued a reciprocal invitation. – You must come and have our Sunday dinner one day – my chicken with apple pie to follow. –

But the invitation was in the same code as 'See you later'. It was not mentioned again. One Sunday Vera shook the grass from her rug. – I'm going for a walk. – And the lodger slowly got up from his chair, put his newspaper aside, and they went through the gate. The neighbours must have seen her with him. The pair went where she led, although they were side by side, loosely, the way she'd seen young men of his kind together. They went on walking a long way, down streets and then into a park. She loved to watch people flying kites; now he was the one who watched her as she watched. It seemed to be his way of getting to know her; to know anything. It wasn't the way of other boys – her kind – but then he was a foreigner here, there must be so much he needed to find out. Another weekend she had the idea to take a picnic. That meant an outing for the whole day. She packed apples and bread and cheese – remembering no ham – under the eyes of her mother. There was a silence between them. In it was her mother's recognition of the accusation she, Vera, knew she ought to bring against herself: Vera was 'chasing' a man; this man. All her mother said was – Are you joining other friends? – She didn't lie. – No. He's never been up the river. I thought we'd take a boat trip. –

In time she began to miss the cinema. Without guile she asked him if he had seen this film or that; she presumed that when he was heard going out for the evening the cinema would be where he went, with friends of his – his kind – she never saw. What did they do if they didn't go to a movie? It wouldn't be bars, and she knew instinctively he wouldn't be found in a disco, she couldn't see him shaking and stomping under twitching coloured lights.

He hadn't seen any film she mentioned. – Won't you come? – It happened like the first walk. He looked at her again as he had then. – D'you think so? –

– Why ever not. Everybody goes to movies. –

But she knew why not. She sat beside him in the theatre with solemnity. It was unlike any other time, in that familiar place of pleasure. He did not hold her hand; only that time, that time in the kitchen. They went together to the cinema regularly. The silence between her and her parents grew; her mother was like a cheerful bird whose cage had been covered. Whatever her mother and father thought, whatever they feared – nothing had happened, nothing happened until one public holiday when Vera and the lodger were both off work and they went on one of their long walks into the country (that was all they could do, he didn't play sport, there wasn't any activity with other young people he knew how to enjoy). On that day celebrated for a royal birthday or religious anniversary that couldn't mean anything to him, in deep grass under profound trees he made love to Vera for the first time. He had never so much as kissed her before, not on any evening walking home from the cinema, not when they were alone in the house and the opportunity was obvious as the discretion of the kitchen clock sounding through the empty passage, and the blind eye of the television set in the sitting-room. All that he had never done with her was begun and accomplished with unstoppable passion, summoned up as if at a mere command to himself; between this and the placing of his hand on hers in the kitchen, months before, there was nothing. Now she had the lips from which, like a doe, she had taken a morsel touched with his saliva, she had the naked body promised by the first glimpse of the naked feet. She had lost her virginity, like all her sister schoolgirls, at fourteen or fifteen, she had been fucked, half-struggling, by some awkward local in a car or a back room, once or twice. But now she was overcome, amazed, engulfed by a sensuality she had no idea was inside her, a bounty of talent unexpected and unknown as a burst of song would have been welling from one who knew she had no voice. She wept with love for this man who might never, never have come to her, never have found her from so far away. She wept because she was so afraid it might so nearly never have happened. He wiped her tears, he dressed her with the comforting resignation to her emotion a mother shows with an over-excited child.

She didn't hope to conceal from her mother what they were doing; she knew her mother knew. Her mother felt her gliding silently from her room down the passage to the lodger's room, the room that still smelt of her brother, late at night, and returning very early in the morning. In the dark Vera knew every floorboard that creaked, how to avoid the swish of her pyjamas touching past a wall; at dawn saw the squinting beam of the rising sun sloped through a window that she had never known was so placed it could let in any phase of the sun's passage across the sky. Everything was changed.

What could her mother have said? Maybe he had different words in his language; the only ones she and her mother had wouldn't do, weren't meant for a situation not provided for in their lives. *Do you know what you're doing? Do you know what he is? We don't have any objection to them, but all the same. What about your life? What about the good firm your father's got you into? What'll it look like, there?*

The innocent release of sensuality in the girl gave her an authority that prevailed in the house. She brought him to the table for meals, now; he ate what he could. Her parents knew this presence, in the code of their kind, only as the signal by which an 'engaged' daughter would bring home her intended. But outwardly between Vera and her father and mother the form was kept up that his position was still that of a lodger, a lodger who had somehow become part of the household in that capacity. There was no need for him to pretend or assume any role; he never showed any kind of presumption towards their daughter, spoke to her with the same reserve that he, a stranger, showed to them. When he and the girl rose from the table to go out together it was always as if he accompanied her, without interest, at her volition.

Because her father was a man, even if an old one and her father, he recognized the power of sensuality in a female and was defeated, intimidated by its obstinacy. *He* couldn't take the whole business up with her; her mother must do that. He quarrelled with his wife over it. So she confronted their daughter. *Where will it end?* Both she and the girl understood: he'll go back where he comes from, and where'll you be? He'll drop you when he's had enough of what he wanted from you.

Where would it end? Rad occasionally acknowledged her among his friends, now – it turned out he did have some friends, yes, young men like him, from his home. He and she encountered them on the street and instead of excusing himself and leaving her waiting obediently like one of those pet dogs tied up outside the supermarket, as he usually had done when he went over to speak to his friends, he took her with him and, as if remembering her presence after a minute or two of talk, interrupted himself: She's Vera. Their greetings, the way they looked at her, made her feel that he had told them about her, after all, and she was happy. They made remarks in their own language she was sure referred to her. If she had moved on, from the pub, the disco, the parents, she was accepted, belonged somewhere else.

And then she found she was pregnant. She had no girlfriend to turn to who could be trusted not to say those things: he'll go back where he comes from, he'll drop you when he's had enough of what he wanted from you. After the second month she bought a kit from the pharmacy and tested her urine. Then she went to a doctor because that do-it-yourself thing might be mistaken.

– I thought you said you would be all right. –

That was all he said, after thinking for a moment, when she told him.

– Don't worry, I'll find something. I'll do something about it. I'm sorry, Rad. Just forget it. – She was afraid he would stop loving her – her term for love-making.

When she went to him tentatively that night he caressed her more beautifully and earnestly than ever while possessing her.

She remembered reading in some women's magazine that it was dangerous to do anything to get rid of 'it' (she gave her pregnancy no other identity) after three months. Through roundabout enquiries she found a doctor who did abortions, and booked an appointment, taking an advance on her holiday bonus to meet the fee asked.

– By the way, it'll be all over next Saturday. I've found someone. – Timidly, that week, she brought up the subject she had avoided between them.

He looked at her as if thinking very carefully before he spoke, thinking apart from her, in his own language, as she was often sure he was doing. Perhaps he had forgotten – it was really her business, her fault, she knew. Then he pronounced what neither had: – The baby? –

– Well . . . – She waited, granting this.

He did not take her in his arms, he did not touch her. – You will have the baby. We will marry. –

It flew from her awkward, unbelieving, aghast with joy: –
You want to marry me! –

– Yes, you're going to be my wife. –

– Because of this? – a baby? –

He was gazing at her intensely, wandering over the sight of
her. – Because I've chosen you. –

Of course, being a foreigner, he didn't come out with
things the way an English speaker would express them.

And I love *you*, she said, I love you, I love you – babbling
through vows and tears. He put a hand on one of hers, as he
had done in the kitchen of her mother's house; once, and
never since.

She saw a couple in a mini-series standing hand-in-hand,
telling them; 'We're getting married' – hugs and laughter.

But she told her parents alone, without him there. It was
safer that way, she thought, for him. And she phrased it in
proof of his good intentions as a triumphant answer to her
mother's warnings, spoken and unspoken. – Rad's going to
marry me. –

– He wants to marry you? – Her mother corrected. The
burst of a high-pitched cry. The father twitched an angry
look at his wife.

Now it was time for the scene to conform to the TV family
announcement. – We're going to get married. –

Her father's head flew up and sank slowly, he turned away.

– You want to be married to him? – Her mother's palm
spread on her breast to cover the blow.

The girl was brimming feeling, reaching for them.

Her father was shaking his head like a sick dog.

– And I'm pregnant and he's glad. –

Her mother turned to her father but there was no help
coming from him. She spoke impatiently flatly. – So that's it. –

– No, that's not it. It's not it at all. – She would not say
to them 'I love him', she would not let them spoil that by
trying to make her feel ashamed. – It's what I want. –

— It's what she wants. — Her mother was addressing her father.

He had to speak. He gestured towards his daughter's body, where there was no sign yet to show life growing there. — Nothing to be done then. —

When the girl had left the room he glared at his wife. — Bloody bastard. —

— Hush. Hush. — There was a baby to be born, poor innocent.

And it was, indeed, the new life the father had gestured at in Vera's belly that changed everything. The foreigner, the lodger — had to think of him now as the future son-in-law, Vera's intended — told Vera and her parents he was sending her to his home for his parents to meet her. — To your country? —

He answered with the gravity with which, they realized, marriage was regarded where he came from. — The bride must meet the parents. They must know her as I know hers. —

If anyone had doubted the seriousness of his intentions — well, they could be ashamed of those doubts, now; he was sending her home, openly and proudly, his foreigner, to be accepted by his parents. — But have you told them about the baby, Rad? — She didn't express this embarrassment in front of her mother and father. — What do you think? That is why you are going. — He slowed, then spoke again. — It's a child of our family. —

So she was going to travel at last! In addition to every other joy! In a state of continual excitement between desire for Rad — now openly sharing her room with her — and the pride of telling her work-mates why she was taking her annual leave just then, she went out of her way to encounter former friends whom she had avoided. To say she was travelling to meet her fiancé's family; she was getting married in a few months, she was having a baby — yes — proof of this now in the rounding under the flowered jumpsuit she wore to show it off. For her mother, too, a son-in-law who was not

one of their kind became a distinction rather than a shame. –
Our Vera's a girl who's always known her own mind. It's a
changing world, she's not one just to go on repeating the
same life as we've had. – The only thing that hadn't changed
in the world was joy over a little one coming. Vera was
thrilled, they were all thrilled at the idea of a baby, a first
grandchild. Oh that one was going to be spoilt all right! The
prospective grandmother was knitting, although Vera laughed
and said babies weren't dressed in that sort of thing any
more, hers was going to wear those little unisex frog suits in
bright colours. There was a deposit down on a pram fit for an
infant prince or princess.

It was understood that if the intended could afford to send
his girl all the way home just to meet his parents before the
wedding, he had advanced himself in the restaurant business,
despite the disadvantages young men like him had in an
unwelcoming country. Upstairs was pleased with the news;
Upstairs came down one evening and brought a bottle of
champagne as a gift to toast Vera, whom they'd known since
she was a child, and her boy – much pleasant laughter when
the prospective husband filled everyone's glass and then
served himself with orange juice. Even the commissionaire felt
confident enough to tell one of his gentlemen at the club that
his daughter was getting married but first about to go abroad
to meet the young man's parents. His gentlemen's children
were always travelling; in his ears every day were overheard
snatches of destinations – 'by bicycle in China, can you
believe it' … 'two months in Peru, rather nice …'
… 'snorkeling on the Barrier Reef, last I heard'. *Visiting her
future parents-in-law where there is desert and palm trees*; not bad!

The parents wanted to have a little party, before she left, a
combined engagement party and farewell. Vera had in mind a
few of her old friends brought together with those friends of
his she'd been introduced to and with whom she knew he still
spent some time – she didn't expect to go along with him, it
wasn't their custom for women, and she couldn't understand

their language, anyway. But he didn't seem to think a party would work. She had her holiday bonus (to remember what she had drawn it for, originally, was something that, feeling the baby tapping its presence softly inside her, she couldn't believe of herself) and she kept asking him what she could buy as presents for his family — his parents, his sisters and brothers, she had learnt all their names. He said he would buy things, he knew what to get. As the day for her departure approached, he still had not done so. — But I want to pack! I want to know how much room to leave, Rad! — He brought some men's clothing she couldn't judge and some dresses and scarves she didn't like but didn't dare say so — she supposed the clothes his sisters liked were quite different from what she enjoyed wearing — a good thing she hadn't done the choosing.

She didn't want her mother to come to the airport; they'd both be too emotional. Leaving Rad was strangely different; it was not leaving Rad but going, carrying his baby, to the mystery that was Rad, that was in Rad's silences, his blind love-making the way he watched her, thinking in his own language so that she could not follow anything in his eyes. It would all be revealed when she arrived where he came from.

He had to work, the day she left, until it was time to take her to the airport. Two of his friends, whom she could scarcely recognize from the others in the group she had met occasionally, came with him to fetch her in the taxi one of them drove. She held Rad's hand, making a tight double fist on his thigh, while the men talked in their language. At the airport the others left him to go in alone with her. He gave her another, last-minute gift for home. — Oh Rad — where'm I going to put it? The ticket says one handbaggage! — But she squeezed his arm in happy recognition of his thoughts for his family. — It can go in — easy, easy. — He unzipped her carryall as they stood in the queue at the check-in counter. She knelt with her knees spread to accommodate her belly, and helped him. — What is it, anyway — I hope not something that's going to break? – He was making a bed for the package. – Just toys for my sister's kid. Plastic. – I could have put them in the suitcase – oh Rad . . . what room'll I have for duty-free! – In her excitement, she was addressing the queue for the American airline's flight which would take her on the first leg of her journey. These fellow passengers were another kind of foreigner, Americans, but she felt she knew them all; they were going to be travelling in her happiness, she was taking them with her.

She held him with all her strength and he kept her pressed against his body; she could not see his face. He stood and watched her as she went through passport control and she stopped again and again to wave but she saw Rad could not wave, could not wave. Only watch her until he could not see her any longer. And she saw him in her mind still looking at her, as she had done at the beginning when she had imagined herself as still under his eyes if she had gone to the pub on a Sunday morning.

Over the sea, the airliner blew up in midair. Everyone on board died. The black box was recovered from the bed of the sea and revealed that there had been an explosion in the tourist-class cabin followed by a fire; and there the messages ended; silence, the disintegration of the plane. No one knows if all were killed outright or if some survived to drown. An inquiry into the disaster continued for a year. The background of every passenger was traced, and the circumstances that led to the journey of each. There were some arrests; people detained for questioning and then released. They were innocent – but they were foreigners, of course. Then there was another disaster of the same nature, and a statement from a group with an apocalyptic name representing a faction of the world's wronged, claiming the destruction of both planes in some complication of vengeance for holy wars, land annexation, invasions, imprisonments, cross-border raids, territorial disputes, bombings, sinkings, kidnappings no one outside the initiated could understand. A member of the group, a young man known as Rad among many other aliases, had placed in the handbaggage of the daughter of the family with whom he lodged, and who was pregnant by him, an explosive device. Plastic. A bomb of a plastic type undetectable by the usual procedures of airport security.

Vera was chosen.

Vera had taken them all, taken the baby inside her; down, along with her happiness.

MARY GORDON

The Thorn

If I lose this, she thought, I will be so far away I will never come back.

When the kind doctor came to tell her that her father was dead, he took her crayons and drew a picture of a heart. It was not like a valentine, he said. It was solid and made of flesh, and it was not entirely red. It had veins and arteries and valves and one of them had broken, and so her daddy was now in heaven, he had said.

She was very interested in the picture of the heart and she put it under her pillow to sleep with, since no one she knew ever came to put her to bed anymore. Her mother came and got her in the morning, but she wasn't in her own house, she was in the bed next to her cousin Patty. Patty said to her one night, 'My mommy says your daddy suffered a lot, but now he's released from suffering. That means he's dead.' Lucy said yes, he was, but she didn't tell anyone that the reason she wasn't crying was that he'd either come back or take her with him.

Her aunt Iris, who owned a beauty parlour, took her to B. Altman's and bought her a dark blue dress with a white collar. That's nice, Lucy thought. I'll have a new dress for when I go away with my father. She looked in the long mirror and thought it was the nicest dress she'd ever had.

Her uncle Ted took her to the funeral parlour and he told her that her father would be lying in a big box with a lot of flowers. That's what I'll do, she said. I'll get in the box with him. We used to play in a big box; we called it the tent and we got in and read stories. I will get into the big box. There is my father; that is his silver ring.

She began to climb into the box, but her uncle pulled her away. She didn't argue; her father would think of some way to get her. He would wait for her in her room when it was dark. She would not be afraid to turn the lights out anymore. Maybe he would only visit her in her room; all right, then, she would never go on vacation; she would never go away with her mother to the country, no matter how much her mother cried and begged her. It was February and she asked her mother not to make any summer plans. Her aunt Lena, who lived with them, told Lucy's mother that if she had kids she wouldn't let them push her around, not at age seven. No matter how smart they thought they were. But Lucy didn't care; her father would come and talk to her, she and her mother would move back to the apartment where they lived before her father got sick and she would only have to be polite to Aunt Lena; she would not have to love her, she would not have to feel sorry for her.

On the last day of school she got the best report card in her class. Father Burns said her mother would be proud to have such a smart little girl, but she wondered if he said this to make fun of her. But Sister Trinitas kissed her when all the other children had left and let her mind the statue for the summer: the one with the bottom that screwed off so you could put the big rosaries inside it. Nobody ever got to keep it for more than one night. This was a good thing. Since her father was gone she didn't know if people were being nice or if they seemed nice and really wanted to make her feel bad later. But she was pretty sure this was good. Sister Trinitas kissed her, but she smelled fishy when you got close up; it was the paste she used to make the Holy Childhood poster. This was good.

'You can take it to camp with you this summer, but be very careful of it.'

'I'm not going to camp, Sister. I have to stay at home this summer.'

'I thought your mother said you were going to camp.'

'No, I have to stay home.' She could not tell anybody, even Sister Trinitas, whom she loved, that she had to stay in her room because her father was certainly coming. She couldn't tell anyone about the thorn in her heart. She had a heart, just like her father's, brown in places, blue in places, a muscle the size of a fist. But hers had a thorn in it. The thorn was her father's voice. When the thorn pinched, she could hear her father saying something. 'I love you more than anyone will ever love you. I love you more than God loves you.' *Thint* went the thorn; he was telling her a story 'about a mean old lady named Emmy and a nice old man named Charlie who always had candy in his pockets, and their pretty daughter, Ruth, who worked in the city'. But it was harder and harder. Sometimes she tried to make the thorn go *thint* and she only felt the thick wall of her heart; she couldn't remember the sound of it or the kind of things he said. Then she was terribly far away; she didn't know how to do things, and if her aunt Lena asked her to do something like dust the ledge, suddenly there were a hundred ledges in the room and she didn't know which one and when she said to her aunt which one did she mean when she said ledge: the one by the floor, the one by the stairs, the one under the television, her aunt Lena said she must have really pulled the wool over their eyes at school because at home she was an idiot. And then Lucy would knock something over and Aunt Lena would tell her to get out, she was so clumsy she wrecked everything. Then she needed to feel the thorn, but all she could feel was her heart getting thicker and heavier, until she went up to her room and waited. Then she could hear it. 'You are the prettiest girl in a hundred counties and when I see your face it is like a parade that someone made special for your daddy.'

She wanted to tell her mother about the thorn, but her father had said that he loved her more than anything, even God. And she knew he said he loved God very much. So he must love her more than he loved her mother. So if she couldn't hear him her mother couldn't, and if he wasn't waiting for her in her new room then he was nowhere.

When she came home she showed everyone the statue that Sister Trinitas had given her. Her mother said that was a very great honour: that meant that Sister Trinitas must like her very much, and Aunt Lena said she wouldn't lay any bets about it not being broken or lost by the end of the summer, and she better not think of taking it to camp.

Lucy's heart got hot and wide and her mouth opened in tears.

'I'm not going to camp; I have to stay here.'

'You're going to camp, so you stop brooding and moping around. You're turning into a regular little bookworm. You're beginning to stink of books. Get out in the sun and play with the other children. That's what you need, so you learn not to trip over your own two feet.'

'I'm not going to camp. I have to stay here. Tell her, Mommy, you promised we wouldn't go away.'

Her mother took out her handkerchief. It smelled of perfume and it had a lipstick print on it in the shape of her mother's mouth. Lucy's mother wiped her wet face with the pink handkerchief that Lucy loved.

'Well, we talked and we decided it would be best. It's not a real camp. It's Uncle Ted's camp, and Aunt Bitsie will be there, and all your cousins and that nice dog Tramp that you like.'

'I won't go. I have to stay here.'

'Don't be ridiculous,' Aunt Lena said. 'There's nothing for you to do here but read and make up stories.'

'But it's for *boys* up there and I'll have nothing to do there. All they want to do is shoot guns and yell and run around. I hate that. And I have to stay here.'

'That's what you need. Some good, healthy boys to toughen you up. You're too goddamn sensitive.'

Sensitive. Everyone said that. It meant she cried for nothing. That was bad. Even Sister Trinitas got mad at her once and told her to stop her crocodile tears. They must be right. She would like not to cry when people said things that she didn't understand. That would be good. They had to be right. But the thorn. She went up to her room. She heard her father's voice on the telephone. *Thint*, it went. It was her birthday, and he was away in Washington. He sang 'happy birthday' to her. Then he sang the song that made her laugh and laugh: 'Hey, Lucy Turner, are there any more at home like you?' because of course there weren't. And she mustn't lose that voice, the thorn. She would think about it all the time, and maybe then she would keep it. Because if she lost it, she would always be clumsy and mistaken; she would always be wrong and falling.

Aunt Lena drove her up to the camp. *Scenery*. That was another word she didn't understand. 'Look at that gorgeous scenery,' Aunt Lena said, and Lucy didn't know what she meant. 'Look at that bird,' Aunt Lena said, and Lucy couldn't see it, so she just said, 'It's nice.' And Aunt Lena said, 'Don't lie. You can't even *see* it, you're looking in the wrong direction. Don't say you can see something when you can't see it. And don't spend the whole summer crying. Uncle Ted and Aunt Bitsie are giving you a wonderful summer for free. So don't spend the whole time crying. Nobody can stand to have a kid around that all she ever does is cry.'

Lucy's mother had said that Aunt Lena was very kind and very lonely because she had no little boys and girls of her own and she was doing what she thought was best for Lucy. But when Lucy had told her father that she thought Aunt Lena was not very nice, her father had said, 'She's ignorant.' *Ingnorant*. That was a good word for the woman beside her with the dyed black hair and the big vaccination scar on her fat arm.

'Did you scratch your vaccination when you got it, Aunt Lena?'

'Of course not. What a stupid question. Don't be so

goddamn rude. I'm not your mother, ya know. Ya can't push me around.'

Thint, went the thorn. 'You are ignorant,' her father's voice said to Aunt Lena. 'You are very, very ignorant.'

Lucy looked out the window.

When Aunt Lena's black Chevrolet went down the road, Uncle Ted and Aunt Bitsie showed her her room. She would stay in Aunt Bitsie's room, except when Aunt Bitsie's husband came up on the weekends. Then Lucy would have to sleep on the couch.

The people in the camp were all boys, and they didn't want to talk to her. Aunt Bitsie said she would have to eat with the counsellors and the K.P.'s. Aunt Bitsie said there was a nice girl named Betty who was fourteen who did the dishes. Her brothers were campers.

Betty came out and said hello. She was wearing a sailor hat that had a picture of a boy smoking a cigarette. It said 'Property of Bobby'. She had braces on her teeth. Her two side teeth hung over her lips so that her mouth never quite closed.

'My name's Betty,' she said. 'But everybody calls me Fang. That's on account of my fangs.' She opened and closed her mouth like a dog. 'In our crowd, if you're popular, you get a nickname. I guess I'm pretty popular.'

Aunt Bitsie walked in and told Betty to set the table. She snapped her gum as she took out the silver. 'Yup, Mrs O'Connor, one thing about me is I have a lot of interests. There's swimming and boys, and tennis, and boys, and reading, and boys, and boys, and boys, and boys, and boys.'

Betty and Aunt Bitsie laughed. Lucy didn't get it.

'What do you like to read?' Lucy asked.

'What?' said Betty.

'Well, you said one of your interests was reading. I was wondering what you like to read.'

Betty gave her a fishy look. 'I like to read romantic comics. About romances,' she said. 'I hear you're a real bookworm. We'll knock that outa ya.'

The food came in: ham with brown gravy that tasted like ink. Margarine. Tomatoes that a fly settled on. But Lucy could not eat. Her throat was full of water. Her heart was glassy and too small. And now they would see her cry.

She was told to go up to her room.

That summer Lucy learned many things. She made a birchbark canoe to take home to her mother. Aunt Bitsie made a birchbark sign for her that said 'Keep Smiling'. Uncle Ted taught her to swim by letting her hold onto the waist of his bathing trunks. She swam onto the float like the boys. Uncle Ted said that that was so good she would get double dessert just like the boys did the first time they swam out to the float. But then Aunt Bitsie forgot and said it was just as well anyway because certain little girls should learn to watch their figures. One night her cousins Larry and Artie carried the dog Tramp in and pretended it had been shot. But then they put it down and it ran around and licked her and they said they had done it to make her cry.

She didn't cry so much now, but she always felt very far away and people's voices sounded the way they did when she was on the sand at the beach and she could hear the people's voices down by the water. A lot of times she didn't hear people when they talked to her. Her heart was very thick now: it was like one of Uncle Ted's boxing gloves. The thorn never touched the thin, inside walls of it anymore. She had lost it. There was no one whose voice was beautiful now, and little that she remembered.

MARY LAVIN

Lilacs

'That dunghill isn't doing anybody any harm and it's not going out of where it is as long as I'm in this house!' said Phelim Molloy.

'But if it could only be put somewhere else,' said his wife Ros, 'and not right under the window of the room where we eat our bit of food!'

'Didn't you tell me, yourself, a minute ago, you could smell it from the other end of the town? If that's the case I don't see what's going to be the good in moving it from one side of the yard to the other.'

'What I don't see,' said his daughter Kate, 'is the need for us dealing in dung at all.'

'There you are!' said Phelim. 'There you are! I knew all along that was what you had in the back of your mind; both of you, and the one inside too!' – he beckoned backwards with his head towards the door behind him. 'You wanted to be rid of it altogether, not just to shift it from one place to another. Why on earth can't women speak out what they mean? That's a thing always puzzles me.'

'Leave Stacy out of it, Phelim,' said Ros; 'Stacy has one of her headaches.'

'And what gave it to her I'd like to know?' said Phelim. 'I'm supposed to think it was the smell of the dung gave it to her, but I know more than to be taken in by women's nonsensical notions.'

'Don't talk so loud, Phelim,' said Ros; 'she might be asleep.'

'It's a great wonder any of you can sleep a wink at all any night with the smell of that poor harmless heap of dung, out there, that's bringing in good money week after week.'

He turned to his daughter.

'It paid for your education at a fine boarding school.'

He turned to Ros.

'And it paid for Stacy's notions about the violin and the piano, both of which is rotting within there in the room; and not a squeak of a tune ever I heard out of the one or other of them since the day they came into the house!'

'He won't give in,' said Ros to her daughter. 'We may as well keep our breath.'

'You may as well,' said Phelim. 'That's a true thing anyway.' He went over to the yard door. When he opened the door the faint odour of stale manure that hung already about the kitchen was thickened by a hot odour of new manure from the yard. Kate followed her father to the door and banged it shut after him.

As the steel taps on Phelim's shoes rang on the cobbles the two women stood at the window looking out at him. He took up a big yard-brush made of twigs tied to a stick with leather thongs, and he started to brush up dry clots of manure that had fallen from the carts as they travelled from the gate to the dung trough. The dung trough itself was filled to the top, and moisture from the manure was running in yellow streaks down the sides. The manure was brown and it was stuck all over with bright stripes of yellow straw.

'You'll have to keep at him, Mother,' said Kate.

'There's not much use,' said Ros.

'Something will have to be done. That's all about it!' said Kate. 'Only last night at the concert in the Town Hall, just after the lights went down, I heard the new people, that took the bakehouse across the street, telling someone that they couldn't open a window since they came to the town with the terrible smell that was coming from somewhere; I could have died with shame, Mother. I didn't hear what answer they got, but when the lights went up for the interval I saw they were sitting beside Mamie Murtagh, and you know what that one would be likely to say! My whole pleasure in the evening was spoiled, I can assure you.'

'You take things too much to heart, Kate,' said Ros. 'There's Stacy inside there, and if it wasn't for the smell of it I don't believe she'd mind us having it at all. She says to me sometimes, "Wouldn't it be lovely, Mother, if there was a smell of lilacs every time we opened the door?"'

'Stacy makes me tired,' said Kate, 'with her talk about lilacs and lilacs! What does she ever do to try and improve things?'

'She's very timid,' said Ros.

'That's all the more reason,' said Kate, 'my father would listen to her if she'd only speak to him.'

'Stacy would never have the heart to cross anyone.'

'Stacy's a fool.'

'It's the smell that gives her the headaches all the same,' said Ros. 'Ever since she came home from boarding school she's been getting her headaches every Wednesday regular the very minute the first cartload comes in across the yard.'

'Isn't that what I'm saying!' said Kate impatiently, taking down a brown raincoat from a peg behind the door. 'I'm going out for a walk and I won't be back till that smell has died down a bit. You can tell him that too, if he's looking for me.'

When Kate went out Ros took down a copper tea-caddy from the dresser and threw a few grains of tea into a brown earthen teapot. Then she poured a long stream of boiling water into the teapot from the great sooty kettle that hung over the flames. She poured out a cup of the tea and put sugar and milk in it, and a spoon. She didn't bother with a saucer, and she took the cup over to the window and set it on the sill to cool while she watched Phelim sweeping in the yard.

In her heart there seemed to be a dark clot of malignance towards him because of the way he thwarted them over the dunghill. But as she looked out at him he put his hand to his back every once in a while, and Ros felt the black clots thinning away. Before the tea was cool enough to swallow, her blood was running bright and free in her veins again and she was thinking of the days when he used to call her by the old name.

She couldn't rightly remember when it was she first started calling herself Ros, or whether it was Phelim started it. Or it might have been someone outside the family altogether. But it was a good name no matter where it came from, a very suitable name for an old woman. It would be only foolishness to go on calling her Rose after she was faded and all dried up. She looked at her hands. They were thin as claws. She went over to the yard door.

'There's tea in the teapot, Phelim,' she called out, and she left the door open. She went into the room where the two girls slept.

'Will I take you in a nice cup of nice hot tea, Stacy?' she said, leaning over the big bed.

'Is it settled?' said Stacy, sitting up.

'No,' said Ros, pulling across the curtain, 'it's to stay where it is.'

'I hope he isn't upset?' said Stacy.

'No. He's sweeping the yard,' said Ros, 'and there's a hot cup of tea in the teapot for him if he likes to take it. You're a good girl, Stacy. How's your poor head?'

'I wouldn't want to upset him,' said Stacy. 'My head is a bit better. I think I'll get up.'

It was, so, to Stacy that Ros turned on the night Phelim was taken bad with the bright pain low in the small of his back. When he died in the early hours of the morning, Ros kept regretting that she had crossed him over the dunghill.

'You have no call to regret anything, Mother,' said Stacy. 'You were ever and always calling him in out of the yard for cups of tea, morning, noon, and night. I often heard you, days I'd have one of my headaches. You've no call at all for regret.'

'Why wouldn't I call him in to a cup of tea on a cold day?' said Ros. 'There's no thanks for that. He was the best man that ever lived.'

'You did all you could for him, Mother,' said Kate, 'and there's no need to be moaning and carrying on like that!'

'Let us not say anything,' said Ros. 'It was you was the one was always at me to talk to him about the dunghill. I wish I never crossed him.'

'That was the only thing you ever crossed him over, Mother,' said Stacy, 'and the smell was really very hard to put up with.'

Phelim was laid out in the parlour beyond the kitchen. He was coffined before the night, but the lid was left off the coffin. Ros and the girls stayed up all night in the room. The neighbours stayed in the house, but they sat in the kitchen where they threw sods of turf on the fire when they were needed, and threw handfuls of tea leaves into the teapot now and again, and brought tea in to the Molloys.

Kate and Stacy sat one each side of their mother and mourned the man they were looking at, lying dead in a sheaf of undertaker linen crimp. They mourned him as they knew him for the last ten years, a heavy man with a red face who was seldom seen out of his big red rubber boots.

Ros mourned the Phelim of the red rubber boots, but she mourned many another Phelim. She mourned him back beyond the time his face used to flush up when he went out in the air. She mourned him the time he never put a hat on when he was going out in the yard. She mourned him when his hair was thick, although it was greying at the sides. She mourned him when he wore a big moustache sticking out stiff on each side. But most of all she mourned him for the early time when he had no hair on his face at all, and when his cheeks were always glossy from being out in the weather. That was the time he had to soap down his curls. That was the time he led her in a piece off the road when they were coming from Mass one Sunday.

'Rose,' he said. 'I've been thinking. There's a pile of money to be made out of manure. I've been thinking that if I got a cart and collected a bit here and a bit there for a few pence I might be able to sell it in big loads for a lot more than I paid for it.'

'Is that so?' she said. She remembered every word they said that day.

'And do you know what I've been thinking too?' he said. 'I've been thinking that if I put by what I saved I might have enough by this time next year to take a lease of the little cottage on the Mill Road.'

'The one with the church window in the gable end?' she said. 'And the two fine sheds,' he said.

'The one with the ivy all down one side?' she said, but she knew well the one he meant.

'That's the very one,' said Phelim. 'How would you like to live there? With me, I mean?'

'Manure has a terrible dirty smell,' she said.

'You could plant flowers, maybe.'

'I'd have to plant ones with a strong perfume,' she said, 'rockets and mignonette.'

'Any ones you like. You'd have nothing else to do all day.'

She remembered well how innocent he was then, for all that he was twenty, and thinking to make a man of himself by taking a wife. His face was white like a girl's, with patches of pink on his cheeks. He was handsome. There were prettier girls by far than her who would have given their eyes to be led in a piece off the road, just for a bit of talk and gassing from Phelim Molloy – let alone a real proposal.

'Will you, Rose?' said Phelim. 'There's a pile of money in manure, even if the people around these parts don't set any store by it.'

The colour was blotching over his cheeks the way the wind blotched a river. He was nervous. He was putting his foot up on the bar of the gate where they were standing, and the next minute he was taking it down again. She didn't like the smell of manure, then, any more than after, but she liked Phelim.

'It's dirty stuff,' she said. And that was her last protest.

'I don't know so much about that,' said Phelim. 'There's a lot in the way you think about things. Do you know, Rose, sometimes when I'm driving along the road I look down at the dung that's dried into the road and I think to myself that you couldn't ask much prettier than it, the way it flashes by under the horses' feet in pale gold rings.' Poor Phelim! There weren't many men would think of things like that.

'All right, so,' she said. 'I will.'

'You will?' said Phelim. 'You will?'

The sun spilled down just then and the dog-roses swayed back and forwards in the hedge.

'Kiss me so,' he said.

'Not here!' she said. The people were passing on the road and looking down at them. She got as pink as the pink dog-roses.

'Why not?' said Phelim. 'If you're going to marry me you must face up to everything. You must do as I say always. You must never be ashamed of anything.'

She hung her head, but he put his hand under her chin.

'If you don't kiss me right now, Rose Magarry, I'll have nothing more to do with you.'

The way the candles wavered round the corpse was just the way the dog-roses wavered in the wind that day.

Ros shed tears for the little dog-roses. She shed tears for the blushes she had in her cheeks. She shed tears for the soft kissing lips of young Phelim. She shed tears for the sunny splashes of gold dung on the roads. And her tears were quiet and steady, like the crying of the small thin rains in windless weather.

When the cold white morning came at last the neighbours got up and stamped their feet on the flags outside the door. They went home to wash and get themselves ready for the funeral.

When the funeral was over Ros came back to the lonely house between her two daughters. Kate looked well in black. It made her thinner and her high colour looked to advantage. Stacy looked the same as ever. The chairs and tables were all pushed against the wall since they took the coffin out. One or two women stayed behind, and there was hot tea and cold meat. There was a smell of guttered-out candles and a heavy smell of lilies.

Stacy drew in a deep breath.

'Oh, Kate!' she said. 'Smell!'

Kate gave her a harsh look.

'Don't remind her,' she said, 'or she'll be moaning again.'

But Ros was already looking out in the yard and the tears were streaming from her eyes again down the easy runnels of her dried and wrinkled face.

'Oh, Phelim,' she said. 'Why did I ever cross you? Wasn't I the bad old woman to cross you over a little heap of dirt and yellow straw?'

Kate bit her lip.

'Don't take any notice of her,' she said to the women. She turned to Stacy. 'Take in our hats and coats,' she said, 'and put a sheet over them.' She turned back to the women. 'Black is terrible for taking the dust,' she said, 'and terrible to clean.' But all the time she was speaking she was darting glances at Ros.

Ros was moaning louder.

'You're only tormenting yourself, Mother,' said Kate. 'He was a good man, one of the best, but he was an obstinate man over that dunghill, so you've no call to be upsetting yourself on the head of that!'

'It was out of the dung he made his first few shillings.'

'How long ago was that?' said Kate. 'And was that any reason for persecuting us all for the last five years with the smell of it coming up under the window, you might say?'

'I think we'll be going, Kate,' said the women.

'We're much obliged to you for your kindness in our trouble,' said Ros and Kate together.

The women went out quietly.

'Are they gone?' said Stacy, coming out of the inside room, looking out the window at the women going down the road.

'Is it the dunghill you were talking about?' she said. 'Because tomorrow is Wednesday!'

'I know that,' said Ros.

'The smell isn't so bad today, is it?' said Stacy. 'Or was it the smell of the flowers drove it out?'

'I wish to goodness you'd look at it in a more serious light, Stacy,' said Kate. 'It's not alone the smell of it, but the way people look at us when they hear what we deal in.'

'It's nothing to be ashamed of,' said Ros. 'It was honest dealing, and that's more than most in this town can say!'

'What do you know about the way people talk, Mother?' said Kate. 'If you were away at boarding school, like Stacy and me, you'd know, then, what it felt like to have to admit your father was making his money out of horse dung.'

'I don't see what great call was on you to tell them!' said Ros.

'Listen to that!' said Kate. 'It's easily seen you were never at boarding school, Mother.'

Stacy had nearly forgotten the boarding school, but she remembered a bit about it then.

'We used to say our father dealt in fertiliser,' she said. 'But someone looked it up in a dictionary and found out it was only a fancy name for manure.'

'Your father would have laughed at that,' said Ros.

'It's not so funny at all,' said Kate.

'Your father had a wonderful sense of humour,' said Ros.

'He was as obstinate as a rock, that's one thing,' said Kate.

'When we knew that was the case,' said Ros, 'why did we cross him? We might have known he wouldn't give in. I wish I never crossed him.'

The old woman folded her knotted hands and sat down by the fire in the antique attitude of grieving womankind.

Kate could talk to Stacy when they were in the far corner

of the kitchen getting down the cups and saucers from the dresser.

'I never thought she was so old-looking.'

'She looked terribly old at the graveside,' said Stacy. 'Make her take her tea by the fire.'

'Will you drink down a nice cup of tea, here by the fire, Mother?' said Stacy, going over to the old woman.

Ros took the cup out of the saucer and put the spoon into it. 'Leave that back,' she said, pushing away the saucer. She took the cup over to the window sill.

'It only smells bad on hot days,' she said, looking out.

'But summer is ahead of us!' said Kate, spinning round sharply and looking at the old woman.

'It is and it isn't,' said Ros. 'In the January of the year it's as true to say you have put the summer behind you as it is to say it is ahead of you.'

'Mother?'

Kate came over and, pushing aside the geranium on the window ledge, she leaned her arm there and stared back into her mother's face.

'Mother,' she said. 'You're not by any chance thinking of keeping on the dunghill?'

'I'm thinking of one thing only,' said Ros. 'I'm thinking of him and he young, with no hair on his lip, one day – and the next day, you might say, him lying within on the table and the women washing him for his burial.'

'I wish you'd give over tormenting yourself, Mother.'

'I'm not tormenting myself at all,' said Ros. 'I like thinking about him.'

'He lived to a good age,' said Kate.

'I suppose you'll be saying that about me one of these days,' said Ros, 'and it no time ago since I was sitting up straight behind the horse's tail, on my father's buggy, with my white blouse on me and my gold chain dangling and my hair halfway down my back. The road used to be flashing by under the clittering horse-hooves, and the gold dung dried into bright gold rings.'

★

'Stacy,' said Kate, that night when they were in bed, 'I don't like to see her going back over the old days like she was all day. It's a bad sign. I hope we won't be laying her alongside Father one of these days.'

'Oh, Kate,' said Stacy, 'don't remind me of poor Father. All the time she was talking about crossing him over the dung I was thinking of the hard things I was saying against him the last time my head was splitting and he was leading in the clattering carts over the cobblestones and the dirty smell of the dung rising up on every wind.'

'You've no call to torment yourself, Stacy,' said Kate.

'That's what you said to Mother.'

'It's true what I say, no matter which of you I say it to. There was no need in having the dunghill at all. It was nothing but obstinacy. Start to say your beads now and you'll be asleep before you've said the first decade. And don't be twitching the clothes off me. Move over.'

It seemed to Stacy that she had only begun the second decade of her beads, when her closed eyes began to ache with a hard white light shining down on them without pity. She couldn't sleep with that hard light on her eyes. She couldn't open her eyes either, because the light pressed down so weightily on her lids. Perhaps, as Kate had said, it was morning and she had fallen asleep? Stacy forced her lids open. The window square was blinding white with hard venomous daylight. The soft night had gone. There was another day before them, but Father was out in the green churchyard where the long grass was always wet even in yellow sunlight.

Stacy lay cold. Her eyes were wide and scopeless and her feet were touching against the chilled iron rail at the foot of the bed. She looked around the whitewashed room and she looked out of the low window, that was shaped like the window of a church, at the cold crinkled edges of the corrugated sheds. Stacy longed for it to be summer, though summer was a long way off. She longed for the warm winds to be daffing through the trees and the dallops of grass to be dry enough for flopping down on, right where you were in the middle of a field. And she longed for it to be the time when the tight hard beads of the lilacs looped out into the soft pear shapes of blossom, in other people's gardens.

And then, as soft as the scent of lilac steals through early summer air, the thought came slowly into Stacy's mind that poor dear Father, sleeping in the long grave-grasses, might not mind them having lilacs now where the dunghill used to be. For it seemed already to Stacy that the dunghill was gone now that poor Father himself was gone. She curled up in the blankets and closed her eyes again, and so it was a long time before she knew for certain that there was a sound of knocking on the big yard-gate and a sound of a horse shaking his brass trappings and pawing the cobbles with his forefoot. She raised her head a little off the pillow. There was the sound of a wooden gatewing flapping back against the wall. There was a rattle of horse-hooves and steel-bound cart-wheels going over the cobbles. 'Kate! Kate!' she shouted, and she shook Kate till she wakened with a flush of frightened red to her cheeks. 'Kate,' she said, 'I thought I heard Father leading in a load of manure across the yard!'

Kate's flush deepened.

'Stacy, if you don't control yourself, your nerves will get the better of you completely. Where will you be then?' But as Kate spoke they heard the dray board of a cart being loosened in the yard and chains fell down on the cobbles with a ringing sound.

Kate sprang out of bed, throwing back the clothes right over the brass footrail, and left Stacy shivering where she lay, with the freezing air making snaps at her legs and her arms and her white neck. Kate stared out of the window.

'I knew this would happen,' she said, 'I could have told you!' Stacy got out of bed slowly and came over across the cold floor in her bare feet. She pressed her face against the icy glass. She began to cry in a thin wavering way like a child. Her nose was running, too; like a child's.

In the yard Ros was leading in a second cart of manure, and talking in a high voice to the driver of the empty cart that was waiting its turn to pass out. She was dressed in her everyday clothes that weren't black, but brown; the dark primitive colour of the earth and the earth's decaying refuse. The cart she led was piled high with rude brown manure, stuck all over with bright stripes of yellow straw, and giving off a hot steam. The steam rose up unevenly like thumby fingers of a clumsy hand and it reached for the faces of the staring women that were indistinct behind the fog their breaths put on the glass.

'Get dressed!' said Kate. 'We'll go down together.'

Ros was warming her hands by the fire when they went into the kitchen. There was a strong odour of manure. Kate said nothing, but she went over and banged the yard door shut. Stacy said nothing. Stacy stood. Ros looked up.

'Well?' said Ros.

'Well?' said Kate, after her, and she said it louder than Ros had said it.

The two women faced each other across the deal table. Stacy sat down on the chair that Ros had just left, and she began to cry in her thin wavy voice.

'Shut up, Stacy!' said Kate.

'Say what you have to say, Kate,' said Ros, and in the minds of all three of them there was the black thought that bitter words could lash out endlessly, now that there was no longer a man in the house to come in across the yard with a heavy boot and stand in the doorway slapping his hands together and telling them to give up their nonsense and lay the table for the meal.

'Say what you have to say,' said Ros.

'You know what we have to say,' said Kate.

'Well, don't say it, so,' said Ros, 'if that's all it is.' She went towards the door.

'Mother!' Stacy went after her and caught the corner of her mother's old skirt. 'You were always saying it would be nice if it was once out of there.'

'Isn't that my only regret, Stacy?' said Ros. 'That was the only thing I crossed him over.'

'But you were right, Mother.'

'Was I?' said Ros, but not in the voice of one asking a question. 'Sometimes an old woman talks about things she knows nothing about. Your father always said it wasn't right to be ashamed of anything that was honest. Another time he said money was money, no matter where it came from. That was a true thing to say. He was always saying true things. Did you hear the priest yesterday when we were coming away from the grave? "God help all poor widows!" he said.'

'What has that got to do with what we're talking about?' said Kate.

'A lot,' said Ros. 'Does it never occur to the two of you that it mightn't be so easy for three women, and no man, to keep a house going and fires lighting and food on the table; to say nothing at all about dresses and finery?'

'I suppose that last is meant for me?' said Kate.

'That's just like what Father himself would say,' said Stacy, but no one heard her. Kate had suddenly moved over near her mother and was leaning with her back against the white rim of the table. When she spoke it was more kindly.

'Did you find out how his affairs were fixed, Mother?' she said.

'I did,' said Ros, and she looked at her daughter with cold eyes. 'I did,' she said again, and that was all she said as she went out the door.

The smell that came in the door made Stacy put her arm over her face and bury her nose in the crook of her elbow. But Kate drew herself up and her fine firm bosom swelled. She breathed in a strong breath.

'Pah!' she said. 'How I hate it!'

'Think if it was a smell of lilacs!' said Stacy, 'Lovely lilacs.'

'I wish you'd stop crying,' said Kate. 'You can't blame her, after all, for not wanting to go against him and he dead. It's different for us.'

Stacy's face came slowly out of the crook of her arm. She had a strange wondering look.

'Maybe when you and I are all alone, Kate?' she said, and then as she realized what she was saying she put her arm up quickly over her face in fright. 'Not that I meant any harm,' she said. 'Poor Mother! poor Mother!'

Kate looked at her with contempt.

'You should learn to control your tongue, Stacy. And in any case, I wish you wouldn't be always talking as if we were never going to get married.'

'I sometimes think we never will,' said Stacy.

Kate shook out the tablecloth with a sharp flap in the warm air.

'Maybe you won't,' she said. 'I don't believe you will, as a matter of fact. But I will.' She threw the tablecloth across the back of a chair and looked into the small shaving mirror belonging to their father that still hung on the wall.

In the small mirror Kate could see only her eyes and nose, unless she stood far back from it. And when she did that, as well as seeing herself, she could see the window, and through the window she could see the yard and anyone in it. And so, after she had seen that she looked just as she thought she would look, she stepped back a little from the glass and began to follow the moving reflections of her mother that she saw in it. There seemed a greater significance in seeing her mother in this unreal way than there would have been in seeing her by looking directly out the window. The actions of Ros as she gathered up the fallen fragments of dung seemed to be symbolic of a great malevolent energy directed against her daughters.

'I didn't need to be so upset last night going to bed,' she said to Stacy bitterly. 'There's no fear of her going after my poor father. She's as hardy as a tree!'

But Ros Molloy wasn't cut out to be a widow. If Phelim had been taken from her before the dog-roses had faded on their first summer together she could hardly have moaned him more than she did, an old woman, cold and shivering, tossing in her big brass bed all alone.

The girls eased her work for her at every turn of the hand, but on Wednesday mornings they let her get up alone to open the gates at six o'clock and let in the carts of manure. They didn't sleep however.

As often as not Stacy got up, on to the cold floor in her bare feet, and stood at the window looking out. She crossed her arms over her breast to keep in what warmth she had taken from the blankets, and she told Kate what was going on outside.

'Did she look up at the window?' Kate asked one morning.

'No,' Stacy said.

'Get back into bed so, and don't give her the satisfaction of knowing you're watching her.'

'Kate.'

'What?'

'You don't think I ought to slip down and see if the kettle is boiling for when she comes in, do you, Kate?'

'You know what I think,' said Kate. 'Will you get back into bed and not be standing there freezing!'

'She has only her thin coat on,' said Stacy.

Kate leaned up on one elbow, carefully humping up the clothes with her, pegged to her shoulder.

'By all the pulling and rattling that I hear, she's doing enough to keep up her circulation, without her having any clothes at all on her.'

'She shouldn't be lifting things the way she is,' said Stacy.

'And whose fault is it if she is?' said Kate, slumping back into the hollows of the bed. 'Get back here into bed, you, and stop watching out at her doing things there's no need in her doing at all. That's just what she wants; to have someone watching out at her.'

'She's not looking this way at all, Kate.'

'Oh, isn't she? Let me tell you, that woman has eyes in the back of her head!'

'Oh, Kate,' said Stacy, and she ran over to the bed and

threw herself in across Kate, sobbing. Kate lay still for a minute listening to her, and then she leaned up on her other elbow and humped the clothes up over the shoulder. Stacy slept between her and the wall. 'What in the name of God ails you now?' she asked.

'Don't you remember, Kate? That's what she used to say to us when we were small. She used to stand up straight and stiff, with her gold chain on her, and say that we had better not do anything wrong behind her back because she had eyes in the back of her head.'

Kate flopped back again.

'We all have to get old,' she said.

'I know,' said Stacy, 'but all the same you'd hate to see the gold chain dangling down below her waist, like I did the other day, when she took it out of her black box and put it on her.'

Kate sat up again.

'She's not wearing it, is she?'

'She put it back in the box.'

Kate flopped back once more. Her face was flushed from the sudden jerks she gave in the cold morning air.

'I should hope she put it back,' she said, 'that chain is worth a lot of money since the price of gold went up.'

Stacy lay still with her eyes closed. There was something wrong, but she didn't know just what it was. All she wanted was to get the dunghill taken away out of the yard and a few lilacs put there instead. But it seemed as if there were more than that bothering Kate. She wondered what it could be? She had always thought herself and Kate were the same, that they had the same way of looking at things, but lately Kate seemed to be changed.

Kate was getting old. Stacy took no account of age, but Kate was getting old. And Kate took account of everything. Stacy might have been getting old too, if she was taking account of things, but she wasn't. It seemed no length ago to Stacy since they came home from the convent. She couldn't tell you what year it was. She was never definite about anything. Her head was filled with nonsense, Kate said.

What do you think about when you're lying inside there with a headache?' Kate asked her once.

'Things,' Stacy said.

She would only be thinking of things; this thing and that thing; things of no account; silly things. Like the times she lay in bed and thought of a big lilac tree sprouting up through the boards of the floor, bending the big bright nails, sending splinters of wood flying till they hit off the window-panes. The tree always had big pointed bunches of lilac blossom all over it; more blossoms than leaves. That just showed, Stacy thought, what nonsense it was. You never saw more blossoms than leaves. But the blossoms weighed down to-wards her where she lay shivering, and they touched her face.

It was nonsense like that that went dawdling through her mind one morning, when the knocking at the gate outside kept up for so long that she began to think her mother must have slept it out.

'Do you think she slept it out, Kate?'

'I hope she did,' said Kate. 'It might teach her a lesson.'

'Maybe I ought to slip down and let them in?'

'Stay where you are.'

But Stacy had to get up.

'I'll just look in her door,' she said.

Stacy went out and left the door open.

'Hurry back and shut the door,' said Kate, calling after her.

But Stacy didn't hurry. Stacy didn't come back either.

'Stacy! Stacy!' Kate called out.

She lifted her head off her pillow to listen.

'Stacy? Is there anything wrong?'

Kate sat up in the cold.

'Stacy! Can't you answer a person?'

Kate got out on the floor.

She found Stacy lying in a heap at her mother's bedside, and she hardly needed to look to know that Ros was dead. She as good as knew – she said afterwards – that Stacy would pass out the minute there was something unpleasant.

No wonder Stacy had no lines on her face. No wonder she looked a child, in spite of her years. Stacy got out of a lot of worry, very neatly, by just flopping off in a faint. Poor Ros was washed, and her eyes shut and her habit put on her, before Stacy came round to her senses again.

'It looks as if you're making a habit of this,' said Kate, when Stacy fainted again, in the cemetery this time, and didn't have to listen, as Kate did, to the sound of the sods clodding down on the coffin.

'But I did hear them, Kate,' Stacy protested. 'I did. I heard them distinctly. But I was a bit confused in my mind still at the time, and I thought it was the sound of the horse-hooves clodding along the road.'

'What horse-hooves? Are you going mad?'

'You remeber, Kate. Surely you remember. The ones Mother was always telling us about. Her hair hung down her back and her gold chain dangled, and while she was watching the road flashing by under the clittering horse-hooves she used to think how pretty the gold dung was, dried into bright discs.'

'That reminds me!' said Kate. 'Tomorrow is Wednesday.'

Although Stacy's face was wet with the moisture of her thin scalding tears, she smiled and clasped her hands together.

'Oh Kate!' she said; and then, in broad daylight, standing in the middle of the floor in her new serge mourning dress that scraped the back of her neck all the time, she saw a heavy lilac tree nod at her with its lovely pale blooms bobbing.

'Which of us will get up?' Kate was saying, and watching Stacy while she was saying it.

'Get up?'

'To let them in.'

'To let who in?'

'Who do you think? The men with the manure of course.' Kate spoke casually, but when she looked at Stacy she stamped her foot on the floor.

'Don't look so stupid, Stacy. There isn't any time now to

let them know. We can't leave them hammering at the gate after coming miles, maybe. Someone will have to go down and open the gate for them.'

When Stacy heard the first rap on the gate she hated to think of Kate's having to get up.

'I'll get up, Kate,' she said. 'Stay where you are.'

But she got no answer. Kate was walking out across the yard at the time, dressed and ready, and she had the gate thrown back against the wall before the men had time to raise their hands for a second rap.

Stacy dressed as quickly as she could, to have the kettle on as a surprise for Kate. It was the least she might do.

But when Stacy went down the fire was blazing up the chimney and there was a trace of tea in a cup on the table. Poor Kate, thought Stacy, she must have been awake half the night in case she'd let the time slip. Wasn't she great! Stacy felt very stupid. She was no good at all. Kate was great. Here was their great moment. Here was the time for getting rid of a nuisance, and if it was up to her to tell the men not to bring any more cartloads she honestly believed she'd be putting it off for weeks and be afraid to do it in the end, maybe. But Kate was great. Kate made no bones about it. Kate didn't say a word about how she was going to do it, or what she was going to say. She just slipped out of bed and made a cup of tea and went out in the yard and took command of everything. Kate was great.

'What did you say?' asked Stacy, when Kate came in.

'How do you mean?' said Kate and looked at her irritably. 'What on earth gave you such a high colour at this hour of the morning? I never saw you with so much colour in your face before?'

But the colour was fading out already.

'Didn't you tell them not to bring any more?' she asked.

Kate looked as if she were going to say something, and then she changed her mind. Then she changed her mind again, or else she thought of something different to say.

'I didn't like to give them the hard word,' she said.

Stacy flushed again.

'I see what you mean,' she said: 'we'll ease off quietly?'

'Yes,' said Kate. 'Yes, we could do that. Or I was thinking of another plan.'

Stacy knelt up on a hard deal chair and gripped the back of it. There was something very exciting in hearing Kate talk and plan. It gave Stacy a feeling that they had a great responsibility and authority and that they were standing on their own feet.

'You mightn't like the idea,' said Kate, 'at first.'

'Oh, I'm sure I'll love it,' said Stacy.

'It's this then,' said Kate. 'I was thinking last night that instead of doing away with the dunghill we should take in twice as much manure for a while till we made twice as much money, and then we could get out of this little one-story house altogether.'

Stacy was looking out the window.

'Well?' said Kate.

Stacy laid her face against the glass.

'Oh for goodness' sake stop crying,' said Kate; 'I was only making a suggestion.' She began to clatter the cups on the dresser. She looked back at Stacy. 'I thought, you see, that after a bit we might move over to Rowe House. It's been idle a long time. I don't think they'd want very much for it, and it's two-story, what's more, with a front entrance and steps going up to the hall door.'

Stacy dried her face in the crook of her arm and began to put back the cups that Kate had taken down from the dresser, because the table was already set. Her face had the strained and terrible look that people with weak natures have when they force their spirits beyond their bounds.

'I'll never leave this house,' she said; 'never as long as I live.'

'Stay in it, so!' said Kate. 'And rot in it for all I care. But I'm getting out of it the first chance I get! And that dunghill isn't stirring from where it is until I have a fine fat dowry out of it.'

She went into the bedroom and banged the door, and Stacy sat down looking at the closed door. Then she looked out the window. Then she got up and ran her hand down over the buttons of her bodice. They were all closed properly. She took the tea-caddy and began to put two careful spoonfuls of tea into the teapot. When the tea was some minutes made, she went over to the closed door. Once again she ran her hand down the buttons of her bodice; and then she called Kate.

'Your tea is getting cold,' she said, and while she waited for an answer her heart beat out its fear upon her hollow chest.

But Kate was in a fine good humour when she came out, with her arms piled up with dresses and hats and cardboard boxes covered with rose-scattered wallpaper. She left the things down on the window sill and pulled her chair in to the table.

'Is this loaf bread or turnover?' she said. 'It tastes very good. Sit down yourself, Stacy,' and after a mouthful of the hot tea she nodded her head at the things on the window sill.

'There's no point in having a room idle, is there?' she said. 'I may as well move into Mother's room.'

There was no more mention of the dunghill. Kate attended to it. Stacy didn't have her headaches as bad as she used to have them. Not giving in to them was the best cure yet. Kate was right. There was only a throbbing. It wasn't bad.

Stacy and Kate got on great. At least there was no fighting. But the house was as uneasy as a house where two women live alone. At night you felt it most. So Stacy was glad at the back of everything when Con O'Toole began dropping in, although she didn't like him and she thought the smell of stale tobacco that was all over the house next day was worse than the smell of the dung.

'Do you like the smell of his pipe, Kate?' said Stacy one day.

'I never noticed,' said Kate.

'I think it's worse than the smell of the dung!' said Stacy with a gust of bravery.

'I thought we agreed on saying "fertiliser" instead of that word you just used,' said Kate, stopping up in the dusting.

'That was when we were at boarding school!' said Stacy, going on with the dusting.

'I beg your pardon,' said Kate, 'it was when we were mixing with the right kind of people. I wish you wouldn't be so forgetful.'

But next morning Kate came into the parlour when Stacy was nearly finished with the dusting. She threw out her firm chest and drew in a deep breath.

'Pah!' she said. 'It *is* disgusting. I'll make him give up using it as soon as we take up residence at Rowe House. But don't say anything about it to him. He mightn't take it well. Of course I can say anything I like to him. He'll take anything from me. But it's better to wait till after we're married and not come on him with everything all at once.'

That was the first Stacy heard about Kate's getting married, but of course if she had only thought about it she'd have seen the way the wind was blowing. But she took no account of anything.

After the first mention of the matter, however, Kate could hardly find time to talk about anything else, right up to the fine blowsy morning that she was hoisted up on the car by Con, in her new peacock blue outfit, and her mother's gold chain dangling. Stacy was almost squeezed out of the doorway by the crowd of well-wishers waving them off. They all came back into the house. Such a mess! Chairs pulled about! Crumbs on the cushions! Confetti! Wine spilled all over the carpet! And the lovely iced cake all cut into! Such a time as there would be cleaning it all up! And Stacy thought that when she'd be putting things back in their places would be a good time to make a few changes. That chair with the red plush would be better on the other side of the piano. And she'd draw the sofa out a bit from the wall.

'Will you be lonely, Miss Stacy?' said someone.

'You should get someone in, to keep you company, Miss Stacy,' said someone else.

'At night anyway,' they all said.

They were very kind. Stacy loved hearing them all making plans for her. It was so good-natured. But this was the first time she'd ever got a chance to make a few plans for herself, and she wished they'd hurry up and go.

They didn't stay so very long. They were soon all gone, except Jasper Kane. Jasper liked Stacy, apart from his being the family solicitor, and knowing her father so well.

'Might I inquire, Miss Stacy, what is the first thing you're planning to do, now that you are your own mistress?'

Stacy went over to the window.

'I'm going to plant a few lilac trees, Mr Kane,' she said, because she felt she could trust him. Her father always did.

'Oh!' said Jasper, and he looked out the window, too. 'Where?' he said.

'There!' said Stacy, pointing out of the back window. 'There where the dunghill is now.' She drew a brave breath. 'I'm getting rid of the dunghill, you see,' she said.

Jasper stayed looking out of the window at the dunghill. Then he looked at Stacy. He was an old man.

'But what will you live on, Miss Stacy?' he said.

OLIVIA MANNING

Innocent Pleasures

It was the tram-car in the Transport Museum that reconstituted Mr Limestone. Before that he had been no more than a little dust buried beneath Emily's rejected and done-for memories of Camber. She had not given him a thought for years. He was probably dead. There might be no one left in Camber who had even heard of him; yet, suddenly, there he was in her mind, as alive as he had ever been, which was not saying much.

When she went closer to read the tram-car's particulars, she was startled, for it was one of Camber's own old tram-cars. There had never been many of them and she must have ridden in this one dozens of times. It had probably taken her again and again to Mr Limestone's door and now, by some afflatus of its own, it had conjured up the man himself. It had said across the floor: 'Limestone', yet she would not have recognized it as a Camber tram-car.

Giving herself distance as though in front of a painting, she viewed the car from the front. She was struck by its elegance. With that tall, narrow prow it might have been built, like a clipper, for speed; instead, it had been a mere public conveyance, scarcely able to get under way before once more grinding to a halt.

The line had run from the north of Camber to the Pier. The tram simply went straight down and back again. She and Edward had called it 'the brown tram' to distinguish it from the green, open-topped tram that went into the country; but now she saw it was not brown at all; it was maroon. The maroon outer casing was beautifully bright. Inside, the slatted honey-coloured seats were polished like satin, the brass-work shone. In its present shape, it was as much a museum piece as some hand-made engine of Victorian times. It certainly had not looked like this when she and Edward, a critical, impatient pair, had watched it come swinging and pinging through the dusty sunlight, or ploughing, like some lighted bathysphere, the sea-blue murk of a winter's afternoon.

Mr Limestone lived half-way between the termini. The Worples were in north Camber, which Emily condemned as 'a nothing place', and when the tram left her at Mr Limestone's door and went on to the sea and pier and the promenade where the band played on Sundays, she wished she were going with it.

The Limestones' house, a carmine semi-detached with yellow brickwork, was finer than the Worples' house, at least on the outside. It had a front garden where a wooden palette stood on an easel and told passers-by that Mr Limestone was a dentist. Because of the palette there was a general belief that Mr Limestone was 'artistic'. Nothing was said about his being a children's dentist but the patients — and these were few enough — all seemed to be children.

There was a dentist in north Camber, but someone had told Mrs Worple that Mr Limestone was good with children. In those early days, when she had to accompany her children, she took the long tram journey in the belief that he, and he alone, could 'manage' them. She boasted that she could not manage them herself, a fact for which she apportioned blame equally between them and their father. Of course there had been uproar before she could persuade them to a first visit. She described the awful remorse suffered by grown-ups who neglected their teeth in childhood: 'You wouldn't like false teeth, would you?' she demanded. 'Why not?' said Edward: 'False teeth don't ache.' When nothing else would move them, she promised them two bars of chocolate apiece. As most occasions began with threats and ended with chocolate bars, the years ahead were filled with visits to Mr Limestone.

Mr Limestone had another virtue: he was cheap. It took him months, years even, to concoct his account, and then several items would be forgotten. But small though his accounts were, and overdue, they led to painful discussions about money and Mrs Worple would say that Emily and Edward did not appreciate the sacrifices that were being made for them.

'In my young day,' she said, 'children looked up to their parents. They were grateful for being alive.'

'I bet,' said Edward, bringing from Mrs Worple the bitter comment:

'Unruly children!'

This riposte, a favourite of hers, dated back to the time when a Mr Greening, a business acquaintance of Mr Worple, had called on the Worples at tea-time and been invited to join them at the table. He was a stout, pompous man who did most of the talking, and while he talked his moustache waggled in a manner that gripped the attention of the children. At first they watched, scarcely believing, then dire amusement set in. They began to laugh until, losing control, their laughter became wild. When Mrs Worple frowned at them, they exploded helplessly and rolled round and round in their chairs. It slowly came to Mr Greening that he, of all people, was the cause of this shocking exhibition. He looked at Mr Worple, but Mr Worple had a weakness. It was a serious weakness of a sort that had been unknown in fathers when Mrs Worple was young. Whenever Emily and Edward started to laugh, Mr Worple had to laugh, too.

He did his best to admonish them: 'Now, Emily,' he said, 'Now, Edward,' but he was already beginning to shake and his face was red and his eyes damp with the effort to suppress his laughter.

Emily's voice rose in a shriek: 'Listen to daddy trying to talk like mummy,' and both children collapsed on the table, weeping in an anguish of mirth.

It was then that Mr Greening, observing them with disgust,

said 'Unruly children!' and Mrs Worple was deeply impressed.
Although he never came back to the Worples' house, she
remembered him as a champion against her unsatisfactory
husband and intolerable children. If he had not made his
historic indictment, she might never have realized the extent
of her own grievance. When things were at their worst –
which usually meant, when some *jeu d'esprit* thrown off by one
of them had thrown both into hysterics – she would say, as
though the phrase might quell them: 'Unruly children!'

In view of this, it was all the more remarkable that Mr
Limestone, with nothing but his professional mystery, could
manage them. He did not look like a manager. Mrs Worple
gave him one look and began to say, 'I'm afraid you'll find
them very difficult. I don't know why they behave so badly.
I'm sure they couldn't have a better home.'

Mr Limestone murmured 'Oh, yes?' without interest, and
the children felt he was on their side.

He was so small that they outgrew him in no time. He was
pale, with sandy hair and a nose that looked over-large
because it was almost the whole of his face. His cheeks, brow
and chin seemed to have receded, leaving the nose in possession. His shoulders, too, had shrunk so his white jackets were
all too big for him and his collar always stood out at the back
as though a hand had seized him by the scruff. He was gentle,
but never smiled. Emily and Edward, used to their father's
quick response, sometimes tried to entertain Mr Limestone,
but it meant nothing to him. Whether he heard them or not,
he remained melancholy, perhaps intent on more serious
things.

When he had to drill a tooth, he kept up a reassuring
murmur of 'There, there, shan't be long now,' and at the
slightest wince or whimper, he withdrew the cutting point,
saying 'Easy does it. No hurry. We'll just take a little rest,'
then he would go and browse among his instruments. The
danger was that he might wander out of the room and not
come back for half an hour or more. Once, returning and

finding Emily, miserable prisoner of the chair, he said as though he had been seeking her all over the house, 'Oh, that's where you are!'

Unlike most other people in those spacious times, the Limestones did not keep a maid. The front door was opened by Mrs Limestone with her pink, empty, melted face above a long neck, a lace blouse and a lace-edged apron. She acted as assistant when her husband was forced to extract a tooth, an extreme measure that he would avoid whenever possible, and would show her strength by letting the patient grip her hand and by wordlessly guiding the movements of Mr Limestone whose fear was such he scarcely knew what he was doing.

When she was home, she kept an eye on the waiting-room and saw that no one was forgotten. When she was out, anything might happen. Once Emily had arrived for a three o'clock appointment and getting no answer, had been about to go when the door was opened by Mr Limestone, hair towsled, eyes pink like those of a white rabbit, who hoarsely whispered, 'Yes, what is it?' Then, recognizing Emily, he put her into the waiting-room where another patient, a small boy, was curled up asleep in a chair. 'Won't be a minute,' Mr Limestone said and left them, and there they remained, Emily and the sleeping boy, until Mrs Limestone came back at five o'clock. 'Better go home,' Mrs Limestone said, waking the boy and packing them off as though she scarcely knew what she might find below.

Emily had spent so long in the waiting-room, she could have listed every item in it. The wall-paper was aflash with shaded squares, orange, fawn and brown. A large yellowish table crowded the centre of the room. It was littered with old copies of *Little Folks* and surrounded by eight straight-backed chairs whose leatherette seats were as good as new. No one sat in them. The children always threw themselves into the broken-down, tapestry arm-chairs that stood, one on either side of the fireplace. Though the grate held nothing but crumpled red paper, the whole area of the fireplace was hung with brass toasting-forks, chestnut pans and ornamental bellows, and there were so many fire-irons, dogs and hobs, it was scarcely possible to fit in the little electric fire which held a bar of heat on very cold days.

On either side of the chimney-breast there were built-in cupboards which, Emily early discovered, were filled with grown-up books. It was years before she took them out and looked at them. On the shelves above the cupboards there were, beside the electro-plated toast-racks, jam-dishes and other useful unused objects, statuettes of tall girls leading Alsatian dogs and small girls cuddling bunnies.

The years passed and there were changes outside in Camber, but none in the waiting-room. Even in Camber nothing changed completely. The tram-cars gave way to buses but the buses followed the arbitrary route of the tram-lines that were still there under the tarmac and could be seen in places when the tarmac rubbed away. The Band of Hope Hall opposite Mr Limestone's house was turned into a cinema, but when the Council permitted it to open on Sunday, the massed Baptist choirs sang outside, making so much noise that people asked for their money back.

As for Emily, waiting in the waiting-room, she had started to rummage in the fireside cupboards, hoping the hidden books would help her to solve some of life's mysteries. They did solve mysteries, but not those of this world. They all treated of one subject: Spiritualism.

At first Emily was excited by them. She had been discouraged by the picture of Heaven given at St Luke's, Camber (N), and had rejected it as soon as she discovered Bernard Shaw. Now she found that people called mediums were in direct touch with the Other Side and showed it to be nothing like the boring hymn-singing Heaven of St Luke's. In fact, the spirits revealed, the Other Side was much like this Side, only nicer. Innocent pleasures enjoyed here by the few, could there be enjoyed by everyone. Supposing, one writer said, you occasionally indulge in the luxury of a cigar! On the Other

Side you had only to wish for a cigar and a box of the Very Best would appear in your hand.

'Chocolates, too,' Emily hoped.

The *mise en scène* where these wonders occurred was all green lawns, trees, roses, lilies, crystal fountains, sweet breezes and balmy airs. Book after book assured the reader that the Other Side was a garden set in perpetual summer. 'It's beautiful,' the mediums said: 'Everything's beautiful.'

'And then what happens?' Emily wondered, but nothing, it seemed, happened. The Other Side was as static as the garden painted on the safety curtain at the Pier concert hall, and soon it looked to Emily just as dusty and faded.

Between visits, caught up in the rough and tumble of reality, she forgot the spirit world, but when she returned to the Limestones' waiting-room, she would remember the nectar of the Hereafter and feel drawn back to it and read avidly a while, then find it as insipid as before.

In one book a seance was described for those who, like Emily, knew nothing of procedure. When she learnt that the researchers sat round a dining-room table, she looked anew at the Limestones' table and imagined them sitting round it, fingers touching, and Mr Limestone with head raised and eyes shut, saying in his sad little voice, 'It's beautiful. Everything's beautiful.'

Emily now towered over Mr Limestone and, feeling there was something ridiculous about their relationship, she resented the hours wasted in the waiting-room and said she should go to a grown-up dentist. Soon it became what Mrs Worple called 'a battle' to get her to go at all, and the battle became grim when Emily was invited to Lilac Mittens' birthday party on the same half-term afternoon that had been appointed for a session with Mr Limestone. Emily demanded that the appointment be changed. Mrs Worple refused to change it.

Though she boasted of her inability to control her children, Mrs Worple could on occasions be adamant. These occasions always related to any suggested alteration in the scheme of things. She could not bear a picture, ornament or piece of furniture to be moved from its place in the household. Arrangements made for the future must not be unmade. Appointments that had been made by letter had a rigidity all their own. Nothing would induce Mrs Worple to write to Mr Limestone and change Emily's appointment, and it was a measure of Emily's immaturity that she dare not write herself or fail to keep it. As a last resort, she burst into tears and Mrs Worple hit back by raising her eyes to heaven and asking, 'Haven't I borne enough?'

When she addressed the Almighty, Mrs Worple would do so in an anguished wail that always defeated Emily. So Emily argued no more, but when the afternoon came she set out early, wearing her party frock under her coat, determined to get Mr Limestone over and done with. Mrs Limestone appeared at the door with her hat on. A bad omen. Emily appealed to her in a confiding manner: 'I'm going to a party, Mrs Limestone. Do you think Mr Limestone could do my tooth straight away?'

'We'll see,' Mrs Limestone said, not committing herself, but she went straight down to the basement where Mr Limestone had his being, and a few minutes later, he appeared, abject, in a newly starched jacket, his wife at his heels, self-satisfied and a little breathless as though she had taken him by the collar and pushed him up the stairs. She now had on her rat-grey coat and imitation silver-fox fur: 'I'm off,' she said, and off she went.

Mr Limestone said resignedly, 'Come along, Emily,' and led the way to the back room where the blue plush dental chair stood in the chilly, silvery light of the half frosted window. The upper pane that sometimes held the distraction of clouds, held nothing now but the flat, grey February sky.

Emily, sitting down, tried to hurry Mr Limestone by mentioning the party. Not listening, he said: 'Put your head back. Open your mouth. *There's* a good girl,' and went with maddening slowness from tooth to tooth. He tapped with his mirror: 'That one ought to come out.' The tooth, crowded sideways into Emily's lower jaw, had been condemned months before and Mr Limestone would never have the nerve to pull it unsupported by his wife. When Emily said nothing, he sighed and moved on to the tooth that had to be filled. Changing the mirror for a sort of button-hook, he picked for several minutes at the decay before saying sombrely: 'I'll have to cut it.'

Snatching at his natural unwillingness to act, she said, 'I could come another time.' He reflected deeply, then said with decision:

'No. Let's get it over.'

He packed her mouth with cotton-wool, an exacting process, then brought over the drill. Knowing that any squeak or shudder would delay the operation, Emily gripped the chair-arms and watched Mr Limestone's nose that moved, too close for comfort, like a half moon around her vision. She could smell the peppermint which he sucked to sustain himself while he worked. Her fortitude was such that he said several times: 'There's a brave girl,' then: 'I think that will do. It's only a small cavity.'

The worst over, Emily relaxed, thinking that even Mr Limestone must soon be done, but it was amazing how long it took him to mix the little dab of filling. As he bent to apply it, hand trembling with creative effort, his anxiety was such that he swallowed his peppermint. He pushed and scraped at the filling, breathing loudly, taking so long that when he stepped back to survey his handiwork, Emily was ready to leap from the chair.

'We're not finished yet,' he warned her and she reluctantly put her head back on the rest and reopened her mouth.

Mr Limestone went to his table and searched among his equipment. He came back with a sliver of whalebone which he wedged between the newly filled tooth and its neighbour, saying: 'Don't touch that. I want the filling to dry out. It's very important it shouldn't be disturbed.'

Gagged with cotton-wool and whalebone, Emily watched Mr Limestone to see he did not leave the room. Should he try to go, she was ready, or almost ready, to jump down and seize him. Yet he got away. One moment he was replacing his instruments in their box, the next he had gone. He went so quickly, quietly and suddenly, he seemed to dissolve among the shadows at the door. She gave a cry, but too late. She listened.

Sometimes, when Mrs Limestone was home, there could be heard slight creaks and murmurs from the rooms below. Now there was no sound at all.

She felt tricked and could do nothing but wait. The waiting went on and on. There were no clocks in the waiting-room or surgery, no means of measuring time except by the change in the light. As she watched the sky turn from grey to pewter, she began to panic.

The party began at four-thirty and tea was at five. In Emily's circle it was not correct to arrive late, and one could lose by doing so. Emily had been late for the first meeting of the Drama Club and found that the elocution mistress had cast the play and left no part for her. She had never got over that and the rebuff may, for all she knew, have destroyed her chance of becoming a great actress. It was possible that Lilac's party had already begun and she sat in agony, imagining the bright room, the talk, the expectation, the brilliance of it all.

At last, unable to bear more, she sat up and considered her position. The silence was such, Mr Limestone might have sunk down into the grave; yet he must be somewhere in the house. As the shadows deepened about her, she began to imagine him down in the basement with his hands on the table, his eyes shut, his little pale face raised as he whispered to himself, 'It's beautiful. Everything's beautiful.' Fearful, she longed for Mrs Limestone to come back. 'Oh, Mrs Limestone,' she pleaded in her solitude, '*please* ask Mr Limestone to finish my tooth!' But Mrs Limestone did not come.

Growing desperate, Emily did what she had never done

before: she disobeyed Mr Limestone. First she took the soaking cotton-wool out of her mouth, then she touched the whalebone filament. It was firmly fixed between the teeth and protruded so slightly, she could not get a grip on it. She might have gone, whalebone and all, but without the protecting cotton-wool, the filament cut into her lip.

She sat for some minutes on the chair edge, listening to silence, giving Mr Limestone a last chance, then she slid down and tip-toed into the hall. She leant over the basement stairs and called in a small voice, 'Mr Limestone.' There was not a breath below.

Had he abandoned her completely? Had he left the house? She descended a few steps and spoke his name more boldly. Her voice died and not a sound returned to her. She went down further, breathing the lower air redolent with cooking-fat and old floor-cloths, and saw through the shadows in the passage a daylight glimmer from a half-open door. When she paused again, she knew he was there. She could hear him breathing.

She stood, daunted by the fact he did not answer, then it occurred to her that he might be ill. He may have fainted or had a heart attack or a stroke. With this excuse for trespass, she ran on down, ready to save Mr Limestone's life. The half-open door led to the kitchen. She saw a scrubbed deal table, an old dresser, a gas-stove, a sink − but no Mr Limestone. Yet he was near. His breathing came more loudly. An inner door led to a scullery or pantry and knowing he must be there, she advanced cautiously until she could see inside. And there he was. An old dental chair, its plush bursting and spilling the interior wadding, stood inside the door and Mr Limestone was sitting in it. She edged round to view him and saw his head propped on the rest, his eyes shut, his breath puffing out between his parted lips. His expression, tranquil, almost felicitous, told her he was not ill. He must be asleep; and before going to sleep, he had pulled up the sleeve of his white jacket and thrust a hypodermic needle into his arm. His poor, thin, little arm lay on his lap with the tip of the needle still clinging to the flesh.

What an extraordinary thing to do! Having a dislike of injections herself, Emily edged nearer, repelled and bewildered, yet curious, and at her movement, Mr Limestone's eyelids fluttered. He gave her an unseeing glance then seemed to sleep again.

She said, 'I must go, Mr Limestone. I'm invited to a party,' and for the first time in their long acquaintance, Mr Limestone smiled. His smile was joyous, as though he had already reached the Other Side where pleasures were innocent and everything was beautiful.

In front of him, on a work-table, there were some small tools and a row of false teeth set in ruby gums and mounted on a base of chalk. Among the tools Emily saw a pair of pliers and, stretching round Mr Limestone's chair, she picked these up and used them to pluck the whalebone cleanly from between her teeth. Her relief was such, she became flippant and said with a giggle:

'I'm sorry, Mr Limestone. I couldn't wait.'

As she spoke, the front door banged on the floor above and the sound sobered Mr Limestone. He did not wake, but his smile was gone in an instant. Emily, guilty, an intruder who must not be discovered, fled from the kitchen and made her escape through the back garden door. Running round the side of the house, she jumped on a bus and reached Lilac's party just as the guests were going in to tea.

Imagining she would be at fault, Emily decided to tell her mother nothing of this episode, but somehow it all came out.

Mrs Worple was surprisingly indignant: 'I sometimes thought . . . I suspected,' she said: 'Well, what a disgraceful thing!'

'What do you mean?' Emily asked. Mrs Worple would say no more but when Emily next complained of Mr Limestone's slowness, her mother at once agreed it was time for both the children to attend a 'grown-up' dentist. They never saw Mr Limestone again.

Almost at once he disappeared from Emily's mind and it was only now, twenty years later, that she remembered and understood Mr Limestone's blissful smile. Her mother had disapproved, yet Emily could not disapprove. His may not have been an innocent pleasure, yet it seemed to her the pleasure of the innocent.

She came to the end of the Transport Museum feeling she had had enough of the past. She had had enough of Mr Limestone, too. Faced with the Clapham traffic and the struggle to get home, she turned her back on his memory and said again, 'I must go, Mr Limestone.'

After a moment she thought to add 'Good-bye.' And that was all she could say to Mr Limestone in an age that had given up innocence and received nothing in return.

The Wrong Vocation

'When God calls you, he is never denied' Sister Mercy told us with a finality which struck terror into our hearts.

She stood at the front of the room with the window behind her, so we were blinded and could not see her features but we knew she smiled.

'He waits patiently until we hear his voice. When that happens, you are never the same.'

It terrified me that this thing called a vocation might come dropping in to my mind out of nowhere one day and wedge there like a piece of grit.

'God is looking now, seeing who is pure of heart and ready to be offered up.'

Every girl shifted uncomfortably. Sister looked at our upturned faces and seemed pleased with the effect she was having. By way of illustration she told us about a young woman from a rich home who was always laughing, with young men waiting to escort her here, there and everywhere, and a big family house with chandeliers in the rooms and a lake in the garden.

'I've seen it. It was on the telly the other night,' Nancy Lyons whispered to me.

'With all these good things in life, she was spoiled. Her wealthy father indulged his daughter's every wish. And do you think she was happy?'

'She damned well ought to be,' Nancy hissed while around us the more pious members of the form shook their heads.

Sister placed her bony hands across her chest and stood up

on her tiptoes as if reaching with her rib cage for something that would constantly evade it.

'Her heart was empty.'

Sister went on to tell us how the young woman resisted the call, but eventually realized she would never be happy until she devoted her life to Christ. Going out beside the lake, she asked him to enter her life.

'She is one of our very own nuns, right here in this convent. Of course I cannot tell you which sister she is, but when you imagine that we were all born as nuns, remember that we were once young girls like yourselves, without a thought in our heads that we should devote our lives to God.'

There was a silence. We all stared out past her head.

'Oh, Sister, it's beautiful,' said a voice. Nancy rolled her eyes to heaven. Lumpy, boring Beatrice who always sat at the front would like it. She was so slow-witted and so good. She was one of the least popular girls in the class, a reporter of bad news and always the first to give homework in. With mini skirts *de rigueur*, her uniform remained stoically unadapted. She must have been the only girl in the school that did not need to have her hemline checked at the end of the day. While we struggled to turn over our waistbands Beatrice always wore her skirt a good two inches below her plump knees and looked like one of the early photographs, all sepia and foggy, of the old girls in their heyday.

Nancy pulled a face.

'But wasn't her rich father angry?' someone asked, and Sister Mercy nodded.

'Mine would sodding kill me. They don't even want me to stay on at school. Me mother's always reminding me how much money they're losing because I'm not bringing any wages home.'

'Do you have something to say, Nancy Lyons?' Sister's stern voice rapped.

'No Sister, I was just saying what a great sacrifice it was to make.'

'Ah yes, a great sacrifice indeed.'

But the sacrifice was not just on the nun's part. Everyone else was made to suffer. There was a woman in our street who never recovered after her eldest daughter joined the Carmelites. Mrs Roddy's daughter was a teacher in the order. It was not the fact that she would never give her mother grandchildren that caused the greatest upset, but the economics of it. All a nun's earnings go straight back into the convent. Mrs Roddy used to wring her hands.

'That money's mine,' she would shout, 'for feeding and clothing her all those years. The church has no right to it!'

Then her daughter went peculiar. We only noticed because they sent her home for a week on holiday, and we thought that was unusual, but it was around the time they were relaxing the rule. Nuns were appearing on the streets with skirts that let them walk easily, skimming their calves instead of the pavement.

During that week she got her cousin to perm her hair, on account of the new headdress. She assured her that it was all right because even nuns had to look groomed now their hair showed at the front, and every night she continued to lead the family in the joyful mysteries.

'I'll tell you Mrs Mac, I'm worn out with all the praying since our Delcia's been back,' her mother would confide to mine as they passed quickly in the street, while her daughter muttered 'God bless you' to no one in particular and with a vague smile.

But indoors, she borrowed her mother's lipstick, deep red because Mrs Roddy still had the same one from before the war. That was when they thought she was going a bit far, when they saw her outmoded, crimson mouth chanting the rosary. She drove her family mad. She had tantrums and kept slamming doors. Then they saw her out in the street asking to be taken for rides on Nessie Moran's motorbike. Everyone said she had taken her vows too young. She crammed all those teenage things she never did into that week. By the end of it they were relieved to send her back.

Her mother hated nuns. She did not mind priests half as much.

'At least they're human' she would say. 'Well, half human. Nuns aren't people. They're not proper women. They don't know what it is to be a mother and they'll never be high up in the church. They'll never be the next pope. They can't even say mass. What good are they? They're stuck in the middle, not one thing or the other. Brides of Christ! They make me sick. Let them try cooking, cleaning and running a home on nothing. I'd have a damned easier life if I'd married Christ, instead of that lazy bugger inside.'

But she was fond of the young priest at her church, a good looking, fresh faced man from Antrim who would sit and have a drink with them at the parish club.

'At least you can have a laugh with him,' she'd say, 'but that stuck up lot, they're all po-faced up at Saint Ursula's. They're no better than any of us. I'm a woman, don't I know what their minds are like. They're no different. Gossipy, unnatural creatures, those ones are. Look what's happened to our poor Delcia after being with them.'

And then the convent sent Delcia home to be looked after by her family. An extended holiday they called it, on account of her stress and exhaustion.

'They've used her up, now they don't want what's left over, so I've got her again. What good is she to anyone now? She can't look after herself. She can't even make a bloody cup of tea. How will she fend for herself if the order won't have her back? I'm dying, Mrs Mac, I can't be doing with her.'

My mother would tut and nod and shut the door.

'It's a shame. What sort of a life has that poor girl had?' she would say indoors, shaking her head at the tragedy.

'I know she's gone soft now, but she was good at school. Her mam and dad thought she'd be something and now she's fit for nothing if the church can't keep her.'

In the evening we would hear Mrs Roddy shouting 'Get in off the street!'

Finally they took her into a hospice and we heard no more about it, but Mrs Roddy always crossed the road to avoid nuns. Once outside Lewis's a Poor Clare thrust a collection box at her and asked for a donation. Mrs Roddy tried to take it from her and the box was pulled back and forth like a bird tugging at a worm. It was not the nun's iron grip, but the bit of elastic which wrapped itself around her wrist that foiled Mrs Roddy's attempt to redistribute the church's wealth.

'They're just like vultures,' she would say, 'waiting to see what they can tear from your limbs. They're only happy when they've picked you clean. Better hide your purses!'

At the collection on Sundays she sat tight lipped and the servers knew better than to pass the collecting plate her way.

'A vocation gone wrong,' was what my father called Delcia Roddy. He would shake his head from side to side and murmur things like 'the shame' or 'the waste'. He had a great deal of sympathy for her tortured soul. It was about this time that I became tortured. He had none for me.

Sister Mercy's words had stung like gravel in a grazed knee. At night I could hear them as her voice insisted, 'You cannot fight God's plan,' and I would pray that God keep his plans to himself.

'You must pray for a vocation,' she told us.

I gritted my teeth and begged His Blessed Mother to intervene.

'I'll be worse than the Roddy girl,' I threatened, 'and look what a disgrace she was.' Then, echoing the epitaph of W. B. Yeats, I would point into the darkness and urge 'Horseman; Pass by!'

'We are instruments of God's will,' Sister Mercy told us and I did not want to be an instrument.

I knew if God had any sense he would not want me, but Sister Mercy frightened us. Beatrice was the one headed for a convent. She had made plain her intentions at the last retreat when she stood up and announced to the study group that she was thinking of devoting her life to Christ.

'She may as well, there's nothing else down for her,' Nancy commented.

Yet Sister Mercy told us that often the ones we did not suspect had vocations, and she looked around the room like a mind-reader scrutinizing the audience before pulling out likely candidates.

The convent terrified me; the vocation stalked my shadow like a store detective. One day it would pounce and I would be deadlocked into a religious life, my will subsumed by one greater than I. Up there was a rapacious appetite which consumed whole lives, like chicken legs. I dreaded that I should end up in a place where every day promised the same, the gates locked behind me and all other escape sealed off. It wasn't that I had any ambitions for what I might do, but I could not happily reconcile myself to an existence where the main attraction was death. I dreaded hearing God's call.

'He can wait for years. God is patient.'

I decided that I would have to exasperate him, and fast.

Down at the Pier Head, pigeons gathered in thousands. The Liver Buildings were obscured as they all rose in unison like a blanket of grey and down. I never knew where my fear came from, but I was terrified of those birds. Harmless seagulls twice their size flew about me, followed the ferry out across the water to Birkenhead and landed flapping and breathless on the landing plank. Their screech was piercing. They never disturbed me. Yet when I stepped out into Hamilton Square and saw the tiny cluster of city birds waiting, my heart would beat in panic. City birds who left slime where they went, their excrement the colour of the new granite buildings springing up. They nodded their heads and watched you out of the corners of their eyes. They knocked smaller birds out of the way and I had seen them taking bread away from each other. They were a fighting, quarrelsome brood, an untidy shambling army, with nothing to do all day but walk around the Pier Head or follow me through Princess Park and make my life a misery.

Once I was crossing for a bus, just as a streak of them flew up into the air. I put my hands over my head, the worst fear being that one should touch my face, and I could think of nothing more sickening than the feel of one of these ragged creatures, bloated with disease, the flying vermin which flocked around the Life Assurance building, to remind us we were mortal.

I had a nightmare at the time of being buried alive under thousands of these birds. They would make that strange cooing noise as they slowly suffocated me. Their fat greasy bodies would pulsate and swell, as satiated, they nestled down onto me for the heat my body could provide. Under this sweltering, stinking mass I would be unable to scream. Each time I opened my mouth it filled with dusty feathers.

Then my nightmare changed. Another element crept into my dreams. Alongside the pigeons crept the awful shape that was a vocation. It came in all colours, brown and white, black and white, beige, mottled, grey and sandy, as the different robes of each order clustered around me, knocking pigeons out of the way. They muttered snatches of Latin, bits of psalms, and rubbed their clawed hands together like bank-tellers. The big change in the dream was that they, unlike the pigeons, did not suffocate me, but slowly drew away, leaving me alone in a great empty space, which at first I thought was the bus terminal, but which Nancy Lyons assured me was the image of my life to be.

Her older sister read tea leaves and was very interested in dreams. Nancy borrowed a book from her.

'It says here, that dreaming about water means a birth.'

'I was dreaming about pigeons, and then nuns.'

'Yeah, but you said you were down at the Pier Head didn't you, and that's water.'

'I don't know if I was at the Pier Head.'

'Oh you must have been. Where else would you get all them pigeons?' Nancy was a realist. 'Water means a birth,' she repeated firmly. 'I bet your mam gets pregnant.'

I knew she was wrong. I was the last my mother would ever have, she told me often enough. But Nancy would not be put off. The book was lacking on nuns so she held out for the water and maintained that the big empty space was my future.

'There's nothing down for you unless you go with the sisters,' she said.

It was not because I lacked faith that I dreaded the vocation. I suffered from its excesses, it hung around me, watching every move, and passing judgement. I was a failed miserable sinner and I knew it, but I did not want to atone. I did not want the empty future I was sure it offered. Our interpretation of the dream differed.

Around this time I had a Saturday job in a delicatessen in town. I was on the cold-meat counter. None of the girls were allowed to touch the bacon slicer. Only Mister Calderbraith could do that. He wore a white coat and must have fancied himself as an engineer the way he carried on about the gauge of the blades. He would spend hours unscrewing the metal plates and cleaning out the bolts and screws with a look of extreme concentration on his face.

His balding head put out a few dark strands of hair which he grew to a ludicrous length and wore combed across his scalp to give the impression of growth. Some of the girls said he wore a toupee after work, and that if we were to meet him on a Sunday we would not know him.

He used to pretend he was the manager. He would come over and ask customers solicitously if everything was all right and remark that if the service was slow, it was because he was breaking in new staff.

'Who does he think he's kidding!' Elsie said after he had leaned across the counter one morning. 'He couldn't break in his shoes.'

Shoes were a problem. I was on my feet all day, and they would ache by the time we came to cash up. I used to catch the bus from the Pier Head at around five-thirty, if I could get the glass of the counter wiped down and the till cashed. The manager and seniors were obsessed with dishonesty. Cashing up had to be done in strict military formation. None of us were allowed to move until we heard a bell and the assistant manager would take the cash floats from us in silence.

Inside his glass office the manager sat on a high stool with mirrors all around him, surveying us. If any of the girls sneezed, or moved out of synch another bell would sound and we would all have to instantly shut our tills while the manager shouted over the loudspeaker system, 'Disturbance at counter number four' or wherever it was. Sometimes it took ages.

They never failed to inform us that staff were all dishonest. Not the management, Mister Calderbraith or senior staff, but the floor workers, and especially the temporary staff, the Saturday workers, because as they told us, we had the least to lose, and we were 'fly by nights' according to the manager, who grinned as he told us that.

I could not imagine anything there worth stealing. It was all continental meats and strange cheeses that smelt strongly, the mouldier the better.

'Have you seen that bread they're selling?' Elsie said to me one Saturday.

'The stuff that looks like it's got mouse droppings on top?'

But people came from all over the city and placed orders.

One Saturday evening I was waiting for the next bus having missed the five-thirty. My feet ached. The manager would not let you sit down. Even when there were no customers in sight you were supposed to stand to attention. I took it in turns with Elsie to duck beneath the wooden counter supports and sit on the floor when business was slack. Whenever Mister Calderbraith was about, we both stood rigidly. He loathed serving customers.

'See to that lady,' he would say if anyone asked him for a quarter of liver sausage.

I had worn the wrong shoes, they had heels. Throughout the week I wore comfortable brown lace-ups, but at the weekend I wanted to wear things that did not scream 'school-girl'. But my mother had been right. I was crippled.

After a few minutes I leant back on the rail and kicked one shoe off. My toes looked puffy and red. I put that one back and kicked off the other. It shot into the gutter. Before I had a chance to hop after it, a pigeon the size of a cat flapped down and stood between it and me. It looked at me, then slowly began to walk around the shoe. I was rigid, gripping the rail and keeping my foot off the pavement. Then the bird hopped inside the shoe and seemed to settle as a hen might in a nest. It began to coo. I was perspiring. I would never be able to take the shoe from it, and even if I managed to I would not be able to put my foot inside after that vile creature had sat in it. I was desperate. Suddenly, as if it sensed my fright, it flew up in the air towards me almost brushing my face with its wings, then it circled and landed squarely back inside the shoe. I did not wait. It could have it. I hopped away from the bus stop and limped towards the taxi stand. I reckoned I had just enough money to get a cab home. It would be all my pay for the Saturday, and I would not be able to go out that night, but I did not care. It would take me, shoeless, right to the front door and away from the pigeon.

Then, I thought it was my mind playing tricks, but I saw three shapes blowing in the breeze, veils flapping behind them. The Pier Head was so windy, I thought they might become airborne. They got bigger and bigger. I was certain that they flew. Soon they would be right on top of me. God was giving me a sign. The Vocation had decided to swoop after so long pecking into my dreams. Three silent figures, as mysterious as the Trinity, crossed the tarmac of the bus terminal. I could not take my eyes from them. They seemed to swell the way a pigeon puffs out its chest to make itself important. They were getting fatter and rounder like brown and white balloons. Carmelites. I could not stay where I was. I had to escape. Some people moved to one side as I hobbled to a grass verge. I tripped on the concrete rim of the grassy area and caught my ankle. As I put my hand down to catch myself, several birds pecking on rubbish, rose into the air just in front of me, and I thought for one deluded second that I was flying with them as the white sky span and I tumbled over. Only when my head came level with a brown paper carrier bag did I smell the grossly familiar scent of cold meats.

'Young lady, are you in some sort of difficulty?'

The voice of Mister Calderbraith pulled me out of my terrified stupor. I lifted my head and came eye to quizzical eye.

'Whatever is wrong with you? Can't you walk properly? Good heavens, what has happened to your shoe? Have you been in some sort of incident?' He straightened up and looked around desperately.

'Tell me who did it,' he insisted. 'Check that you still have your front door keys.'

I raised myself up on one knee and obediently opened my bag. Everything was intact. Mister Calderbraith's eyes opened wide.

'I really don't understand . . .' he began.

Behind him I could see a triangle formation moving against the empty sky. The three sisters seemed to glide inside its rigid outline like characters in the medals people brought back from Fatima. Behind them flapped wings, veils, patches of brown, and feathers. Dark against the white sky they enveloped me, just as my dream had forewarned. I could not speak. My hands shook.

'What is it? Have you seen the culprit?'

I nodded, still struggling to rise.

'They often work in a gang, these hoodlums,' Mister Calderbraith continued. 'Oh, yes. I've watched enough detective programmes to know how they operate.' He glanced from side to side furtively.

'They've probably left their lookout nearby. Acting casual.' He glowered menacingly at the passers-by.

They were closing in behind Mister Calderbraith. They peered over his shoulder. Inhuman, they cheeped and shrieked. I could not understand a thing. Mister Calderbraith nodded at me, his head pecking up and down. I reached out and pointed and a dreadful magnetic force pulled me towards them. I was on my feet in seconds.

Mister Calderbraith turned round and saw the three. He shrank away from them.

'You don't mean these, surely?' he said. 'That is stretching it. Have you been drinking? Tell me, were you on relief at the spirit counter?'

'She's had a bit of a fall,' a passer-by said.

'I think she fell on her head,' Mister Calderbraith nodded.

Then turning to the spectators who had crossed from the bus shelter, he reassured them that everything was all right.

'She is one of my staff members, it's all under control. I know this young lady. Let me deal with it.'

The smallest nun, a tiny frail sparrow, hopped lightly towards me, concern marked by the way she held her head on one side. Her scrawny hand scratched at the ground and she caught up a carrier bag that lay askew on the grass verge. The others clucked solicitously. Then there was a stillness. All fluttering seemed to stop. She handed the bag to me and I took it as my voice returned to tumble out in hopeless apologies while my face burned. Hugging the carrier bag to me, I stumbled towards a taxi which had pulled up. I fell inside and slammed the door. I breathed deeply, thinking that I was going to cry from embarrassment. Out of the back window I could see the nuns standing with Mister Calderbraith who was looking about as if he had lost something.

'Where to, love?' the driver asked.

My voice was thin and wavery as I told him. I put my

head back and sighed. Only when we were halfway along the Dock Road did I realize that I was still hugging the bag. I peered inside. It was stuffed with pieces of meat, slivers of pork and ends of joints, all wrapped up in Mr Calderbraith's sandwich papers. There was a great knuckle of honey roast ham. It would be a sin to waste it.

Then I started to laugh. I couldn't stop. Tears ran down my face. Sister Mercy had told us that we had to be spotless, our souls bleached in God's grace. We had to repent our past and ask Him to take up residence in our hearts. I put my hand into the bag and drew out a piece of meat. I crammed it into my mouth. I swallowed my guilt, ate it whole and let it fill my body. As I chewed I wondered at how I still felt the same. I was no different, only now I had become the receiver of stolen goods. I wondered if Mister Calderbraith would be nicer to me? I would not be surprised if he let me have a go on the bacon slicer, next weekend.

'Are you all right love?' the driver asked.

I was choking on a piece of meat.

'I'm fine,' I coughed, scarcely waiting long enough before I stuffed another bit into my mouth. I ate with frenzied gulping sounds. When I looked up I saw the driver watching me in his mirror.

'God, but you must be starving,' he said.

I nodded.

'Well you're a growing girl. You don't know how lucky you are to have all your life in front of you.'

'I do, I really do,' I told him as I pulled another bit of meat off a bone with my teeth. Between mouthfuls I laughed. My one regret was that it wasn't a Friday – I could have doubled my sin then without any effort. Then I realized that I had subverted three nuns into being accomplices. What more did I need?

I slapped my knees and howled. God would have to be desperate to want me now.

As the taxi pulled up outside the house, I saw the curtains twitch. I did not know how I was going to explain losing my shoe, but nothing could lower my spirits, not even hiccups.

CANDIA McWILLIAM

Sweetie Rationing

'In the main a discriminating man, Davey, would you not say? Not the sort to get in with . . . leave alone engaged to . . .' Mrs McLellan's voice fell and joined those of her companions, good women in woolly tams.

With its freight of sugar ('freight' pronounced 'fright' to rhyme with bite and night in those days when the Clyde was still an ocean-going river), the cake-stand flowered high among the women. At each of the six tables in the tearoom there was such an efflorescence, encircled by blunt knives for spreading the margarine, and white votive cups. The celebrants sat in small groups. They had all been born in another century.

'Old ladies, that's the business. There's always more of them. The men don't hold on the same way. Then there was that war, too.' Erna's mother had told her right when she nagged her to take over the tearoom, even though it meant a move into the city. Erna's mother was known as a widow. Erna had not met her father. He was gone long before he was dead.

'What are you, Mother, if you're no' an old lady?' asked Erna.

'An old woman.'

Erna wondered about the difference. Her mother wore a scarf munitions-factory style and had brass polish round her fingernails from cleaning the number on the front door. Out by the lochan they'd had no number, but good neighbours. Now, in Argyle Street, the old woman went to kirk to get her dose of grudge at whatever new daft thing God had let happen. She had a top half which she kept low down in her apron-bib till the Sabbath, when it went flat under a sateen frock with white bits under the arms in summer and a serviceable coat over that in winter. Erna had always had shoes.

Well, now they had the tearoom, and Erna's mother had silver polish round her fingernails, from all the paraphernalia ladies use to take their tea in style. Cleaning the cake-stands was a long job because of the ornamental bits, curly at the top and four feet like the devil's at the bottom. Without the silver plates for the cakes, three of them getting smaller towards the top, the things were just tall skeletons. The plates were all right to clean. Wire wool made them shine up softly, like metal that has been at sea. Erna's father was said to have been in the Merchant Navy. Erna did not know whether she herself was destined to become an old woman or an old lady. Marriage would tell. It would be soon, she guessed, from the way he was on at her.

At Mrs McLellan's table, the cakes on the bottom level of the cake-stand were almost finished. Not that it would be right to progress upwards until every crumb had gone.

'Discriminating?' Mrs Dalgleish, as though her hand were just a not totally reliable pet she had given shelter among her tweeds, took the penultimate iced fancy. 'You might say that, Mrs McLellan, but I might not.' The last cake, pink like nothing on earth, was reflected in the silver dish which bore it. Its yellow fellow was in the throat of Mrs Dalgleish, and then even more intimately part of her. When she had truly swallowed and licked all possible sugar from her lips and extracted all sweetness from the shimmery silence she had brewed among her friends, she went on.

Miss Dreever, who was excitable, never having been married, could not stop herself; she took the pink cake. She forgot in her access of pleasure to use the silver slice, but impaled it on her cake fork with its one snaggle tooth.

A doubly delicious moment: the ladies were free to progress

up the shaft of sugar and to slip deeper into the story. Mrs Macaulay eased off one of her shoes at the heel. The ladies wore lace-ups perforated all over as though for the leather's own good. They were good shoes and kept up to the mark by shoe trees and Cherry Blossom; the good things in life do not grow on trees. Mrs Dalgleish had at home a shoe-horn, which she sometimes showed the lodgers; the late Mr Dalgleish had given it her, she explained, before he died. Only one lodger had ever dared to respond, 'Not after, Mrs Dalgleish, then?' The shoehorn was to save her bending. 'Though a widow has to do worse things than bend,' Mrs Dalgleish would say. She was not having a joke.

Nor was she today. 'Davey is no more discriminating than any of them when it comes to . . . women. And he's been cooped up in engine rooms for half his natural life. All that oil and steam. Not to mention foreign parts.' Mr Dalgleish too had been to foreign parts, but without the fatal admixture of oil and steam. Davey was an engineer, the sort with prospects. After the war, he'd done university.

'But the girl's not foreign, is she? Is her mother not from Kilmahog? Didn't you say that? And the wean brought up on Loch Lomondside?' Miss Dreever had a grouse-claw brooch which she touched with her own thin hand as she spoke. Since the war, she'd not got about so much, with her mother and the breakdown, but she did pride herself on her penetration beyond the Highland Line. So many people lived in a country and didn't know the half of it.

'Yes, but a father from where, that's what I'm asking myself.' Mrs Dalgleish looked down at her wedding ring. 'Maybe I'll just try one of those coconut kisses.'

She gave a hostess's inclusive smile. 'Will you none of yous join me?'

In stern order of precedence, Miss Dreever last, the lowest in order below the sugar, the ladies took the cakes. The coconut was friable and soapy as Lux flakes, which the ladies hoarded to care for their good woollens. Today, Mrs Macaulay was in a lovat pullover, Mrs Dalgleish in ancient red, and Mrs McLellan (who had always been a redhead) had a heather twinset which had lasted well. Miss Dreever did not dress to please. She had the proper pride not to be eyecatching.

'Would the girl's father be an islander, then, Janice?' Only Mrs McLellan was allowed to call Mrs Dalgleish Janice. Sometimes they took tea in each other's houses. Mrs McLellan had a tiger skin on brown felt backing, which had seen better days not long ago.

Although the second rung of cakes had been reached, Mrs Dalgleish was not sure that the perfect moment for familiarity had arrived.

'Not an islander *or* a Highlander, Ishbel. And now we've all had quite enough of nephew Davey. What of your family, Miss Dreever?'

It was a bony, unappetising topic, though it had to be tackled at some point during these teas. Miss Dreever was an only child. Her fiancé (had he existed? the other ladies wondered) had been killed. No meat there, of the sort at any rate which you could really chew. Certainly no fat.

Miss Dreever's mother could not be discussed in safety because she intermittently went mad which upset Miss Dreever who had been raised in a tenement and bettered herself through reading. What a true relief for her to get out and about like this then, the once a week.

'You know me,' said Miss Dreever, 'always busy. There's Mother and the teaching and there is a chance I'll be the one to take the form outing this year. We're hoping the petrol will stretch to a beauty spot.'

Magnanimous, placated – how dull could be the lives of others – Mrs Dalgleish turned to Miss Dreever and looked at her. She was a poor skinny thing and probably had nothing in the evening but her books. Mrs Dalgleish had any number of activities. She never wasted a thing, not a tin, not a thread; there was all that putting away, all that folding, saving, sorting, to be done. She often had to stay in to do it, specially.

'Miss Dreever, dear, take that cream horn.' Mrs Dalgleish referred to a sweetmeat on the topmost rung of the cake-stand. The horn was of cardboard pastry and the cream was the kind whipped up from marge and hope and dairy memory, but it was a lavish token. The horn stood for plenty. The sugar on it was hardly dusty. In reverse order of precedence, the ladies took their cakes. Mrs Dalgleish was grace itself as she hung back.

Erna took away the teapot and freshened it in the kitchen at the back. She had torn the sole of her shoe jumping on old cans to flatten them for the dustbin man. She was glad she could get away with just drawing a brown line down the back of her leg to look like the seam of a nylon. All those old ladies had gams like white puds, and then there'd be the darning. With her shade skin anyhow she'd no need for stockings. He said so. She'd let him draw the line once, with her eyebrow pencil, but it got dangerous. Then it was her had to draw the line.

'Seemingly,' Mrs Dalgleish said as she distributed the tea, 'seemingly – though it could be talk, to do with which I will as you know have nothing – Davey's girl's father wasn't all he might have been. In the colour department.'

Miss Dreever wondered, in the instant before she understood, whether this future relative by marriage of Mrs Dalgleish could have worked in a paint shop. Then, clear as in a child's primer, came the bright image of a pot of tar, and the soft, dark, touching tarbrush. She bit the sweet horn.

ALICE MUNRO

The Peace of Utrecht

I have been at home now for three weeks and it has not been a success. Maddy and I, though we speak cheerfully of our enjoyment of so long and intimate a visit, will be relieved when it is over. Silences disturb us. We laugh immoderately. I am afraid — very likely we are both afraid — that when the moment comes to say goodbye, unless we are very quick to kiss, and fervently mockingly squeeze each other's shoulders, we will have to look straight into the desert that is between us and acknowledge that we are not merely indifferent; at heart we reject each other, and as for that past we make so much of sharing we do not really share it at all, each of us keeping it jealously to herself, thinking privately that the other has turned alien, and forfeited her claim.

At night we often sit out on the steps of the verandah, and drink gin and smoke diligently to defeat the mosquitoes and postpone until very late the moment of going to bed. It is hot; the evening takes a long time to burn out. The high brick house, which stays fairly cool until midafternoon, holds the heat of the day trapped until long after dark. It was always like this, and Maddy and I recall how we used to drag our mattress downstairs onto the verandah, where we lay counting falling stars and trying to stay awake till dawn. We never did, falling asleep each night about the time a chill drift of air came up off the river, carrying a smell of reeds and the black ooze of the riverbed. At half-past ten a bus goes through the town, not slowing much; we see it go by at the end of our street. It is the same bus I used to take when I came home from college, and I remember coming into Jubilee on some warm night, seeing the earth bare around the massive roots of the trees, the drinking fountain surrounded by little puddles of water on the main street, the soft scrawls of blue and red and orange light that said BILLIARDS and CAFE; feeling as I recognized these signs a queer kind of oppression and release, as I exchanged the whole holiday world of school, of friends and, later on, of love, for the dim world of continuing disaster, of home. Maddy making the same journey four years earlier must have felt the same thing. I want to ask her: is it possible that children growing up as we did lose the ability to believe in – to be at home in – any ordinary and peaceful reality? But I don't ask her; we never talk about any of that. No exorcising here, says Maddy in her thin, bright voice with the slangy quality I had forgotten, we're not going to depress each other. So we haven't.

One night Maddy took me to a party at the Lake, which is about thirty miles west of here. The party was held in a cottage a couple of women from Jubilee had rented for the week. Most of the women there seemed to be widowed, single, separated or divorced; the men were mostly young and unmarried – those from Jubilee so young that I remember them only as little boys in the lower grades. There were two or three older men, not with their wives. But the women – they reminded me surprisingly of certain women familiar to me in my childhood, though of course I never saw their party-going personalities, only their activities in the stores and offices, and not infrequently in the Sunday schools, of Jubilee. They differed from the married women in being more aware of themselves in the world, a little brisker, sharper and coarser (though I can think of only one or two whose respectability was ever in question). They wore resolutely stylish though matronly clothes, which tended to swish and rustle over their hard rubber corsets, and they put perfume, quite a lot of it, on their artificial flowers. Maddy's friends were considerably modernized; they had copper rinses on their hair, and blue eyelids, and a robust capacity for drink.

Maddy I thought did not look one of them, with her slight figure and her still carelessly worn dark hair; her face has grown thin and strained without losing entirely its girlish look of impertinence and pride. But she speaks with the harsh twang of the local accent, which we used to make fun of, and her expression as she romped and drank was determinedly undismayed. It seemed to me that she was making every effort to belong with these people and that shortly she would succeed. It seemed to me too that she wanted me to see her succeeding, to see her repudiating that secret, exhilarating, really monstrous snobbery which we cultivated when we were children together, and promised ourselves, of course, much bigger things than Jubilee.

During the game in which all the women put an article of clothing – it begins decorously with a shoe – in a basket, and then all the men come in and have a race trying to fit things on to their proper owners, I went out and sat in the car, where I felt lonely for my husband and my friends and listened to the hilarity of the party and the waves falling on the beach and presently went to sleep. Maddy came much later and said, 'For heaven's sake!' Then she laughed and said airily like a lady in an English movie, 'You find these goings-on distasteful?' We both laughed; I felt apologetic, and rather sick from drinking and not getting drunk. 'They may not be much on intellectual conversation but their hearts are in the right place, as the saying goes.' I did not dispute this and we drove at eighty miles an hour from Inverhuron to Jubilee. Since then we have not been to any more parties.

But we are not always alone when we sit out on the steps. Often we are joined by a man named Fred Powell. He was at the party, peaceably in the background remembering whose liquor was whose and amiably holding someone's head over the rickety porch railing. He grew up in Jubilee as we did but I do not remember him, I suppose because he went through school some years ahead of us and then went away to the war. Maddy surprised me by bringing him home to supper the first night I was here and then we spent the evening, as we have spent many since, making this strange man a present of our childhood, or of that version of our childhood which is safely preserved in anecdote, as in a kind of mental cellophane. And what fantasies we build around the frail figures of our child-selves, so that they emerge beyond recognition incorrigible and gay. We tell stories together well. 'You girls have got good memories,' Fred Powell says, and sits watching us with an air of admiration and something else — reserve, embarrass-ment, deprecation — which appears on the faces of these mild deliberate people as they watch the keyed-up antics of their entertainers.

Now thinking of Fred Powell I admit that my reaction to this — this *situation* as I call it — is far more conventional than I would have expected; it is even absurd. And I do not know what situation it really is. I know that he is married. Maddy told me so, on the first evening, in a merely informative voice. His wife is an invalid. He has her at the Lake for the summer, Maddy says, he's very good to her. I do not know if he is Maddy's lover and she will never tell me. Why should it matter to me? Maddy is well over thirty. But I keep thinking of the way he sits on our steps with his hands set flat on his spread knees, his mild full face turned almost indulgently toward Maddy as she talks; he has an affable masculine look of being diverted but unimpressed. And Maddy teases him, tells him he is too fat, will not smoke his cigarettes, involves him in private, nervous, tender arguments which have no meaning and no end. He allows it. (And this is what frightens me, I know it now: he allows it; *she needs it*.) When she is a little drunk she says in tones of half-pleading mockery that he is her only real friend. He speaks the same language, she says. Nobody else does. I have no answer to that.

Then again I begin to wonder: *is* he only her friend? I had forgotten certain restrictions of life in Jubilee — and this holds good whatever the pocket novels are saying about small towns — and also what strong, respectable, never overtly sexual friendships can flourish within these restrictions and be fed by them, so that in the end such relationships may consume half a life. This thought depresses me (unconsummated relationships depress outsiders perhaps more than anybody else) so much that I find myself wishing for them to be honest lovers.

The rhythm of life in Jubilee is primitively seasonal. Deaths occur in the winter; marriages are celebrated in the summer. There is good reason for this; the winters are long and full of hardship and the old and weak cannot always get through them. Last winter was a catastrophe, such as may be expected every ten or twelve years; you can see how the pavement in the streets is broken up, as if the town had survived a minor bombardment. A death is dealt with then in the middle of great difficulties; there comes time now in the summer to think about it, and talk. I find that people stop me in the street to talk about my mother. I have heard from them about her funeral, what flowers she had and what the weather was like on that day. And now that she is dead I no longer feel that when they say the words 'your mother' they deal a knowing, cunning blow at my pride. I used to feel that; at those words. I felt my whole identity, that pretentious adolescent construction, come crumbling down.

Now I listen to them speak of her, so gently and ceremoniously, and I realize that she became one of the town's possessions and oddities, its brief legends. This she achieved in spite of us, for we tried, both crudely and artfully, to keep her at home, away from that sad notoriety; not for her sake, but for ours, who suffered such unnecessary humiliation at the sight of her eyes rolling back in her head in a temporary paralysis of the eye muscles, at the sound of her thickened voice, whose embarrassing pronouncements it was our job to interpret to outsiders. So bizarre was the disease she had in its effects that it made us feel like crying out in apology (though we stayed stiff and white) as if we were accompanying a particularly tasteless sideshow. All wasted, our pride; our purging its rage in wild caricatures we did for each other (no, not caricatures, for she was one herself; imitations). We should have let the town have her; it would have treated her better.

About Maddy and her ten-year's vigil they say very little; perhaps they want to spare my feelings, remembering that I was the one who went away and here are my two children to show for it, while Maddy is alone and has nothing but that discouraging house. But I don't think so; in Jubilee the feelings are not spared this way. And they ask me point-blank why I did not come home for the funeral; I am glad I have the excuse of the blizzard that halted air travel that week, for I do not know if I would have come anyway, after Maddy had written so vehemently urging me to stay away. I felt strongly that she had a right to be left alone with it, if she wanted to be, after all this time.

After all this time. Maddy was the one who stayed. First, she went away to college, then I went. You give me four years, I'll give you four years, she said. But I got married. She was not surprised; she was exasperated at me for my wretched useless feelings of guilt. She said that she had always meant to stay. She said that Mother no longer 'bothered' her. 'Our Gothic Mother,' she said, 'I play it out now, I let her be. I don't keep trying to make her *human* any more. You know.' It would simplify things so much to say that Maddy was religious, that she felt the joys of self-sacrifice, the strong, mystical appeal of total rejection. But about Maddy who could say that? When we were in our teens, and our old aunts, Aunt Annie and Auntie Lou, spoke to us of some dutiful son or daughter who had given up everything for an ailing parent, Maddy would quote impiously the opinions of modern psychiatry. Yet she stayed. All I can think about that, all I have ever been able to think, to comfort me, is that she may have been able and may even have chosen to live without time and in perfect imaginary freedom as children do, the future untampered with, all choices always possible.

*

To change the subject, people ask me what it is like to be back in Jubilee. But I don't know, I am still waiting for something to tell me, to make me understand that I am back. The day I drove up from Toronto with my children in the back seat of the car I was very tired, on the last lap of a twenty-five-hundred-mile trip. I had to follow a complicated system of highways and sideroads, for there is no easy way to get to Jubilee from anywhere on earth. Then about two o'clock in the afternoon I saw ahead of me, so familiar and unexpected, the gaudy, peeling cupola of the town hall, which is no relation to any of the rest of the town's squarely-built, dingy grey-and-red-brick architecture. (Underneath it hangs a great bell, to be rung in the event of some mythical disaster.) I drove up the main street – a new service station, new stucco front on the Queen's Hotel – and turned into the quiet, decaying side streets where old maids live, and have birdbaths and blue delphiniums in their gardens. The big brick houses that I knew, with their wooden verandahs and gaping, dark-screened windows, seemed to me plausible but unreal. (Anyone to whom I have mentioned the dreaming sunken feeling of these streets wants to take me out to the north side of town where there is a new soft-drink bottling plant, some new ranch-style houses and a Tastee-Freez.) Then I parked my car in a little splash of shade in front of the house where I used to live. My little girl, whose name is Margaret, said neutrally yet with some disbelief, 'Mother, is that your house?'

And I felt that my daughter's voice expressed a complex disappointment – to which, characteristically, she seemed resigned, or even resigned *in advance*; it contained the whole flatness and strangeness of the moment in which is revealed the source of legends, the unsatisfactory, apologetic and persistent reality. The red brick of which the house is built looked harsh and hot in the sun and was marked in two or three places by long grimacing cracks; the verandah, which always had the air of an insubstantial decoration, was visibly falling away. There was – there *is* – a little blind window of coloured glass beside the front door. I sat staring at it with a puzzled lack of emotional recognition. I sat and looked at the house and the window shades did not move, the door did not fly open, no one came out on the verandah; there was no one at home. This was as I had expected, since Maddy works now in the office of the town clerk, yet I was surprised to see the house take on such a closed, bare, impoverished look, merely by being left empty. And it was brought home to me, as I walked across the front yard to the steps, that after all these summers on the Coast I had forgotten the immense inland heat, which makes you feel as if you have to carry the whole burning sky on your head.

A sign pinned to the front door announced, in Maddy's rather sloppy and flamboyant hand: VISITORS WELCOME, CHILDREN FREE, RATES TO BE ARRANGED LATER (YOU'LL BE SORRY) WALK IN. On the hall table was a bouquet of pink phlox whose velvety scent filled the hot air of a closed house on a summer afternoon. 'Upstairs!' I said to the children, and I took the hand of the little girl and her smaller brother, who had slept in the car and who rubbed against me, whimpering, as he walked. Then I paused, one foot on the bottom step, and turned to greet, matter-of-factly, the reflection of a thin, tanned, habitually watchful woman, recognizably a Young Mother, whose hair, pulled into a knot on top of her head, exposed a jawline no longer softly fleshed, a brown neck rising with a look of tension from the little sharp knobs of the collarbone — this in the hall mirror that had shown me, last time I looked, a commonplace pretty girl, with a face as smooth and insensitive as an apple, no matter what panic and disorder lay behind it.

But this was not what I had turned for; I realized that I must have been waiting for my mother to call, from her cough in the dining-room, where she lay with the blinds down in the summer heat, drinking cups of tea which she never finished, eating — she had dispensed altogether with mealtimes, like a sickly child — little bowls of preserved fruit and crumblings of cake. It seemed to me that I could not close the door behind me without hearing my mother's ruined voice call out to me, and feeling myself go heavy all over as I prepared to answer it. Calling, *Who's there?*

I led my children to the big bedroom at the back of the house, where Maddy and I used to sleep. It has thin, almost worn-out white curtains at the windows and a square of linoleum on the floor; there is a double bed, a washstand which Maddy and I used as a desk when we were in high school, and a cardboard wardrobe with little mirrors on the inside of the doors. As I talked to my children I was thinking — but carefully, not in a rush — of my mother's state of mind when she called out *Who's there?* I was allowing myself to hear — as if I had not dared before — the cry for help — undisguised, oh, shamefully undisguised and raw and supplicating — that sounded in her voice. A cry repeated so often, and, things being as they were, so uselessly, that Maddy and I recognized it only as one of those household sounds which must be dealt with, so that worse may not follow. *You go and deal with Mother*, we would say to each other, or *I'll be out in a minute, I have to deal with Mother*.

It might be that we had to perform some of the trivial and unpleasant services endlessly required, or that we had to supply five minutes' expediently cheerful conversation, so remorselessly casual that never for a moment was there a recognition of the real state of affairs, never a glint of pity to open the way for one of her long debilitating sieges of tears. But the pity denied, the tears might come anyway; so that we were defeated, we were forced — to stop that noise — into parodies of love. But we grew cunning, unfailing in cold solicitude; we took away from her our anger and impatience and disgust, took all emotion away from our dealings with her, as you might take away meat from a prisoner to weaken him, till he died.

We would tell her to read, to listen to music and enjoy the changes of season and be grateful that she did not have cancer. We added that she did not suffer any pain, and that is true — if imprisonment is not pain. While she demanded our love in every way she knew, without shame or sense, as a child will. And how could we have loved her, I say desperately to myself, the resources of love we had were not enough, the demand on us was too great. Nor would it have changed anything.

'Everything has been taken away from me,' she would say. To strangers, to friends of ours whom we tried always unsuccessfully to keep separate from her, to old friends of hers who came guiltily infrequently to see her, she would speak like this, in the very slow and mournful voice that was not intelligible or quite human; we would have to interpret. Such theatricality humiliated us almost to death; yet now I think that without that egotism feeding stubbornly even on disaster she might have sunk rapidly into some dim vegetable life. She kept herself as much in the world as she could, not troubling about her welcome; restlessly she wandered through the house and into the streets of Jubilee. Oh, she was not resigned; she must have wept and struggled in that house of stone (as I can, but will not, imagine) until the very end.

But I find the picture is still not complete. Our Gothic Mother, with the cold appalling mask of the Shaking Palsy laid across her features, shuffling, weeping, devouring attention wherever she can get it, eyes dead and burning, fixed inward on herself; this is not all. For the disease is erratic and leisurely in its progress; some mornings (gradually growing fewer and fewer and farther apart) she wakes up better; she goes out to the yard and straightens up a plant in such a simple housewifely way; she says something calm and lucid to us; she listens attentively to the news. She has wakened out of a bad dream; she tries to make up for lost time, tidying the house, forcing her stiff trembling hands to work a little while at the sewing machine. She makes us one of her specialties, a banana cake or a lemon meringue pie. Occasionally since she died I have dreams of her (I never dreamt of her when she was alive) in which she is doing something like this, and I think, why did I exaggerate so to myself, see, she is all right, only that her hands are trembling –

At the end of these periods of calm a kind of ravaging energy would come over her; she would make conversation insistently and with less and less coherence; she would demand that we rouge her cheeks and fix her hair; sometimes she might even hire a dressmaker to come in and make clothes for her, working in the dining room where she could watch – spending her time again more and more on the couch. This was extravagant, unnecessary from any practical point of view (for why did she need these clothes, where did she wear them?) and nerve-racking, because the dressmaker did not understand what she wanted and sometimes neither did we. I remember after I went away receiving from Maddy several amusing, distracted, quietly overwrought letters describing these sessions with the dressmaker. I read them with sympathy but without being able to enter into the once-familiar atmosphere of frenzy and frustration which my mother's demands could produce. In the ordinary world it was not possible to re-create her. The picture of her face which I carried in my mind seemed too terrible, unreal. Similarly the complex strain of living with her, the feelings of hysteria which Maddy and I once dissipated in a great deal of brutal laughter, now began to seem partly imaginary; I felt the beginnings of a secret, guilty estrangement.

I stayed in the room with my children for a little while because it was a strange place, for them it was only another strange place to go to sleep. Looking at them in this room I felt that they were particularly fortunate and that their life was safe and easy, which may be what most parents think at one time or another. I looked in the wardrobe but there was nothing there, only a hat trimmed with flowers from the five-and-ten, which one of us must have made for some flossy Easter. When I opened the drawer of the washstand I saw that it was crammed full of pages from a loose-leaf notebook. I read: 'The Peace of Utrecht, 1713, brought an end to the War of the Spanish Succession.' It struck me that the handwriting was my own. Strange to think of it lying here for ten years — more; it looked as if I might have written it that day.

For some reason reading these words had a strong effect on me; I felt as if my old life was lying around me, waiting to be picked up again. Only then for a few moments in our old room did I have this feeling. The brown halls of the old High School (a building since torn down) were re-opened for me, and I remembered the Saturday nights in spring, after the snow had melted and all the country people crowded into town. I thought of us walking up and down the main street, arm in arm with two or three other girls, until it got dark, then going in to Al's to dance, under a string of little coloured lights. The windows in the dance hall were open; they let in the raw spring air with its smell of earth and the river; the hands of farm boys crumpled and stained our white blouses when we danced. And now an experience which seemed not at all memorable at the time (in fact Al's was a dismal place and the ritual of walking up and down the street to show ourselves off we thought crude and ridiculous, though we could not resist it) had been transformed into something curiously meaningful for me, and complete; it took in more than the girls dancing and the single street, it spread over the whole town, its rudimentary pattern of streets and its bare trees and muddy yards just free of the snow, over the dirt roads where the lights of cars appeared, jolting towards the town, under an immense pale wash of sky.

Also: we wore ballerina shoes, and full black taffeta skirts, and short coats of such colours as robin's egg blue, cerise red, lime green. Maddy wore a great funereal bow at the neck of her blouse and a wreath of artificial daisies in her hair. These were the fashions, or so we believed, of one of the years after the war. Maddy; her bright skeptical look; my sister.

★

I ask Maddy, 'Do you ever remember what she was like before?'

'No,' says Maddy. 'No, I can't.'

'I sometimes think I can,' I say hesitantly. 'Not very often.'
Cowardly tender nostalgia, trying to get back to a gentler truth.

'I think you would have to have been away,' Maddy says, 'You
would have to have been away these last — quite a few — years to get
those kind of memories.'

It was then she said: No exorcising.

And the only other thing she said was, 'She spent a lot of time sorting things. All kinds of things. Greeting cards. Buttons and yarn. Sorting and putting them into little piles. It would keep her quiet by the hour.'

I have been to visit Aunt Annie and Auntie Lou. This is the third time I have been there since I came home and each time they have been spending the afternoon making rugs out of dyed rags. They are very old now. They sit in a hot little porch that is shaded by bamboo blinds; the rags and the half-finished rugs make an encouraging, domestic sort of disorder around them. They do not go out any more, but they get up early in the mornings, wash and powder themselves and put on their shapeless print dresses trimmed with rickrack and white braid. They make coffee and porridge and then they clean the house, Aunt Annie working upstairs and Auntie Lou down. Their house is very clean, dark and varnished, and it smells of vinegar and apples. In the afternoon they lie down for an hour and then put on their afternoon dresses, with brooches at the neck, and sit down to do hand work.

They are the sort of women whose flesh melts or mysteriously falls away as they get older. Auntie Lou's hair is still black, but it looks stiff and dry in its net as the dead end of hair on a ripe ear of corn. She sits straight and moves her bone-thin arms in very fine, slow movements; she looks like an Egyptian, with her long neck and small sharp face and greatly wrinkled, greatly darkened skin. Aunt Annie, perhaps because of her gentler, even coquettish manner, seems more humanly fragile and worn. Her hair is nearly all gone, and she keeps on her head one of those pretty caps designed for young wives who wear curlers to bed. She calls my attention to this and asks if I do not think it is becoming. They are both adept at these little ironies, and take a mild delight in pointing out whatever is grotesque about themselves. Their company manners are exceedingly lighthearted and their conversation with each other falls into an accomplished pattern of teasing and protest. I have a fascinated glimpse of Maddy and myself, grown old, caught back in the web of sisterhood after everything else has disappeared, making tea for some young, loved, and essentially unimportant relative – and exhibiting just such a polished relationship; what will anyone ever know of us? As I watched my entertaining old aunts I wonder if old people play such stylized and simplified roles with us because they are afraid that anything more honest might try our patience; or if they do it out of delicacy – to fill the social time – when in reality they feel so far away from us that there is no possibility of communicating with us at all.

At any rate I felt held at a distance by them, at least until this third afternoon when they showed in front of me some signs of disagreement with each other. I believe this is the first time that has happened. Certainly I never saw them argue in all the years when Maddy and I used to visit them, and we used to visit them often – not only out of duty but because we found the atmosphere of sense and bustle reassuring after the comparative anarchy, the threatened melodrama, of our house at home.

Aunt Annie wanted to take me upstairs to show me something. Auntie Lou objected, looking remote and offended, as if the whole subject embarrassed her. And such is the feeling for discretion, the tradition of circumlocution in that house, that it was unthinkable for me to ask them what they were talking about.

'Oh, let her have her tea,' Auntie Lou said, and Aunt Annie said, 'Well. When she's *had* her tea.'

'Do as you like then. That upstairs is hot.'

'Will you come up, Lou?'

'Then who's going to watch the children?'

'Oh, the children. I forgot.'

So Aunt Annie and I withdrew into the darker parts of the house. It occurred to me, absurdly, that she was going to give me a five-dollar bill. I remembered that sometimes she used to draw me into the front hall in this mysterious way and open her purse. I do not think that Auntie Lou was included in that secret either. But we went on upstairs, and into Aunt Annie's own bedroom, which looked so neat and virginal, papered with timid flowery wallpaper, the dressers spread with white scarves. It was really very hot as Auntie Lou had said.

'Now,' Aunt Annie said, a little breathless. 'Get me down that box on the top shelf of the closet.'

I did, and she opened it and said with her wistful conspirator's gaiety, 'Now I guess you wondered what became of all your mother's clothes?'

I had not thought of it. I sat down on the bed, forgetting that in this house the beds were not to be sat on; the bedrooms had one straight chair apiece, for that. Aunt Annie did not check me. She began to lift things out, saying, 'Maddy never mentioned them, did she?'

'I never asked her,' I said.

'No. Nor I wouldn't. I wouldn't say a word about it to Maddy. But I thought I might as well show you. Why not? Look,' she said. 'We washed and ironed what we could and what we couldn't we sent to the cleaners. I paid the cleaning myself. Then we mended anything needed mending. It's all in good condition, see?'

I watched helplessly while she held up for my inspection the underwear which was on top. She showed me where things had been expertly darned and mended and where the elastic had been renewed. She showed me a slip which had been worn, she said, only once. She took out nightgowns, a dressing gown, knitted bed-jackets. 'This was what she had on the last time I saw her,' she said. 'I think it was. Yes.' I recognized with alarm the peach-coloured bed-jacket I had sent for Christmas.

'You can see it's hardly used. Why, it's hardly used at all.'

'No,' I said.

'Underneath is her dresses.' Her hands rummaged down through those brocades and flowered silks, growing yearly more exotic, in which my mother had wished to costume herself. Thinking of her in these peacock colours, even Aunt Annie seemed to hesitate. She drew up a blouse. 'I washed this by hand, it looks like new. There's a coat hanging up in the closet. Perfectly good. She never wore a coat. She wore it when she went into the hospital, that was all. Wouldn't it fit you?'

'No,' I said. '*No.*' For Aunt Annie was already moving towards the closet. 'I just got a new coat. I have several coats. Aunt Annie!'

'But why should you go and buy,' Aunt Annie went on in her mild stubborn way, 'when there are things here as good as new.'

'I would rather buy,' I said, and was immediately sorry for the coldness in my voice. Nevertheless I continued, 'When I need something, I do go and buy it.' This suggestion that I was not poor any more brought a look of reproach and aloofness into my aunt's face. She said nothing. I went and looked at a picture of Aunt Annie and Auntie Lou and their older brothers and their mother and father which hung over the bureau. They stared back at me with grave accusing Protestant faces, for I had run up against the simple unprepossessing materialism which was the rock of their lives. Things must be used; everything must be used up, saved and mended and made into something else and used again; clothes were to be worn. I felt that I had hurt Aunt Annie's feelings and that furthermore I had probably borne out a prediction of Auntie Lou's, for she was sensitive to certain attitudes in the world that were too sophisticated for Aunt Annie to bother about, and she had very likely said that I would not want my mother's clothes.

'She was gone sooner than anybody would have expected,' Aunt Annie said. I turned around surprised and she said, 'Your mother.' Then I wondered if the clothes had been the main thing after all; perhaps they were only to serve as the introduction to a conversation about my mother's death, which Aunt Annie might feel to be a necessary part of our visit. Auntie Lou would feel differently; she had an almost superstitious dislike of certain rituals of emotionalism; such a conversation could never take place with her about.

'Two months after she went into the hospital,' Aunt Annie said. 'She was gone in two months.' I saw that she was crying distractedly, as old people do, with miserable scanty tears. She pulled a handkerchief out of her dress and rubbed at her face.

'Maddy told her it was nothing but a check-up,' she said. 'Maddy told her it would be about three weeks. Your mother went in there and she thought she was coming out in three weeks.' She was whispering as if she was afraid of us being overheard. 'Do you think she wanted to stay in there where nobody could make out what she was saying and they wouldn't let her out of her bed? She wanted to come home!'

'But she was too sick,' I said.

'No, she wasn't, she was just the way she'd always been, just getting a little worse and a little worse as time went on. But after she went in there she felt she would die, everything kind of closed in around her, and she went down so fast.'

'Maybe it would have happened anyway,' I said. 'Maybe it was just the time.'

Aunt Annie paid no attention to me. 'I went up to see her,' she said. 'She was so glad to see me because I could tell what she was saying. She said Aunt Annie, they won't keep me in here for good, will they? And I said to her, No. I said, No.

'And she said, Aunt Annie ask Maddy to take me home

again or I'm going to die. She didn't want to die. Don't you
ever think a person wants to die, just because it seems to
everybody else they have got no reason to go on living. So I
told Maddy. But she didn't say anything. She went to the
hospital every day and saw your mother and she wouldn't
take her home. Your mother told me Maddy said to her, I
won't take you home.'

'Mother didn't always tell the truth,' I said. 'Aunt Annie,
you know that.'

'*Did you know your mother got out of the hospital?*'

'No,' I said. But strangely I felt no surprise, only a vague
physical sense of terror, a longing not to be told – and
beyond this a feeling that what I would be told I already
knew, I had always known.

'Maddy, didn't she tell you?'

'No.'

'Well she got *out*. She got out the side door where the
ambulance comes in, it's the only door that isn't locked. It
was at night when they haven't so many nurses to watch
them. She got her dressing gown and her slippers on, the first
time she ever got anything on herself in years, and she went
out and there it was January, snowing, but she didn't go back
in. She was away down the street when they caught her.
After that they put the board across her bed.'

The snow, the dressing gown and slippers, the board across the bed.
It was a picture I was much inclined to resist. Yet I had no
doubt that this was true, all this was true and exactly as it
happened. It was what she would do; all her life as long as I
had known her led up to that flight.

'Where was she going?' I said, but I knew there was no
answer.

'I don't know. Maybe I shouldn't have told you. Oh,
Helen, when they came after her she tried to run. She tried to
run.'

The flight that concerns everybody. Even behind my
aunt's soft familiar face there is another, more primitive old

woman, capable of panic in some place her faith has never touched.

She began folding the clothes up and putting them back in the box. 'They nailed a board across her bed. I saw it. You can't blame the nurses. They can't watch everybody. They haven't the time.

'I said to Maddy after the funeral, Maddy, may it never happen like that to you. I couldn't help it, that's what I said.' She sat down on the bed herself now, folding things and putting them back in the box, making an effort to bring her voice back to normal – and pretty soon succeeding, for having lived this long who would not be an old hand at grief and self-control?

'We thought it was hard,' she said finally. 'Lou and I thought it was hard.'

Is this the last function of old women, beyond making rag rugs and giving us five-dollar bills – making sure the haunts we have contracted for are with us, not one gone without?

She was afraid of Maddy – through fear, had cast her out for good. I thought of what Maddy had said: nobody speaks the same language.

When I got home Maddy was out in the back kitchen making a salad. Rectangles of sunlight lay on the rough linoleum. She had taken off her high-heeled shoes and was standing there in her bare feet. The back kitchen is a large untidy pleasant room with a view, behind the stove and the drying dishtowels, of the sloping back yard, the CPR station and the golden, marshy river that almost encircles the town of Jubilee. My children who had felt a little repressed in the other house immediately began to play under the table.

'Where have you been?' Maddy said.

'Nowhere. Just to see the Aunts.'

'Oh, how are they?'

'They're fine. They're indestructible.'

'Are they? Yes I guess they are. I haven't been to see them for a while. I don't actually see that much of them any more.'

'Don't you?' I said, and she knew then what they had told me.

'They were beginning to get on my nerves a bit, after the funeral. And Fred got me this job and everything and I've been so busy —' She looked at me, waiting for what I would say, smiling a little derisively, patiently.

'Don't be guilty, Maddy,' I said softly. All this time the children were running in and out and shrieking at each other between our legs.

'I'm not guilty,' she said. 'Where did you get that? I'm not guilty.' She went to turn on the radio, talking to me over her shoulder. 'Fred's going to eat with us again since he's alone. I got some raspberries for dessert. Raspberries are almost over for this year. Do they look all right to you?'

'They look all right,' I said. 'Do you want me to finish this?'

'Fine,' she said. 'I'll go and get a bowl.'

She went into the dining room and came back carrying a pink cut-glass bowl, for the raspberries.

'I couldn't go on,' she said. 'I wanted my life.'

She was standing on the little step between the kitchen and the dining room and suddenly she lost her grip on the bowl, either because her hands had begun to shake or because she had not picked it up properly in the first place; it was quite a heavy and elaborate old bowl. It slipped out of her hands and she tried to catch it and it smashed on the floor.

Maddy began to laugh. 'Oh, hell,' she said. 'Oh, hell, oh *Hel*-en,' she said, using one of our old foolish ritual phrases of despair. 'Look what I've done now. In my bare feet yet. Get me a broom.'

'Take your life, Maddy. Take it.'

'Yes I will,' Maddy said. 'Yes I will.'

'Go away, don't stay here.'

'Yes I will.'

Then she bent down and began picking up the pieces of broken pink glass. My children stood back looking at her with awe and she was laughing and saying, 'It's no loss to me. I've got a whole shelf full of glass bowls. I've got enough glass bowls to do me the rest of my life. Oh, don't stand there looking at me, go and get me a broom!' I went around the kitchen looking for a broom because I seemed to have forgotten where it was kept and she said, 'But why can't I, Helen? *Why can't I?*'

GRACE PALEY

The Immigrant Story

Jack asked me, Isn't it a terrible thing to grow up in the shadow of another person's sorrow?

I suppose so, I answered. As you know, I grew up in the summer sunlight of upward mobility. This leached out a lot of that dark ancestral grief.

He went on with *his* life. It's not your fault if that's the case. Your bad disposition is not your fault. Yet you're always angry. No way out but continuous rage or the nuthouse.

What if this sorrow is all due to history? I asked.

The cruel history of Europe, he said. In this way he showed ironic respect to one of my known themes.

The whole world ought to be opposed to Europe for its cruel history, Jack, and yet in favour of it because after about a thousand years it may have learned some sense.

Nonsense, he said objectively, a thousand years of outgoing persistent imperial cruelty tends to make enemies and if all you have to deal with these enemies is good sense, what then?

My dear, no one knows the power of good sense. It hasn't been built up or experimented with sufficiently.

I'm trying to tell you something, he said. Listen. One day I woke up and my father was asleep in the crib.

I wonder why, I said.

My mother made him sleep in the crib.

All the time?

That time anyway. That time I saw him.

I wonder why, I said.

Because she didn't want him to fuck her, he said.

No, I don't believe that. Who told you that?

I know it! He pointed his finger at me.

I don't believe it, I said. Unless she's had five babies all in a row or they have to get up at 6 a.m. or they both hate each other, most people like their husbands to do that.

Bullshit! She was trying to make him feel guilty. Where were his balls?

I will never respond to that question. Asked in a worried way again and again, it may become responsible for the destruction of the entire world. I gave it two minutes of silence.

He said, Misery misery misery. Grayness. I see it all very very gray. My mother approaches the crib. Shmul, she says, get up. Run down to the corner and get me half a pound of pot cheese. Then run over the drugstore and get a few ounces cod-liver oil. My father, scrunched like an old gray foetus, looks up and smiles smiles smiles at the bitch.

How do *you* know what was going on? I asked. You were five years old.

What do you think was going on?

I'll tell you. It's not so hard. Any dope who's had a normal life could tell you. Anyone whose head hasn't been fermenting with the compost of ten years of gluttonous analysis. Anyone could tell you.

Tell me what? he screamed.

The reason your father was sleeping in the crib was that you and your sister who usually slept in the crib had scarlet fever and needed the decent beds and more room to sweat, come to a fever crisis, and either get well or die.

Who told you that? He lunged at me as though I was an enemy.

You fucking enemy, he said. You always see things in a rosy light. You have a rotten rosy temperament. You were like that in sixth grade. One day you brought three American flags to school.

That was true. I made an announcement to the sixth-grade assembly thirty years ago. I said: I thank God every day that I'm not in Europe. I thank God I'm American-born and live on East 172nd Street where there is a grocery store, a candy store, and a drugstore on one corner and on the same block a shul and two doctors' offices.

One Hundred and Seventy-second Street was a pile of shit, he said. Everyone was on relief except you. Thirty people had t.b. Citizens and noncitizens alike starving under the war. Thank God capitalism has a war it can pull out of the old feed bag every now and then or we'd all be bored. Ha ha.

I'm glad that you're not totally brainwashed by stocks, bonds, and cash. I'm glad to hear you still mention capitalism from time to time.

Because of poverty, brilliance, and the early appearance of lots of soft hair on face and crotch, my friend Jack was a noticeable Marxist and Freudian by the morning of his twelfth birthday.

In fact, his mind thickened with ideas. I continued to put out more flags. There were twenty-eight flags aflutter in different rooms and windows. I had one tattooed onto my arm. It has gotten dimmer but a lot wider because of middle age.

I am probably more radical than you are nowadays, I said. Since I was not wiped out of my profession during the McCarthy inquisitions, I therefore did not have to go into business for myself and make a fortune. (Naturally many have remained wiped out to this day, gifted engineers and affectionate teachers . . . This makes me think often of courage and loyalty.)

I believe I see the world as clearly as you do, I said. Rosiness is not a worse windowpane than gloomy grey when viewing the world.

Yes yes yes yes yes yes yes, he said. Do you mind? Just listen:

My mother and father came from a small town in Poland. They had three sons. My father decided to go to America, to 1. stay out of the army, 2. stay out of jail, 3. save his children from everyday wars and ordinary pogroms. He was helped by the savings of parents, uncles, grandmothers and set off like hundreds of thousands of others in that year. In America, New York City, he lived a hard but hopeful life. Sometimes he walked on Delancey Street. Sometimes like a bachelor he went to the theatre on Second Avenue. Mostly he put his money away for the day he could bring his wife and sons to this place. Meanwhile, in Poland famine struck. Not hunger which all Americans suffer six, seven times a day but Famine, which tells the body to consume itself. First the fat, then the meat, the muscle, then the blood. Famine ate up the bodies of the little boys pretty quickly. My father met my mother at the boat. He looked at her face, her hands. There was no baby in her arms, no children dragging at her skirt. She was not wearing her hair in two long black braids. There was a kerchief over a dark wiry wig. She had shaved her head, like a backward Orthodox bride, though they had been serious advanced socialists like most of the youth of their town. He took her by the hand and brought her home. They never went anywhere alone, except to work or the grocer's. They held each other's hand when they sat down at the table, even at breakfast. Sometimes he patted her hand, sometimes she patted his. He read the paper to her every night.

They are sitting at the edge of their chairs. He's leaning forward reading to her in that old bulb light. Sometimes she smiles just a little. Then he puts the paper down and takes both her hands in his as though they needed warmth. He continues to read. Just beyond the table and their heads, there is the darkness of the kitchen, the bedroom, the dining room, the shadowy darkness where as a child I ate my supper, did my homework and went to bed.

The Fifteen Dollar Eagle

There are other tattoo shops in Madigan Square, but none of them a patch on Carmey's place. He's a real poet with the needle and dye, an artist with a heart. Kids, dock bums, the out-of-town couples in for a beer put on the brakes in front of Carmey's, nose-to-the-window, one and all. You got a dream, Carmey says, without saying a word, you got a rose on the heart, an eagle in the muscle, you got the sweet Jesus himself, so come in to me. Wear your heart on your skin in this life, I'm the man can give you a deal. Dogs, wolves, horses and lions for the animal lover. For the ladies, butterflies, birds of paradise, baby heads smiling or in tears, take your choice. Roses, all sorts, large, small, bud and full bloom, roses with name scrolls, roses with thorns, roses with Dresden-doll heads sticking up in dead centre, pink petal, green leaf, set off smart by a lead-black line. Snakes and dragons for Frankenstein. Not to mention cow-girls, hula girls, mermaids and movie queens, ruby-nippled and bare as you please. If you've got a back to spare, there's Christ on the cross, a thief at either elbow and angels overhead to right and left holding up a scroll with 'Mount Calvary' on it in Old English script, close as yellow can get to gold.

Outside they point at the multi-coloured pictures plastered on Carmey's three walls, ceiling to floor. They mutter like a mob scene, you can hear them through the glass:

'Honey, take a looka those peacocks!'

'That's crazy, paying for tattoos. I only paid for one I got, a panther on my arm.'

'You want a heart, I'll tell him where.'

I see Carmey in action for the first time courtesy of my steady man, Ned Bean. Lounging against a wall of hearts and flowers, waiting for business, Carmey is passing the time of day with a Mr Tomolillo, an extremely small person wearing a wool jacket that drapes his non-existent shoulders without any attempt at fit or reformation. The jacket is patterned with brown squares the size of cigarette packs, each square boldly outlined in black. You could play tick-tack-toe on it. A brown fedora hugs his head just above the eyebrows like the cap on a mushroom. He has the thin, rapt, triangular face of a praying mantis. As Ned introduces me, Mr Tomolillo snaps over from the waist in a bow neat as the little moustache hairlining his upper lip. I can't help admiring this bow because the shop is so crowded there's barely room for the four of us to stand up without bumping elbows and knees at the slightest move.

The whole place smells of gunpowder and some fumey antiseptic. Ranged along the back wall from left to right are: Carmey's work table, electric needles hooked to a rack over a Lazy Susan of dye pots, Carmey's swivel chair facing the show window, a straight customer's chair facing Carmey's chair, a waste bucket, and an orange crate covered with scraps of paper and pencil stubs. At the front of the shop, next to the glass door, there is another straight chair, with the big placard of Mount Calvary propped on it, and a cardboard file-drawer on a scuffed wooden table. Among the babies and daisies on the wall over Carmey's chair hang two faded sepia daguerreotypes of a boy from the waist up, one front-view, one back, from the distance he seems to be wearing a long-sleeved, skin-tight black lace shirt. A closer look shows he is stark naked, covered only with a creeping ivy of tattoos.

In a jaundiced clipping from some long-ago rotogravure, these Oriental men and women are sitting crosslegged on tasselled cushions, back to the camera and embroidered with seven-headed dragons, mountain ranges, cherry trees and waterfalls. 'These people have not a stitch of clothing on,' the blurb points out. 'They belong to a society in which tattoos are required for membership. Sometimes a full job costs as much as $300.' Next to this, a photograph of a bald man's head with the tentacles of an octopus just rounding the top of the scalp from the rear.

'Those skins are valuable as many a painting, I imagine,' says Mr Tomollilo. 'If you had them stretched on a board.'

But the Tattooed Boy and those clubby Orientals have nothing on Carmey, who is himself a living advertisement of his art – a schooner in full sail over a rose-and-holly-leaf ocean on his right biceps, Gypsy Rose Lee flexing her muscled belly on the left, forearms jammed with hearts, stars and anchors, lucky numbers and name scrolls, indigo edges blurred so he reads like a comic strip left out in a Sunday rainstorm. A fan of the Wild West, Carmey is rumoured to have a bronco reared from navel to collar-bone, a thistle-stubborn cowboy stuck to its back. But that may be a mere fable inspired by his habit of wearing tooled leather cowboy boots, finely heeled, and a Bill Hickock belt studded with red stones to hold up his black chino slacks. Carmey's eyes are blue. A blue in no way inferior to the much sung about skies of Texas.

'I been at it sixteen years now,' Carmey says, leaning back against his picture-book wall, 'and you might say I'm still learning. My first job was in Maine, during the war. They heard I was a tattooist and called me out to this station of WACs.'

'To tat*too* them?' I ask.

'To tattoo their numbers on, nothing more or less.'

'Weren't some of them scared?'

'Oh, sure, sure. But some of them came back. I got two WACs in one day for a tattoo. Well they hemmed. And they hawed. "Look," I tell them, "you came in the other day and you knew which one you wanted, what's the trouble?"

' "Well it's not what we want but where we want it," one

of them pipes up. "Well if that's all it is you can trust me," I say. "I'm like a doctor, see? I handle so many women it means nothing." "Well I want three roses," this one says: "one on my stomach and one on each cheek of my butt." So the other one gets up courage, you know how it is, and asks for one rose . . .'

'Little ones or big ones?' Mr Tomolillo won't let a detail slip.

'About like that up there,' Carmey points to a card of roses on the wall, each bloom the size of a Brussels sprout. 'The biggest going. So I did the roses and told them: "Ten dollars off the price if you come back and show them to me when the scab's gone."'

'Did they come?' Ned wants to know.

'You bet they did.' Carmey blows a smoke ring that hangs wavering in the air a foot from his nose, the blue, vaporous outline of a cabbage-rose.

'You wanta know,' he says, 'a crazy law? I could tattoo you anywhere,' he looks me over with great care, 'anywhere at all. Your back. Your rear.' His eyelids droop, you'd think he was praying. 'Your breasts. Anywhere at all but your face, hands and feet.'

Mr Tomolillo asks: 'Is that a *Federal* law?'

Carmey nodds. 'A Federal law. I got a blind,' he juts a thumb at the dusty-slatted venetian blind drawn up in the display window. 'I let that blind down, and I can do privately any part of the body. Except face, hands and feet.'

'I bet it's because they *show*,' I say.

'Sure. Take the Army, at drill. The guys wouldn't look right. Their faces and hands would stand out, they couldn't cover up.'

'However that may be,' Mr Tomolillo says, 'I think it is a shocking law, a totalitarian law. There should be a freedom about personal adornment in any democracy. I mean, if a lady *wants* a rose on the back of her hand, I should think . . .'

'She should *have* it,' Carmey finishes with heat. 'People

should have what they want, regardless. Why, I had a little lady in here the other day,' Carmey levels the air with the flat of his hand not five feet from the floor. 'So high. Wanted Calvary, the whole works, on her back, and I gave it to her. Eighteen hours it took.'

I eyed the thieves and angels on the poster of Mount Calvary with some doubt. 'Didn't you have to shrink it down a bit?'

'Nope.'

'Or leave off an angel?' Ned wonders. 'Or a bit of the foreground?'

'Not a bit of it. A thirty-five dollar job in full colour, thieves, angels, Old English — the works. She went out of the shop proud as punch. It's not every little lady's got all Calvary in full colour on her back. Oh, I copy photos people bring in, I copy movie stars. Anything they want, I do it. I've got some designs I wouldn't put up on the wall on account of offending some of the clients. I'll show you.' Carmey opens the cardboard file drawer on the table at the front of the shop. 'The wife's got to clean this up,' he says. 'It's a terrible mess.'

'Does your wife help you?' I ask with interest.

'Oh, Laura, she's in the shop most of the day.' For some reason Carmey sounds all at once solemn as a monk on Sunday. I wonder, does he use her for a come-on: Laura, the Tattooed Lady, a living masterpiece, sixteen years in the making. Not a white patch on her, ladies and gentlemen — look all you want to. 'You should drop by and keep her company, she likes talk.' He is rummaging around in the drawer, not coming up with anything, when he stops in his tracks and stiffens like a pointer.

This big guy is standing in the doorway.

'What can I do for you?' Carmey steps forward, the maestro he is.

'I want that eagle you showed me.'

Ned and Mr Tomolillo and I flatten ourselves against the

side walls to let the guy into the middle of the room. He'll be
a sailor out of uniform in his pea jacket and plaid wool shirt.
His diamond-shaped head, width all between the ears, tapers
up to a narrow plateau of cropped black hair.

'The nine dollar or the fifteen?'

'The fifteen.'

Mr Tomolillo sighs in gentle admiration.

The sailor sits down in the chair facing Carmey's swivel,
shrugs out of his peajacket, unbuttons his left shirt cuff and
begins slowly to roll up the sleeve.

'You come right in here,' Carmey says to me in a low,
promising voice, 'where you can get a good look. You've
never seen a tattooing before.' I squinch up and settle on the
crate of papers in the corner at the left of Carmey's chair,
careful as a hen on eggs.

Carmey flicks through the cardboard file again and this
time digs out a square piece of plastic. 'Is this the one?'

The sailor looks at the eagle pricked out on the plastic.
Then he says: 'That's right,' and hands it back to Carmey.

'Mmmm,' Mr Tomolillo murmurs in honour of the sailor's
taste.

Ned says, 'That's a fine eagle.'

The sailor straightens with a certain pride. Carmey is dancing
round him now, laying a dark-stained burlap cloth across his lap,
arranging a sponge, a razor, various jars with smudged-out labels
and a bowl of antiseptic on his work-table – finicky as a priest
whetting his machete for the fatted calf. Everything has to be
just so. Finally he sits down. The sailor holds out his left arm as
Ned and Mr Tomolillo close in behind his chair, Ned leaning
over the sailor's right shoulder and Mr Tomolillo over his left.
At Carmey's elbow I have the best view of all.

With a close, quick swipe of the razor, Carmey clears the
sailor's forearm of its black springing hair, wiping the hair off
the blade's edge and on to the floor with his thumb. Then he
anoints the area of bared flesh with vaseline from a small jar
on top of his table, 'You ever been tattooed before?'

'Yeah.' The sailor is no gossip. 'Once.' Already his eyes are locked in a vision of something on the far side of Carmey's head, through the walls and away in the thin air beyond the four of us in the room.

Carmey is sprinkling a black powder on the face of the plastic square and rubbing the powder into the pricked holes. The outline of the eagle darkens. With one flip, Carmey presses the plastic square powder-side against the sailor's greased arm. When he peels the plastic off, easy as skin off an onion, the outline of an eagle, wings spread, claws hooked for action, frowns up from the sailor's arm.

'Ah!' Mr Tomolillo rocks back on his cork heels and casts a meaning look at Ned. Ned raises his eyebrows in approval. The sailor allows himself a little quirk of the lip. On him it is as good as a smile.

'Now,' Carmey takes down one of the electric needles, pitching it rabbit-out-of-the-hat, 'I am going to show you how we make a nine dollar eagle a fifteen dollar eagle.'

He presses a button on the needle. Nothing happens.

'Well,' he sighs, 'it's not working.'

Mr Tomolillo groans. 'Not again?'

Then something strikes Carmey and he laughs and flips a switch on the wall behind him. This time when he presses the needle it buzzes and sparks blue. 'No connexion, that's what it was.'

'Thank heaven,' says Mr Tomolillo.

Carmey fills the needle from a pot of black dye on the Lazy Susan. 'This same eagle,' Carmey lowers the needle to the eagle's right wingtip, 'for nine dollars is only black and red. For the fifteen dollars you're going to see a blend of four colours.' The needle steers along the lines laid by the powder. 'Black, green, brown and red. We're out of blue at the moment or it'd be five colours.' The needle skips and backtalks like a pneumatic drill but Carmey's hand is steady as a surgeon's. 'How I *love* eagles!'

'I believe you *live* on Uncle Sam's eagles,' says Mr Tomolillo.

Black ink seeps over the curve of the sailor's arm and into the stiff, stained butcher's apron canvas covering his lap, but the needle travels on, scalloping the wing feathers from tip to root. Bright beads of red are rising through the ink, heart's blood bubbles smearing out into the black stream.

'The guys complain,' Carmey singsongs. 'Week after week I get the same complaining: What have you got new? We don't want the same type eagle, red and black. So I figure out this blend. You wait. A solid colour eagle.'

The eagle is losing itself in a spreading thundercloud of black ink. Carmey stops, sloshes his needle in the bowl of antiseptic, and a geyser of white blooms up to the surface from the bowl's bottom. Then Carmey dips a big, round cinnamon-coloured sponge in the bowl and wipes away the ink from the sailor's arm. The eagle emerges from its hood of bloodied ink, a raised outline on the raw skin.

'Now you're gonna see something.' Carmey twirls the Lazy Susan till the pot of green is under his thumb and picks another needle from the rack.

The sailor is gone from behind his eyes now, off somewhere in Tibet, Uganda or the Barbados, oceans and continents away from the blood drops jumping in the wake of the wide green swaths Carmey is drawing in the shadow of the eagle's wings.

About this time I notice an odd sensation. A powerful sweet perfume is rising from the sailor's arm. My eyes swerve from the mingling red and green and I find myself staring intently into the waste bucket by my left side. As I watch the calm rubble of coloured candy wrappers, cigarette butts and old wads of muddily-stained Kleenex, Carmey tosses a tissue soaked with fresh red on to the heap. Behind the silhouetted heads of Ned and Mr Tomolillo the panthers, roses and red-nippled ladies wink and jitter. If I fall forward or to the right, I will jog Carmey's elbow and make him stab the sailor and ruin a perfectly good fifteen-dollar eagle not to mention disgracing my sex. The only alternative is a dive into the bucket of bloody papers.

'I'm doing the brown now,' Carmey sings out a mile away, and my eyes rivet again on the sailor's blood-sheened arm. 'When the eagle heals, the colours will blend right into each other, like on a painting.'

Ned's face is a scribble of black India ink on a seven-colour crazy-quilt.

'I'm going . . .' I make my lips move, but no sound comes out.

Ned starts towards me but before he gets there the room switches off like a light.

The next thing is, I am looking into Carmey's shop from a cloud with the X-ray eyes of an angel and hearing the tiny sound of a bee spitting blue fire.

'The blood got her?' It is Carmey's voice, small and far.

'She looks all white,' says Mr Tomolillo. 'And her eyes are funny.'

Carmey passes something to Mr Tomolillo. 'Have her sniff that.' Mr Tomolillo hands something to Ned. 'But not too much.'

Ned holds something to my nose.

I sniff, and I am sitting in the chair at the front of the shop with Mount Calvary as a back-rest. I sniff again. Nobody looks angry so I have not bumped Carmey's needle. Ned is screwing the cap on a little flask of yellow liquid. Yardley's smelling salts.

'Ready to go back?' Mr Tomolillo points kindly to the deserted orange crate.

'Almost.' I have a strong instinct to stall for time. I whisper in Mr Tomolillo's ear which is very near to me, he is so short, 'Do *you* have any tattoos?'

Under the mushroom-brim of his fedora Mr Tomolillo's eyes roll heavenward. 'My gracious no! I'm only here to see about the springs. The springs in Mr Carmichael's machine have a way of breaking in the middle of a customer.'

'How annoying.'

'That's what I'm here for. We're testing out a new spring

now, a much heavier spring. You know how distressing it is when you're in the dentist's chair and your mouth is full of what-not . . .'

'Balls of cotton and little metal siphons . . .?'

'Precisely. And in the middle of this the dentist turns away,' Mr Tomolillo half-turns his back in illustration and makes an evil, secretive face, 'and buzzes about in the corner for ten minutes with the machinery, you don't know what.' Mr Tomolillo's face smooths out like linen under a steam iron. 'That's what I'm here to see about, a stronger spring. A spring that won't let a customer down.'

By this time I am ready to go back to my seat of honour on the orange crate. Carmey has just finished with the brown and in my absence the inks have indeed blended into one another. Against the shaven skin, the lacerated eagle is swollen in tricoloured fury, claws curved sharp as butcher's hooks.

'I think we could redden the eye a little?'

The sailor nods, and Carmey opens the lid on a pot of dye the colour of tomato ketchup. As soon as he stops working with the needle, the sailor's skin sends up its blood beads, not just from the bird's black outline now, but from the whole rasped, rainbowed body.

'Red,' Carmey says, 'really picks things up.'

'Do you save the blood?' Mr Tomolillo asks suddenly.

'I should think,' says Ned, 'you might well have some arrangement with the Red Cross.'

'With a blood bank!' The smelling salts have blown my head clear as a blue day on Monadnock. 'Just put a little basin on the floor to catch the drippings.'

Carmey is picking out a red eye on the eagle. 'We vampires don't share our blood.' The eagle's eye reddens but there is now no telling blood from ink. 'You never heard of a vampire doing that, did you?'

'Nooo . . .' Mr Tomolillo admits.

Carmey floods the flesh behind the eagle with red and the

finished eagle poises on a red sky, born and baptized in the blood of its owner.

The sailor drifts back from parts unknown.

'Nice?' With his sponge Carmey clears the eagle of the blood filming its colours the way a sidewalk artist might blow the pastel dust from a drawing of the White House, Liz Taylor or Lassie-Come-Home.

'I always say,' the sailor remarks to nobody in particular, 'when you get a tattoo, get a good one. Nothing but the best.' He looks down at the eagle which has begun in spite of Carmey who is waiting for something and it isn't money. 'How much to write Japan under that?'

Carmey breaks into a pleased smile. 'One dollar.'

'Write Japan, then.'

Carmey marks out the letters on the sailor's arm, an extra flourish to the J's hook, the loop of the P, and the final N, a love-letter to the eagle-conquered Orient. He fills the needle and starts on the J.

'I under*stand*,' Mr Tomolillo observes in his clear, lecturer's voice, 'Japan is a centre of tattooing.'

'Not when *I* was there,' the sailor says. 'It's banned.'

'Banned!' says Ned. 'What for?'

'Oh, they think it's *bar*barous nowadays.' Carmey doesn't lift his eyes from the second A, the needle responding like a broken-in bronc under his masterly thumb. 'There are operators, of course. *Sub rosa*. There always are.' He puts the final curl on the N and sponges off the wellings of blood which seem bent on obscuring his artful lines. 'That what you wanted?'

'That's it.'

Carmey folds a wad of Kleenex into a rough bandage and lays it over the eagle and Japan. Spry as a shopgirl wrapping a gift package he tapes the tissue into place.

The sailor gets up and hitches into his peajacket. Several schoolboys, lanky, with pale, pimply faces, are crowding the doorway, watching. Without a word the sailor takes out his wallet and peels sixteen dollar bills off a green roll. Carmey transfers the cash to his wallet. The schoolboys fall back to let the sailor pass into the street.

'I hope you didn't mind my getting dizzy.'

Carmey grins. 'Why do you think I've got those salts so close to hand? I have big guys passing out cold. They get egged in here by their buddie and don't know how to get out of it. I got people getting sick to their ears in that bucket.'

'She's never got like that before,' Ned says. 'She's seen all sorts of blood. Babies born. Bull fights. Things like that.'

'You was all worked up.' Carmey offers me a cigarette, which I accept, takes one himself, and Ned takes one, and Mr Tomolillo says no thank you. 'You was all tensed, that's what did it.'

'How much is a heart?'

The voice comes from a kid in a black leather jacket in the front of the shop. His buddies nudge each other and let out harsh, puppy-barks of laughter. The boy grins and flushes all at once under his purple stipple of acne. 'A heart with a scroll under it and a name on the scroll.'

Carmey leans back in his swivel chair and digs his thumbs into his belt. The cigarette wobbles on his bottom lip. 'Four dollars,' he says without batting an eye.

'Four dollars?' The boy's voice swerves up and cracks in shrill disbelief. The three of them in the doorway mutter among themselves and shuffle back and forth.

'Nothing here in the heart line under three dollars.' Carmey doesn't kowtow to the tight-fisted. You want a rose, you want a heart in this life, you pay for it. Through the nose.

The boy wavers in front of the placard of hearts on the wall, pink, lush hearts, hearts with arrows through them, hearts in the centre of buttercup wreaths. 'How much,' he asks in a small, craven voice, 'for just a name?'

'One dollar.' Carmey's tone is strictly business.

The boy holds out his left hand. 'I want Ruth.' He draws an imaginary line across his left wrist. 'Right here . . . so I can cover it up with a watch if I want to.'

His two friends guffaw from the doorway.

Carmey points to the straight chair and lays his half-smoked cigarette on the Lazy Susan between two dye-pots. The boy sits down, schoolbooks balanced on his lap.

'What happens,' Mr Tomolillo asks of the world in general, 'if you choose to change a name? Do you just cross it off and write the next above it?'

'You could,' Ned suggests, 'wear a watch over the old name so only the new name showed.'

'And then another watch,' I say, 'over that, when there's a third name.'

'Until your arm,' Mr Tomolillo nods, 'is up to the shoulder with watches.'

Carmey is shaving the thin scraggly growth of hairs from the boy's wrist. 'You're taking a lot of ragging from somebody.'

The boy stares at his wrist with a self-conscious and unsteady smile, a smile that is maybe only a public substitute for tears. With his right hand he clutches his schoolbooks to keep them from sliding off his knee.

Carmey finishes marking R-U-T-H on the boy's wrist and holds the needle poised. 'She'll bawl you out when she sees this.' But the boy nods him to go ahead.

'Why?' Ned asks. 'Why should she bawl him out?'

'Gone and got yourself tattooed!' Carmey mimics a mincing disgust. 'And with just a name! Is *that* all you think of me? — She'll be wanting roses, birds, butterflies . . .' The needle sticks for a second and the boy flinches like a colt. 'And if you *do* get all that stuff to please her — roses . . .'

'Birds and butterflies,' Mr Tomolillo puts in.

'. . . she'll say, sure as rain at a ball game: What'd you want to go and spend all that *money* for?' Carmey whizzes the needle clean in the bowl of antiseptic. 'You can't beat a woman.' A few meagre blood drops stand up along the four letters — letters so black and plain you can hardly tell it's a tattoo and not just inked in with a pen. Carmey tapes a

narrow bandage of Kleenex over the name. The whole operation lasts less than ten minutes.

The boy fishes a crumpled dollar bill from his back pocket.
His friends cuff him fondly on the shoulder and the three of
them crowd out of the door, all at the same time, nudging,
pushing, tripping over their feet. Several faces, limpet-pale
against the window, melt away as Carmey's eye lingers on
them.

'No wonder he doesn't want a heart, that kid, he wouldn't
know what to do with it. He'll be back next week asking for
a Betty or a Dolly or some such, you wait.' He sighs, and
goes to the cardboard file and pulls out a stack of those
photographs he wouldn't put on the wall and passes them
around. 'One picture I would like to get,' Carmey leans back
in the swivel chair and props his cowboy boots on a little
carton. 'The butterfly. I got pictures of the rabbit hunt. I got
pictures of ladies with snakes winding up their legs and into
them, but I could make a lot of sweet dough if I got a picture
of the butterfly on a woman.'

'Some queer kind of butterfly nobody wants?' Ned peers in
the general direction of my stomach as at some high-grade
saleable parchment.

'It's not what, it's where. One wing on the front of each
thigh. You know how butterflies on a flower make their
wings flutter, ever so little? Well, any move a woman makes,
these wings look to be going in and out, in and out. I'd like a
photograph of that so much I'd practically do a butterfly for
free.'

I toy, for a second, with the thought of a New Guinea
Golden, wings extending from hip-bone to knee-cap, ten
times life-size, but drop it fast. A fine thing if I got tired of
my own skin sooner than last year's sack.

'Plenty of women *ask* for butterflies in that particular spot,'
Carmey goes on, 'but you know what, not one of them will
let a photograph be taken after the job's done. Not even from
the waist down. Don't imagine I haven't asked. You'd think

everybody over the whole United States would recognize them from the way they carry on when it's even mentioned.'

'Couldn't,' Mr Tomolillo ventures shyly, 'the wife oblige? Make it a little family affair?'

Carmey's face screws up in a pained way. 'Naw,' he shakes his head, his voice weighted with an old wonder and regret. 'Naw, Laura won't hear of the needle. I used to think the idea of it'd grow on her after a bit, but nothing doing. She makes me feel, sometimes, what do I see in it all. Laura's white as the day she was born. Why, she *hates* tattoos.'

Up to this moment I have been projecting, fatuously, intimate visits with Laura at Carmey's place. I have been imagining a lithe, supple Laura, a butterfly poised for flight on each breast, roses blooming on her buttocks, a gold guarding dragon on her back and Sinbad the Sailor in six colours on her belly, a woman with Experience written all over her, a woman to learn from in this life. I should have known better.

The four of us are slumped there in a smog of cigarette smoke, not saying a word, when a round, muscular woman comes into the shop, followed closely by a greasy-haired man with a dark, challenging expression. The woman is wrapped to the chin in a woolly electric-blue coat; a fuchsia kerchief covers all but the pompadour of her glinting blonde hair. She sits down in the chair in front of the window regardless of Mount Calvary and proceeds to stare fixedly at Carmey. The man stations himself next to her and keeps a severe eye on Carmey too, as if expecting him to bolt without warning.

There is a moment of potent silence.

'Why,' Carmey says pleasantly, but with small heart, 'here's the wife now.'

I take a second look at the woman and rise from my comfortable seat on the crate at Carmey's elbow. Judging from his watchdog stance, I gather the strange man is either Laura's brother or her bodyguard or a low-class private detective in her employ. Mr Tomolillo and Ned are moving with one accord towards the door.

'We must be running along,' I murmur, since nobody else seems inclined to speak.

'Say hello to the people, Laura,' Carmey begs, back to the wall. I can't help but feel sorry for him, even a little ashamed. The starch is gone out of Carmey now, and the gay talk.

Laura doesn't say a word. She is waiting with the large calm of a cow for the three of us to clear out. I imagine her body, death-lily-white and totally bare – the body of a woman immune as a nun to the eagle's anger, the desire of the rose. From Carmey's wall the world's menagerie howls and ogles at her alone.

MARY SCOTT

Language

Unlike many people, Rita did not write to *The Times* deploring modern standards of English. She preferred to make corrections on the spot.

Sometimes she did this by offering an incentive. This afternoon in the market she negotiated the amendment of 'Brokkoli' on a hand-written sign by agreeing to buy two pounds of the vegetable – or to be precise, flower used as a vegetable. Tom would resent having broccoli for dinner again, she knew. But unfortunately it was misspelt far more often than peas or spring greens or even aubergine, although that, too, was a difficult word.

On other occasions Rita found, as she did with the children, that a certain sharp authority was more effective. Today she decided that 'house clearences' lettered on a junk shop window was intolerable. She went into the shop.

For a moment she stood in the doorway, allowing her eyes to adjust to the gloomy interior. On either side furniture was piled in high, precarious heaps. She could distinguish desks, torn chairs, filing cabinets and Beautility tables. Further away, in the dim recesses of the shop, the individual items merged together, with just a leg discernible here, an upholstered arm protruding there. She stepped forward and discovered, sitting at a desk which stood the right way up, a small dark man.

'Your business cannot hope to succeed,' she announced, her voice booming in the narrow space. 'First impressions count. The impression your shop gives will deter potential customers.' She pointed her finger at the lettering on the window. 'The "E" should be an "A".'

Later that afternoon, when she had finished her shopping and passed the shop a second time, she found the E had been changed to an A. Just as, when she informed her class of noisy fourteen-year-olds that there was to be 'no more of that', there was no more.

When she arrived at the bus station she saw on the wall behind her bold, splashy writing in foreign characters, Arabic maybe or Urdu, and small, disordered scribbles around the glass faces of the timetables, which, although an irritation, caused Rita no real pain. 'Fred was here', 'Mandy loves Greg', 'Joey sucks' were inane, but neither the grammar nor the spelling could be faulted.

On the bus home she passed, as usual, the new industrial estate. Someone had painted an 'I' between the words 'TO' and 'LET' on the boarded up windows.

She left the bus, walked down the main road to the corner, turned into her own road and saw scrawled in black beneath her feet 'cunt'. The word had not been there when she left that morning. 'Shit' was painted on the next flagstone. She scuffed at it with the tip of one brown brogue but it did not even smudge. 'Balls' was the next word she came across, a few yards further on. She accepted this was the kind of thing children wrote on the pavement nowadays. But what had happened to hopscotch? She remembered drawing with white chalk the six squares for hopping and, at the far end, a semicircle which she labelled 'BED'.

The words on the pavement were common currency nowadays; although Rita's mother would have found them deeply offensive. 'Language!' her mother would cry when Rita or her brother Bob said even 'crikey' or 'blimey'. Her mother's voice would fill with outrage. Their grandmother, she said, would have washed out their mouths that instant with carbolic soap. The threat was enough to stop Rita and Bob going as far as their friends with real rude words. Instead they went in for archaic exclamations such as 'Botheration!' or made up their own: 'Slitherkins!' 'Pistoops!' and the somehow more daring 'Oh zags!'.

Rita wheeled her tartan shopping trolley past 'cock' and 'tit'. Remarkable, she thought, how many of these terms were familiar to quite young children. Certainly, in her classroom, sex was the topic on which she knew their vocabulary to be widest, in spite of the fact that it didn't receive the level of attention she insisted they devote to the subjects on the curriculum. She wheeled on. 'Brest' stared up at her from the pavement. She wheeled on again. She reached her house.

Rita let herself into the house with the Yale. The kitchen was already dark. She looked through the french windows. The back garden was a small square of lawn bordered by rhododendrons which, in turn, were surrounded by a high wattle fence. Neither Rita nor Tom used the garden for anything apart from mowing and weeding. She drew the curtains.

She went into the living room where she settled down at the dining table to mark compositions. Why did so many of the children put the 'e' and the 'i' the wrong way round again in 'their'? She circled 'unneccessary' in one effort, wrote in the margin of another 'participal phrase must refer to grammatical subject'.

Tom arrived at twenty to eight – on schedule for his daily journey from London. He awarded Rita the customary homecoming kiss. It was a brief kiss but Rita no longer felt aggrieved by that.

'Had a good day? What's for dinner?' he asked. She told him. 'Broccoli again,' he said with little real enthusiasm. He went upstairs. There he would remove his jacket, his waistcoat and his tie, roll up his sleeves and wash his hands. Possibly he also washed his face, she did not know, never having asked him. Until bedtime, no further kiss would be offered in which, had it been, she might, or might not, have detected the scent of soap.

'How about your day?' she asked, over dinner.

'Trouble with the trains again. All very well them claiming these improvements to commuter lines. No seven fifty-three this morning. No eight o two. I'd have taken my overcoat if I'd known. You know how damp it was this morning. I think I might have caught a cold.'

'For them to claim' would not have jarred the ear in the same way, she thought, but did not say.

After dinner he leaned back on the sofa, she sat upright across the room in a matching easy chair. They watched *News at Ten*. A junior Defence Minister attempted to explain that a bomb might easily be planted in a barracks: 'Anyone could walk in as long as they were carrying a package which did not look suspicious.'

'He means,' said Rita, slowly, in her loud classroom voice, 'anyone could walk in as long as he or she were not carrying a package that did look suspicious.'

'I wanted to hear what else he had to say,' complained Tom.

'An early night for me,' was the next thing from him, while she stayed as always, to complete the *Guardian* crossword.

'You go on up,' she said. 'There's some Lem Sip in the medicine cabinet.'

'What about you?'

'I'll just finish up in the kitchen.'

For once her motive for staying downstairs was not to avoid the bedroom routine – his request and her reluctant compliance. Tonight, her craving to correct had the sharp tingle of sherbert.

Silence upstairs. Tom had settled down swiftly. He might read for a while but he would not come downstairs, would not hear anything if she were quiet. She found black paint in one of the kitchen cupboards, left over from the time Tom had painted the front door, and a brush. She levered the lid off the pot with a screwdriver, stirred the contents, replaced the top lightly and loaded the lot, along with a small torch, into a shopping bag.

Less than half an hour later she cleaned the brush in white spirit, and pressed the lid of the tin noiselessly down. She went upstairs and completed the usual preparations for bed. In the bathroom she slid dental floss in and out between her teeth. She washed her face and smoothed cream over her skin. In the bedroom she took off her blouse and skirt and hung them carefully in the wardrobe. She folded her slip and draped it over a chair. She added her underwear to Tom's Y-fronts in the laundry basket. She slipped into her nightie and slid into bed beside Tom, who was asleep and breathing through his mouth. She would not wake him or touch him or even lie close enough to feel his warmth.

In the beginning, more than fifteen years ago, when she was much slimmer and wore flared trousers, she seemed to enter a magnetic field whenever she came close to Tom. Once within range, parts of her body could not be prevented from touching parts of his. If she sat beside him her head would loll onto his shoulder and stay there for long moments. If they were both standing, perhaps having drinks with friends, she would lean towards him and her glass would tilt and spill. Her hands also behaved unexpectedly. The heel of one of them might massage his arm or the rough texture of his cheek. Some of these incidents occurred, regrettably, in public.

Even after marriage, even in the bed in which she was now trying to lie disturbingly still, Tom was embarrassed by the caresses that brought Rita such pleasure. With effort, vast at first, diminishing by slow degrees, she suppressed her body's compulsions. And bit by bit their lovemaking turned into a dry ritual which caused Rita no actual pain, only a lingering, grey regret. Eventually she found other things to do when, in his view, it was time to do that.

In the morning Tom said he had a cold. Not bad enough, he judged, for him to stay in bed but bad enough to keep him at home. Rita made sure that he had a supply of Kleenex and

Lem Sip and left for school, approving on the way the neatness with which she had changed 'brest' to 'breast'. Though to be really professional she should make corrections in red as she did in the children's books.

On the way back that afternoon she bought a can of red spray paint in a car accessories shop. At home she found Tom looking better, though serious. He blew his nose and said: 'I don't have a cold. I stayed home so we'd have time this evening. I want to talk to you.'

'Can it wait till I've started dinner? And corrected 4b's grammar?'

'Can't you ever think about anything but correcting grammar?'

'The compositions are always so bad I can only face them if I do so right away.'

'This is important.'

'4b's are the worst of all.'

'I'm seeing someone else.'

'Why do none of the children distinguish between "it's" and "its"? I've told them often enough.'

'I've fallen in love with someone.'

'They sprinkle commas around for absolutely no reason.'

'She wants me to move in with her. I told her I'd tell you today.'

'Restrictive clauses, for instance. There is just no justification.'

'She wants to have children and you never did.'

'Nominative not objective pronoun in a comparison where the verb is understood.'

'I want to marry her. I want a divorce.'

'Imagine putting two "ts" in writing.'

'We can still be friends. You know you've not been interested in sex for years.'

She picked up the bag that held the can of red spray paint and left the living room in silence. She stepped out of the front door and closed it behind her.

She stood on the pavement and pointed the spray can at the low brick wall of their front garden. 'Unclean' she sprayed in bold script and below that 'adulterer'. She moved to the neighbours' wall and sprayed 'fornicator' and 'debauchee'. Next door but one came in for 'concupiscence' and 'whore-monger'. By the third house she completed 'lecher', 'libertine' and 'licentious' before she heard Tom mutter: 'Rita, please. People are looking.'

She turned the spray and stained the white front of his shirt blood red, then turned back and slowly wrote 'carnal knowledge', 'impudicity'.

Had she looked she would indeed have seen many faces peeking from behind twitched curtains, but she was too busy with 'copulation', 'coition', 'clitoris', 'testicles' and 'fuck'.

By the time someone called the police the street boasted red descriptions of every aspect of straight sex along with some more arcane terms such as 'fellatio', 'cunnilingus' and 'onanism'.

'It's quite all right,' she said to the young, pink faced WPC. 'The can is, in any case, almost empty.'

Rita sat in the back of the police car as she was told to do. A broad shouldered constable sat beside her. The young WPC drove.

At the police station Rita sat on a wooden bench and answered questions. The policeman typed his version of what she said on an old manual Remington.

He finished typing, took the paper from the machine and gave it to her. She examined the statement.

'Too many passive verbs,' she said. 'Very common nowa-days and makes for flabby, colourless prose. I said I was "loath" not "loathe". Occurrence with an "e" not an "a". When a quotation is followed by an attributive phrase, the comma is placed within the quotation marks. In all other respects I agree it is an entirely accurate record of the event.'

HELEN SIMPSON

What Are Neighbours For

Mrs Brumfitt crossed the room sideways and at speed, making for the comparative obscurity of the corner chair. She was tree-limbed, with beetling unplucked eyebrows that gave her a false scowl. Hilary thanked her for the Mr Kipling Almond Slices, and they talked for a minute or two about *The Jungle Book*, which neither of them had read though Mrs Brumfitt had seen the film. And Mowgli? asked Hilary: any news of Mowgli? Mrs Brumfitt's eyes dimmed to pebbles and she shook her head roughly.

Chitra arrived next and understood at once.

'Ah, poor Mowgli,' she sighed. 'It is the fur coat gang, I saw it on television.'

'You look nice,' said Mrs Brumfitt enviously, wiping her eyes, angry again that her own clean crimplene was the best Large Lady mail order could manage for under fifty pounds.

'Terribly pretty,' agreed Hilary. Her own jeans and sweat-shirt appeared churlish now that she saw they had both made an effort. The lilac of Chitra's shot-silk sari caused her skin to glimmer like verdigris. In her left nostril was a star-shaped diamond, and big silver filigree bells hung from her ears. Her feet peeped out in crimson beaded slippers.

'Here are some cakes from my husband's favourite shop,' she said, 'and here are some pakora which I made myself.'

She arranged herself on the sofa, beaming around her with appreciative delicacy.

'What a lovely room,' she said.

You must be joking, thought Hilary, who had hated this

dreary back parlour from the very first day. She unpacked the cakes, which were pistachio green, amber and cream-coloured globes and bars.

'They are made with milk curds that take twelve hours to cook,' called Chitra from the sofa.

'Twelve hours!' said Mrs Brumfitt. 'Some people must have time on their hands.'

Hilary wondered what to do with the pakora, placing them at last between the egg sandwiches and the Scotch pancakes. When she went to open the door for her last guest, Chitra and Mrs Brumfitt were muttering together with some vehemence about their husbands. Only yesterday she had spied Mr Brumfitt from the bathroom window, perched up a ladder fixing a new plastic downpipe while his wife yelled at him, 'You poxy old devil.' Or perhaps it had been, 'You foxy old devil.' Mrs Brumfitt was deeply dissatisfied with him, for the way he refused to eat spiced foods or go out and about or paint the house. When Hilary had asked her to tea, she had responded with immediate wrath: 'I can't invite anyone round till *he's* decorated.'

Stefania stood puffing in splendour after her climb to Hilary's upstairs maisonette. She was bearing a large pannetone in a sky-blue box.

'For you,' she said, with a grand gesture as though they were both on stage. Her aquamarine dress and della Robbia eyelids dazzled Hilary, who had only seen her before in shapeless coats, generally with a bag on wheels in tow.

'And who else, I wonder, will be here at your tea party?' said Stefania as they walked along the hall. The smile slid from her face like an omelette from its pan when she caught sight of Mrs Brumfitt in the corner. She turned stonily, rearranged her features into some fresh approximation of sweetness, and greeted Chitra with a lordly smile.

'I almost did not come, Hilary,' she said, sinking into a chair. 'I have had *such* a headache all the morning. I said to my husband, this is too much to bear, perhaps I will not go.'

'I hope you feel better now,' said Chitra.

Stefania smiled bravely through half-closed lids, and pressed her temples with her index fingers.

'What about a paracetamol,' said Hilary.

'That's a doctor speaking,' said Mrs Brumfitt.

Stefania shook her head and closed her eyes completely.

'Give me two minutes only,' she whispered.

Hilary thought, if you turned up in my surgery with an act like that, I'd give you short shrift. She was practical and careful in her approach to her work, but a shade underpowered on the empathizing front; she took some satisfaction in sending moaning minnies away with fleas in their ears.

'How brave and clever you are to be a doctor,' said Chitra, once they were sitting in a circle around the tea table. 'All that blood.'

'Girls today,' said Mrs Brumfitt. 'There's no stopping them. My Jill, the one who's in computers – you met her, Chitra – well, she makes all her own loose covers and curtains, plays squash, goes to Spanish conversation *and* cooks Rob a hot meal every night.'

'How does she have time for preparing hot meals after work?' asked Chitra.

'She does it all beforehand in a Slow Hotpot,' said Mrs Brumfitt triumphantly, 'then she bungs some baked potatoes in the microwave. That girl is so organized it makes my head spin. She's made time for everything except babies.'

Hilary passed the sandwiches round. She was twenty-nine and had been qualified for two years. She had just managed to land a partnership in a local practice, starting in three weeks' time, after lengthy stints of locum work. Now it looked as though things were about to grind to a close with Philip, more from apathy than for any dramatic reason, plus the fact that he seemed incapable of behaving like an adult. Well, she would be earning enough to be able to buy him out. The question was, whether she should see if she couldn't get pregnant before he left, without telling him, of course. Caroline had managed it before Archie went, and claimed the child was infinitely preferable to the man. This new job gave fairly decent maternity leave, too. She wouldn't be able to afford a nanny yet but she'd have quite enough to pay child-minders, although they'd obviously need to be backed up by a dependable neighbour or two. She looked thoughtfully around the table.

The conversation had turned to animals.

'You know Mowgli has disappeared,' said Chitra to Stefania.

'It was a fox,' said Stefania firmly. 'My Sammy came back four nights ago with deep tooth marks each side of his muzzle. You're not telling me a dog did that.'

'Poor Mrs Brumfitt,' said Chitra softly, watching her next-door neighbour sag in her chair. They had been on friendly terms for a decade now, but Mrs Brumfitt remained on surname terms with everyone and had done so ever since she got married, blighted as she had been with an unmentionable Christian name. Fanny? Boadicea? Whatever it was, nobody was likely to find out. Even her children did not know it. She gnawed savagely at a Grantham gingerbread, fighting back the tears. What that cat had meant to her was nobody's business. Now all she had left to think about was her growth, maybe benign, King's had said, and maybe not. Nobody knew about it except the hospital. It might have been some relief to ask Hilary, her being a doctor, though she probably didn't know much since she was only just out of medical school. Also, she never seemed to have much time for you – she was always in such a tearing hurry – *very* like Jill. This tea was a turn-up for the books. She must be bored waiting for her new job. Either that, or she was after something.

Chitra said, 'In my former life I had cats, dogs, geese, goats, parrots, so it was a full day running around playing with them all.'

'Spiders are the only one of God's creatures I cannot love,' declared Stefania with an elaborate shudder. 'My God, there was one the size of this teacup on the kitchen floor when I came down this morning.'

'What did you do?' asked Mrs Brumfitt.

Stefania ignored her. Mrs Brumfitt's forehead flushed livid. Chitra became as agitated as a bird.

'Snakes make me full of horror,' she twittered, her eyes large and bright.

'I'm not too keen on eels,' said Hilary.

'Eels!' said Stefania in low thrilling tones. 'I *love* eels! From Condon's I ordered two live eels last February and I carried them home wrapped up in newspaper.'

'Didn't they struggle?' said Hilary.

'No. There is something about being rolled in the newspaper that transfixes them. When I was a young girl in Palinuro, we used to get up in the middle of the night and go down to the stream with forks. Then we stabbed the eels as they swam. How beautiful they were to fry.'

'I like them jellied,' mumbled Mrs Brumfitt, determined to stay in the conversation.

'How delightful, Hilary – chocolate éclairs,' said Stefania, artificial as a West End farce.

'Marks and Sparks,' said Hilary brusquely. She poured more tea.

'I have been reading a book on etiquette,' announced Chitra, 'and it says to add the milk afterwards.'

'*You* put *hot* milk in tea, Chitra, don't you,' said Mrs Brumfitt with interest.

'Oh yes, my first husband always insisted on hot milk,' said Chitra, and sighed. 'He was a banker. We were used to an enormous social circle. We knew a thousand people. I have gone steadily down. We moved; we knew then maybe five hundred. We moved again. A hundred. Then fifty. Now barely twenty. I have come from the heights in my own country to nothing here in Herne Hill.'

'Herne Hill,' spat Stefania. 'My God, sometime I stand at my front gate and stare at the view of all these red bricks, I think, my *God* how came I into Herne Hill, I who used to look from my front door out over the blue sea.'

'After the war, wasn't it,' commented Mrs Brumfitt. 'No work down your part of Italy.'

Stefania's features writhed.

'How long have you lived here?' asked Hilary hastily.

'Thirty-eight years,' said Stefania, composing herself with an effort.

'Ever since I got married to *him*,' said Mrs Brumfitt, jerking her chin in the direction of her own house.

'How nice it must have been when you both had young children,' said Chitra daringly. 'Did they play together in your gardens?'

'A fair bit,' said Mrs Brumfitt, 'Though Heather and Maria-Grazia used to fight something shocking. I had to throw a bucket of water over them once.'

'Small babies are best,' beamed Chitra. 'All day you can pick them up, put them down, wash them, put them down, clean them up, put them down. But toddlers! Great heavens! Always running here and there! What you must do is get a big strong playpen.'

'I have seven children,' announced Stefania. 'In Italy we love our bambini.'

'Babimbi?' repeated Chitra, tasting the word.

Stefania discharged a cackle of hard-boiled merriment. 'Babimbi, babimbi, babimbi,' she mimicked. Then, as though to an idiot, she leaned across to Chitra and enunciated, 'Bambeen-ee!' She rolled her eyes at Hilary, sharing the joke with someone Educated.

'I do not know Italian,' murmured Chitra, who had, however, a full command of Urdu, Punjabi and Parsee.

'Seven children is a lot,' said Hilary, rather coldly.

'Yes,' shrugged Stefania. 'They came easily. Like rabbits.'

'You love your . . . bambini,' suggested Chitra, polite to the bitter end.

'Of course,' said Stefania. 'I am a good mather. A *very* good mather. They are my life and joy.'

Mrs Brumfitt crumbled the remains of a flapjack between strong nicotine-ochred fingers. Stefania knew that she knew that Stefania had not spoken to her married daughter Paola for two years, even though she was only down the road in Crystal Palace and had a six-month-old baby to cope with. Stefania had not even set eyes on this her first grandchild, and all because of a quarrel which had shot up like a beanstalk from a Boxing Day squabble concerning Darwin's ideas about monkeys. There was also Valerio, with his off-the-back-of-a-lorry dealings and his dodgy nocturnal hours, while Lorella's boohooing, clearly audible through the party wall, regularly kept her awake at night. And Maria-Grazia had gone *right* off the rails. Mrs Brumfitt clamped her mouth shut. This was the umpteenth time over the years that Stefania had decided she wasn't speaking to her for some daft reason or other. Well, she wasn't going to eat dirt again, today or any other day.

'It is a good party, Hilary,' said Chitra, nodding her head and smiling. 'How nice it is to sit here talking about such things with friends. In my country I talk only with the men; I cannot put up with more than twenty minutes with the women because always they talk of the same things: clothes and jewellery, clothes and jewellery.'

'Well, they've got nothing else, have they,' commented Mrs Brumfitt.

'Myself, I like art and the creative life,' Chitra continued. 'I have written poetry, in other places where there was society. Most of it I wrote in Urdu. One only has been English – I wrote about how I was happy to be here but I did not like to see the sad old people stuffed away in Homes.'

It's a toss-up between her and Mrs Brumfitt, thought Hilary. Stefania is obviously a *complete* nightmare.

'Last year I went to pottery classes,' continued Chitra. 'We made beautiful ducks to hang on the wall.' She petered out, dispirited by their lack of interest.

Silence descended over the tea table. Stefania had retreated beneath half-closed azure canopies, brooding on some private bitterness, not bothering to conceal the fact that she was not listening. Mrs Brumfitt was concentrating on the stabbing pains which had started up two or three minutes ago. Were they simple indigestion, or to do with you-know-what?

Hilary felt restless and wondered when she could decently start winding up proceedings. A tea party was the only feasible way she could have got them together without their husbands, but she found all this bread and cake rather disgusting, nothing but refined sugar and carbohydrate. These three looked as though they could do with losing a few stone between them. In fact most of the people she saw wandering around this part of London looked acutely in need of some brisk exercise, as she told them in no uncertain terms when they turned up at her surgery. Out shopping for the cakes that morning she had shaken her head over the sign in the dentist's high street window: 'Free McDonald's voucher with every check-up.'

'I must go now,' said Stefania without warning, waking from her reverie.

'If you must,' said Hilary, who had already mentally dismissed her anyway. She showed her to the door.

Mrs Brumfitt was telling Chitra about her last Sunday outing to Jill's in Lewisham.

'We had a ploughman's lunch in a pub, a piece of cheese *this* size' – folding her napkin into a large triangle – 'stacks of bread, pickle, I don't know how much else, and all for two pounds fifty.'

Hilary looked assessingly at Mrs Brumfitt's mulberry cheeks and meaty forearms; she considered her heavy way of walking, and the coughing sessions she could hear every morning through the kitchen wall as she worked through her bowl of muesli. No, she decided, not without regret; Mrs Brumfitt wouldn't be up to the demands of a young baby for more than an hour at a time, though it might be possible to leave it with her during trips to Safeways or while out jogging. Chitra, on the other hand, looked fit and energetic for her age, and would probably be quite grateful for something like this to help fill her days.

Chitra was fiddling with a bangle, smiling, trying to keep at bay the thought that next month her husband's overbearing, critical and diabetic mother was coming to live with them. The old woman did not speak English and would doubtless do all she could to keep Chitra in the house all day long. She would criticize her to her husband and enlist his support in everything. When she fell ill, she would expect to be nursed as tenderly as a baby. And she would force Chitra to give up her local friendships, dismissing good, kind Mrs Brumfitt as uncouth and this unmarried doctor girl as immoral.

'Those pakora really were super,' said Hilary, in an unaccustomed attempt at ingratiation. 'I'd love the recipe.'

Chitra fluttered her hands.

'They are very easy, but you must have time and patience,' she said. 'One day before your new job begins you must come to my house and watch me make them.'

'You should see her do nan bread,' Mrs Brumfitt chimed in, smacking her lips. 'All puffed up and blistered under the grill.'

'Yes, nan bread too!' said Chitra. 'And also stuffed paratha! We will have another tea party.'

'Just so long as you don't ask the Perfect Mother,' said Mrs Brumfitt. 'Her and her precious bambini. Did you ever? I see nobody's touched those almond slices. Well, I'm not too proud to eat shop-bought. Pass them over, Hilary. By the way, I've been meaning to ask you a favour, I've got something funny here on my side and I was wondering if you'd take a look at it for me one day when you've got a spare minute.'

'Of course,' said Hilary crossly, thinking: honestly! give them an inch.

FRANCES TOWERS

Violet

The only person Violet couldn't handle was the mistress herself. From the very first, Mrs Titmus refused, in her obstinate way, to take to Violet; partly, perhaps, because Sophy had engaged her without taking up her references. So lazy of her, and dangerous. At her age, thought Mrs Titmus, I could have done the work of this house and thought nothing of it. I would have been glad to do something useful. Utterly selfish, thought Mrs Titmus, and bone-lazy, eager to grab at the first thing that offered to save herself a little effort.

But to Sophy, who had coped alone with the house for six weeks, it had become a monster that fed on the very marrow of her bones. So that Violet, stepping in and taking the reins in her absurdly small and fluttering hands, seemed like an angel of deliverance. From the beginning, the monster ate out of her hand. In less than no time it had resumed the orderly and polished look of former days. Skirtings acquired a dark glow, furniture a patina of port-wine richness, silver shone as if newly-minted. Any qualms that Sophy may have had that such a large house was too much for such a dot of a thing were quieted by her unruffled and competent air. But she had an effect in ways other than the merely physical.

It seemed to Sophy afterwards that it wasn't till Violet came to the house that the pattern of their lives emerged to her eyes. She was the focal point that related the different planes on which they lived to each other. She drew the design together, so that one became aware of values that had hitherto been submerged below the level of consciousness.

With her smirks and the sudden gleam of light in her opaque eyes, her nods and becks, she illumined the hidden corners of their minds, she twitched aside curtains and revealed the fears and passions of their hearts, she smelt out their secrets, pounced on them and laid them out like dead mice, and she took a hand in their destinies.

On the first morning, when she brought the early tea into Sophy's room, in her neat pink dress with the turned-back white cuffs at the elbows, Sophy was aware of those dense black eyes taking in the rather tousled and puffy-eyed look which she knew only too well she presented on first awaking.

With an odd, humiliating feeling of being unworthy of the attentions of this crisp handmaid, she accepted the meticulously prepared tray.

'But you've given me the Queen Anne teapot,' she said, taken by surprise at the sight of this treasure reserved for guests of consequence.

'I like to be dainty first thing in the morning. It kind of sets the tone for the day,' said Violet, surprisingly. 'Madam's been down to see if I'd lighted the fire. When I saw her in her dressing-gown and her little plait sticking out, I didn't know she was the mistress. She fair frightened me. Must be nice to wake up in this room, miss, with flowers and that. They say you shouldn't sleep with flowers in the room; but I must say it's nice – ever so gentle and feminine. Makes you feel all glorious within, I expect. Madam said only toast for breakfast – is that right? But what about the master? Gentlemen like a couple of rashers and a fried egg. He looks a bit thin to me, kind of hungry-like. He was up ever so early catching slugs in the garden, and I took him out a cup of tea. He seemed ever so surprised. Poor old gentleman, ever so gentle and kind, he seemed. I think I'll do him a proper breakfast.'

'You must do as my mother says,' said Sophy, sipping her tea.

'Righty-ho!' Violet tripped out on her high heels.

But Sophy saw with dismay when she descended to breakfast that the girl had taken the law into her own hands.

Oh, dear! How tactless of her. And Mr Titmus must needs make it worse.

'Ho, ho, ho! It looks as if I'm going to be spoilt.'

Mrs Titmus looked down her nose. When her eyes had that pale, blind look, as if all the blue had been withdrawn from them, Sophy, expert at interpreting signs and portents, knew that trouble was brewing. Her sisters swallowed their coffee and fled to catch the 8.15 to London. They had their careers and were apt to shelve domestic problems.

'Someone,' said Mrs Titmus, fixing the old gentleman with that glazed fishy look, 'seemed to be creaking about the house all night, pulling the plugs. I couldn't sleep a wink.'

Sophy began to chatter wildly about the news in the morning paper. The year was 1938.

'How silly you are, getting all worked up! You don't know a thing about it,' Mrs Titmus said, with a venom that seemed quite unnecessary.

'Really, mother, I may be allowed to express an opinion, I suppose.'

'I don't know when,' said Mr Titmus, seeking to throw oil on troubled waters, 'I've had a nicer breakfast.'

Was it possible, wondered Sophy, exasperated, that one so dense, so innocent, could have begotten her?

'I think there'll be war, and we shall all be blown to bits,' she said loudly and vindictively.

The prospect of war seemed a lesser calamity at the moment than the loss of Violet, which was probably imminent.

'Well, if we are, we are. It can't be helped, and there's nothing we can do about it,' said Mrs Titmus, with the bored manner of one who wished to hear no more of a tiresome subject.

She rose and pushed back her chair.

'Ring the bell,' she said, 'for that girl to clear.'

'We must give her time to finish her own breakfast, poor little scrap,' remarked Mr Titmus, genially.

There was a hideous pause. Mrs Titmus stared at her husband, her eyes pale again with venom.

'What did you say? What term did you apply to the maid-of-all-work?'

'I know what father means, mother.' Sophy rushed in where no angel would have ventured so much as the tip of a toe. 'She really is the tiniest thing I've ever seen – like a little marmoset or something.'

'Well, I don't care for marmosets about *my* house,' was her mother's parting shot as she went out of the room.

'Dear, dear, dear! Your mother seems upset about something. You've not been cheeky to her, my dear, I hope. You girls are inclined to be cheeky, I've noticed.'

'Father,' said Sophy, 'you don't use a word like that about bitter females in their dim thirties.' She began to clear the breakfast plates with thin, nervous hands that shook a little.

'Now, what's the matter with her?' wondered Mr Titmus. Deep in the recesses of his consciousness, he asked himself why one should have married a shrew and become the father of shrews.

'I don't like 'em, not one of 'em,' he said wickedly to himself in the dark depths of his being. 'This yaller girl, she's as nugly as an 'orse,' he thought, regarding her sorrowfully with his innocent, filmy blue eyes.

Oh, what an old dog he was in his deep inwardness! How ugly and vicious! He had a private atrocious language of his own, when things got too much for him, to express the exasperation that boiled within him. They thought he was old Father Christmas, did they? They thought he was a gentle old pet? Ho! Sometimes he was shocked at his own wickedness. Sometimes he was afraid of God's punishment. Suppose He were to take one of the girls! When little Beatrice had pneumonia, he couldn't eat or sleep, he couldn't keep his food down. If God did a thing like that, it could break his heart.

But sometimes he knew such flashes of glory, it was like the gates of Heaven opening. Suddenly a line of poetry would come into his head – or he would hear the strings of his heart playing *Sheep may safely graze*, and he would feel as light and holy as a sainted spirit.

He looked so wistful that Sophy had a twinge of conscience.

'Sorry, father. It's because I'm so tired. This undercurrent of drama all the time . . . Do you ever wish you were dead?'

'No, no!' said Mr Titmus, shocked. '*With worms that are thy chambermaids*,' he said in a whisper, looking into vacancy, and stole away furtively, his shapeless slippers flapping at his heels.

Sophy's hands dropped to her sides. If she had opened a cupboard and found a grinning skeleton inside, she could hardly have felt more chilled.

'I couldn't help hearing what you said,' said Violet, suddenly appearing from nowhere with a tray in her hands. 'If you wish evil, miss, you attract it to you. It would be more sensible, excuse me, to wish to get married. One never knows,' she added, darkly. Her soft black eyes fastened on Sophy's face and clung there, like persistent bees. They were so jetty dark, you couldn't tell if there were compassion in them, or brazen impudence.

Sophy gave her a quelling look, and stalked out of the room with a giraffe-like dignity.

Seeking refuge a few days later from domestic tension, she went to her room and took a leather-bound book out of the bookcase. It was tooled in gold, with the title '*Morte D'Arthur* by Malory', and its pages were blank except for such as were covered by her small pointed script.

'Notre domestique', wrote Sophy, in the green ink she affected, 'is no ordinary scullion. She might have washed up the wine-cups of the Borgias, or looked through the keyholes of the Medici. I have an idea that she can hear the mice scampering furtively behind the panels of our minds. I heard one the other day in an unaccustomed place. Father quoted Shakespeare and frightened me. I know now that he is a very

lonely old man. La domestique knows it too. He loves his
roses better than wife or daughters. It hurts him to have
them picked by careless hands. Lalage is ruthless. She snips
where she will and fills the vases. She comes into a room and
stirs up flowers arranged by someone else, gritting her teeth,
as though to say, How inartistic! What insensitiveness! She is
a lazy, exquisite person, and, like a saint, exudes a delightful
odour. It comes, of course, from a bottle and not from her
bones; but is so much hers that the latter source seems the
true one. She has the most charming hands and eyebrows, and
is about the only person whose bath water one could use
without distaste.

'I am deeply concerned about Bee. The other day a
wedding-ring dropped out of her handbag. She swooped on it,
and I pretended not to see. It was sinister, like finding a
snake's egg in a drawer and knowing that strange rustlings
must have occurred while one slept. A mouse behind the
panels. And yet her small, rather cynical, face is quite untroubled, and she laughs still in her silent, inward way. It's the
secrecy that hurts, so furtive. And yet, what would you, in
our household? V., I fear, has heard that mouse. "There's
something about Miss Beatrice that calls to mind a divorced
lady – ever so worldly and stylish. A woman of the world,
miss, if you know what I mean. Now, if you was to wear one
of her hats, why, you'd look ridiculous!"

'I told Bee and she went into one of her silent convulsions
of laughter. "Poor old Sophy!" she said. "Mind you keep her
on the right side of mother! Your face was beginning to look
like an old leather bag." She meant it kindly.

'Does mother hate Violet for some deep, intuitive reason?

'"Lord, madam. I never did see so many pill-boxes and
medicine bottles. Makes one think of hospitals and death. It
doesn't do to dwell so much on one's health – makes the end
come all the quicker, I daresay."

'I heard mother's voice, with an edge in it. "You can leave
my room. I prefer to do it myself." She didn't prefer it, when

I was doing all the housework. She preferred to write her lectures for the Women's Institute.'

Sophy closed her book and returned it to the shelf. In that household, with such a title, it was safe from prying eyes. It was her consolation, her other self.

Lalage and Beatrice drew Violet out and compared notes. She was a source of infinite amusement to them.

Violet's young man had thrown her over. 'That's all right. I'm not breaking me heart,' she said. 'It wasn't love, it was lust.'

She cast a glance at a photograph on Lalage's mantelpiece.

'Excuse me, miss, but that gentleman's got ever such a nice face. I expect if he gives you flowers, they are real nice ones, gardenias and that. But he's not one to be kept dangling. He's got his pride. Never ask you twice, he wouldn't.' She sighed. 'I never had nothing from Bert, except a bit of dried heather he got off a gipsy. Mean he was. Everything for nothing was his motto. I suppose you'll be getting married, miss, before long?'

'What makes you think so?'

'Red hair and brown eyes, and then, your legs, miss . . . like champagne bottles. Miss Sophy, now, she's different. Only a very spiritual gentleman would single out Miss Sophy, and then he'd love her to the world's end. She's an acquired taste, as they say – and that kind's the most lasting.'

'The little devil,' said Sophy, when these remarks were repeated to her, and for some reason she looked at the same time disconcerted and gratified.

Bee might have noticed it. Her small green eyes might have peeped out of their lashes with a piercing glint. 'Spiritual . . . aha! So that accounts for all these attendances at St Petroc's.'

But Lalage was too lazy, too indifferent. One's heart might crack in two, and she would never guess.

It was a strange thing, but Christian Todmarsh did send her one day not gardenias, but orchids. She looked thoughtfully at his photograph. Yes, he had a proud face. He would easily be lost beyond recall. She rang him up, and their engagement was announced a few days later.

'Things always seem to happen when I come into a house,' remarked Violet, dropping her eyelids.

'The master and his roses,' she said one day, looking out of the window with a duster in her hand. 'It's as well to have a passion, even if it's only for flowers. My last gentleman had one for pictures. Ever so queer they were. You didn't hardly like to look at them. He said a thing I've never forgotten. He said there was some foreign painter that painted women as if they were roses, and roses as if they were women. That isn't a thing you'd be likely to forget. It makes a difference to your life . . . gives you ideas and that. Madam isn't a bit like a rose,' she added reflectively, almost under her breath; 'but Miss Lalage is. It comes out in her.'

Violet continued to skate blithely over thin ice. It seemed a shame that a gentleman with such a passion for roses should have no rose in his heart. Madam was like an east wind. She fair shrivelled one up. But she wasn't going to drive Violet away. So long as there were those that appreciated her, Violet would stay put. They needed her. Oh, but how desperately they needed her! How they had ever got on without her she didn't know.

She seemed to be moving all the time to some secret tune. Mrs Titmus hated the way she laid the table, posturing and pirouetting like a ballet-dancer, setting down glasses and pepper-pots with a turn of the wrist, as though she were miming to unheard music, stepping back theatrically and regarding her handiwork with her head on one side, waiting for the next beat of the invisible baton. Even more irritating was it to hear her singing below stairs, in raucous abandonment to emotion, with that awful, vulgar scoop of the street singer who seeks to wring the heart.

But there were other and worse things.

'I don't like the girl, and I never shall,' said Mrs Titmus.

'She pesters your father. I caught her taking him a cup of cocoa in the middle of the morning. He's so foolish that I've no doubt he drank it.'

'But what harm in that? She meant it kindly. She isn't a bad little thing,' said Sophy nervously, though she knew it was worse than useless to attempt palliation of Violet's offences.

'Nonsense! You girls are idiotic about her. She's *evil*. She's always *saying* things,' said Mrs Titmus, with a pinched look about her mouth. 'Yesterday, she was putting clean sheets on my bed, and she said, "Look, madam, diamonds all down the middle fold."'

'Diamonds?' asked Sophy, blankly.

'Yes; the sheet had been badly folded, the way they do in this laundry, and there were little squares. I wouldn't have noticed them. "That means death," she said. I didn't like the look she gave me. If I were ill and alone, I wouldn't care to be at the mercy of that girl.'

Morbid, thought Sophy. It was a new aspect of her. Was there to be no end to the discoveries one made about one's nearest and dearest?

She looked at her mother as if she were seeing her for the first time. The thin face, hooked nose and Greek knot at the back of the head gave her the look of a teapot – was it? Or the Indian idol of massive brass that had stood on the hall table ever since she could remember, the head of Lakshmi, the goddess, brought back by some ancestor and bearing on her forehead the red seal of the Brahmin.

Teapot or goddess. She had something of both in her composition. She had comforted her children, and inspired them with fear. 'And now that one is middle-aged,' thought Sophy (who prided herself on facing unpleasant facts, to the extent of being guilty, more often than not, of overstatement) 'there is no longer need of comfort, but vestiges of the fear remain. I am still afraid sometimes that she can read my thoughts. I still tremble when her eyes go pale. This house, so shabby and so beautiful, is in part her creation, but she has long ceased to take any interest in it. She has become warped about money and won't spend a penny.'

Atmosphere is a mysterious thing. Like wallpapers superimposed to a thickness, maybe, of inches, atmosphere settles upon atmosphere with the succeeding tenants of an old house. The Titmus atmosphere, one felt (if one were a somewhat precious and fantastic creature like Sophy), owed something of its richness and duskiness to those others that it had absorbed since the days of Queen Anne. The sound of the harpsichord, she liked to think, had gone into the old wood. The scent of pomander balls was, perhaps, part of the peculiar Titmus smell . . . faintly peppery, with a hint of Russian leather and petal dust, that clung about the house and permeated all their belongings and even stole out of parcels sent across the seas. All their selves had left slimy invisible trails. The furniture knew it. It had that dumb but sentient look, as if something of their personalities had passed into it and fed and enriched it. Was it too fantastic, Sophy wondered, to imagine that lately it had taken on a darker, stranger glow, a glint as of the reflection of soft black eyes?

One sound had certainly haunted the house since the day it was first built, the sound of the bells of St Petroc's. They had a magical significance now for Sophy, like the aromatic poplars in the churchyard and the light that shone through the east window.

'The Vicar is in the drawing-room with Madam. But it's you he came to see, miss,' announced Violet, bursting in one afternoon when Sophy was communing with her book. Her heart turned over.

Violet fixed her with her soft black stare. There seemed to be the faintest trace of a smirk on her face.

'Did he ask for me?' enquired Sophy, turning away.

'Not to say, *asked*, but there are some things that are known without words. Madam doesn't go to his church, does she? Of course, this isn't his parish. You're St Matthew's, reelly. He preaches lovely, I think. Ever so deep. The silver tea service, I suppose, miss? And I'll soon make some scones.'

Sophy went slowly down the stairs. If she had been summoned to meet an archangel she could hardly have felt more frightened, more inadequate. Never had she sought the acquaintance of this man who had been so much hers in dreams that she could not bear to face the bleakness of reality. She could not rid herself of the feeling that unwanted love is the basest kind of treachery towards the beloved. She had made herself free of his mind and his heart without his knowledge. How could he ever forgive her? She had created a world in which he was her lover because she could not help herself. But she knew that one breath of reality would blow her world to smithereens, and dash her to pieces. And yet there was a terrible, painful excitement in her heart.

'I am the Rose of Sharon and the lily of the valleys,' she said to her reflection in the dim Venetian mirror in the hall, speaking out of her dream-world. For surely it must still be a dream. It couldn't be that he had intruded into the real world in which one shook hands and took tea and made conversation.

The odd thing was that when she came into the room, Mr Chandos's heart gave a sudden leap of recognition. A voice deep inside him said – 'This is the face I have been waiting for. This is the woman for me.'

But Sophy as she looked into the bright pale eyes that were the colour of the sea, that were as cold as aquamarines, was thinking – 'I shall not be able to endure the agony of loving this man.' The touch of his hand chilled her. There was something alien and terrifying in it, like the feel of a frog in her palm. Her mind felt cold and tingling, as though contact with the strange flesh of the beloved had frozen it. She rubbed it against the folds of her skirt, and still there was this queer, icy glow.

'Sophy,' thought Mrs Titmus, 'is behaving like a fool. If one could only *teach* them.' For in her reveries, she was still the girl she had once been; another Lalage, but much more vivid and vivacious. Lalage would never know the triumphs that had been hers. She remembered that dress she wore that everyone raved about at the Hunt Ball that year. He had kissed her shoulder in the dark. She could never hear the *Invitation to the Valse* without remembering. What a lover he was! But she had lost him a long time ago. She never identified him with old Mr Titmus, though they were one and the same person. It seemed strange that she should be married now to this old changeling. Once she had overheard him saying to himself in the bathroom – 'Now, where has she hidden my razor, the old . . . *puss*!' So treacherous! She had been shocked to the heart.

She came to the rescue of her awkward, helpless child.

'My daughter says the singing at St Petroc's is so beautiful. She is very musical, and has perfect pitch – which is quite uncommon, isn't it? So they tell me.'

Mr Chandos smiled and looked at Sophy. He couldn't take his eyes off that face. It made a pattern that fascinated him, like a map of olden times with its 'Here are dragons', and other strange indications. It was a unique face. New faces are seldom unfamiliar. They do not come upon us with a shock of strangeness, but are easily relegated to the different categories of faces which we draw up in our minds. Only out of history does a face sometimes look out with a hint of alien ineluctable charm. To Mr Chandos, the face of Sophy Titmus had that quality. Her soft mouse-like name enchanted him.

'You are not a communicant. I should have remembered you,' said Mr Chandos, making a pyramid with the joined tips of his fingers and resting his chin upon them.

'No, no. I am a lost sheep. I came in one evening to hear the anthem, and then you preached; and you quoted Donne. And then I had to join your congregation. But how did you know?'

'A member of your household, Violet Wilson, told me.' (That girl! thought Mrs Titmus with a little shiver as though a goose had walked over her grave, and thoughts of witchcraft came into the head of Sophy, already bemused and laid under a spell, so that her own voice, sounding out of the midst of the threefold circle that seemed to have been woven round her, was strange to her ears.) 'Did you like my sermon, Miss Titmus?'

'Have I not already told you? I see that priests have their vanities, like other artists.'

How hollow and far-away her voice sounded, like the voice of a stranger echoing in a cave.

A few weeks later, she was saying to herself amazedly – 'I had no idea it was as easy as this. I had no idea. I had no idea.'

For the unimaginable had come to pass. He was no longer an archangel, but her own Paul.

She had thought everyone must know it when she came into the house, when she floated in with the moon in her hair. But when she looked in at the drawing-room door, no one seemed aware that something tremendous had happened. They were doing silly, unimportant things, poor earthbound wretches, and glanced at her indifferently with lack-lustre eyes.

She retreated and caught Violet coming out of Mr Titmus's study. She was carrying a tea-tray. The old gentleman had been treated to his wife's best china and the silver muffin-dish, which still contained what was left of the forbidden dripping-toast he enjoyed so much. A little posy of wild flowers in a wine-glass added to the general effect of festivity and loving-kindness. Violet was playing her favourite game of circumventing the mistress. She was watering the withered old heart. She was shedding the beams of love upon it and re-awakening it. She was queering the old cat's pitch.

'Poor old gentleman!' she said, with a sidelong glance. 'He does like a little attention.' She smirked self-righteously, and then, catching sight of Sophy's face, nearly dropped the tray.

'Oh, miss! Whatever is it? Your heart's desire come true, that's what it is! I'm *ever* so glad.'

There was a strange look of triumph on her face.

After all, it was her doing, thought Sophy.

'Things always seem to happen when I come into a house,' said Violet, *sotto voce*. And suddenly Sophy remembered a greasy pack of cards she had found when looking for something in a drawer in the kitchen.

'Do you play patience alone down here in the evenings?' she had asked, with a spasm of pity.

'Not me,' Violet had replied. 'They fall for me the way I want them. It's wonderful what they tell you, if you have the gift.'

Sophy was moved now to put an arm about the girl. 'I shall never forget that I owe it to you,' she said softly.

'That's all right, miss,' said Violet, dropping her eyelids. There was an inscrutable expression on her face, as if she knew what she knew.

'And now there's Miss Beatrice. But the cards don't come out right for her. Not yet, they don't. A married man, I should think, miss.'

'What do you mean? You mustn't say such things. I've never heard such nonsense!' said Sophy, deeply alarmed.

'Oh, it's all right, miss! You can trust me. I'm as secret as the grave.' And she disappeared through the baize door to her own quarters. To the ace of spades and the mice, thought Sophy, with a little shiver. Love, she thought, and Death, dealt out on the kitchen table by those small, clever hands.

So that, in a way, she was prepared for that frightening moment when Mrs Titmus mounted the stairs to her room.

There was a look on her face, a sick and abject look, as if her pride had crumpled up in her, that hurt Sophy and shocked her.

She gave a backward look over her shoulder and closed the door furtively.

'Sophy,' she said, pitiably, in a strange whispering voice, 'that girl . . . I saw her. She was *pinching* diamonds into the table-cloth.'

'Oh, darling mother, she must go at once!' cried Sophy, flinging her arms round the gaunt figure.

For she knew now that Violet with a death-wish in her heart was about as safe to have in the house as a tame cheetah.

CHRISTA WOLF
Translated by
Heike Schwarzbauer and Rick Takvorian

June Afternoon

A story? Something firm, tangible, like a pot with two handles, to be touched and drunk from?

A vision, perhaps, if you understand what I mean.

Although the garden was never more real than this year. In all the time we have known it — of course it has only been three years — it has never had the opportunity to show what it is capable of. Now it turns out that it was the dream of being a green, rampant, wild, lush garden, no more, no less. The archetype of a garden. Garden incarnate. I have to say, this touches us. We exchange approving comments about its growth and understand secretly that it exaggerates its lushness; that, at present, it cannot but exaggerate, for how could it not exploit greedily the rare occasion of profiting from the falls, the still frequent rainfalls of near and far storms?

Whatever is sauce for the goose is gravy for the gander.

What is a gander? The child sat at my feet, doggedly carving a piece of bark which was first supposed to become a ship, later a dagger, and then something from the umbrella family. Now, however, unless all signs failed, it was turning into a gander. And in the process we would find out what this darned gander actually was. Although one can't carve with such a dull knife, you must admit. As if it had not been proven that one cuts oneself much more often with a dull knife than with a sharp one! Yet I, experienced in ignoring concealed reproaches, leaned back in my deck chair and read on, no matter what kind of criticism might be brought against a dull carving knife.

Listen, I said a little later to my husband, whom I could not see; however, his pruning shears were audible: he was probably at the vine, for it had to be continually thinned out this year, since it was acting as if it grew on a Mosel hillside and not on a skimpy trellis under a Brandenburg March pine. Listen, I said, you were right after all.

Didn't I say so, he said. Why you never wanted to read it, I don't know!

She knows how to write, I said.

Although not everything is good, he said, so I wouldn't be in danger of going too far again.

That goes without saying! But the way she deals with the country . . .

Yes, he said with a superior air. Italy!

And the sea? I asked challengingly.

Yes, he exclaimed, as if that alone was irrefutable proof. The Mediterranean!

But that's not it at all. One very exact word next to the other. That's what it is.

Although the Mediterranean is perhaps not entirely to be scoffed at either, he said.

Why do you always have to use foreign words! said the child, full of reproach.

The sun, rare as it was, had already started to bleach her hair. Within the course of the summer and especially during the vacation on the eastern seaboard, that golden helmet, which the child wore with dignity like something that was her due, and which we forgot year after year, would evolve again.

I turned a page and the sweetish odour of almost withered acacias mingled with the foreign smell of macchia bushes and stone pines, but I took care not to introduce any more foreign words and stuck my nose obediently into the handful of thorny leaves the child held up to me, full of malicious glee at the inconspicuous origin of peppermint tea. She stood like a stork in the midst of an island of wild chives and rubbed one skinny leg against the other. I remembered that, in summer as well as winter, she smelled of chives and mint and hay and all manner of herbs we did not yet know but which had to exist, for the child smelled of them.

Snails exaggerate their slowness, don't you think? she said, and it could not be denied that, within the course of an entire hour, the snail had not managed to crawl from the wooden leg of my deck chair to the rain barrel. Although one could not be completely sure to what extent it had understood and accepted our bet earlier on and whether a snail can plan such an undertaking: the rain barrel in one hour, if at all.

By the way, did you know that they are crazy about plum leaves? I have tested it.

I did not know this. Never in my entire life had I seen a snail eat, least of all plum leaves, but I kept my ignorance and my doubts to myself and let the child go off and look for something that was less disappointing than the snail.

As soon as she was out of hearing, there was suddenly no sound at all for seconds. Neither a bird nor the wind nor any sound at all, and believe me, it is disturbing when our quiet area becomes truly quiet. You never know why everything is holding its breath. This time, however, it was only one of those good old passenger aircrafts; I'm not saying that it can't be incredibly quick and comfortable, for these airlines flying overhead are in cutthroat competition with one another. I only mean, clearly visible to everybody, it flew from east to west, to use these designations for nothing but direction for once; in the opinion of most of its passengers the plane was probably flying from West to west; that is, because it had taken off in West Berlin, since the air corridor – a word one could ponder over for a long time – is just over our yard and the rain barrel and my deck chair, from where I observed, not without satisfaction, how without the slightest effort this airplane absorbed not only its own buzzing but the entire collection of sounds of our garden.

I do not know whether the sky is just as densely occupied elsewhere as it is here. If one lay down flat on the ground and stared up at the sky, one could get to know different types of aircraft from all over the world within the space of an hour. Yet this is of no use to me, for I was not taught even by the war to differentiate between airplanes of different make and function. I do not even know whether they blink red on the right and green on the left when they fly over our house at night, or vice versa.

And do they actually care about us in the least? Well then, I have flown often enough to know that an aircraft has no eyes to see and no soul to care. But I would bet any amount that more than an undersecretary of state, a banker, and a business mogul are drifting along above us this afternoon. I'd even bet there's one of those princesses who has recently become so active. Within the course of the week one has done one's bit and strengthened the feeling of being on outpost duty in oneself and in others, and flies home on Saturday with a clear conscience. During takeoff one shows a fleeting interest in the country down there, its roads, bodies of water, houses and gardens. Somewhere there are three dots in a green area (of course, I am leaving out the snail). What do you know, people. Well. Wonder what kind of life they lead around here. Unfavourable area, too. Not much can be done about this from the sky.

Don't think that I'm going to let you sleep now, said the child. She had crept up on me like an Indian and was satisfied to see me jump. She crouched down next to me to look up at the sky as well and scan it for ships and castles, wild mountain chains and gilded oceans of bliss. No battleships today. No storm alarm far and wide. Only the sound of cars in the distance and the breathtaking development of an oasis in the desert, its palm-tree tops graced by the sun and its animal world changing with amazing speed, for up there they had discovered the trick of letting one thing develop from another, of letting one thing merge into another: a camel into a lion, a rhinoceros into a tiger, and, in spite of the fact that this was a little strange, a giraffe into a penguin. We were suddenly overcome by a sense of insecurity about the reliability of celestial landscapes, but we hid this from each other.

Do you remember how you always used to say Engupin? I asked.

Instead of penguin? I was never that stupid!

How long is never for an eight-year-old child? And how long is forever? Four years? Or ten? Or the unimaginable gap between her age and mine?

Engupin, I insisted. Ask your father.

However, we could not ask him. I could not hear him laugh and say Engupin, in the same tone that he had four years ago. For Father stood at the fence speaking to the next-door neighbour. The usual conversation: What? You're not thinking of cutting the wild Lactarius on your tomatoes even more? You can't be serious! We listened to the argument with haughty amusement, the way one listens to something one is not really concerned about. By the way, we agreed with Father. Out of principle and because the neighbour had lost our last bit of respect during spring, when he demanded in all seriousness that the child pick all of the at least six hundred dandelions in our garden, so they could not turn into puffballs and their seeds threaten his pedantically manicured yard. We had a lot of fun over the thought of armies of puffball parachutes — six hundred times thirty, roughly calculated — drifting toward the neighbour's yard one day in a favourable southwesterly wind, with him standing there groaning, since he is growing too fat, and armed to the teeth with hoe, spade, and garden hose, his straw hat on his head and his furious little cur at his feet. Yet all of them together are no match for the puffball seeds leisurely sailing along and alighting wherever they happen to drop, without the least hurry or reluctance, for there will be no problem at all in finding that little piece of soil and dampness needed to gain ground and germinate. We were completely on the side of the puffballs.

Still, the neighbour was right in complaining about the fact that the strawberries are rotting on their stems and that nobody knows where it will end if a sunny afternoon like this is a rare exception.

The dry, sharp, truly bloodcurdling sonic boom of a jet invaded this weary talk, the subdued laughter from another garden, the slightly sad dialogue in my book. It's always right above us, said the child, insulted but not frightened, and I did not reveal how easily shock can still pull the ground out from under my feet. It can't manage any other way, I said. What? The sound barrier. It has to get through. Why? It has been specially made for this purpose, and now it has to get through. Even if it boomed twice as loud. He must be embarrassed about it himself. Don't you think? Perhaps the pilot puts cotton in his ears? But he doesn't hear anything. That's the whole point: the sound stays behind him. Practical, don't you think? said the child, and added in the same tone, I'm bored.

I do know that one should fear the boredom of children, and that it cannot be compared with the boredom of adults, unless their boredom has become deadly. What do we have to fear more than the deadly boredom of entire races? However, that does not apply in this case. I had to cope with the boredom of the child and said vaguely and ineffectually, Then do something!

It says in the newspaper that children should be given tasks, says the child. That's what educates them.

You read the newspaper?

Of course. But Father takes the best articles away from me. For example, 'Husband's Corpse Found in Window Seat'.

You really wanted to read that?

That would have been exciting. Did the wife murder the husband?

No idea.

Who was it that hid him in the window seat?

But I haven't read the article!

When I'm big I'll read all those articles. I'm bored.

I told the child to get water and a rag and wipe off the table and chairs, and I saw the body of the husband in the window seat swim through her dreams, saw wives flitting about with the intention of murdering their husbands with — what? With a hatchet? With the kitchen knife? With the clothesline? Saw myself standing by her bed: What is it? Did you have a bad dream? and saw her frightened eyes: Nothing. There's nothing wrong with me. Are you all there? At some point in the future the child will tell her children about an early nightmare. The garden will have sunk into oblivion a long time before; she will shake her head in embarrassment at an old photo of me, and will hardly remember anything about herself. The husband's body in the window seat, however, will have been preserved in her memory, impudent and pale, the same way I am still tortured by a man my grandfather once told me about: on account of a horrible murder he had been sentenced to madness by drops of water which fell on his shaved head in regular intervals, day in and day out.

Hey, said my husband, can't you hear today?

I was thinking of my grandfather.

Which one — the one who was still standing on his head at eighty?

The one who died of typhoid fever in '45.

The one with a moustache like a seal?

Yes. Him.

Strange how I always get your grandfathers mixed up!

That's your problem. One can't be mistaken for the other.

He continued to complain about my grandfathers and I continued to defend them, as if we had to fool an invisible spectator about our true thoughts and intentions. He stood next to the little apricot tree, which, surprisingly, overcame its stunted existence this year, although it did not manage to bear more than one single fruit, and we pretended to look at this tiny green apricot. I don't know what he was really looking at. I, in any case, was amazed at the light, which now surrounded the apricot tree and everything in its vicinity, so that one could look at it for quite a while without getting the least bit bored. Even if one proceeded from the grandfathers to something else in the meantime, for example the book I still held in my hands, the advantage of which was that it did not interrupt the contemplation of apricot trees. Instead, it contributed its bit, in all modesty, as is expected of a third party.

Yet there were still a few too many recluses and prophets and bewitched people in it, we agreed about that, and I obtained permission to skip a story, which supposedly describes all the gory details of a people's revenge on a traitor; I confessed that I could no longer cope with all these mutilations and killings of men before the eyes of their trussed-up wives; I admitted that, as of late, I have begun to be afraid of the next drop that falls on our bare heads.

Just at that moment our daughter appeared, and next door, the engineer pushed his new frog-green car out of the garage for its Saturday-night wash. As regards the car, none of us would have had the sad courage to tell the engineer that his car is frog-green, because it says 'linden-green' on the car's registration, and that's what he adheres to. He goes by printed matter in general. You only need to look at his haircut to know about the most recent recommendations of the magazine *Your Hairdo* and at his apartment to know what *Interior Design* considered a must two years ago. He is a friendly, flaxen-haired man, our engineer; he is not interested in politics but looks helpless when we call the most recent editorial boring. He never reveals anything, and neither do we, for we are more than convinced that the flaxen-haired engineer with his frog-green car has the same right to be on this earth as we do, with our puffballs and celestial landscapes and this or that slightly sad book. If only our thirteen-year-old daughter, yes, the one who is just now entering through the garden door, had not set her mind on finding everything connected with the engineer modern. And if only we didn't know what catastrophic dynamite that word contains for her.

Have you seen the chic sunglasses he is wearing today? she asked as she drew closer. With one glance I was able to prevent Father from calling the sunglasses we hadn't even noticed impossible, and we watched in silence as she stalked across the bit of lawn, throwing a very long shadow, as she lowered herself in a complicated fashion next to the apricot tree and smoothed out her blouse in order to make it clear to us that the person sitting in front of us was no longer a child.

Have I already mentioned that she was coming from a rehearsal for a school recital?

It isn't working, she said. Nothing is working at all. What do you think of that?

Normal, said her father, and to this day I believe that it was nothing but revenge for the engineer's chic sunglasses.

You! said the daughter angrily. You probably find it normal if the speakers do not know their poems and the choir keeps hitting the wrong notes and the solo dancer keeps falling on her bottom?

You teach me all these expressions, stated the child, who was sitting on the edge of the rain barrel and taking care not to miss a single word from the nerve-racking life of her big sister. This caused their father to explain that it was a regrettable fact if a solo dancer fell on her bottom, but not an expression. However, the real question was whether a solo dancer was really needed at a school party.

How can I make you understand in so many words that the argument which now started had deep roots which were not so much nourished by the coincidental performance of a solo dancer as by a principal difference in opinion about the taste of the teacher, who has been organizing all school events since our children started attending the school. Up to now she had always found some well-built girl in the ninth or tenth grade who was willing to drift across the stage in a dress of red veils and mime longing to piano music. If you ask me, these girls deserved neither bitter disapproval nor uncritical rapture, but as I said before, this has nothing to do with

them. This does not even have anything to do with the
teacher's penchant for Bengal lights, for we should have
learned by now to come to terms with all possible kinds of
illumination. No, in reality Father cannot bear his daughter's
painful devotion to everything she deems perfect; cannot bear
the sight of her vulnerability; keeps standing in the empty
field, whenever there is a thunderstorm, in order to attract
the lightning bolts meant for her. For which he wins alter-
nately stormy tenderness and furious ingratitude, so that he
has said a thousand times, From this second onward I'll never
get involved in these women's affairs, I swear. However, we
did not listen to his oaths, for he is involved, with or without
oaths. By hook or by crook.

Crook-jail, said the child inquiringly testing the waters:
Will they continue to ignore me? The answers, which she got
from us in quick succession and which I record here faithfully,
will seem odd to you: Rain worm, I said. Fortune cookie, said
her father. Night ghost, said the daughter. With such a good
collection of words our game could begin at once, and the first
round was: Rainjail, crookcookie, fortuneghost, and night-
worm, and then we really got going, got carried away with
holeworm and crookghost and rainfortune and cookienight,
after which point there was no stopping us, the dams broke
and flooded the land with the most exquisite monstrosities,
what with wormghost and crookrain and nightjail and cookie-
worm and jailfortune and nighttrain and cookiecrook gushing
out.

Excuse me. But it is difficult not to get carried away. It is
quite possible that there are better words. And of course five
or six players are better than four. We once tried it with the
engineer. Do you know what he said? You'll never guess. Of
course he cheated. One of the rules of the game is that
everybody name the word at the tip of his tongue, without
stopping to think. The engineer, however, racked his brains
for seconds before our very eyes; he made a great effort until,
very relieved, he came up with reconstructionhour. Of course

we didn't want to let him show us up and racked our brains as well and served him up work brigade and extra shift and union paper, and the child in her confusion articulated pioneer leader. Yet unionreconstruction and brigadehour and extrawork and shiftleader and paperpioneer failed to turn into a proper game; we went on for a while listlessly, dutifully gave a small laugh at leaderunion, and broke off.

None of us said a word about this abortive attempt in order not to hurt the daughter's feelings, but it visibly occupied her until, at night, she defiantly said, So he's got consciousness!

Snow goose, said her father back then, the same thing he says today, because the daughter once more comes up with the solo dancer, who had been previously disposed of, and states in her defence that, wonderfully enough, this time she would perform in a sea-green dress. Sea-green snow goose! He took the child by the hand and they went off with expressions on their faces as if they were leaving us forever and not just for the short walk to their secret clover spot, for fortunecookie had naturally made them think of a lucky four-leaf clover. The daughter, however, looked after them triumphantly. He always says snow goose when he runs out of arguments, doesn't he? Do you happen to have a comb?

I gave her the comb, and she took a mirror out of her little basket and clumsily fastened it in the branches of the little apricot tree. The she took the ribbon out of her hair and began to comb it. I waited because it was not worth starting a new page. I saw her trying to control herself, but it had to be said: Looks awful, don't you think? Who? My hair. There's no use washing it right before going to bed. Now it had been said. This hairdo strongly emphasized her big nose – Have a heart, I hastily interjected. Your nose isn't too big! – even though it had the advantage of making its wearer look a little older. The bus conductor, for example, had just treated her like a grownup: Listen, miss, pull in your legs a bit! This had been embarrassing for her, but not only embarrassing, do you understand? Couldn't you have put him in his place? I said, purposely changing the subject ever so slightly. Perhaps in the following fashion: Were your polite remarks perhaps addressed to me? Oh no. She never thought of anything like that when she needed it, and apart from that, this was not about the impoliteness of the bus conductor but about the form of address. However, to get back to her hair: Listen, my daughter said. What would you rather be, beautiful or intelligent?

Do you know the feeling when a question hits you like a thunderbolt? I knew immediately that this was the question of all questions and that it got me into an insoluble dilemma. I expatiated at great length, and saw in the face of my daughter that she thought me guilty of each and every offence which was thinkable in my answer, and I silently asked an unpresent authority for a happy inspiration and thought, How she is beginning to resemble me; hopefully she doesn't notice it yet! and I suddenly said out loud, Now you listen to me. If you're going to look at me like that and not believe a word I'm saying anyway, why do you ask me in the first place? At which point she threw her arms around my neck, but that had been the purpose of the question anyway. The comb lay in the grass as if forever, and her soft lips were all over my face and very welcome protestations at my ear, such as 'I-only-really-love-you' and 'want-for-ever-to-stay-with-you' and 'always-listen-to-you,' in short, the kinds of promises one rashly makes for one's own protection shortly before one has to break them for good. And I believed every word and scoffed at my own weakness and my penchant toward cheap self-deception.

Now they're licking each other again, said the child disdainfully, and casually dropped a bouquet of clover into my lap, seven little stalks of clover, each one of them with four properly formed leaves, I could go ahead and see for myself. No optical illusion, no false bottom, no glue spit involved. Solid, four-leafed luck.

Seven! the daughter cried, electrified. Seven is my lucky number. In short, she wanted the leaves. All seven of them for herself. We had difficulty finding words for this immoderate claim and did not even think of reminding her that she had never shown any interest in four-leaf clovers and had never found a single four-leaf clover herself. We only looked at her with widened eyes and kept silent. But she was so set on luck that she did not become the least bit embarrassed.

Yes, the child said finally. Seven is her lucky number, that's true. On our way to school she always takes seven steps from one tree to the next. It drives me crazy. As if this were an act of inevitable justice, she took the clovers out of my lap and gave them to her sister. By the way, I got them back right after the daughter had firmly pressed them against her supposedly oversized nose; I should store them in my book for the time being. I was carefully observed as I put them between stone pines and macchia bushes at the edge of the foreign Mediterranean, on the steps of those stairs to the oracle who lied out of compassion, on the wooden table where the young landlord had waited on his guests as long as he was still happy and had not yet been marked as the victim of a dark evil. I left out the pages on which that gruesome act of revenge is committed, for what do I know about four-leaf clover and the lucky number seven, and what gives me the right to challenge certain forces?

Better to be on the safe side.

Now which one of you took my string again? From one moment to the next the foreign flora and fauna slipped off behind the horizon, which is where it belongs anyway, and what concerned us was the father's look of gloom.

String? Nobody, we said bravely. What kind of string? Didn't we have eyes in our heads to see that the roses had to be tied up?

The child pulled one of the pieces of string she always carries with her out of her pocket and offered it to him. This made us aware of the gravity of the situation. The daughter proposed getting new string. However, the father did not want any new string, just the six pieces he had just measured and cut and put down here somewhere and which we naturally had to take away. You see, our looks said to each other, we should not have left him to his own devices for so long, one should at least have put a clover in his pocket, for everyone needs protection from evil spirits when he is alone. We saw ourselves searching for string for the rest of the afternoon and, on top of that, heard Father bemoan a fate which had thrown him among three women. So we sighed and were at our wits' end. Then along came Frau B.

Frau B. came waddling across the meadow, because she has to shift her entire weight from one leg to the other at every step, and in her left hand she carried her shopping bag, which she doesn't leave the house without, but in her right hand she held the six pieces of string. Well, she said, hasn't somebody forgotten these by the fence? Afterward you have to look for them and then all hell breaks loose.

Oh yes, said Father, actually these are just what I need. He took the string and went off to the roses.

Thank you very much, Frau B., we said. But won't you sit down?

The daughter went to get one of the garden chairs we had just wiped off, and we looked on, slightly uneasy, as it completely disappeared under the voluminous bulk of Frau B. Frau B. panted a little, because for her, every little walk becomes a chore; she took a deep breath and subsequently informed us that excessive chemical fertilization had ruined our strawberries. For Frau B. is accustomed to even the oddest behaviour of any living creature; she sees at a glance the disease and its roots where other people spend a long time looking. Our meadow should have been mown long ago and the weeds in the carrot patch thinned out, she told us, and we did not argue. But then Frau B. astonished us by asking whether we had already looked at the inside of the yellow rose, the first one on the left of the rose bed. No, we hadn't yet looked inside the rose and we sensed that we owed her something as a result. The child immediately ran off to make up for it and came back breathlessly with the announcement that it was worth it. Deeper inside, the rose became a darker yellow and finally almost pink. Although this was a pink which does not exist otherwise. However, the greatest thing was how deep this rose was. Really, one would not have thought so.

Just like I told you, said Frau B. It's a superior variety. The hazelnuts are also growing well this year.

You're right, Frau B., we said. It is a superior variety. And only now, after Frau B. had noticed it, the hazelnuts were doing well and it seemed to us that everything which her gaze had graced with approval or reproof, even the strawberries that had bolted to seed, had received its proper blessing only now.

At this point Frau B. opened her mouth and said, The standing crop is going to rot this year.

Now, Frau B.! we exclaimed.

It's true, she said, unmoved. That's how it is. Just like the Hundred Years' Calendar says: Storms and rain and thundershowers and floods. The harvest will stay outside and rot.

This silenced us. We saw the harvest perishing according to the Hundred Years' Calendar, with Frau B. calmly looking on, and for the space of a second we may have thought that it was she herself who had the power to rule over the harvest and the hazelnuts and the strawberries and the roses. After all, there is a possibility that, through a lifetime's work with the products of nature, one can earn a certain say in their fates. In vain I attempted to imagine the floods of fruit juice, the mountains of jams and jellies which had passed over Frau B.'s kitchen table within the course of forty years; I saw the freight cars full of carrots and green beans which had grown beneath her hands and been cleaned by her fingers, the thousands of chickens she had fed, the pigs and rabbits she had fattened, the goats she had milked, and I had to admit that it would only be fair if *one* now told her in front of all the others, Now listen, dear Frau B., as far as this year's harvest is concerned, *we* were thinking . . .

For, after all, no one has seen the Hundred Years' Calendar with their own eyes.

Here they are again, said Frau B. contentedly. I'm just amazed that they aren't getting sick of it.

Who, Frau B.? What?

But then we saw them as well: the helicopters. Do I have to apologize for the busy air traffic over our area? The fact is that at this hour of the afternoon two helicopters are flying along the border, whatever they may hope or fear to see beyond the wire fence. We, however, should we happen to have time, can see how close the border is, can see the long propellers turning and show one another the light spots inside the cockpit, the pilots' faces; we can wonder whether they are always the same ones who have been assigned to this flight or whether they take turns. Perhaps they only send them so that we can get used to them. After all, one is not afraid of things one sees every day. Yet, not even the nightly searchlights and the red and yellow signal flares going up against the bell-jar glow of the city move the border as close to us as the harmlessly curious helicopters, which do not shun the daylight.

To think that he could be from Texas, said Frau B. Where my boy is now.

Who, Frau B.?

The pilot up there. He could just as well be from Texas, couldn't he?

Sure he could. But what on earth is your son doing in Texas?

Playing soccer, said Frau B.

And then we remembered all about her deaf-mute son, who lived in the West with his deaf-mute wife and who was now in Texas with the soccer team of the deaf, never dreaming what his mother was saying at the sight of a foreign helicopter pilot. We also thought of Anita, Frau B.'s daughter, who was deaf as well and who was training on a job, alone in a distant town, although within reach, and sent her laundry home every week. We took another look at Frau B., searching for traces of fate in her face. Yet we did not detect anything special.

Everyone look straight ahead, said the child, and made a face.

Standing at the fence was our neighbour the Widow Horn.

Well, good night, then, said Frau B. I'm leaving.

Yet she stayed and turned the entire mass of her body toward the fence, facing the Widow Horn: the woman who does not add an onion to the potato pancakes and does not have her blocked drainpipe repaired and who does not grant herself a change of headscarf, out of pure naked stinginess. She had come to talk to us about the train accident in her penetrating, indifferent voice.

Now there are twelve, she said, in place of a greeting.

How are you, we answered uneasily. What do you mean by twelve?

Twelve bodies, said the Widow Horn. Not nine like they wrote in the paper only yesterday.

Good heavens, said Frau B., and gave our neighbour a look as if *she* had killed the three people who hadn't been in the newspaper the day before. We knew that Frau B. thought her capable of anything, for whoever loves money can also steal and kill people; however, this was going too far. Although we didn't like the sparkle in the eyes of the Widow Horn either.

How do you know this we asked, and is it really certain that three people from our village are among them?

Four, our neighbour said casually. But the wife of that actor had good insurance, anyway.

Oh no, we said, and turned pale. Is she dead as well?

Of course, said the Widow Horn severely.

Then we kept a few seconds' silence for the wife of the actor. For the last time she came up the street to our garden door with her two dachshunds, for the last time she complained in earnest as well as in jest about the dogs' bad habits, let herself be dragged reluctantly from tree to tree, and smoothed back her long black hair. Yes, now we all saw that she had beautiful hair, just slightly touched up, and that she was slim and looked good for her age. However, we could not tell her this, she was already over, had turned her back on us in an irrevocable manner which we had never seen in her, and we could not hope that she would turn back or even come back to us so that we, the inattentive living, could see her face one more time and impress it on our minds — forever.

What an unsuitable word for the actor's wife who had been vital but always bogged down by everyday worries.

He is not back, anyway, said our neighbour, who hadn't noticed anybody passing by.

Who?

Well, the actor. They didn't find any more of her, just her pocketbook and her passport. That must have really confused her husband. He is not back yet.

It happened as it had to happen. The child opened her mouth and asked, But why? Why didn't they find any more of her?

All of us stared at the Widow Horn, as if she would now proceed to describe what the rails can look like after a train accident such as this, but without so much as heeding our imploring glances, she said, It takes time. They're still searching.

Why don't you come over, I said. Why don't you sit down.

However, our neighbour could only smile at that. One never sees her smile unless something unnatural is expected of her, that she should give something away, for example. Or that she should sit down in the middle of the day. Whoever is sitting down thinks. Whoever carts manure onto his cornfield or digs up his piece of land or slaughters chickens has to think much less than a person sitting in her parlour and staring at the cupboard with the collector's cups. Who could guarantee that a man would not suddenly stand in front of the cupboard, at the very spot where he always stood to take down his newspaper; a man who deserves to be hated, who recently found his punishment for leaving his wife through death, as one hears. Or grandchildren one doesn't know since one kicked out the daughter-in-law, that slut, along with the son, after all. Then one jumps up and puts the wire cage with the chickens in the parlour; who cares if they fill the empty apartment with their chirping, who cares if their feathers fly about so that one can hardly breathe, who cares if everything goes to hell. Or one runs into the kitchen and colours eggs and gives them as Easter presents to the neighbour's children, those good-for-nothings who ring the doorbell at night and then scatter so that there is no one there when one comes rushing out, keeps rushing out, but nothing is there. Nothing and no one, no matter how one may crane one's neck.

Bye, said the Widow Horn, I didn't really want anything else. Frau B. went with her. Every single one of her heavy steps intimated that she had no dealings with the gaunt woman tripping along beside her. It was imperative to protect the boundary forever separating undeserved fate and misfortune incurred through one's own fault.

A fight broke out between the children to which I paid no attention. It got worse and in the end they chased one another beneath the trees; the child held up a torn-off scrap of paper and screamed, She loves somebody, she loves somebody! and the daughter, beside herself, demanded her scrap of paper back, her secret which was just as hard to hide as it was to reveal. I leaned my head back on the pillow of my deck chair. I closed my eyes. I wanted neither to see nor to hear anything. The woman of whom one had found nothing but her pocketbook no longer saw or heard anything either. No matter which game she had had her hand in, it had been slapped away, and the game had gone on without her.

The entire feather-light afternoon hung on the weight of this minute. A hundred years are as one day. One day is as a hundred years. The sinking day is what they say. Why shouldn't one feel it sinking: past the sun, already dipping down into the lilac bushes, past the little apricot tree, the loud children's screams, even past the rose which is yellow on the outside and pink on the inside only today and tomorrow. Yet one begins to be afraid if one still sees no ground; one jettisons superfluous ballast, this and that, only in order to get up again. After all, who is to say that the hand which will pull one away from everything is already set to pounce? Who is to say that, this time, it is our turn? That the game will go on without us?

The children had stopped fighting. They were catching grasshoppers. The sun was barely visible. It began to get chilly. Father called out that we should clear everything away, it was time. We tilted the chairs toward the table and put the rakes in the stuffy little shed.

As we left, the air was full of June bugs. At the garden door we turned around and looked back.

When was all that about the Mediterranean, anyway? asked the child. Today?